C000153461

SUSAN A JENNINGS

Sarah's Choice

Book 3 – The Sackville Hotel Trilogy

Contents

A Loving Dedication To...   i
Author's Notes   ii
Sarah's Choice   iv
Graduation Day - June 1960   1
The Penthouse   9
Summer at Bexhill   17
First Impressions   23
Commune and Conflict   30
Good News for Lizzy   37
Passions and Dreams Revealed   44
Ghosts From the Past   50
London   58
Darkening Storms   66
Le Papillon Gallery of Art   74
Inheritance and Inner Conflict   82
A Conference of Secrets   89
Elusive Men   97
Tides of Change   106
Lizzy's Wedding   114
Sarah in Canada   122
Surprises   129
The Canadian and Totem Poles   137
Whispering Trees   144
Futures in Jeopardy   153
All About Art   161

Art and Spies   170
All Sorts of Love   178
Solutions and More Problems   186
Sarah Does it All   194
Royal College of Art's Annual Exhibition   203
Solving the Sackville Problems   211
Christmas 1962 - Ringing in 1963   219
Sarah is Famous   227
Treason and Trickery   236
Secrets and Truths   246
True Colours   252
Summer 1963   259
Troubles in Bexhill   267
Anna and Bill Make Decisions   276
Sadness and Joy   283
Exhaustion Takes Over   291
Christmas 1963   301
Independence   311
Shattered Dreams   319
The Demon Drink   327
Anna's Reflective Dream   335
Hard Goodbyes   339
The Truth   347
What Happened Next?   354
About Susan   356
Acknowledgements   357
More Books by Susan   359
Ruins in Silk   361
Research Resources   362

A Loving Dedication To...

Mothers, Daughters, Granddaughters, Grandmothers

And especially to...

My granddaughters Annabelle and Karoline

My daughter Rosemary

My mother Betty

My grandmothers Anne and May

The most precious relationships experienced by most women are those relationships with her grandmothers, mother, daughters and granddaughters. During her lifetime a woman will experience at least two of these relationships and some are lucky enough to experience them all.

Author's Notes

Writing The Sackville Hotel Trilogy has been quite a journey inspired by my mother and grandmother. *Book I, The Blue Pendant* intertwined true events in my grandparents' and mother's lives with a mostly a fictitious story, which grew into something bigger than one novel and spilled into the sequel, *Book II, Anna's Legacy*, which was a completely fictitious story. However, I still had more story to write, and one book turned into a trilogy as I planned, *Book III, Sarah's Choice*.

It is both rewarding and sad to bring this trilogy to a conclusion. As I write, I'm transported to Bexhill, to London, to Toronto and to British Columbia. I live the lives of the characters. I cry with them and feel their pain, I laugh with them and feel their happiness, I love them and feel their love. I think you will agree that this trilogy has been quite the roller coaster ride.

I hope with all my heart that you enjoy Anna's Journey of love, loss, happiness, hope and destiny from 1913 to 1964.

There is one fact that I can declare as true, which is mentioned in the Epilogue. The Sackville Hotel was eventually bought by developers and converted into retirement apartments. While I was writing this book, I was contacted by Duncan Humber, the building manager and Roy Haynes a retired BBC journalist, both residents of The Sackville Apartments and intrigued by my association with Bexhill. Concierge, Val Crowson, came across *The Blue Pendant Book I of The Sackville Hotel Trilogy* during an online search for books for the Sackville reading group. Serendipitous indeed!

As I was never able to visit either the apartments or Bexhill, I relied heavily on Googling information and reading material for research. I can only hope that my research, even if not entirely correct, did justice to the Sackville and its residents, past and present.

*More about **Susan** – Follow her on social media.*
***Website & Blog** - http://susanajennings.com*
***Facebook** – facebook.com/authorsusanajennings*
***The Sackville Hotel News & Updates** - http://eepurl.com/bgY6kb*

Free Prequel - *Ruins in Silk* -https://dl.bookfunnel.com/hj6em-bawkt

Sarah's Choice

One

Graduation Day – June 1960

*M*iss Sarah Anne Wexford."

Sarah didn't move as the metal chairs screeched around her—all other sounds were muted and fuzzy. Abandoned on an island in a sea of people—students, friends, loved ones and proud parents—her own parents weren't there. Her mother dead more than ten years and her father…well, no one knew where he was and no one seemed to care. But she did.

"SARAH ANNE WEXFORD," Sarah looked up as her name bellowed into the convocation hall.

Lizzy, her best friend, jabbed her in the ribs. "Sarah, that's you! You've won the Victoria Award for best artist." Lizzy hugged her and pushed her up from her chair. "Go!"

Sarah squeezed past her fellow students, nervous as she stepped on stage in front of that sea of people, seeing only two, Anna and Bill Blaine her grandparents on their feet cheering and clapping wildly. Her heart so full of love and gratitude the tears spilled unashamedly down her cheeks. In that moment, she knew she could not disappoint them.

She shook hands as she accepted the symbolic modern sculpture of an artist poised with a paint brush from Miss Berkley, head of the fine arts department. Miss Berkley kissed her on each cheek and said, "In all my years of teaching I have never met anyone as talented as you, Miss Wexford. Take this prize and use it wisely." She handed her a cheque for £100. "One day you will be famous and your art work will hang in the best galleries in the world."

Completely overwhelmed, Sarah could barely say thank you. Miss Berkley smiled, squeezed her hand and whispered "Good luck. You deserve it."

The applause abated as the diploma-clutching graduates took their seats and the hall fell momentarily silent before bursting into applause as Mr. Robin Darwin, Principal of the Royal College of Art, stepped up to the podium and began his closing speech.

Sarah tried to stay focused, but his ramblings about the graduates having a duty to Great Britain and the world of art seemed irrelevant to what she intended to do with her National Diploma in Design - Diploma of Art & Design.Her fingers felt the smooth lapis pendant: Would Great Uncle Bertie's "follow your dream" message work for her? She doubted it. Quite unexpectedly her throat tightened and tears filled her eyes at the realization that her aspirations of owning an art studio would probably remain only a dream. Her inheritance, The New Sackville Hotel, was waiting for her in Bexhill. It had been her mother's desire to take over the hotel, not hers. Another round of applause signalled the end of Mr. Darwin's speech.

Sarah turned around, scanning the seats for Marcus. He'd run off just before the ceremony, saying it was a waste of time and that he'd got better things to do. *What?* she had thought, not daring to answer, knowing the consequences if she argued. She'd started dating Marcus in second year. He was different, laid-back and fun, but recently he'd been moody and aloof.

**

Sarah and Lizzy's exit from the hall took some time as fellow graduates stopped her to view the trophy. Overwhelmed, Sarah stayed quiet, letting Lizzy do the talking. Lizzy had graduated in fashion design. Although talented, Lizzy's main interest had been catching a husband rather than studying fashion—except her own, of course. Sarah wondered how they could be such close friends. The white picket fence couldn't have been further from Sarah's ambitions, although life with a free-spirited boyfriend like Marcus had crossed her mind.

"Lizzy, have you seen Marcus?"

"No. Why didn't he come to the ceremony?"

Sarah found herself making excuses for him. "Oh, you know Marcus. Doesn't like the fuss and I don't think his parents could make it. But I don't know where he went. He was supposed to be joining us for dinner and celebrations, but he changed his mind."

"What are you going to do when you are in Bexhill and he's in London?"

"It's okay, we've worked out a plan." Sarah quickly glanced downwards, changing the subject.

"I see your mother, she's waving," Sarah said, waving to Mrs. Elliot and calling goodbye as Lizzy ran towards her parents.

"I'll see you on Saturday in Bexhill," Lizzy shouted.

Sarah glanced through the crowd again but there was no sign of Marcus. Anna and Bill were approaching, beaming with pride, followed by their closest friends, Lord and Lady Thornton, who had known Sarah since she was a baby.

"We are so proud of you," Anna said, hugging her tightly with glassy eyes. Bill hugged them both.

"Congratulations!" Belle Thornton said, followed by more hugs.

Darcy Thornton stepped forward saying, "Well done, champion. What a great honour, the Victoria prize. Very well deserved."

Her cheeks blushed pink as she fidgeted with the trophy, unsure that she deserved all these accolades.

"Thanks everyone. I was very surprised. There are many talented artists here at college. I guess I got lucky."

"Luck has nothing to do with it." At the sound of the familiar deep baritone voice, Sarah swung around. Belle and Darcy's son, Felix, stood behind her in his bespoke Savile Row suit, looking like the handsome solicitor that he was. Her heart missed a beat. Eight years her senior, Felix was her oldest and after Lizzy her dearest friend.

"Felix! I didn't know you were here. Thanks for coming."

"I was late. Sorry, I was in court today and couldn't get away early, so I crept in the back and I did see you get your award. And as I was saying, luck had nothing to do with it. You have more talent in your little finger than of the others have in their whole bodies." He bent down and kissed her cheek. She felt the familiar tingle. There were times when she wondered if there was more than friendship but quickly pushed the thought from her mind. Anything more would spoil things.

"We'll start with cocktails at my club, then we'll go back to the townhouse to change for dinner and dancing at the Savoy." Darcy, Lord Thornton, looked at his watch. "The car will be waiting for us. Is everybody ready?"

"Where's Marcus? I thought you had invited him to join us. Did his parents make it after all?" Anna asked, staring at Sarah.

"Oh, he had to go somewhere. He won't be joining us."

"Is everything all right?"

"Yes, his plans changed, that's all." She was making excuses again. Sarah hated telling lies to Anna, but in truth she didn't know where he was or why he had declined dinner.

Darcy's Rolls Royce was waiting at the main entrance. The chauffeur, Harris, doffed his cap as he opened the car door. "Congratulations, Miss Sarah."

Aware that her college friends were staring at her and the Rolls, she felt awkward. Not that it was unusual to see chauffeur driven cars at the college, but it was unusual for quiet, unassuming Sarah. Felix had visited a few times, but her friends knew him as a fancy London solicitor not the Earl of Hillcrest's son and heir.

She stepped back to allow Belle and Anna to enter first and from the corner of her eye she saw Marcus, his face as dark as thunder. She smiled and waved for him to come but he dodged behind a car and disappeared. He would have been surprised, as when she invited him to join the family, she had omitted any reference to the Thorntons, and part of her was relieved he had run off. She told herself she didn't want to embarrass him, but in truth his anti-establishment beatnik ideals sometimes scared her and she was afraid he might embarrass the group.

She adjusted the headband that was tight around her forehead; practical because it held her shoulder length, wayward and very curly red hair in place. She fiddled with the cord of her white blouse, brushing the coloured embroidery and hitching up the too-long, red cotton dirndl skirt that had been hidden by her graduation robe. Was she showing defiance against the establishment? Suddenly self-conscious of her outfit, which was more suitable for college than for Darcy's club, she was pleased she had agreed that Anna should pack her a change of clothes as well as evening wear for the Savoy.

**

The Thorntons' London townhouse accommodated as many as six guests, the family and the staff of a cook, maid and butler and of course Harris the chauffeur. Three times the size of any ordinary house, Sarah smiled when Felix called it the little townhouse, but she acknowledged it was minute compared to Hillcrest Hall.

Feeling woozy, she clung to the bannister as she followed the maid to her room. Not used to drinking, two martinis at the club had gone to her head. She needed to lie down. As soon as her head hit the pillow she fell asleep.

"Sarah! Wake up."

Sarah opened her eyes. "Nana, what time is it? I must have nodded off."

"You needed the rest and there is plenty of time to get changed. Darcy wants us in the drawing room for cocktails at 7:30, he's booked dinner for 8:30. Come and join Bill and I when you're ready and we'll go down together."

Sarah gave a cat-like stretch and smiled at Anna. "I needed that sleep, I feel much better. Give me half an hour." Anna nodded and disappeared through the door to the adjoining room.

She hadn't even noticed that the maid had laid out the dress and accessories that Anna had packed at home. *Nana knows me so well,* she thought, admiring her favourite dress, a peacock blue strapless taffeta, the watermarked fabric shimmered green to blue, catching the green in her hazel eyes. She applied her makeup and looked in the mirror at her big hair and sighed. "Now, what do we do to you?" she said, winding the hair around her fist, trying to smooth the tight, springy curls. She heard a knock on the door and thinking it was Anna she called, "Come in."

"Good evening, Miss Wexford. Lady Thornton sent me to see if you needed any help to dress."

"Thank you, ...um..." Sarah hesitated, embarrassed that she couldn't remember the maid's name.

"Connie, miss. My name is Connie."

"Connie, thank you." Sarah looked at her more closely, priding herself on treating everyone equally. Connie was her age, nineteen or perhaps a year younger. Sarah wondered why she was a maid. "Are you any good at dressing hair? Mine is like a bird's nest, at best." Sarah glanced at her apologetically. "I'm sorry I forgot your name, it won't happen again."

"That's all right, miss. I'm just a maid."

"Don't say that, Connie. You are an excellent maid."

Connie blushed and touched Sarah's hair. "May I?"

"Yes, I'll hug you if you can tame this mop."

Connie's cheeks were now a deep pink as she took the brush and tugged as gently as she could through Sarah's hair. With a copious amount of bobby pins, Connie pinned and piled the hair on top of Sarah's head and threaded blue and green ribbons in and out of the curls before finally freeing a few wisps of hair around Sarah's neck and face.

Staring in the mirror, Sarah said, "It's wonderful, thank you. I love the ribbons."

"Thank you, miss. I thought the ribbons would suit your style," Connie said, glancing at the skirt and blouse on the chair as she helped Sarah into her dress.

Sarah smiled. "My Bohemian style might be a little out of place here."

"I like it, miss. It's like a breath of fresh air. It can be a bit stuffy round here." Connie chuckled softly as she left the room.

"Wow!" Bill's voice came from the doorway. "I can't believe how grown up you are, my little Sarah. I wish your mother could see you."

"I know, I miss her too."

"I see you're wearing the blue pendant, it looks lovely on you," said Anna with a sentimental smile as she followed Bill into the room.

"Oh, do you want it back?"

"Heavens no! It is yours to keep. Great Uncle Bertie would want me to pass it on to you. I was the same age as you, preparing to leave home and take up my position as receptionist at the Sackville hotel when he gave this to me. I know I've told you this before but his words are so important. 'Follow your dreams and never let anyone destroy them.' For me, it was close a couple of times but I clasped the pendant and thought of Uncle Bertie's words. It used to have a black velvet ribbon and the day it broke I thought disaster would befall us but Grandpa Bill bought this silver chain and made it strong again. As sad as I am that your mother never received Uncle Bertie's pendant, I think you will treasure it more." Anna smiled and nodded towards Bill.

"We have something else for you." He took her hand and led her into the next room.

"Congratulations! We are so proud of you." Sarah heard the quiver in Anna's voice as she handed her a small box. Sarah pulled the blue ribbon and removed the lid and stared inside. Anna pointed to the items in the box. "The bracelet Uncle Bertie gave to me years ago, although I never wore it much, and the earrings are a gift from Grandpa Bill and me."

Bill put his hands on his waist and motioned for Anna and Sarah to link their arms in his. He kissed them both on the cheek and said, "Now, lets go celebrate."

Two

The Penthouse

*W*hat happened last night? Sarah thought as London streets whizzed by the car window. *Too much wine perhaps, but the look in his eyes had nothing to do with wine.* Confused, she allowed her head to fall back onto the leather seat. Closing her eyes, she heard dance music, the last waltz, and felt his warm breath on her neck as he whispered, "I wish this dance would go on forever." His hold tightened around her back. Felix always made her feel safe and secure. She looked up to him as an older brother, a dear friend; romance had never entered her head. Frowning, she thought, *Well, not often. After all, I'm in love with Marcus. Aren't I?*

Felix played the role of rich playboy well. He always had women of notoriety, either wealthy or titled, hanging off his arm, and he had a reputation for affairs and relationships that never lasted long enough to be considered serious marriage possibilities—much to his father's disappointment. That he behaved quite differently around Sarah often made her defend him; she knew his flirtatious behaviour was a cover up for a sensitive, caring man.

Bill's voice shook her from her thoughts, "You look tired. Did you have fun last night?" She glanced up and saw his kind, unusual, aqua eyes in the rear-view mirror. His smile told her he had seen them dancing and she didn't want Anna and Bill to have any expectations of romance associated with Felix.

"It was a long day yesterday, but I had fun. It's been a busy few days. I'll be glad to relax in Bexhill."

Anna turned around and Sarah smiled, seeing the familiar broad Cheshire cat grin and understood the pride. "Have you given any thought about what you want to do next?"

Sarah went quiet, sensing the full meaning of the question she didn't know how to answer. She needed to think. "I'd like to enjoy the summer at Bexhill with Lizzy and perhaps work on some sketches. Marcus might come down for a few days. I could earn my keep and help you or Miss Jenkins at the hotel." Sarah hoped she sounded vague, offering to help without commitment.

"I wondered if you could use your art talent and help with the posters and advertising."

Bill interrupted before she could answer. "Here we are." Henry the doorman opened the car door for Anna.

Sarah jumped out of the car. "It feels good to be home. Henry, have my bags sent up to the penthouse, please." The confidence in her voice belied her feelings. Part of her wanted to stay in the security of her bedroom in her grandparents' suite where she'd lived since she was eight. In fact, no one had lived in the penthouse for over ten years. Distancing herself from the hotel, or to be honest Nana's suite, was important; she was ready to grow up. And in a practical sense, the penthouse was large enough to set up an art studio. She could do her own cooking. She hadn't told Bill yet that she was vegetarian; an executive chef whose whole life had been about food would not understand. Was she convinced or was it Marcus's influence, she wondered.

Cheers and congratulations rang through the lobby. Miss Dorothy Jenkins, the events co-ordinator, and Mr. James Lytton, the general manager, came out of their offices and Mrs. Amy Peterson, the head housekeeper, stood on the stairs with several maids behind her. Sarah looked around at the old familiar faces, people who had watched her grow up, and she couldn't help noticing how everyone had aged in the three years she had been away. She smiled at Woody, the handyman, and Balaji, the maître d' and the youngest among them. She looked at Anna and Bill, both in their late sixties, and felt an involuntary shudder at the thought of losing them. And who would take over the hotel? It should have been Isabelle, her mother, leaving Sarah the freedom to do what she wanted—paint and dream of owning an art studio with a public gallery. Miss Berkley's words flashed through her head and anger clenched her stomach, anger at her mother for putting her in this impossible position.

**

The penthouse reflected Sarah's personality; funky artwork hung on the walls and modern sculptures decorated the tables. The sitting room had the most light, with two big dormer windows and a skylight in the ceiling, so she'd chosen to use it as her studio. She had enjoyed setting up her new home, but at first, her mind had played tricks—she imagined she saw her mother walking through the flat or heard her father crying and sobbing. The memories were vague and childlike, not surprising as her mind went back to being eight years old. She remembered feeling scared as her father shouted, drunk and angry, and the relief when Nana came up and took her things down for her to live in Suite 305. She couldn't shake the sense of guilt that it was her fault that her father left because she had abandoned him. Underneath those dark thoughts she remembered happiness; her parents laughing, kissing and hugging in this very room. And then, it all changed one day and her mother was dead, murdered by thugs, and her father, crippled with grief, had disappeared.

The studio was no longer the lounge with bad memories but was now her creative place, filled with her parents' energy from happier times. Taking a piece of charcoal, she sketched the view of the beach and Promenade from her window. There was a knock on her door, she was about to greet her first guest.

"Lizzy, come in." Sarah led her into the section of the L-shaped room that now served as her sitting area with an archway into the kitchen.

"It looks so different. I like what you've done to the place, the art work and your studio," Lizzy said, walking around. "I wish I had my own place. Mother is fussing and father wants me to get a job."

"What kind of job?"

"That's just it, there isn't much to do with fashion design around here or in Eastbourne. I could work in a boutique but I want to design, not sell clothes. What do you want to do?"

"I want to paint, but I know they expect me to work in the hotel. I'm guessing I have the summer before I'm asked to work full time."

"Yes, my mum said I could enjoy the summer here. But then what? Even the men are idiots. Remember Spotty Dick, he worked for his father renting deckchairs to tourists?"

"Oh yes, he had a thing for you."

"Well, his acne has gone and he calls himself Rick now, still works for his father. He took me to the pictures on Saturday night; his creepy hands were all over me. I couldn't watch the film. All he talked about was deckchairs and women in bikinis."

"What about Dave Turner? You had a crush on him and I think he's a solicitor now. Didn't he join his brother's practice here in Bexhill?"

"He's dating someone from Brighton. The chances of finding a decent job or husband here in this backwater are remote. Have you heard from Marcus?"

"No, and I'm worried. He saw me getting into the Rolls Royce with the Thorntons. I hadn't told him they were friends. He hates society people, capitalists as he calls them. He probably thinks I betrayed him."

"Sarah, let him go. He's bad news. I heard he was into drugs."

"No, he's not." Sarah sounded emphatic, but she wasn't sure. The day before graduation he'd seemed out of it, giggling and his eyes were bloodshot. It wasn't the first time but she had been afraid to say anything. "I phoned his digs but he wasn't there. I left a message for him to call me. I miss him. We had planned to visit every second weekend, alternating between London and Bexhill, starting this Saturday in Bexhill."

"Be careful, Sarah. I see the way he speaks to you. He's disrespectful and hurtful."

"That's just his way; he teases me. He loves me and…I love him."

"Do you? You hesitated, I don't think you are sure about that."

Sarah sighed. "You're right, I'm not sure. So why do I want to see him?"

"I don't know, but if you are planning to commit to him you'd better be sure. There are lots more fish in the sea. Just not round here," Lizzy said with a laugh. "How would you feel about going back to London?"

"I hadn't thought about it. I just got home. I want to spend the summer here. I liked London and I would go back, but I can't leave Nana and Grandpa Bill."

"You keep saying that but they seem to be managing just fine without you. Have you talked to them about what you want to do?"

"No, I don't want to disappoint them. But I'd love to go back to London and work on my art, maybe get known in a few galleries. I'm dreaming."

"With your talent, it isn't a dream. Will you think about it?"

"Yes, I'll think about it." Sarah nodded. "But we stay here for the summer."

"Agreed. There's a dance at the drill hall tonight. What do you have to wear? And none of that Bohemian stuff." The two friends walked into the bedroom and Sarah opened the wardrobe door. Grabbing a yellow dress, Lizzy held it against Sarah. "Perfect. Scoop neck, tight bodice and full skirt; add a frilly petticoat and it'll be great for dancing. Do you have a head band to match?"

Sarah pulled a yellow scarf from her chest of drawers and folded it into a head band, wrapping it around her wild curls and tying it behind her right ear.

"I'm going home to change. My dad said he'd drive us there and pick us up. He wants to make sure we don't run off with undesirable men." Lizzy giggled. "We'll pick you up at seven."

**

It was midnight when Mr. Elliot dropped Sarah off at the hotel.

"Good evening, Miss Sarah. I trust you had a pleasant evening." Dan the night doorman said, opening the car door.

"I had a fabulous evening but my feet are killing me from dancing." She bent down, flipping her high heels off and looping her fingers through the straps. She walked barefoot, laughing and twirling as the dance music still played in her head.

Dan coughed and stalled with his hand on the brass door handle. "Miss Sarah, you have a visitor. He arrived about two hours ago and insisted on waiting to see you." Dan gave her a worried, quizzical look. "He said he's your boyfriend from London and that you are expecting him." He coughed again. "Miss, he's a bit odd looking. If you want me to throw him out, just say the word."

Sarah peered through the frosted glass door panel. "It's Marcus." Her heart gripped her chest. She stood riveted to the spot, her ears thrumming with emotion, joy or fear she couldn't tell which. And then horror struck her—she didn't want him here, he didn't belong. Dan pulled the door open.

Marcus jumped up. "Surprise!" He opened his arms looking like a Jesus figure in his loose fitting shirt, long, mousy and not-too-clean hair and two strings of wooden beads hanging around his neck. He spun round in circles. "Wow! Man, you didn't tell me you lived in a palace with a butler dude."

"Dan is not a butler dude, he's our night doorman and this is a hotel not a palace and yes, I am surprised." Irritation clipped Sarah's words. "What are you doing here?"

"Following our plan. Remember, alternate weekends in London and Bexhill."

"Why didn't you answer my phone call? I didn't think you were coming."

"Sorry, I wanted to see my girl and a mate offered me a drive, and here I am." He stopped spinning around and looked at Sarah. "What's with the new duds, you look different. Pretty dress."

"Lizzy and I went dancing at the drill hall."

"Dancing!" Marcus's smile disappeared into a dark cloud. "Who with and who drove you home?"

Sarah attempted a laugh, but it sounded forced. "Marcus, don't be silly. Lizzy's dad drove us. We went to listen to the music and we danced with each other." Sarah felt the warmth on her cheeks as she lied. They had both danced all night with young officers from the military camp.

Marcus grabbed the top of her arm and Sarah winced. "I don't want you fooling around. You're my girl."

Sarah pulled her arm free and glared at Marcus. She sensed Dan taking a step towards them, but then the front doors opened and he greeted a hotel guest. She pushed Marcus into the chair and sat next to him. Her back to the guests, she sensed a look of disapproval as they walked to the lift. She wanted to get Marcus out of sight.

"We'll talk tomorrow. Where are you staying tonight?"

"Here, of course."

Sarah gulped, she had never thought about sleeping arrangements. They had never slept together, as in overnight. There had been plenty of pretty intensive necking but she had managed to avoid 'going all the way'. Living in tight student quarters didn't offer much privacy, but her penthouse was very private. Was she asking for trouble? Maybe, but where else could she take him?

"Come on then, we'll go to the penthouse." Dan gave her a disapproving look. "It's okay, Dan, I have two bedrooms," she said with confidence, but underneath she wondered if Marcus would respect her wishes.

"Yes, miss. If you need anything—anything at all—just ring me."

"Thank you, we'll be fine."

The ornate brass gate clanged shut and the lift began moving. As they reached the third floor Sarah whispered, "Be very quiet, we have to pass my grandparents' suite. I'd rather not surprise them. I'll do the introductions tomorrow."

Three

Summer at Bexhill

S tretching cat-like, part of Sarah's morning routine, she glanced at the clock: 9 a.m. She twisted the stiffness from her feet, smiling as she remembered the previous night's dancing. Then she said aloud, "Oh no! Marcus!"

"Did I hear my name?" Marcus stood in the doorway with a steaming cup of coffee. "Hot milk, no sugar, just how you like it."

"Good morning. You remembered," she said, swinging her legs out of bed, glad that she had slept in pyjamas. As she reached for the cup, Marcus pulled it away.

"Kiss first." He placed the cup and saucer on the side table.

Sarah moved away from the bed and kissed him on the cheek. He clasped his hands roughly around her head, pulling her face to his and kissed her full on the mouth. She gasped feeling the sweet sensation ripple from head to toe; she couldn't help herself and kissed him back with such intensity it frightened her and she pushed him away.

Breathing heavily, she said, "No, Marcus. This isn't right." Her words the opposite of the lust that churned inside. He leaned forward, laughing as he tried to pull her back into his arms. "Marcus, no!"

"I'm not good enough for you, now that you are back in your fancy place."

"No, I love you and I'm scared."

"Scared of what? Me!"

"Of course not." She stared into his eyes and thought, *There are times I'm scared of you, like right now. Your eyes are wild with temper.* She hesitated; should she be honest and risk an outburst? No not now. "I'm scared of my feelings for you. I'm afraid we'll go too far." She felt her cheeks blush. "I don't want to make promises I can't keep, whether they are implied or spoken. I want to be free and spend the summer here painting and having fun. You said you wanted to chill out and be free this summer."

"I do. I thought maybe we could go to the commune, but after seeing who your friends are and how you live, it's obvious the simple life of living off the land wouldn't suit you."

"Commune? What are you talking about?" Sarah frowned. "You're talking nonsense. Are you going to tell me what is really upsetting you?"

"All right, I'm shocked and angry." Sarah felt the spittle on her cheeks as he spat the words in her face. "I saw you getting into that Rolls Royce graduation day. You looked chummy and quite at home with the toffs. Bleeding capitalists by the look of their fancy clothes and posh words. Who are they?"

Sarah didn't like his tone, it sounded envious and devious—something she had never seen in Marcus before. Controlling her own temper, she answered cautiously, "Darcy and Belle Thornton. My grandmother used to work for Darcy's mother and Grandpa Bill met Darcy when he was under-chef. Years later they met up and became friends."

"Your grandparents used to work here? And now they own the hotel. Who gave them a hand-out, their rich capitalist friends?"

"Don't you dare speak about my grandparents in that way. They worked hard and saved all their lives and invested their savings in this hotel. Darcy and Belle have their own problems keeping the estate afloat."

"Estate!" Marcus yelled. Sarah backed away and moved into the sitting room, regretting her slip of the tongue.

"Are these *friends* society people?"

"If you must know they are Lord and Lady Thornton of Hillcrest Hall and they are kind, generous, hard-working people. They had to open their home to strangers to pay the bills. Belle runs the gift shop and house tours and Darcy looks after his tenant farmers and the estate. They work hard."

"You expect me to feel sorry for them, taking money from poor people to show off their expensive treasures and art work? I think that is as capitalist establishment as you can get, and you are a part of it."

"It's not like that. You are taking the situation out of context." Sarah wondered how out of context it was. The Thorntons were part of the establishment, albeit they worked hard and they were nice people. She had known them all her life so they seemed normal to her. But to someone like Marcus maybe not, and she sensed there was more to it—his anger was personal.

"Unbelievable! My little orphan Sarah, miss goodie two shoes, is a capitalist. A member of the establishment. Who would have known?"

The sarcasm hurt. Unable to answer as tears sprang into her eyes, the room fell silent except for the sound of Marcus pacing and breathing rapidly. The pacing, gradually slowed his breathing to normal. He stopped and put his arm on her shoulder, she held her breath afraid to move away. He brushed the tears from her cheeks. "I'm sorry, I didn't mean what I just said. I get so angry when I think about what those people did to my family."

Sarah realized that because he avoided talking about them ,she knew very little about his family,. All she really knew was that one of his grammar school teachers had recognized his talent for art and sculpting and helped him apply for a scholarship at RCA.

"What happened?"

"My dad lost his job and couldn't pay the rent. They kicked us out of the farm. We finished up in a crummy, dirty council house in city squalor. My mum was never the same." Moisture rimmed his eyes and his tone changed. He looked contrite and sad, the temper gone.

"I'm sorry," Sarah frowned not totally convinced he was telling the truth. "I had no idea you were tenant farmers."

"We weren't, dad just rented the house. I don't want to talk about it."

"Okay, but perhaps you can tell me more about this commune." She didn't really want to know, communal living was not her style but she needed to change the atmosphere.

"I like living in the country. Paul, he gave me a lift here, was heading up to a commune near Hastings. That's why I mentioned the commune." Marcus's eyes lit up as he continued, "Everyone lives in this big farmhouse, eating together and pitching in to cook and clean. The idea is to be self sufficient, farming and growing our own food, doing whatever we want to do. There are no rules or regulations and everyone lives in love and peace. No wars, no establishment. Man, it is perfect. Sarah, come with me. You can paint all day, I'll sculpt and we'd be together." He put his arms around her and kissed her, gently this time. "I love you and I can't bear the thought of living without you. Neither of us want the marriage thing—living free with friends is the answer."

Stunned, Sarah didn't react to the embrace as her mind frantically digested what she had just heard. Some of her college friends talked about the new free living, which included sleeping with and having sex with anyone you fancied and sometimes with more than one person. She shuddered, repulsed by the thought. Marcus had made the commune sound wholesome, but he hadn't mentioned getting high on weed, or worse, tripping on LSD. Some people hallucinated for days.

Is this the kind of life I want? It's what Marcus wants and if I want Marcus... Her thoughts stopped as she realized that Marcus would fit right in. Would he fall into the drug trap? She'd seen it in London. Could she get used to drugs? She'd never tried. Fear gripped her insides at the thought of losing Marcus.

"I don't know what to say." She knew she should tell him now that this wasn't what she wanted. So why didn't she?

"What do you want?" Marcus asked, mirroring her thoughts.

"I need to think about it. I want to stick to our plan for the summer and spend weekends together, going to the beach and swimming in the sea and I can come up to London a couple of times. When you're not here, I need some space and alone time so I can paint and think about my future."

"Does your future include me?"

"You know it does. But there are other things to consider." Sarah was choosing her words carefully. She had far more questions than answers, especially about Marcus and the latest commune thing had added more confusion."

"I'm sorry I made you cry. Am I forgiven?"

The phone rang as Sarah nodded yes. Pleased the argument was over, she picked up the phone. "Hello, Nana." She paused, "Yes, he is. We'll be down in about fifteen minutes."

Sarah looked at Marcus. "Well, word travels fast. Dan must have mentioned your arrival. Nana wants to meet you; late breakfast in the dining room. I need to get dressed and you need to clean up a bit."

"What's wrong with me?"

"You have to ask?" Sarah touched his stringy hair. "At least comb your hair and change your shirt, and those baggy trousers look as though you slept in them."

"I did," he replied with a note of defiance.

"A good wash wouldn't hurt. When was the last time you took a bath? There are clean towels in the bathroom cupboard." She took his hand and grimaced at the black fingernails and pointedly looked at his sandaled feet, grey with grime. "I'd like my boyfriend to make a good first impression and get my grandparents' approval." Sarah was quite aware that Anna and Bill would be pleasant and polite to

Marcus, *But approval might be stretching it,* she thought.

"Like it or not, this hotel caters to the establishment and my grandparents mean a lot to me. If you want to be my boyfriend and expect me to consider a commune, you had better behave and be polite while you're in the hotel. And don't mention the commune, I doubt they have heard of such a thing and if you explain how it works they will freak out."

Marcus smiled and kissed her on the cheek. "That's the first time I've heard you say, 'My boyfriend,' and I like the sound of it. I will play the part well because I love you."

Sarah slipped on a short black skirt and black and white striped blouse. She pulled the collar up and tied a white scarf around her head, leaving the tails dangling on her right shoulder. She liked the scarf look that Lizzy had suggested yesterday for the dance, it tamed and held her hair in place.

"Will I do? Am I good enough for you—*girlfriend?*"

Marcus appeared from the bathroom clean-shaven, shiny and polished. His hair was combed back, his shirt clean, buttoned at the neck and cuffs, and tucked into slim fitting trousers. He straightened and patted the hand-knitted sleeveless Argyle pullover. "My mum knitted this for me." His voice softened with sadness as he looked down at his feet. "I don't have any socks, so it's sandals and bare feet, but they are clean."

Sarah flinched slightly at the emphasis on girlfriend, but she couldn't help but smile upon looking at his feet. "The sandals are fine and you look...so different."

"Don't get too used to it, I'm only doing it to please you for the introductions."

Four

First Impressions

⚜

Balaji, the maître d', greeted Anna as she walked into the quiet Emily Carr Dining Room; most of the guests had eaten and moved on to their days at the beach or sightseeing.

"Good morning, Balaji. Sarah and a guest will be joining me." Balaji flipped his fingers and the waiter held the chair for Anna. She looked up, smiling. "Good morning, Eddie. Coffee for me please and menus for Sarah and her guest, and would you ask Chef Bill to join us?"

She was worried about Sarah's guest. One of those arty, beatnik types, Dan had informed her and then commented that he had been invited to spend the night in the penthouse. Anna was shocked. It was something Isabelle, Sarah's mother would have done, but not innocent, vulnerable Sarah. Anna had been reluctant to let Sarah go to art school in London, even if it was the best in the country. Bill had persuaded her that she would be fine and needed to spread her wings. Anna predicted that exposing her to London and arty types would be too much and she had been right.

Undeniably, three years at art school had moved Sarah's natural gift far beyond good or excellent, but people didn't make a living from art. Anna's eyes scanned the Emily Carr paintings that adorned the dining room walls. She didn't need to compare. In Anna's opinion, Sarah's genius surpassed even that of Emily Carr.

Emily Carr, a Canadian artist and Anna's favourite, had many talents. Anna had studied her work and career, enjoying her evolving themes and phases as she developed her unique skills. It bothered Anna that Carr had never made much money and lived a pauper's life in the forests of Canada's West Coast.

She wanted more for Sarah. Sarah's mother had discouraged her art, always pushing math and English instead; skills Sarah would need for business—specifically running the hotel. Since Isabelle's death, Anna had encouraged Sarah's talent, knowing that she found peace in her art. But now she wasn't sure she'd done the right thing. Perhaps Isabelle had been right. Assuming that Sarah would abandon her art and take over the hotel had been a mistake. She could see the conflict in Sarah's eyes.

"Penny for them, Nana." Sarah bent down and kissed Anna.

"Sarah, darling. I'm sorry, I was miles away. And this must be Marcus." Anna reached out and shook his hand. "Marcus, I am pleased to meet you at last. Please take a seat. Would you like some coffee or there's tea if you prefer?" Anna couldn't take her eyes off his red and grey diamond argyle pullover, not the beatnik she had expected but the pullover might have been a legacy from his grandfather. Wondering if he had matching socks, she couldn't stop her eyes seeking his feet. *Ah, there's the beatnik—open sandals and no socks.*

"Coffee is fine." Marcus took the menu as the waiter poured the coffee.

"Nana and Grandpa Bill spent time in Canada and America and got used to coffee in the mornings." Sarah explained. "Where is Grandpa Bill?"

"The new sous chef is not working out too well. You know Bill. His standards are high so he's giving him some extra training. He said he'd pop by to meet Marcus and… speak of the devil."

Marcus shot up from his chair and shook Bill's hand. The table went quiet as it seemed nobody wanted to speak first. Sarah wondered what her grandparents were thinking. The arrival of breakfast broke the ice as the waiter placed a tray of fresh fruit and toast in front of Sarah and a full English breakfast of fried eggs, rashers of crispy bacon, sausage, fried black pudding, mushrooms, tomatoes and baked beans in front of Marcus.

Sarah's mouth dropped open. "Marcus, I'm sorry, you don't like the meat. Do you want to order something else?"

"No, this looks real cool. Oh, man I haven't had a breakfast like this since ..."

"But I thought you were vegetarian?" Sarah tried to hide her surprise at the meaty breakfast while thinking of all the disgusting vegetarian dishes she'd suffered to please him. Marcus scowled directly at Sarah, "My mother always cooked us a big breakfast on Sunday morning," he paused, "after church." With raised eyebrows, Sarah wanted to giggle at his last words. *Church? That's a new one,* she thought, biting into a large strawberry.

Anna chimed in quickly. "What do you two have planned for today?"

"If the weather holds, I thought I'd show Marcus around Bexhill. Walk on the beach and may be swim if it's warm enough."

"Didn't we decide to go to Hastings?" Marcus mumbled

The commune, Sarah thought. *Not what I had in mind.* "We don't have a car and I doubt we can get to where you want to go on the bus."

"You can use the old Hillman if you like," Bill offered. "It's ten years old but it runs fine."

"Thanks, Grandpa. But you'll need it for the guests. We can go another time."

"We don't need it, we only use it as a spare. We have the Rover if guests need to be picked up or taken anywhere."

"Thanks, Mr. Blaine. I would like to visit my friend Dave," Marcus said as he deliberately wiped his plate with an oversized crust, shoving the too-large hunk of yolk and grease soaked bread in his mouth. Sarah gave him a sharp look of disapproval, recognizing his behaviour as truculent and wondered why he was acting this way.

Bill gave her a little smile; he had seen it too, but she knew he wouldn't say anything. "Sarah, come with me and I'll give you the car keys." Once out of earshot Bill turned to Sarah. "Is everything all right, Sarah? You look upset."

"Of course." Sounding but not feeling confident, she added, "I was a bit shocked at his lack of table manners. I guess I hadn't noticed it at college. And I really would rather go to the beach."

"Oh sorry, my offer of the car is not helping. Why don't you come back and swim this afternoon? I could suddenly remember I needed the car."

Sarah gave him a hug. "Thanks, but we'll be fine. We'll go swimming tomorrow."

As Sarah returned to the table with the car keys, Marcus stood up, ready to leave. "Let's get going. I need to get something from the flat."

Sarah hesitated, bent and kissed Anna. "Sorry, Marcus isn't much for small talk."

"I can see that," Anna replied. "Have fun in Hastings."

Bill sat down with Anna and took her hand. "She's fine. He's a bit weird, but artsy types often are."

"I'm worried. He's strange. I can see it in your eyes that you are worried too. The hair combed back and the argyle pullover were obviously for our benefit. We don't know anything about him or his family, and judging by his table manners, he's from the wrong side of the tracks. Sarah mentioned he was on a scholarship."

"It's not like you to be judgmental, but I have to agree about his manners. And I don't like his attitude of…I'm not sure of the word, entitlement maybe."

Anna nodded in agreement and then motioned towards the lobby. "Dan's description was more like that." Marcus walked through the lobby in a loose oversized shirt and baggy trousers and carrying a small bag.

The lines on Bill's brow creased, showing his age. "I don't want him sleeping in the flat. Can you find him a guest room?"

"I can, but do you think it will make any difference? There are two bedrooms in the flat and Amy told me that both beds had been slept in."

"Um, devious! You had Amy check on them. I trust Sarah but I don't trust him. But you might be right. You could give him one of the staff rooms and Sarah could lock herself in the penthouse. Then it would be up to her if she let him in."

Anna laughed. "A bit excessive, don't you think? The days of the chastity belts are long gone. I don't like the man, but she is almost twenty and a grown woman."

"You're right," Bill said, laughing. "I knew there was a good reason why I loved you. I must get back to the kitchen." He brushed a curl from her forehead and let his lips linger on her cheek before leaving.

Anna watched him disappear through the service door, his steps uneven from sore feet, a legacy of years of standing in a busy kitchen. She put her hand to her cheek, feeling the warmth and love of his kiss. She wanted Sarah to feel the same kind of love, but she wasn't going to get that from Marcus.

Smiling, happy guests greeted her as she walked through the lobby but she had noticed bookings were down from last year. People were going abroad for holidays not that it was so easy now to drive your car onto the ferry and cross the English Channel. The New Sackville's younger clientele who had money wanted to explore new horizons and the guests who came year after year were elderly and suffering health issues. *And so are my staff,* she thought as James Lytton, general manager, leaned heavily on his cane and hobbled towards her, his face contorted with pain from an old war wound.

"Is the leg bothering you today?"

"Just a bit." He tapped his leg with his cane. "Best weather barometer there is. It will rain before the day is out. I came to remind you that we have a meeting with Dorothy in few minutes."

"On my way. I just met Sarah's boyfriend. I'm not impressed, I need something to take my mind off him." Anna asked Mrs. Robertson, the secretary, to take notes as Dorothy Jenkins, the events co-ordinator, followed behind.

Anna opened the meeting. "As I'm sure you are all aware, summer bookings are down by twenty-five percent in spite of our efforts with the children's program and guided tours. Times are changing and people are going further afield for holidays. Seaside holidays are not as exciting. But thanks to Dorothy's hard work the corporations are more than filling the gap."

"I'm working with two big companies." Dorothy passed a sheet of paper to James and Anna. "Doggie Grub is a pet food company," Dorothy said, laughing, "as the name implies, and they want to book a managers' meeting in late August. We've always had a policy not to book corporate meetings during high season. We do have rooms available that week if they take double occupancy, and the company is fine with that, but it would put us to full capacity."

"Let's do it," Anna said, "I have no problem with the hotel being full. It's unlikely we'll get many more holiday bookings and corporate business is booming. We need to go after the business money. Everyone agree?" Nods of assent went around the table.

Dorothy continued, "The second company wants to take over the whole hotel for five days at the end of November. But they are actually only booking twenty-five rooms."

Anna's eyes lit up. "November is our worst month. We never get more than five or six bookings at that time. It sounds wonderful."

"I'm concerned, as this company is being extremely secretive. The director gave his name as Mr. Jack Jones and the company's name Willingate & Company. It's supposedly an investment company but I cannot find it listed anywhere and nobody in the financial or investment industry has heard of them. Beyond the fact that Mr. Jones did have a Welsh lilt to his voice, it is hard to know if he is genuine. And they insist the hotel be closed to the public, including the restaurant. When I asked for more details he said he would only speak to the owner in person. He's calling back this afternoon to confirm an appointment. He wouldn't even give me a phone number."

"What do you think, James?"

"From what Dorothy has described, it sounds classified to me; a military operation or something to do with the government. It could be the mafia, although I doubt that." James laughed. "Joking aside, it sounds classified rather than cloak and dagger. No harm in talking to them."

"It wouldn't be difficult to close the hotel at that time; even the restaurant is quiet then. Go ahead and book an appointment with Mr. Jones, Dorothy. Invite him for lunch next week, whatever afternoon I have free and co-ordinate it with Bill and James."

"I've had an idea to boost summer bookings," Dorothy said. "What do you think of offering a program to encourage wives to accompany the men at the conferences?"

"I like that idea. James do you have any ideas?"

"I wondered if we could get Rolls Royce interested in the car festival again?"

"I think Dorothy has more than enough to do at the moment. Let's give Rolls Royce some thought for next year. I don't have anything else. Any more questions? Good, lets get back to work."

Five

Commune and Conflict

S hiny and new looking, it was hard to believe Bill's green Hillman Minx was more than ten years old. Sarah handed the keys to Marcus as Henry held the passenger door open. Marcus stood by the door blocking her from getting into the car. "I forgot my driver's license."

Sarah sat in the driver's seat. Pulling away from the hotel, she glanced at Marcus. "You don't drive, do you? I can teach you to drive this summer. Grandpa won't mind us using this car."

Marcus shrugged his shoulders; his arms spread wide holding the unfolded map in his face. "The village is called Clover's Corner. It's here on the map, about twenty miles north of Hastings, and Clover Farm Commune is ten miles north of the village. Dave said to turn off onto Barn Road and keep going until we reach a big old farmhouse.

"Hastings isn't far. Dave must be expecting you if he gave you detailed directions. I'm wondering why you didn't mention it?"

"I wasn't sure you'd want to come."

Sarah stared straight ahead and drove on without answering, annoyed that he ignored the fact that she didn't in fact want to come.

Clover's Corner amounted to about four houses and had there not been a sign they would have missed it.

"How much further to Barn Road?" Sarah asked, slowing down.

"It should be here." Marcus pointed to a sign post. "There!"

"Are you sure this is right?" Sara turned the steering wheel and the car bumped and groaned as she navigated around large holes. Long grass and low bushes brushed the sides of the car. Finally, they arrived at an old rundown farmhouse. Chickens wandered around the yard, clucking and pecking. A tall, spindly man was unhitching a horse and maneuvering a cart into a barn.

Sarah stopped the car and Marcus jumped out. "Hey Dave! I told you I'd come." Two white geese waddled at quite a speed towards the car, wings flapping. The man shooed them away.

"Marcus! Welcome to Clover Farm. Love and peace, man." Dave held up his hand in the familiar vee peace sign. "And you persuaded Sarah to come. Jenny, look who's here."

Jenny, a small, round woman in her mid-thirties with waist-length brown hair, dressed in men's trousers and a paisley blouse, came out of the barn and greeted Sarah with a hug. "Welcome to Clover Farm and peace be with you, sister."

Not quite sure how to respond to the sisterly greeting, Sarah timidly said, "Hello."

"Come into the house and I'll make some coffee. The others will be in soon. Tina and John are in the meadow and I sent Summer to get some eggs. We're a small group today as the others went into town for supplies to repair the barn."

"How many people live her?' Sarah asked, looking around the kitchen dominated by a large wooden table and mismatched wooden chairs.

"There are seven of us right now. You and Marcus make nine, and there's six bedrooms upstairs so I reckon there's room for fifteen or more." Jenny breathed hard and her ample breasts jiggled as she pressed the pump handle vigorously. It seemed she was pumping air until water finally swished into the enamel coffee pot. "Dave and I have lived here for five years and the most we've had is twelve. Tina and John have been here three years and the others come and go.

31

Not everyone can handle living so close to nature. Marcus told you that we are self-sufficient, right?" Sarah gave a nod, not wanting to admit that Marcus had told her nothing. "We grow our own grains and vegetables." The coffee pot sizzled as she placed it on the cooker. Staring at the cut wood piled at the side, Sarah realized the cooking stove was fueled by wood, which explained the heated kitchen on a warm July day.

A little girl of about five years old came skipping into the kitchen carrying a basket. Sarah found herself glancing at the door, waiting for Hansel to follow this fairy tale Gretel into the room.

"How many did Mrs. Hen lay for you today?" Jenny bent down, peering in the basket, and kissed the little girl on the head.

"Summer, we have a visitor. Meet Sarah, our new friend." After putting the basket on the table, Summer politely extended her hand to Sarah.

"I'm pleased to meet you, Summer. Do you fetch the eggs every day?" Summer nodded and skipped away into another room.

Jenny placed two steaming cups on the table and motioned to Sarah. "Sit and chill. Help yourself to scones, I made them fresh this morning. Bought flour I'm afraid, we've run out of our own until the next crop of wheat. Flour is hard to grind, so we often run out. We are mostly vegetarian, but we do eat dairy products. When I was pregnant with Summer and then breast feeding, I felt I needed milk and now Summer needs it for her growing bones."

The aroma coming from the steam didn't smell like normal coffee, Sarah took a sip and it vaguely tasted like coffee but was sweet, she liked it and added milk. "What kind of coffee is this? It has a sweet taste."

"Dandelion root. What an amazing plant. We roast and grind the big tap roots, add hot water and it makes coffee. The leaves make a tasty salad; we'll have some at dinner. We make our own tea too." Jenny grabbed a tin from the shelf. "We use dried herb leaves and sometimes fruit peels." She took the lid off and pushed the open tin towards Sarah's face. The leaves looked brown and inedible, but the fragrance of lemon was pleasant. "This is my favourite—lemon grass with dried chopped lemon peel."

It had been a long time since breakfast and Sarah enjoyed the homemade scone. Finishing her coffee, she asked, "How long have you known Marcus?"

"We only met him a few years ago. Apparently, he and Dave grew up in the same neighborhood in Liverpool, but they didn't know each other back then." Jenny shook her head. "He told us the story. Unimaginable, losing both parents that way and then the horror of the accusations. Such a tragedy." Jenny's eyes scanned Sarah. "He didn't tell you?"

"No. He doesn't talk about his past. What happened?"

"I can't tell you, the records were sealed. I only mentioned it because I thought you knew. You'll have to ask Marcus. What I can tell you is that the scholarship to the Royal College of Art and meeting you saved his life."

Sarah felt sick. She'd always had the feeling that there was something not right in Marcus's past, but Jenny's words of tragedy, sealed records and unimaginable horror confirmed Sarah's instinct that something bad had happened. Why had he not told her? She felt betrayed. Tears burned the back of her eyes. Instinctively, Jenny wrapped her arms around her, and Sarah welcomed her warmth and kindness.

"I'm sorry, I've upset you. I should have known. Marcus never talks about it, but he's so close to you I thought he would have. He went through a bad patch and he and Dave lost touch when Marcus went to London. Dave is happy to have him back in his life, especially as he wanted to bring you and live here."

"Pardon?" Sarah wasn't sure she'd heard right, but then nothing she'd heard in the last hour seemed right. *Am I dreaming? This farm, Jenny, dandelion coffee and girls called Summer—nothing seems right and I don't know who Marcus is anymore.*

"I don't know what Marcus told you, but we're not staying. My grandparents are expecting us back at the hotel by dinner time." Sarah's voice clipped as it did when she was annoyed.

"Let's go see what Dave and Marcus are up to," Jenny said, leading the way across the yard towards the barn.

"Dave, I made some coffee. Come join me in the kitchen." Dave and Marcus came out of the barn.

Jenny stroked Sarah's shoulder. "We'll leave you to talk to Marcus." Sarah didn't want to talk, she wanted to get in the car and leave. She found herself staring Marcus in the face.

He frowned. "What do you want to talk about?"

"Why didn't you tell me about your life in Liverpool?"

"There's nothing to tell. I don't like taking about personal stuff." Marcus gripped the top of both Sarah's arms, she flinched as his thumbs pressed into her flesh. She saw that wild look in his eyes again and tried to pull away. "What did Jenny tell you?"

"Let go of me, you're hurting me. Jenny said you had a tragedy in the family and to ask you as she couldn't tell me."

Marcus released his grip. "Oh, I'm sorry. It's something I've put behind me and dredging it up is too upsetting."

"I don't understand, you say you love me but I know nothing about you. I told you about the tragedy in my family and yet you kept your family secret from me. You don't trust me."

He grabbed her arms again. "I do trust you. I just don't want you to hate me." Sarah didn't answer because she thought it might be true. She realized he had seen it in her body language and his tone changed. "Don't let's fight. Let's enjoy the day in the countryside."

"Are you sure it's only one day? Jenny tells me you arranged for *us* to stay here. Our room is ready for us."

"It's beautiful here, who wouldn't want to stay? I thought you'd like it, living in nature, painting and living free."

"Well, you thought wrong. Whether I like it or not is beside the point. You didn't ask me! I'm tired of your secrets and manipulation.

I'm going back to Bexhill and it's up to you whether you come with me or stay." Sarah walked back into the farmhouse. Dave and Jenny were at the table.

"It has been lovely to meet you but I am heading back to Bexhill."

Marcus called from the door, "Go back and collect your things and come back, even if it's just for the summer."

"No!" Sarah marched passed him and held her breath, seeing the fire in his eyes. Dave jumped up and moved him roughly into the kitchen. Jenny took Sarah's arm and walked her to the car.

"He's upset because he loves you."

"I think you are making excuses for him. I saw how he looked at me and that was anger not love."

"Dave'll take care of him. I will miss you, sister. I think we could have been good friends."

Sarah smiled. "I agree, and I would have liked to get to know you. You are very kind. I'm not sure I could get used to the sisterly thing." They both laughed. "If ever you're in Bexhill, I'm easy to find at The New Sackville Hotel. I have my own flat, which belonged to my parents, above the hotel and I would love you to visit."

"I'd like that. Drive safely, and I'm sorry it didn't work out."

"Me too." Sarah giggled. "A sisterly hug?"

The Hillman bounced into a particularly big hole as Sarah took her eyes off the road to wave goodbye to Jenny, secretly hoping that Marcus might appear. But the doorway remained empty.

When she turned onto the main road, an audible sigh escaped on her breath as she said, "I'm glad that's over. Am I relieved I didn't hit a pothole or relieved I got away?" Hesitating, she thought, *From the farm or from Marcus?*

She was surprised at how matter fact she felt; the only emotion was disappointment. Disappointed he hadn't tried harder to make her stay, or agreed to come back with her. She had never doubted that he loved her, and yet he had let her go too easily. She glanced in the rear-view mirror, hoping to see him pull out of Barn Road—a prince chasing his princess. She began laughing, the only way he could reach her would be on the back of an old cart-horse.

Marcus wanted her on his terms. She had known that all along, but only now did she admit it. *It's over and I'm not even upset, but I am curious about his past.* She shuddered, a sealed record meant he had done something bad in his youth, and his parents were dead. But she realized she didn't quite believe his story. His fiery eyes flashed before her and she rubbed the top of her arm feeling the bruise where his fingers had been. Was he a violent man? *I'll never know because I doubt I'll ever see him again.* Even as the thought crossed her mind, her gut told her she wasn't rid of him. She did feel a little emotion—after all, they had been together for two years. Why wasn't she bawling her eyes out with grief over a lost love? She felt sadder that she wouldn't be able to get to know Jenny.

Sarah drove up the hill to Lizzy's house to tell her the news. She wasn't quite ready to tell Anna and Bill. She could hear a " We told you so," coming, although neither would say the words out loud.

Six

Good News for Lizzy

~⚭⚭⚭~

"Y ou're back. What happened?" Lizzy asked as she opened her
front door.

"Quite a lot. Come for a drive and I'll tell you all about it."
Sarah drove out of Bexhill to a quiet beach away from the holidaymakers. At first they sat with their knees tucked under their chins in
the kind of silence only close friends understand.

The calm sea rolled onto the shingle beach, each wave positioning
itself to fall with a delicate whoosh, the pebbles waiting to sing as
the salty water receded back into the sea. The blue sky was peppered
with fluffy white clouds floating over the sun, easing the afternoon
heat. It was one of those perfect summer days.

Sarah moved her gaze from the horizon to Lizzy. Wisps of her
usually neatly-flipped blond hair blew across her face.

"I broke up with Marcus."

"Why?" Lizzy's eyes widened in surprise. "How do you feel? You
don't look sad."

"That's just it, I'm not at all sad. I'm relieved. I keep thinking I
should be upset, but I'm happy. And it's probably a really good thing;
I discovered he has a troubled past."

"I never understood what you saw in him."

After Sarah related the visit to the commune, meeting Jenny and how Marcus had just let her go, they both stretched out on their backs, closing their eyes to the bright sun and fell into silence again.

Lizzy lifted her head on one elbow, facing Sarah. "It's for the best. I never liked him. I've heard of communes, they smoke drugs and practice free love."

"You know, it wasn't like that. Dave and Jenny were really nice people. I didn't see any drugs. They were a couple with a cute little girl; a happy family living with nature. I wouldn't want to live like that and," Sarah began laughing, "and you, dear Lizzy, would die without electricity."

"No electricity! How did she dry her hair?"

"Trust you to think of your hair!"

Lizzy rolled on her back, "I have some news too. I had a letter this morning from Jacob's Fashions offering me a job as an assistant to a junior fashion designer.

"Wow. Lizzy, that sounds wonderful. That means you'll have to move back to London." Sarah frowned. "What's wrong with the job?"

"I had applied for a junior designer's position. Assistant means mostly secretarial work and practically no designing. The pay isn't even enough to live in London."

"It's a start. And once you start you can work your way up to designer."

Lizzy's lips pouted. "I thought you'd understand. I'm not a cheap secretary. I'm a fashion designer." She jumped up and threw pebbles into the waves. "It's not fair!" She picked up a rock and slammed it into the water. "My dad said I should take it. Actually, he ordered me to take the job and gave me a lecture about being grateful and how it would do me good to start at the bottom. He said he'd pay the rent on a flat until I was on my feet."

Sarah put her arm around Lizzy. She knew how hard it was for her friend, she had always had everything she wanted. Her wealthy parents spoiled her and now her father was expecting her to take an entry level job, which most people would accept as normal, but not

Lizzy.

"I know it's disappointing," Sarah said, squeezing her shoulders. "When do they want you to start?"

"September first."

'That's not so bad. We have almost the whole summer here, and something else might come up."

Lizzy smiled and brushed her eyes. "You always know the right things to say. Sarah, would you come to London and live with me?" Seeing Sarah hesitate, Lizzy rambled on, "You could find work at one of the art galleries or continue your studies. We could find a place where you can have an art studio. Please, Sarah!"

"I haven't really thought beyond the summer. You know my grandparents expect me to learn the hotel business, but I would rather come to London. It sounds perfect; I could work on my art and maybe sell a few paintings. And yes, I'd like to study more, but I don't have the money for more classes."

"Is the hotel business what you want?"

Sarah shook her head. "I don't have a choice."

"Will you think about it? Promise."

"I promise to think about it. Now let's have some fun. Is there a Saturday night dance anywhere? What about the De la Warr Pavillon?"

**

The dance turned out to be a dinner dance and not what the girls were looking for, so they joined friends at The Pitt, a trendy coffee shop. Laughter and conversation prattled noisily around their table of mostly old friends from school. Sarah glanced towards a smooching couple and felt an unexpected pain in her heart. She wanted to leave, but Lizzy was having a good time flirting.

"Lizzy, it's getting late. Let's go!" Sarah said, pulling on her arm.

Waving good night, she dropped Lizzy off at her house and drove on to the hotel, hoping Anna and Bill would have already retired for the evening. She didn't feel like answering questions about Marcus, so she crept in the service entrance. Surprised that even at eleven at night the service area was abuzz with activity, she heard Bill's voice saying good night to the staff and walked right into him.

"Sarah, what are you doing down here?"

"I just parked the car and this entrance was closer." Sarah felt like a teenager sneaking in past curfew as Bill gave her a quizzical look. She would normally leave the car under the portico for the valet to park.

"When did you get back from Hastings? Where's Marcus?"

"He's staying with friends. I spent the evening with Lizzy."

"Are you going to tell me what's wrong?"

Sarah shrugged. "Nothing is wrong." She didn't want to admit how she felt. It had seemed okay and devoid of emotion when she told Lizzy about Marcus. But sitting in the coffee shop watching young couples in love had triggered a sense of loss and sadness—she missed Marcus. Lizzy, too busy making eyes at a handsome young man across the table, hadn't seen Sarah's mood change. Her emotions raw, bumping into Grandpa Bill had triggered tears. His hand tipped her chin and he scanned her face, his gaze resting on her eyes and the tears flowed. He wrapped his arms around her and whispered, "It's okay." He led her to the back door and they sat on the bench in the courtyard. He lit a cigarette and let her cry, not saying a word.

Sarah leaned on his shoulder and said, "Marcus and I broke up and it hurts so much."

"I know, sweetheart." He cuddled and comforted her, staring up at the stars. It was a clear night with a warm, gentle breeze. He felt Sarah's pain but was relieved that Marcus had gone. He remembered that pain of losing a loved one when Anna had chosen to marry Alex; they had not been much older than Sarah. But sometimes things worked out for the best. He felt blessed for marrying Alex's widow and gaining a stepdaughter and step-granddaughter.

"In my early days here, I would sit on this bench having a smoke trying to escape Chef Louis." Bill chuckled and continued, "He was a tyrant but he taught me all I know."

"You aren't a tyrant so I'm not sure what Chef Louis taught you."

"His creative cooking and chef skills were second to none. And because he was such a tyrant, he taught me not to be one, which is why I treat my staff well."

"That makes sense."

"I fell in love with your grandmother on this bench. She was in tears, thinking she was going to be fired only days after she started working here." Bill's eyes smiled and he gently hugged Sarah.

"You loved her for a long time, Grandpa."

Bill nodded. "But I doubt you want to talk about love tonight. This bench has a story or two to tell. I first met Darcy Thornton here, before he was Lord Thornton." Bill pointed into the darkness. "I remember seeing an orange glow coming towards me—Darcy's cigar. He sat down where you are and told me I was a good chef. I didn't know what to do. It was so inappropriate, a mere sous-chef talking to a guest, and not just an ordinary guest, but Lady Thornton's son. But Darcy didn't care. He had a habit of popping up in unusual places."

"That's the first time I've heard that story."

"I haven't thought about it in years. How are you feeling? Are you going to tell me what happened?"

Sarah raised her head and wiped her face. "It's lovely out here, peaceful like Clover Farm—that's where Marcus took me. It's a commune, but nothing like what I expected." Sarah poured out the whole story about Jenny and Dave and what she had heard about Marcus.

"I think you are better off without him. It's hard, but it will get easier. Now, it's getting late and Nana will be wondering what has kept me." As they walked up the stairs together, Sarah noticed Bill was breathing hard. "Time to give up those cigarettes, Grandpa"

"Did anyone tell you you're getting bossy?" He smiled and kissed her cheek. "Good night, sweetheart."

Sarah climbed the last flight of stairs to the penthouse. She was glad she had told Bill, but the empty flat prompted thoughts of her parents. Memories of her mother were clear, there were photos and Nana and Grandpa talked of her often. But memories of her father were fading. No one ever spoke of him. Her first memories of him were his strong arms lifting her in the air, making her giggle, and playing games on the floor when she was a toddler.

But, she thought, *it wasn't here.* She'd been told they used to live in Scotland. The memories were vague and had a dark feeling to them. In contrast, she had been excited about moving to live at Nana's big hotel. Her most precious memories were of her father arriving at this flat and the laughter and happiness of being a family. And then a demon intruded: her mother was dead. She had tried to comfort her father's sobbing, but had failed. She cringed as her mind heard his drunken yelling, and relaxed with relief when Nana had rescued her from the penthouse. Then he had disappeared.

Ten years was a long time, and she didn't know where to start. Why the shroud of secrecy? Did Nana know where he was? Had he tried to contact her? Were they protecting her, and if so, from what? She vowed to ask Nana and find a lead—just somewhere to start.

Yawning, suddenly tired after an eventful day, she went to bed but her eyes wouldn't close in sleep. Thoughts of things that might have happened to her father merged with the secrets of Marcus's past, and both had deliberately walked out of her life.

The only people in her life she could rely on were Nana, Grandpa Bill, Lizzy and maybe Felix. They meant the world to her. It didn't seem fair that now they needed her in different places—she had to disappoint one of them. Wide awake, she went into the sitting room and sat on the window seat, marveling at how the plankton glowed on the crests of the waves in the otherwise dark sea. It seemed to have some significance, a glowing light in the darkness. The clouds covered the moon, the wind rattled and thunder rumbled in the distance—a summer storm was brewing. She pulled her knees up, wrapping her arms around them, making herself small. She wanted to be invisible, disappear so she disappointed no one. A flash of lightning startled her, and then, for a brief second, the light surrounded her as though transporting her to a quiet place as the rumbling thunder drifted away. A second flash bathed her in warmth. Her head cleared and she heard a voice tell her she didn't have to choose, but she did have to fulfill her dream. "Where did the voice come from?" she asked. But even as she turned her head, she realized it was her own voice and she knew what she had to do.

Seven

Passions and Dreams Revealed

It seemed to Sarah that she had barely closed her eyes when the alarm rattled on her nightstand. Her arm flayed around until her fingers hit the button. She stretched and rubbed her eyes: six o'clock, much too early for a creative artist, but this was the best time to catch Anna and Bill together and alone. They always had coffee and toast in Anna's office before their day began. She didn't bother to get dressed; wrapping a cotton housecoat over her baby doll pyjamas, she ran down the stairs. Bill was carrying a tray across the lobby.

"Good morning. Can I join you for coffee?"

"Of course, I'll fetch another cup." Bill frowned as Sarah took the tray and walked into Anna's office.

"Sarah? You're up early this morning. Is something wrong?"

"No, but I need to talk to you." She sat on the sofa, tucking her legs underneath her. Not sure where to start, she stared through the window. The sun, well above the horizon, glistened on the Promenade, still wet from last night's storm. "Let's wait for Grandpa Bill. He went to get another cup and saucer."

"Bill told me about Marcus. I'm sorry." Anna reached across and took Sarah's hand. "I know it hurts and I wish I could make it better like I did when you were little." Anna's tender smile tightened her throat and her resolve began to wane. Taking a deep breath, she reminded herself why she was there.

"I'm okay. I had a good cry on Grandpa's shoulder last night. I think it's for the best. The part that hurt the most was the way he just let me go—deserted me. It's the same feeling I have when I think of my father. How can you just let go of someone you love and forget about them unless you don't truly love them?"

"I can't speak for Marcus, although from what I saw I think he was hiding a lot of old pain, making him self-absorbed and insecure. But your father loved you very much."

"You are amazing, Nana. It took me two years to see what you saw in Marcus in less than an hour." She hesitated, suddenly afraid she would hear something about her father she didn't like. She had deflected the conversation to avoid talking about the hotel and her future. Talk of her father caused inner turmoil; everything was getting mixed up. She was relieved when Bill placed a cup and another plate of toast on the coffee table and Anna began pouring coffee.

Bill sat next to her, tapping her arm. "What do you want to talk about?"

"Oh, it's nothing. It can wait for another time."

Anna gave Sarah a stern look and said, "It is something. Now let's hear it."

"I've been thinking about my future." She glanced from Anna to Bill, concern etched in age lines; they both looked tired. *How can I tell them that I don't want to run a hotel, at least not now but possibly never? I can't. They need me, but without my art my soul will die.*

Exchanging knowing looks, Bill nodded to Anna to speak. "It goes without saying that the hotel will be yours one day and it is crucial that you understand the business. I know your art is important to you and you have more talent than most, but art doesn't pay the bills. We're not suggesting you give it up, but that you treat it as a hobby and work in the hotel, learning how it operates. We would pay you of course."

Sarah's heart sank; the people she loved the most had dismissed her passion and talent. Anger bubbled inside her. She wanted to fight back. Make them understand.

"I thought you understood! Treating my art as a hobby is abandoning my dreams. What was it you said to me when you gave me Uncle Bertie's blue pendant? 'Follow your dreams and don't let anyone destroy them.' Isn't that what you did Nana? Followed your dreams, and now you have all this." Sarah waved her arms around the office. She felt like a runaway train—she couldn't stop the hurtful words coming out of her mouth. "This dream might have been my mother's but its not mine. I'm not my mother!" She stamped her feet. "My dream is to be an artist and for my art to be appreciated and hung in galleries. Just like Miss. Berkley said, I will be famous one day." Close to tears she stopped as shock and hurt registered on their faces—the tears flowed. She had disappointed them, something she had vowed not to do.

"I'm sorry."

Silence.

"I am too." Anna paused, "You are partly right, not long before she died your mother did learn to love the hotel and would have taken over from us. If I'm honest, I'm not sure it was her dream or more my dream for her. I encouraged you to study art against your mother's wishes." Anna tried a weak smile. "The blue pendant and Uncle Bertie's words kept me going when I wanted to give up. Your mother had no faith in such things, but I knew it would mean something to you. I'm sorry, I assumed the hotel was your dream too. Grandpa knew better and said so before you left for college. I didn't believe him." Bill's eyes connected with Anna's with gentle understanding. Sarah couldn't help wondering if she would ever find such love.

Bill spoke up. "Sarah, what is it you want to do? Was that why you wanted to talk to us?"

"Lizzy has been offered a job at a fashion house in London and she wants me to live with her. Her father offered to pay the rent on a flat. I thought I could work at an art gallery and sell my paintings and…" Sarah paused, "and maybe take some classes."

"You'll get mixed up with arty beatnik types like Marcus. How can you live off art?" Anna's voice wavered.

Sarah felt her throat tighten. *She's afraid. Nana's afraid for me because of Marcus.* An image of Marcus flashed through her mind. *And she probably has cause.*

"I will be able to make money from my paintings. Miss Berkley told me I had a gift and predicted my art would hang in galleries all over the world. I can and will sell my paintings. I won't starve. And not all artists are like Marcus. In fact, most of my fellow artists are more like me, quiet and passionate about art."

"I noticed Miss Berkley whispered to you at the ceremony. Was it then that she told you that you had a gift?"

"Yes. Lizzy isn't due to start her job until September. I can work here until then and as you say, learn the business. If my art sells, I could come back in the summer and help out. Are you wanting to retire?"

Bill answered, "Not now, but maybe in another four or five years. None of us is getting any younger. We were planning on hiring and training new staff to run things and we'd oversee the operation until you took over. Perhaps you could do both: art and the hotel."

Sarah leaned her head to one side. "Perhaps. I do have an art studio upstairs, which I love. If I work in the hotel all summer, can you manage if I move to London with Lizzy in September?"

"You can start by working in the office."

"And moving to London?" Sarah paused, assessing whether it was a good time to ask about furthering her art studies, aware that the fourth year Silver Medal program required a commitment of time and money. She didn't care, she wanted this more than anything. "I want to register in the Silver Medal program," she blurted the words out, regretting her tone upon seeing Anna stiffen.

Bill touched Anna's arm, and directed his question to Sarah, "How long is the program?"

"It's an academic year. I'd have to apply, and if approved I'd work under a professor, most likely Miss Berkley. At the end of the year if I have met all the college's criteria, I'm awarded the medal. I could use the money I earn here to pay for the program and get a part-time job to support myself while in London." Her eyes flashed from Anna to Bill. "I promise to come home at Christmas to help and possibly by the next summer I could do both." She brushed off a brief sense of guilt as she said the last words. *Would* she come back and do both? "I had better go and get dressed before the guests come down."

Anna said, "You can start tomorrow with Miss Jenkins. And apply for the program, we'll pay for that. Keep your earnings for the London flat. Bill and I can manage until then."

Sarah jumped up and kissed them both before leaving the office. She was excited by the outcome. She had a year to prove to Anna that she could earn a living as a true artist. Whether she would commit to running the hotel, only time would tell.

**

Anna moved over to the sofa, seeking the comfort of Bill's warmth. "I got things very wrong, didn't I?" she leaned on his shoulder. "I forced Isabelle's or my desires onto Sarah. How will we manage? Bill, you can't keep working the hours you do, on your feet all day in the kitchen. There are days you can hardly stand, and that cough is getting worse. I'm tired of dealing with staff and guests; we are way past retiring age. And I know James wants to retire; his leg hurts more each day. Amy wants to spend time with her grandkids, Dorothy seems quite happy at the moment. But if we all retire at the same time, what happens to The New Sackville?"

"I think we need to put our plan into practice. Hire and train staff, cut back on our own hours, and supervise. The other alternative is to sell. But if we do, Sarah won't have her inheritance."

"Mr. Kendrick managed the hotel for years without being here. I'm sure we could too. I'll miss Sarah when she leaves for London. It will be more permanent than when she went to college."

"Let's enjoy the summer. And she'll be home for visits; you heard her, she has her art studio here," Bill reassured Anna, but he wasn't so sure she would come back.

"I just remembered. When you were getting a cup and saucer for Sarah, she mentioned her father. Should we tell her what happened to him?"

Bill shook his head. "Not yet. I think we have enough to deal with right now."

Eight

Ghosts From the Past

*A*n infusion of energy shot into her legs as Sarah ran up the stairs two at a time. *I'll write to Miss Berkley today,* she thought. "I'm going back to London," she squealed, almost bumping into a startled guest. "Oh, pardon me, sir."

Opening the penthouse door, she thought her heart would jump out of her chest with joy. Picking up the phone to tell Lizzy the good news, she glanced at the clock. At seven-thirty it was too early to call, but desperately wanting to share her news, she took some writing paper from the bureau and began penning a letter to Miss Berkley asking for her advice. Feeling calmer, she sat in the window seat and curled her knees up under her chin and stared at the sea.

A partially painted canvas sat on the easel by the window. Her eyes moved slowly from the canvas to the promenade scene. Overwhelmed by a sense of déjà vu, her imagination saw ladies with spinning parasols in long dresses, arms linked with gentlemen, strolling along an old-fashioned promenade. As though in a dream, she floated to her easel and began painting.

A familiar voice intruded, but she ignored it. The voice came again, closer this time. "Sarah…" She turned, suddenly aware of her surroundings.

"Nana, I didn't hear you come in." Sarah put her paint brush down.

Wiping her hands, paint streaked all down her pyjamas before she realized she wasn't wearing her painter's smock. She went to hug Anna but stopped. "What's wrong? You look as though you've seen a ghost." Sarah's hazel eyes widened with fear as she observed Anna's pasty complexion and static stare. "Nana, talk to me."

Staring at the painting Anna said, "The painting. That scene…how did you know?"

"Know what? Nana, you're scaring me."

"The painting! I saw that exact scene from this very window on the first day I arrived in Bexhill almost fifty years ago." Anna's voice dropped into a murmur, "Doll-like figures, ladies spinning parasols with gentlemen at their sides. I was in tears, not sure I had done the right thing coming to The Sackville. My room-mate, Sophie, hated me and I introduced myself to the staff by fainting in the staff dining hall." Anna laughed, rubbing her head. "I made quite the impression. I was wearing a large, unsuitable blue hat, and when I fainted the hatpin jabbed painfully into my head."

"Was that when you met Grandpa Bill? He told me about sitting on the bench with you in tears."

"No, that was a few days later. My first few days here were traumatic. The painting?"

"I can't explain. I was staring out of the window, waiting to phone Lizzy, and the scene came to me and I started painting. I must call Lizzy, she'll be up now."

"I would think so it's two o'clock."

"I've been painting for six hours? Something weird happened here."

"It sure did, but the painting is beautiful."

"A few little touch ups and the painting is yours, Nana."

"I'll hang it in the Emily Carr Dining Room." Emotion crept into Anna's face. She couldn't explain it, but the painting had bridged a void that she had not been aware was there. It filled her heart with more love than she thought possible; linking Sarah to her past.

"Thank you," Sarah said, her voice uneven with emotion. Anna had given her the highest compliment possible. Sarah knew at last that Anna truly appreciated her talent and believed in her art. *I was meant to paint that scene,* she thought.

**

Lizzy was delighted with Sarah's news. Having only half a day to celebrate, they spent it on the beach swimming and talking. Lizzy's father had found her a job as a filing clerk at his office for the summer, and he had convinced her to accept the job at Jacob's Fashions.

"My mother has contacted a friend who knows a lady who rents bed-sitting rooms in Kensington with shared kitchen and bathroom for five shillings a week. Nothing fancy, but it's clean. I suspect the landlady will be told to keep an eye on us." Lizzy rolled her eyes. "But the price is right and it's convenient. Just one Underground stop to both the college and Jacob's."

"I'm excited. My grandparents are paying for my classes, but I'll have to find a job. I'll save through the summer, but that won't last long."

"Stop worrying, Sarah. Let's enjoy the summer."

Lizzy and Sarah didn't see much of each other through the summer. Lizzy worked all day and had found a boyfriend to take up the rest of her time, while Sarah worked afternoons and evenings in the hotel and painted in the morning. Miss Berkley had written to her personally, expressing delight at being her mentor for the silver medal program. Anna pushed her to apply at hotels for part-time work. Grateful that Anna sort of understood Sarah's love of art, she suspected her grandmother still believed it impossible to make a living from creative work. Sarah wondered if Anna was trying to fulfill her own dream. If daughter Isabelle couldn't inherit The New Sackville Hotel, Anna would bequeath the inheritance to next in line—Sarah. Overcoming Anna's concern about earnings would be easy, but rejecting an inheritance would be complicated.

She thought about Felix. He had no choice but to inherit his father's title and estate. On her graduation night, they had danced and talked most of the evening. He had confided in her that he really wanted to be a barrister, with aspirations of becoming a Queen's Counsel, or silk as it was known in the profession. To be appointed QC was the highest honour barring a judicial appointment. The term silk came from the gown a QC wore, which was made of silk. But his father treated Felix's law career the same way Anna treated Sarah's art career—something to dabble in while waiting for the inheritance. Eventually he would have to give up his law practice and move to the Hillcrest Hall Estate permanently. She had felt his helplessness, and today she understood it. She missed Felix, aware of her neglectfulness because of Marcus. Felix understood her dilemma over the hotel. How had she not thought to call him? He'd always been there for her, ever since she was a little girl.

**

Sarah enjoyed working with Dorothy Jenkins, planning the corporate conferences and advertising program. She wrote ad copy, discovering she also liked graphic design but not as much as illustrating. Her painting mornings produces a series of old Bexhill scenes. She intended it as a surprise for Anna before she returned to London.

Reluctantly, Sarah had given up a morning of painting to be briefed on a meeting about an important government client. Bill had laid out coffee and fresh pastries for the three of them. Sarah detected a strange, even sombre atmosphere in Anna's office.

"Is it my imagination or has something bad happened?"

Anna replied, "Not so much bad as clandestine. Mr. Carter, the government official, is coming to 'Inspect the property for security and suitability for a classified meeting,' to use his exact words. They are considering the Sackville for a conference in November."

Sarah laughed. "It sounds as though James Bond is coming to tea, or perhaps more appropriately, cocktails…," she paused. "And by the looks of your faces, I'm right. I was only joking."

"It's not James Bond," Bill chuckled. "Now, that would be fun and interesting; I have read all of Ian Fleming's novels."

"Me too," Sarah said. "But this sounds as though it's the real thing."

"We're not sure if it's MI6," Bill said, rubbing his forehead, "but it does have something to do with the British Secret Service. All they have said so far is that they want the hotel closed, including the restaurant, for three days. We are to tell guests we are fully booked, but in fact they have only booked a block of thirty rooms and a meeting room for ten delegates. We assume the other rooms are for security people, which seems excessive."

"I'm not sure whether to be scared or excited. Do you think it's a conference for spies? How do I figure into all this?"

"I think it more likely to be with the head people and strategists. They insist on speaking with the owners, I have listed you as an owner with Bill and me." Anna said.

"What do you want me to do?"

"We'll know more after meeting Mr. Carter. You and I are responsible for all the arrangements at the hotel, connecting directly with their representative and basically doing their bidding. We meet here at eleven o'clock." Anna glanced at Sarah. "Business attire?"

"Okay, Nana, for James Bond I'll wear a suit, although I think he would prefer a low-cut cocktail dress." Sarah kissed her on the cheek before returning to the penthouse to change.

She took off the pink and white summer dress that Sarah thought was quite conservative enough for summer business attire and sighed. She took a suspender belt from her drawer giving it a disapproving look and fastened it around her waist and carefully pulled on nylon stockings, clipping them on to the suspenders, front and back. She chose a simple, slim-fitting black skirt, noting that it was actually the only black skirt she owned. She added a white blouse and matching black jacket and slipped her stockinged feet into black high heels.

Pulling at a handful of hair, she thought, *It looks as though I've been drawn through a hedge backwards.* She stopped, feeling sad, remembering her mother used to say that about her unruly red curls. The memory prompted her to open her jewelry box. As she picked up her mother's string of pearls, a vision of her father fastening them around her mother's neck flashed in front of her. Unbidden tears sat on her eyelids. Overcome with a profound sadness, she clipped the pearls around her neck and wrapped the curls as tightly as she could into a French roll and pinned it to her head. "Mother, you would be proud of me," she said, staring in the mirror. The tears escaping down her cheeks were not for her mother, they were for Sarah; for a lifestyle she didn't want and for a lifestyle she might have to give up. "Stop being silly," she reprimanded her reflection, brushing invisible fluff from her skirt. "This is just a costume, playing a part for a government official."

Mr. Carter arrived as Sarah stepped into the lobby. A large black Bentley pulled up and three tall, serious-looking men in black suits, each carrying identical brief cases, walked through the main doors. She wanted to giggle. *Triplets,* she thought.

"Gentlemen, welcome to The New Sackville Hotel. My name is Miss Sarah Wexford, Mr. and Mrs. Blaine's granddaughter. We are expecting you."

Shaking Sarah's hand, Mr. Carter introduced his secretary and security man and then he asked an odd question. "Are you related to Sandy Wexford?" She froze, her breath stuck in her throat. *Why is he asking about my father?*

"Miss Wexford?" His eyes pierced into hers, she felt uncomfortable.

"Yes, my father's name is Sandy Wexford. He disappeared after my mother died. I was only eight or nine and I have never seen or heard from him since." Suddenly she felt a glimmer of hope. "Do you know him?"

"No, it's part of our security screening to know how everyone is related and his name came up on your birth certificate." She didn't believe him. Her father's nickname was Sandy, but his real name was Alexander, which was what was written on the birth certificate she had spent many hours staring at, willing it to tell her his whereabouts. Carter had lied, but why? Sarah led the way to Anna's office. Catching an approving nod from Dorothy Jenkins, she straightened her jacket and smiled.

The suits cleverly revealed little about the purpose of the conference or their role, beyond admitting a connection to the British Secret Service. Anna, Bill and Sarah were bombarded with questions and found it creepy to realize how much they already knew about the family and hotel.

They seemed fixated on someone called Ravi Smyth and his brother, who they announced had both died in prison. Mr. Carter kept asking if they knew any of their associates. Sarah had a vague memory of Mr. Smyth the maître d' and remembered he'd had something to do with her mother's death. She noticed Anna wince at his name. Bill assured them they had not had any contact since the arrest and trial and they had not been aware that he was dead. Mr. Carter seemed satisfied with the answers and asked for a tour of the hotel's guest and service areas. A lump sum was agreed upon for the three days and Anna committed to closing the hotel and all three of them were sworn to secrecy. Mr. Carter declined lunch and left.

"I'm quite breathless," Anna said. "That was pretty intense. November 13, 14 and 15 are going to be interesting." She glanced at Sarah, a smile of pride on her face. "You look so much like your mother."

"Don't get used to it, businesswear is not my style," she said with conviction. Seeing the hurt in Anna's face she wished she had not said anything. "I'll dress appropriately for Mr. Carter." She debated whether to tell Anna about the mention of her father but decided to keep it to herself.

"Well, I had Chef Brian prepare a special lunch for James Bond," Bill said. "Let's go and enjoy lunch so we can chat about the meeting. At this hour the dining room will be empty."

"I was surprised they didn't ask about Marcus. He strikes me as the activist type." Bill directed his comment to Sarah.

"Marcus talked a lot, but honestly, I don't think I really knew him. According to Jenny at the commune, he had secrets, but not the espionage kind." As Sarah said the words, she gave an involuntary shudder, recalling odd behaviour and unexplained disappearances.

Nine

London

Only two more days and Sarah would be in London. The summer had turned out quite differently than expected. She and Lizzy had planned to have fun, but both of them wound up working. Even Sarah's work at the hotel had changed; for the last month she had worked with Anna, planning the James Bond Conference as they had jokingly nicknamed it. She admitted she enjoyed the work and had learned the business well. Painting had not been so productive and that irritated her, making her escape to London all the more exciting.

Sarah was satisfied that she had eased Anna's burden during the busy season, but still concerned. Working with her every day, Sarah noticed how she tired easily and on damp mornings she eased the pain in her knees by holding on to furniture—but she never complained. Today they had received the report from Mr. Carter; Anna dropped the letter opener; her swollen fingers had no grip.

"Nana, let me do that."

Anna slowly spread her fingers. "My rheumatism says it's going to rain."

Sarah took the envelope and gently held Anna's hand. "Are your knees bad too?"

"As long as I keep moving the stiffness goes away. Now don't go worrying about me, I'm fine." Anna brushed a stray curl from Sarah's forehead. "It will be better when the sun comes out. Now, lets look at this report."

Sarah scanned the page, which was sparse in detail. Each employee had either a check mark or question mark beside their name. The check mark meant they were okay and would be sworn to secrecy and the question mark meant more investigation was either ongoing or required. There was one red X beside Lionel, one of the bell-boys, with a note that said, *Prison record must be fired.* Above Lionel's name was that of Balaji, with two question marks and the word *Investigating.*

"Did you know Lionel had done time?" Sarah's forehead creased with puzzlement. "Quiet little Lionel? I think they have that wrong. And Balaji, he's been with us forever."

"I suspected Lionel had a past when I hired him, but I wanted to give him a chance, and he has proven himself. I won't fire him, but I'll find away to give him a holiday during the meeting. It's not unusual to lay staff off in November and we don't need everyone here for only thirty guests. Balaji: that is his past association with Ravi Smyth, but as Smyth is dead…" Anna's voice trailed off and her face tightened with emotion. "I don't know what happened, but I hope the bastard *suffered!*" Sarah gasped, she had never heard Anna express such hatred, nor had she heard her swear but she knew why she was doing so now. Smyth had been the cause of her mother's murder.

"You were so little and it was so long ago, but that man's name—and his father's, Ebenezer Pickles—brings back terrible memories."

"I know," Sarah said.

Anna looked at the list. "Thank goodness Dorothy is in the clear but James has a red squiggle at the side of his name. I wonder what that means?" Anna placed Mr. Carter's report in the file folder and locked the cabinet. "Sarah, there isn't anything left to do. Why don't you finish your packing?"

"I'm packed, but come up to the penthouse with me. I have a surprise."

**

Speechless, Anna stared as Sarah unveiled two large, framed paintings of old Bexhill. "I intended to paint three, but the conference interfered and I didn't have time. Do you like them?"

"Of course! They are…I can't find the right words. I will be so proud to hang them with Emily Carr."

"I've asked Woody to rearrange the pictures. He's in the dining room now waiting for you to tell him where to hang them."

**

Mr. Elliot had a large car and had offered to drive Lizzy and Sarah with all their belongings to London. At eight in the morning, Sarah, Anna and Bill stood under the portico beside two large suitcases, wooden paint boxes, a large easel and various smaller items Sarah deemed necessary for life in London. Henry opened the boot, already overflowing with Lizzy's luggage.

"There's no room." Sarah declared, looking at Bill and thinking he would have to drive her.

Henry rubbed his chin. "No worries, Miss Sarah. If Mr. Elliot doesn't mind, I will rearrange the boot. I'm used to this."

Henry rearranged the luggage; fitting the large items in the boot, smaller items, of which there were many, on the spare passenger seat, leaving Sarah's easel the only item not yet stowed. He studied it for a minute and then slid it at an angle between the seats, leaving just enough room for Sarah.

"You're amazing." She hugged a startled Henry, kissed Anna and Bill and slid into the narrow space. Sarah stared through the rear window, waving as the car pulled onto the main road.

Mr. Elliot said, "This is it girls. You are on your way to make your fortunes." Lizzy giggled. It was unusual for her father to say anything, and in fact that was all he said for the rest of the journey. Lizzy and Sarah were quiet too. A mixture of emotion swirled around Sarah—excited to be continuing her art but sorry to leave the hotel. Although she wasn't sure that was true, she did worry about Anna.

She assumed Lizzy was having mixed thoughts too. The job at Jacob's was not what she wanted and the boyfriend in Bexhill had seemed serious. Sarah concluded that returning to London was what they were celebrating.

**

Avonmore Road was a quiet London suburban lane of identical row houses. As they pulled up to number twenty-three, the lace curtains of the bay window parted slightly to allow Mrs. Debinski to asses her new tenants.

After brief introductions, Mrs. Debinski directed the girls to the second floor. Mr. Elliot helped them unload the car and gave the surroundings a disapproving glance as he paid for two months in advance. He kissed Lizzy, whispering something in her ear, and disappeared back to Bexhill.

Mrs. Debinski handed them each a set of keys while spouting a long list of rules about cleanliness, gentleman friends, curfews and the use of the telephone. She opened the only kitchen cupboard, which was technically in the hall over the stairs and pointed to two meters.

"You'll need shillings for the meters. That's for the electrics and the other one's gas for the fires, and it heats the bath water.

The rooms were small and the furnishing old, worn and sparse. Each room had a single bed, a chair and wardrobe; not what either of them was used to. The kitchen was no bigger than a cupboard with a sink and the smallest cooker either of the girls had ever seen. The only storage was in the meter cupboard, with one shelf that contained a miss-matched dinner set, a fry pan and a battered saucepan. The bathroom had a chipped washbasin, taps that squeaked, reluctant to allow more than a drip of water to flow. The hot water geyser hung over a rust-speckled bathtub and a pull-the-chain toilet next to it. But it was clean, like the rest of the house. Sarah surmised Mrs. Debinski had fallen on bad times. She sounded angry when she spoke, although she spoke well, and her clothes were smart, if worn and out of date.

"Well, what do you think?" Lizzy asked.

"It'll do, it's clean." Sarah shrugged, disappointed that there was nowhere bright to set up her easel—the rooms where dark and small.

"My dad said he'd talk to mother and see if he could find us something better."

"Better still, we could look for our own flat. If I get a job we could afford a small one, but for now, this is it." Resigned to the rooms being home for a while, Sarah unpacked her things and rearranged the furniture, finding a spot by the window for her easel. Hearing the doorbell, she glanced out of the window to see the Thornton's Rolls Royce at the curb and she heard voices and a loud, "No gentlemen friends allowed, this is a respectable house." Followed by Harris's voice, "Madame, you flatter me. I am Lord Thornton's chauffeur, come to pick up Miss Wexford and Miss Elliot to join the family for dinner."

Sarah ran to the stairs. "Harris, what are you doing here?"

"Miss Sarah, sorry for the intrusion. Lady Thornton thought you might like to join the family for dinner."

"We would love to, but how did you know where to find us?"

"I believe your grandmother telephoned her ladyship. I was to tell you, its informal, family only, so not to dress for dinner. I'll wait in the car." Harris doffed his hat at Mrs. Debinski, "Good day Madame." Her face bright red, a *tut* sound emitted from her pursed lips as she flung the door closed. Sarah thought her intention was to hit Harris's back.

She looked up at the girls. "Friends in high places I see." Her cheeks still flushed, she tipped her chin up and said, "Rules are rules." Sarah and Lizzy held their breath trying not to laugh.

Ten minutes later, as Harris held the car door open, Sarah turned to see Mrs. Debinski's parlour curtains move. She frowned, seeing two shadows watch them leave. Was there a Mr. Debinski? *No,* Sarah thought, *she's a widow. So who was the other shadow?*

Harris steered the Rolls into the traffic. They could contain their laughter no longer: *"Rules are rules,"* Sarah mimicked. "I feel sorry for the poor lady. She must have wondered who you were, Harris."

"Yes, Miss Sarah." Harris gave a rare smile, "I've never been called a gentleman friend before."

Stepping out of the car, Sarah caught a glimpse of Felix as he opened the door, the stained-glass panel catching the evening sunlight; her heart caught the same warm light. She had missed Felix over the summer and she had so much to tell him.

He gave Lizzy a hug, kissing her on each cheek. "It's good to see you. Come on in." He pushed the door wide open and turned to Sarah. "Sarah, it has been too long." He wrapped his arms around her, his lips lingered on her cheek slightly longer than a friendly peck. "I've missed you. I'm so glad you are back in London."

"Me too. I have so much I want to tell you and to ask your advice." Sarah took his arm and walked into the hall where Belle waited for them.

"Sarah, you are glowing. Happy to be back in London no doubt. I want to hear all about your plans. Anna tells me you are doing a post-graduate program."

"How did you know we were here? We only arrived this afternoon. I was so surprised to see Harris, and so was our landlady." Both girls laughed.

"I happened to telephoned Anna this morning and she said you had just left for London. She sounded sad; she misses you."

"I know. It was hard leaving." Sarah felt the familiar guilt and glanced towards Belle. Was she looking for Belle's approval?

"Just because Anna misses you doesn't mean she doesn't want you to be happy."

"I know you are right. Sometimes I'd like to divide myself in two. Half in Bexhill and the other half in London."

"Anna will manage, she's one of the strongest women I know. Darcy and I plan to visit Bexhill after we leave here." Belle said with a distinct note of reassurance.

**

Harris pulled the Rolls up in front of Mrs. Debinski's and wished the girls a good night. As Sarah put the key in the lock, the door sprang open as a tirade of abuse flew from Mrs. Debinski.

"What in the world is wrong?" Sarah said. "Please slow down. I can't understand what you are saying."

"Curfew is ten o'clock. I will not have…"

Sarah interrupted, "Mrs. Debinski, we are twenty years old and do not require curfews or chaperones. We were quite safe and there is no need for you to worry on our behalf."

"Rules are rules and if you want to stay here, there will be a curfew."

"Very well, the rent has been paid for two months. That will give us time to find other more suitable accommodation." Sarah marched past her and up the stairs, Lizzy close on her heels.

"You can't do that. I'll speak to your father."

Sarah leaned over the bannister. "Oh yes we can. Take my word for it, we are giving you notice and Lizzy's father Mr. Elliot will be quite happy to help us move out of this dump."

"Well, I'll sue you for the year's rent. Mrs. Elliot said you'd be here for a year."

"You do that. My solicitor, Lord Thornton's son would be happy to meet you in court. Good night!"

"Huh!" The bannister shook as Mrs. Debinski slammed her door.

"Sarah, what's got into you?" Lizzy said, her eyes wide. "We have nowhere to go. What if she throws us out?"

"She won't. Did you see the look of horror on her face? *Rules are rules.* I'm going to bed, we'll talk in the morning."

Sarah plumped the pillows and leaned against them. *What an evening*, she thought. Belle and Darcy were so kind, and she knew Belle would keep an eye on Anna. Felix was like an old shoe, comfortable and familiar. She had really wanted to talk, and she'd sensed an urgency in him. He seemed troubled, but after several attempts to have a private conversation had failed, they agreed to meet alone later in the week.

She almost laughed aloud remembering Mrs. Debinski's face, and wondered where she had found the courage to confront her. Recalling how she had managed to be honest with Anna and Bill about her art studies, she mused, "Perhaps, there is more of my mother in me than I realize." She had always assumed she was like her father, quiet and uncomplaining. Hearing Mrs. Debinski refer to Mr. Elliot, as *her* father had sounded good—a father to protect her. "Where are you, Daddy, and what happened to you?" The word daddy came to her naturally-- a little girl again. She felt the warmth of his hand holding hers as they walked to school; she saw his face as clear as if it was yesterday. "I need a place to start, a clue about his whereabouts." Suddenly she sat bolt upright. "Of course. Mr. Carter, how could I have forgotten? How does he know Sandy Wexford?"

Ten

Darkening Storms

Anna replaced the telephone receiver feeling more comfortable knowing that the Thornton's had checked on Sarah. She didn't know why she was so anxious, Sarah had proven she could take care of herself. But she missed her and wished with all her heart that... Tears sprang into her eyes realizing how much she wished Isabelle was alive and poised to take over the hotel.

"Excuse me, Anna. Have you got a minute?" James's voice intruded on her thoughts.

"Of course, James. Come in." Anna removed her glasses and brushed her eyes, gesturing towards the chair.

"I was looking over Mr. Carter's latest list. It looks as though we'll have to lay off several staff. And now he wants them gone two days before. It's beginning to get tiresome. He has offered to pay us for those extra days. I guess that is something." Anna looked at James, his face taut with anxiety. "What is it?"

"There is no easy way to say this, Anna. I want to retire. My roommate, Jeremy, retired last year. He inherited his father's cottage in the Cotswolds and we spend weekends there fishing. Now that he's not working, he wants to move there permanently," James paused. "He's asked me to join him." He gave Anna a sheepish grin. "I think you know that Jeremy is more than just a roommate."

Anna didn't answer and the room went quiet. James's anxiety pulsated as he stared at Anna. It had not occurred to Anna that Jeremy was anything more than a friend, but now that she thought about it, it had seemed an unusually close friendship. James had lodged at Mrs. Bromley's boarding house, now run by her daughter, ever since she and Alex had lived there in 1919. Jeremy had moved in only eight or nine years ago. Two men living in a boarding house was not unusual and she thought a good cover up—homosexuality was a criminal offense. She couldn't remember James having any particular male friends, but then he'd never had a girlfriend either.

James cleared his throat, stirring Anna from her thoughts. She glanced up to see fear in his eyes. "James, it's okay. I'm not judging you. I didn't mean to be silent for so long, but I didn't know you and Jeremy were… Now I do, and it's okay."

James let out a long sigh before answering, "Thank you. You and Bill are like family to me. I've been so afraid to tell you. Until Jeremy came into my life I was quite content to be a bachelor. In case you are wondering, there hasn't been anyone else." He paused again. "Jeremy make me very happy."

Anna smiled. "I'm pleased you have found someone to share your life with. It's a comfort to know there is someone there for you. I'm not sure what I'd do without Bill. Does Bill know?"

"I haven't told him, so unless he guessed, no he doesn't know. In fact, you are the first person to know officially. Jeremy and I agreed it was easier if people didn't know."

"And that must be difficult, having to hide how…" Anna looked at him not sure how to finish the sentence. James was a man of integrity and to keep his love a secret must be painful.

James rescued her. "Yes, at times it is difficult, but we manage. Most people pretend they don't know and good friends like you and Bill know and accept us. But people like Mr. Carter make me feel paranoid."

"I'll deal with Mr. Carter. Will you talk to Bill?" Anna asked.

"Yes, but no one else is to know."

"No, there is nothing to tell. The staff will of course be told you are retiring, but that was to be expected." The lines on Anna's forehead formed deep furrows. "Two men boarding at Mrs. Bromley's is easy to explain, but how will you cope living in a village with nosy neighbours?"

"The village thinks we're brothers-in-law. Jeremy has been married—no children and his wife died ten years ago. The neighbours met his wife when they visited his father. He introduced me as his late wife's brother, soon to retire from a prestigious hotel in Bexhill, which impressed the village." James smiled. "Jeremy is offering a family member retirement sanctuary at his cottage. The neighbours are nice people and we're almost accepted as newcomers."

"Excellent. However, getting back Mr. Carter. I think he might know something." Anna showed James the red mark against his name.

James's pallor paled. "This is not good, I wonder if they found out about Jeremy's cottage? It wouldn't take much to discover I'm not Jeremy's brother-in-law."

"It's hard to say. Even if they have, they wouldn't tell us. But if you are not here, there isn't any need to investigate. You didn't say when you wanted to retire. Do you have a date in mind?"

"Yes, I thought I'd see you through this Bond conference and Christmas. I planned to retire December 31st. Giving you time to find my replacement."

Anna thought for a minute. "We have a couple of options. You could retire now, although that might look suspicious as I hadn't indicated you would retire. But Mr. Carter already knows the seasonal staff are let go at the end of September, and I regularly give the permanent staff holidays in November. It only needs myself and one other person to manage the conference and Sarah said she would be home. I'm also expecting them to clear Dorothy. I'll put you on the list for annual leave. I suggest you go somewhere without Jeremy. Come back after this is all over and take up your duties until December 31st."

James still looked worried. "I could go to prison."

"That is unlikely, the most they can find out is that you lied to the villagers. I don't think that is a crime. Mr. Carter is coming by to discuss the final staffing list at the end of the week. He only seems interested in the staff on duty. Don't worry, make your holiday arrangements and carry on as normal."

"Thank you," James said, leaving the office.

Anna stood at the window; litter and dried leaves flew by like strange birds, airborne in a sudden gust of wind. The temperature had dropped and dark clouds rolled along the horizon. She shuddered and clasped her arms around her middle, pulling her shoulders to her ears. *Why am I protecting myself, and against what?* she thought. The gusting wind rattled the window as a clap of thunder and a fork of lightening caused her to jump back. Holidaymakers ran along the Promenade looking for shelter as the rain came down in sheets. *We'll do well with afternoon tea today,* she thought, smiling briefly. But a cloud as dark as the charcoal sky came over her. Anna's intuition was never wrong, something dark was in the air—something was about to happen.

She heard the door open and Bill's voice, "Quite the storm. I brought you some tea."

Anna turned. Comforted by Bill's presence, she gave him a peck on the cheek. "Tea sounds wonderful. James came to see me today, he wants to retire."

"I know, I was just talking to him."

"He also told me about Jeremy. Did you know?"

"Yes, I think I did but I never thought about it. James is family and I'm glad he's found someone. He said he would retire at the end of the year. It will be a challenge finding a replacement. We'll need someone capable of running the hotel." Bill's eyes hovered expectantly on Anna's face. "Anna darling, we need to plan our own retirement."

"Not yet. Let's wait and see what Sarah wants to do."

"Anna, she's an artist; talented and with a career in art waiting for her. You have to see that. Expecting her to come and run the hotel and only do her art on the side is unfair."

"She did well during the summer and she liked working here. She's coming back to help us with James Bond. How can she make a living with art? I know she has talent but…"

"She'll make a living. How many guests have already asked about those paintings of Bexhill in the dining room?"

"Oh, that was just a whim—holiday memorabilia."

Bill looked at her crossly. "You know that isn't true. We don't cater to whimsical guests; these are people who know good art."

"She can do both. She has the penthouse, and if we hire a good general manager and we are still here to guide her, she can paint here."

"Stop it Anna!" Bill took a breath to control his voice, but the words came out harsh and cold. "I can't sit back and watch you make her feel guilty because she's not her mother. I know you miss Isabelle and I know you wanted Isabelle to take over, but she's dead and Sarah is not her replacement."

Anna sat down heavily, unable to digest Bill's words. In all the years she had known him she had never heard him speak like that to her, or anyone else for that matter. The hurt was the most debilitating pain she had ever felt. As if to amplify Bills words, an enormous crack of thunder and a brilliant flash of lightning shook the building. Tears burst like the rain and Bill grabbed her and gently held the back of her head, pushing her sobbing face into his shoulder. "I am so sorry. I'm so sorry." Bill's voice choked with tears as he whispered the words.

Anna sniffed her tears away and moved her head to speak, "You are right, and I'm sorry too. Some days are harder than others."

Bill held her at arm's length. "I really am sorry. I shouldn't have said that." He took his hanky from his pocket and wiped her tears before wiping the wetness from his own face, then pulled her towards him and kissed her. "That will never happen again."

A loud voice yelled in panic, "Dorothy, dial 999! We need the fire brigade and ambulance." James flung open the office door. "Amy's been hurt. The lightening struck the penthouse."

As they turned onto the third floor landing the smell of smoke hit them. The fire alarm was ringing and guests were scrambling down the stairs. Anna called out, "Bill, you stay with James. I'll see to the guests." She turned, bumping into Dorothy. "Dorothy, you take this floor and tell the guests to assemble under the portico. I'll take the second and first floor."

Back in the lobby after clearing the upper floors, Anna sent Lionel to tell the staff downstairs to leave the building and wait in the courtyard. Henry had directed the fire truck to the back of the building and fireman were running up the stairs followed by ambulance attendants carrying a stretcher. Anna went outside to find Henry surrounded by guests huddled under the portico trying to stay dry. Others were under umbrellas or just getting wet in the garden. Holding the registration book, he called each guest's name and checked them as present. Because of the storm and it being late in the day only two guests were missing and both had spoken to Henry as they left for the evening.

Anna waited for Henry to finish before addressing the guests. "Thankfully everyone is here and unhurt. I'm sorry for the inconvenience. It appears the top floor of the west wing was hit by lightening. I know it is wet and cold, but I'm afraid we have to wait for the fire brigade's instructions before we can re-enter the hotel."

Bill tugged at her elbow. "They are taking Amy to the hospital; she's unconscious, but alive. I'm going to find her husband so he can be with her. The fire is out and the fire chief said he'd be down to talk to you soon." Bill started coughing, "The smoke," he squeaked between coughs. Leaning on his knees he gasped for air until he began to breathe normally.

"You need the medics to check you out." Anna rubbed his back.

"I'm fine, I need to find Sam. I'll get it checked at the hospital."

"Mrs. Blaine, can I speak to you?" the fire chief said, gesturing towards the lobby. "The fire is out, but we will be watching for any smouldering for a while. Fortunately, the lightening hit the kitchen but didn't spread to the rest of the flat. It could have been nasty, I noticed paints, canvas and sketch pads, all flammable things, especially the oil paints."

"The flat belongs to my granddaughter. She's an artist but away at art school."

"Other than a sooty residue, the living room is fine. The kitchen is a mess from fire, smoke and water damage, but your insurance will deal with that. The only guest rooms affected are those immediately below the apartment. It is safe for the guests to come into the lobby and lounge, but we need to check the bedrooms."

"Can the staff go back to their duties downstairs?"

"Yes, but not on the guest floors yet."

"Thank you." Anna turned to Henry, "Please invite the guests back into the lobby and lounge. I will have the staff make tea and the bar will be open. We'll let them know when they can return to their rooms."

As Anna went into her office, she glanced at her watch: Bill had been gone a long time. She thought about poor Amy and then hoped Bill had had the sense to get his chest looked at. Perhaps that's what was keeping him.

James came into the office, smeared with black soot. He was always so immaculately dressed that Anna found his condition comical and chuckled.

"I know, I have soot on me. But I wanted to check Suites 203 and 303; they are both water damaged. 103 seems clear. We'll have to move the 03s on the second and third floors and ask them to check if any of their belonging have been damaged. It was a fluke, but neither were in their rooms when the lightning struck. It would have been pretty loud. I'll call the insurance agent right away. Have you heard from Bill?"

Anna shook her head, she was worried about Bill and Amy. "Did they say anything before they took her to hospital?"

"Not really. They tried to wake her up. The blast had thrown her across the kitchen and knocked her out. Bill ran into the smoke-filled kitchen and pulled Amy away from the fire. Then the fire brigade arrived and took over, but Bill was coughing hard from the smoke. Is he all right?"

"He went to find Sam and said he'd get checked out at the hospital—that's why he's late," Anna said with a great deal more assurance than she felt. In truth, she felt uneasy, but brushed it aside to calm the guests.

Eleven

Le Papillon Gallery of Art

*M*rs. Debinski shoved the phone in Sarah's face, narrowly missing her cheek. "It's for you *again!* This is not a public telephone booth and if you insist on using it all the time I'll have to charge you extra."

Sarah placed the receiver to her ear and waited for Mrs. Debinski to disappear into the parlour.

"Sarah, are you there?"

"Yes, Nana. Sorry about that."

"Is she always so nasty?"

"Yes, that's pretty normal; she's bad tempered all the time." Sarah heard a *tut* and turned to see the parlour door ajar. "And she listens in to my conversations. Felix called earlier, two calls in one night is too many," Sarah laughed. "Nana, it's not like you to call this late. Is something wrong?"

Anna had waited several days to tell Sarah about the fire, hoping to have a report from the insurance company and good news about Amy and Bill. Sarah listened carefully about the lightning strike and subsequent fire. Anna reassured her that the penthouse would be restored to its original state and the insurance company had already started the cleanup. Amy had recovered from a head injury and was out of hospital but not back at work yet. Bill had suffered smoke inhalation and had a bad cough.

"I can get the train home tomorrow," Sarah said, trying to quell her panic. She had heard something in Anna's voice, or was it that the confidence and certainty was missing?

"No. It's okay, really. I just wanted you to know. The staff and guests have been marvelous. It's more important that you come home for James Bond."

"James Bond indeed. Nana, you make me laugh. If you are certain that you're all right, I'll wait until November. Are you sure Grandpa Bill is okay? Take him to see Dr. Gregory."

"We are fine. I didn't call you to worry you. How is Felix?"

"You know Felix, he has yet another society girlfriend; a blond bimbo called Pip, who thinks she has found her Prince Charming. Is she in for a surprise! He's introducing me to Le Papillon Gallery of Art, not far from here in Kensington. It's a small, private studio and gallery, quite well known in London. Darcy buys art from them and knows the owner."

Anna took a breath, "Are they considering your art?"

"Oh no, there's a job opening for the show season. If I get the job it will be perfect, as I would only be needed for their evening and weekend art shows. So it won't affect school and I can be home for the conference and to help with Christmas. I'll be there for you Nana, don't worry."

"That sounds wonderful. Good night, sweetheart. See you soon."

Sarah took a deep breath. Replacing the receiver, her hand lingered on the Bakelite surface. *Am I feeling guilty? Nana's good at that. Or is there something she's not telling me? Lightning striking the penthouse, was that some kind of warning?* Suddenly, she was attacked from behind. Strong arms wrapped around her and wet lips slobbered a kiss on the side of her face. Someone was towering over her. She screamed.

Mrs. Debinski shouted, "Johnny, let her go!"

Sarah turned to see a large, juvenile-looking man with soft, gentle grey eyes. As his eyes caught hers, he dropped his gaze to the floor.

Mrs. Debinski's demeanour changed—for once she was contrite. Sarah spoke first, "It's okay, Johnny; I'm sorry I screamed. You frightened me."

"Go into the kitchen, now." She pointed down the passageway and turned to Sarah. "Johnny is my son, he's not right in the head. The doctors said he had infantile psycho-something and they blamed it on me, saying I was a cold mother. They want me to put him in an institution." Mrs. Debinski's speech wobbled, "I can't do that. He's harmless, but because he's so big, people are afraid of him. He wasn't attacking you, he wanted to give you a hug."

Up until five minutes ago, Sarah would have agreed that Mrs. Debinski was cold, but seeing her anguish and love for her son, Sarah realized there was a whole other layer to this woman.

Sarah gently touched her arm. "I realized that as soon as I saw his gentle eyes. Johnny doesn't have to hide from us." Sarah glanced up to see Lizzy at the top of the stairs.

"My grandmother's handyman at the hotel, Woody, he's like your Johnny; big and strong but very gentle. I used to play with Woody when I was little. I know Johnny is harmless."

Wiping tears on her apron, Mrs. Debinski said, "Please don't leave. I rely on the rent to keep us going. The last two tenants left because of Johnny."

"We are not planning on leaving and we welcome Johnny, but there will be boundaries."

"You'll stay. Do you mean that?"

"Yes, but it would help if you eased up on the rules and yelling and made our stay more comfortable. We don't need protecting."

Sarah beckoned for Lizzy to come down stairs, calling out, "Johnny would you like to meet my friend Lizzy?" Johnny peered round the kitchen door, watching for his mother's approval. She nodded and he came bounding down the hall.

"Steady on there." Sarah looked him in the eye. "Johnny, I would like you to say hello to Lizzy. No hugging yet, but you can shake her hand."

Mrs. Debinski's watched in awe as her son took Lizzy's hand and shook it, albeit staring at his feet and the shake was rather hard. He said, "I'm Johnny."

"Pleased to meet you, Johnny. My name is Lizzy."

He hesitated and for a minute and Sarah thought he was going to hug Lizzy anyway, but to her surprise he swung around and hugged Sarah. "Thank you, Miss Sarah."

"Yes, thank you both." Mrs. Debinski led Johnny by the hand back to the kitchen.

Lizzy and Sarah climbed the stairs. "Well that's one mystery solved. Now we know what the scurrying down the hall is all about and why there are two shadows behind the parlour curtains." Sarah said.

"You are marvelous with him," Lizzy said, adding, "I am glad he didn't hug me. Perhaps she'll leave us alone now that we know about Johnny."

"I doubt it. She's still a nosy gossip with a bad temper and this place is still a dump, but maybe she'll let us spruce it up a bit if we promise to stay. I've been wondering about that box room in the front. I wonder what's in there?"

"Why?"

"If she would rent that room to me I could turn it into a studio. I'm sure she would welcome the extra rent. What do you think about turning one of the rooms into a sitting room and we share the bedroom?"

"I like the idea, we'd have our own flat. My mother has some spare furniture she doesn't want. Do you think Mrs. Debinski would mind if we brought our own?"

"It sounds like a great idea. But if we throw out the old stuff we might have to leave your mother's furniture here."

"Mother will throw it away anyway. I can't see that as a problem."
**

Mrs. Debinski agreed to rent the box room and gave Sarah the key.

The smell of sweet apples wafted out of the unlocked door. Sarah remembered her Great Aunt Lou had a bedroom at the farm that smelled of apples. The not-quite-ripe apples would have been picked from the orchard and stored for the winter in neat rows in a drawer lined with newspaper. There was a small pale blue chest of drawers nestled in the corner of the box room. Sarah opened the drawers, which were empty except for the lingering aroma of apples. "This is perfect for my art supplies," she said aloud. The only other piece of furniture was an old wooden rocking chair with some blue flowers painted on the back. Sarah thought perhaps it had been Johnny's rocking chair when he was a baby. She imagined a young, happy Mrs. Debinski rocking her newborn son and Mr. Debinski looking on, long before they knew he wasn't normal. Taking a second look around the room she realized this had been Johnny's nursery. She sat in the rocking chair, feeling a little sad, understanding that Mrs. Debinski had known happier days. As she rocked to and fro she felt inspired—this was a good place for her art.

"Sarah," Lizzy called, "my dad is here with the furniture. Can you ask Johnny to help him carry it up the stairs?"

Johnny had helped them move the furniture and would do anything for Sarah but he still didn't trust Lizzy. Sarah went downstairs and knocked on the kitchen door. Johnny came out and gave Sarah a hug.

"Johnny, can you help Mr. Elliot with the couch and table? I might have a treat for you."

He gave her a wide grin. "Johnny help. Miss Sarah do you have chocolate?"

"I do, Cadbury's milk chocolate, your favourite."

In less than an hour, the girls had a sitting room with a couch, two comfy chairs, a small polished wood dining table with two dining chairs and a small sideboard, which provided welcome storage space. Mrs. Elliot had even sent a set of curtains that matched the couch; slightly short for the long window but Lizzy, having spent a good deal of time learning housekeeping skills from her mother, said she

could drop the hem and make them fit.
**

High Street bustled with happy, animated passers-by. Sara laughed, *Is it the street or is it me?* She felt bubbly, her feet barely touching the pavement. Nana and Grandpa Bill were coping and keeping well, the flat was amazing, and she and Lizzy were perfect roommates. Creativity flowed from her paint brush and Miss Berkley had high praise for her work.

She hesitated as her hand pulled the large chrome handle of the big glass door with Le Papillon Gallery of Art etched into the glass in swirling letters. Taking a deep breath and holding it, she stepped inside. Faint, soothing music floated by her ear. Afraid to release her breath in the silent ambience, she glanced around for Madame. Sarah found it odd that the owner of a prestigious art gallery didn't appear to have a normal name, assuming she must be a bit eccentric. Felix said nobody knew what her real name was and not to ask.

A variety of paintings were suspended on walls that appeared not to exist; each beautiful piece of art an intrinsic part of the whole, more beauty than Sarah could remember seeing in her whole life.

"Miss Wexford, how nice of you to come early." Sarah thought her heart had flown out of her chest as she gasped, releasing her captive breath.

"I startled you." Madame gave a loud, affected laugh and added, "It can't be helped when an artist is faced with such magnificent art. I expect my clients to be in awe. But you are here to work. I must say, I'm pleased that you appreciate art; the last girl was quite ignorant. I hope you are as good as the Thorntons have led me to believe."

Sarah nodded finding it difficult to take her eyes off this tiny woman with an incredibly large presence, mostly due to her colourful, loose-fitting, flowing outfit; a bright yellow turban was wrapped tightly around her head, her small delicate face spoiled by thin, dark, pencilled-in eyebrows that arched above her pale blue eyes, rouge red cheeks and brilliant red lips that secured a long cigarette holder.

Eccentric indeed, Sarah thought, and her sarcasm had not escaped her either. Had she encountered another jaded woman, a more cultured version of Mrs. Debinski? As she followed Madame around the gallery, the serenity and beauty of the rooms made it impossible to feel anything but happiness.

**

Sarah was used to visiting art galleries and shows, but this was her first time working at an art show. It would be her job to take orders and keep track of the destination of sold pieces and make note of clients who had enquiries to be followed up by Madame.

As the guests arrived, the silence soon turned into escalating, celebratory chatter and laughter. The peaceful ambience of beautiful art changed to clinking glasses and the mixed aromas of hot hors d'oeuvres and pungent perfumes. By nine o'clock the place was elbow to elbow with glittering cocktail dresses, sparkling diamonds and large, lacquered hair-dos. The men in black dinner jackets with bow ties paled in contrast. This was not an arty crowd; these people had money and hung the art in their mansions, estates and London townhouses.

Sarah smiled as she was taking orders, in awe at the number of zeros on the cheques and praising the buyers on their wise choices of art. *One day,* she thought, *Madame will host a showing of my art; she just doesn't know it yet.*

"Which is your favourite painting? I'd like to buy it."

Sarah knew that voice. "Felix, what are you doing here?"

"Buying a painting for a dear friend, and wondering if she would join me for a late dinner."

"I love them all, but there is no need to buy me a painting. Dinner sounds nice, I'm starving. Can you wait? I have no idea when the show closes."

"Madame will be shutting this down soon and taking her favourite clients to dinner. I know because my parents are often included in that group. I'll wait until you're finished."

Sarah was thankful the buying had slowed down and wondered if anything was left for sale. As she stared into the crowd, her heart suddenly jumped into her throat. Was it him? She hardly recognized him with short hair, dressed in black tie and dinner jacket, but there was no mistaking that the man was Marcus Perkins. What was he doing here? She scanned the room, giving the sculptures a closer look, but she didn't recognize any of his work. Why hadn't he come and talked to her? She looked again; he was talking to Madame and they seemed to know each other. There was something about his demeanour that stopped her approaching him. He had an air of slyness, of deception—more than just secretive. She couldn't hear the conversation but his body language and mannerisms were of a cultured, well-educated person, not the working-class background he displayed at college or in the commune. Who was this man she had known as Marcus?

"Penny for them?" Felix said.

"Sorry, I was miles away. Do you see who is over there?"

"Yes, I went over to talk to him and he walked away—disappeared. He looks as though he's come up in the world. Are you ready?"

Twelve

Inheritance and Inner Conflict

*D*inner was casual, in a small bistro near the gallery. As soon as they sat down, Felix explained to Sarah that Pip, his latest bimbo, had hinted at a commitment so he had walked away. Sarah listened to his explanation and wondered why he picked such unsuitable women. With his wealth, eventual title, status as a solicitor as well as being a pretty decent guy, he could date any debutante or young society woman, and yet he allowed gold diggers and bimbos to fall into his lap. Love was never part of it, and she doubted he even liked these women. He wasn't unkind, just dismissive. He hid behind a reputation of being a playboy, which prevented him from making any kind of commitment to more suitable, marriageable partners. His mother thought he had plenty of time at twenty-eight to settle down, but his father was eager for him to marry and produce an heir. Perhaps he was stalling the inevitable.

"Felix, how do you deal with being the heir to the estate and knowing you can't pursue your own path?"

"It's the way it is. I was born knowing that one day the estate would be mine. Unlike my dad, who was the second son—my Uncle Felix, the eldest son, died in Africa, a military man, hating the estate not wanting his inheritance. Ironically, dad was expected to be the military man but loved working on the estate. By the time he inherited, he'd lost interest or something, because he left his manager to look after everything and lived in Chicago, where he met my mother."

"I knew Grandpa Bill and your father had history in Chicago, but I never knew your father wasn't the first heir. I guess that's why you are called Felix. I don't think you want the estate any more than your uncle did?"

"I do like Hillcrest Hall, it's home and I like running the estate. I just like the law more. But not as a solicitor; it can be somewhat boring. I haven't been called to the bar yet. Serving Her Majesty on two years conscription has put me behind. Whenever I get a criminal case or even litigation that is exciting and complex I have to hand it over to a barrister, but that will change shortly." He glanced at Sarah. "Keep this to yourself, as I haven't told Dad. It's a few more years of study, exams to pass, court experience and gaining a reputation among peers, which is extremely important because…" Felix paused, "Once I'm a barrister I would like to get my silk." Felix leaned back in his chair, his eyes almost closed, a slight smile on his lips. Sarah recognized the intensity of the want and felt that same desire.

Sarah frowned. "Silk, that means becoming a Queens Counsel, right?"

Felix nodded and moved forward, leaning across the dinner table and whispered, "I would like to add QC after my name. Maybe work for the Crown on high-profile criminal cases." He sighed, "Pipe dreams I guess"

"I don't think so. I understand. My dream is that one day Madame will present an exhibition of my art at Le Papillon. It's about this very subject that I wanted to talk to you. I have a similar inheritance dilemma. My mother loved the hotel life and she expected to take over from Nana. And now, Nana assumes I'll take over. My passion is art. I know I have a gift, so I want to study and perfect my craft. I don't dislike hotel life and I could run the hotel, but it is not my passion. I feel as though I am in the wake of my mother's ghost."

"Our lives are parallel, although I think you have a bit more choice than me, in the sense that people could be hired to run the hotel or it could be sold. Neither of those things can happen for me."

"True, but I am indebted to Nana for raising me and taking care of me. If it wasn't for her and Grandpa Bill I don't know what I would have done. I'm torn: part of me wants to help and run the hotel and let them retire. Nana's rheumatism is so painful at times, and Grandpa Bill's feet can hardly hold him up some days, to say nothing of his cough. But the other part of me, the bigger part," Sarah hesitated and a pink blush coloured her cheeks as she blurted out, "I want to be a famous artist. I have the talent."

Felix put his head to one side saying, "I love it when you blush. Sarah, it's okay to tell everyone that you are a talented artist because you truly are."

Sarah's chin dropped to her chest, and she stared at the blue pendant around her neck. She held it between her fingers. "Nana told me that her Uncle gave her this with the words, 'Follow your dreams and never let anyone destroy them.' Nana has far surpassed her dreams and there was something in her demeanour that came from deep inside as she recalled Uncle Bertie's words; Nana knows my dreams, but still hopes I'll run the hotel. Perhaps she is as conflicted as me."

They slipped into silence. Felix's eyes fixed on Sarah with a gentleness that more than understood. Her heart tingled ever so slightly. She had felt it before, a tenderness beyond friendship; often fleeting, causing her to question its reality. He looked away, clearing his throat.

"Hum…there doesn't seem to be a solution for either of us. Except, for whatever reason, we are both being allowed to continue along our chosen paths, at least for now. Maybe they think we'll change our minds." He laughed briefly and continued, "But that's not likely to happen for either of us." Felix stifled a yawn. "I think it's time to get you home, I have a day full of client interviews tomorrow: two wills, a divorce and a strange case of child abandonment. It sounds interesting, not quite the normal case."

**

Lizzy stood at the top of the stairs, excitement written across her face. "I thought you'd never get home. I have some terrific news."

Sarah ran up the stairs, hearing Mrs. Debinski door click open and a *tut, tut* followed her upstairs as the clock chimed midnight. Lizzy grabbed Sarah's arm and pulled her into their sitting room, closing the door behind her. Eavesdropping was Mrs. D's favourite pastime, but since the girls had accepted Johnny she left them alone most of the time.

"Don't keep me in suspense. What happened?"

"You won't believe it, Mr. Jacob has asked me to assist him with the spring fashion show. He said I have a good eye for detail and get this, an exceptional eye for fashion accessories. I, *me, moi…*, I'm going to be working with him as he designs the spring collection."

"Lizzy, that is wonderful! What does what's-her-name, your boss, think about it?"

"Crystal, she's not happy. Miss know-it-all, Mr. Jacob this and Mr. Jacob that has been slighted. Honestly, you would think she was married to him or something."

"Do you think she's sweet on him?"

"Sarah," Lizzy dropped her hip to one side, flipped her hand in the air and let it fall limp at the wrist. "I doubt he has any interest in Crystal or any other woman, if you get my meaning. But his creative talent with fashion is just second to none. I am so looking forward to working with him; I will learn so much."

"How did the art exhibit go?"

"Great I think. I'm sure we sold most of the exhibits and probably have orders for more—I passed a lot of enquiries on to Madame. Guess who turned up at the show in black tie? Marcus, but he avoided both Felix and me. Weird?"

"Marcus in black tie, that I would like to have seen. And Felix was there too?"

"He took me out for dinner. That was why I was so late."

"If ever you get tired of him you can send him my way."

"Felix is a long-time friend; there is no romance but believe me you don't want to date him. He's doing everything he can to stay away from marriage and he doesn't treat his girlfriends too well. Now, Peter in his office is good marriage material. I think you'd get along well. I'll see if Felix can arrange a foursome." Sarah rubbed her eyes, trying not to yawn. "I'm really happy Mr. Jacob is recognizing your flair for fashion but I can't talk anymore. I'm beat and need to get to bed. Good night."

**

The following morning, Sarah leapt onto the train, already late for class when she came face to face with Marcus, he stiffened with fear as he stared at her.

"Marcus, fancy meeting you here. I saw you at the art exhibition last night." Now it was Sarah's turn to stare as he remained silent, not responding. She frowned. "What the hell is wrong with you, Marcus? Why are you ignoring me?"

"It's complicated. I didn't see you last night. Are you still at the RCA?"

"Yes, I'm in the silver medal program with Miss Berkley. I see you didn't stay at the commune with Jenny and Dave. I really liked them, they are good people."

The train slowed down. "This is my stop. I can't say it was good to see you, but should you want to connect, I can be reached at the college." Sarah jumped onto the platform, annoyed at his arrogance. She glanced over her shoulder and stopped in her tracks. The man behind her bumped into her, cursing. Marcus was standing on the platform. He caught her eye and walked off in the opposite direction and within seconds he had disappeared. Sarah felt chilled. Was he stalking her? He had to have seen her last night. Why was he pretending he hadn't? And she was quite sure that if she had ignored him on the train he would have walked away without speaking.

Speaking. She thought his voice was different, naturally cultured; there was no sign of a Liverpool accent. She glanced at her watch and began running; she was beyond late for class.

The day passed slowly. She kept thinking about Marcus and she struggled to focus; her last session with Miss Berkley was close to a disaster. Her concentration was so poor that Miss Berkley halted the session and looked her straight in the eye.

"Miss Wexford, I don't know what it is, but something is wrong. Can you tell me about it?"

"I'm sorry. I had a strange encounter with Marcus Perkins on my way to class and I can't get it out of my mind." Sarah relayed the story, including the art show.

"Is he stalking you?"

"I don't think so because he keeps disappearing, and he did the same to Felix last night."

"I don't want to frighten you, but if he appears again I think you need to call the police. Be very aware of your surroundings at all times, Sarah. He was a weird one here at college. Be careful."

Sarah nodded. "Yes, I will. It's a bit creepy."

"Let's call it a day, you look tired. Get an early night and you'll be fresh in the morning."

Sarah spent most of her journey home looking over her shoulder, but there was no sign of Marcus. She decided to ask Madame how she knew Marcus; perhaps her association would throw some light on his behaviour.

**

It was late October before Sarah had a chance to ask Madame about Marcus, and by then it seemed irrelevant as there had been no sign of him since the Underground incident. Even though a month had passed, Sarah still felt uneasy and any unusual sudden noise caused her head to spin around, requiring many apologies as unsuspecting passers-by were stared at for no reason.

Madame had returned from an exhibition in Scotland in extremely good humour as one of the largest galleries in Edinburgh had asked Le Papillon to host a show. Madame displayed three distinct traits: her ego which needed constant feeding, her eccentricities in her appearance—she had returned from Scotland with a tartan turban and matching cigarette holder. The third trait was her uncanny ability to spot exquisite art, often including art that other dealers ignored as unsellable and Madame would make a fortune.

Sarah had become accustomed to Madame's unusual fashion but the tartan turban looked ridiculous and she was trying not to giggle as she unpacked the crates of works that were to be featured in a tribute to the Scottish moorlands.

Madame was not very forthcoming with compliments, but she liked Sarah, possibly because she was good with clients. Sarah had honed this skill with hotel guests from a young age, so it came naturally to her. As she helped Madame unpack an exceptionally large painting, Sarah asked, "Madame, I couldn't help noticing you talking with Marcus Perkins at the last show. Marcus and I are old college friends; he is an amazing sculptor. I thought you might have some of his work, but I don't recognize any here. I wondered what he was doing these days?"

"I don't know a Marcus Perkins and certainly not a sculptor by that name. I talk to a lot of people, I don't remember them all."

Do I pursue this or let it go? Sarah wanted to find out more, but it was obvious Madame did not know him as Marcus, but she had definitely spoken with him the night of the show. *I bet he's using a different name.*

"Back to work, Miss Wexford."

Engrossed in thought, she had stopped pulling the wrapping off the painting. "I'm so sorry," Sarah said, returning to her work.

Thirteen

A Conference of Secrets

The steady rhythm of the train as it gathered speed leaving Paddington Station comforted Sarah. She needed to get away to sort through the million things in her head. Her studies were suffering because she couldn't focus. Miss Berkley was getting quite cross, with good reason. Closing her eyes, she thought of Marcus. Even though he had not made another appearance, she constantly prepared herself to bump into him. She wanted to talk to him, find out why he was being so weird. His behaviour hurt. He had loved her once; more than she loved him, if you could call it love. It didn't seem to fit the criteria of love. She chuckled at the idea, thinking of Felix. He had a new girlfriend, a Canadian teacher from Toronto in London on an exchange program. Felix seemed quite smitten with her and treated her differently. Sarah tried to brush off her feelings of annoyance and even a touch of jealousy. It surprised her that she resented the time he spent with this woman. She couldn't be bothered to remember her name and dismissed the thought.

The train pulled into Reading station where Sarah had to change for Bexhill. An old school friend joined her in the compartment, so her thoughts were put on hold.

**

Sarah waved frantically when she spotted Grandpa Bill on the platform in Bexhill. She hugged him tightly, not wanting to let him go.

He hugged and kissed her and held her at arms length. "Hey there, you only hug me that tightly when there is something wrong."

"Nothing's wrong, Grandpa. I'm just happy to be home."

Bill gave her a quizzical look, not quite convinced. "The Hillman is right outside."

"When are you going to give this car up?"

Bill laughed. "Never! I love this car and it works fine. Good to have you home, sweetheart. Nana is looking forward to you being here. It's going to be busy. I sense this group may be small but demanding. And the secrecy? Mr. Carter arrived yesterday with two burly men and they are checking the hotel, I'm assuming for listening bugs. Most of the staff is on holiday. They don't want the rooms cleaned during their stay, so there is no housekeeping other than Amy. Dorothy is here, I have sous-chef Brian and a couple of prep guys, and two waiters for the dining room and room service. The doors are locked and officially we are closed for repairs. Henry is on the door but only for the arrivals."

"Grandpa, are you teasing me?"

"No, it's for real. We were convinced it was British Secret Service but the bill for the rooms and meals is going to the Prime Minister's private secretary."

"Is the Prime Minister coming?"

"It looks like it, but then nothing is what it seems."

"When do the delegates arrive?"

"Tonight." Bill pulled the car up and Henry took Sarah's bag.

Sarah headed straight into Anna's office. The hotel sounded eerily quiet; not only were there no guests, but there was no bustling staff. The clatter of the typewriter keys was exceptionally loud in the quiet hotel. Dorothy Jenkins had moved from her events manager's office to the reception desk to staff the phones during the conference. She looked up and waved hello to Sarah as she entered Anna's office.

"Sarah, darling. Oh, I'm so glad to see you." Anna stood up, her hands supporting her weight on the desk. She carefully moved from the desk and hugged Sarah.

"It's good to be home. Although it feels quite odd—everything is so quiet. So, what do you want me to do?"

"Mr. Carter is joining us for dinner with his final instructions. Don't ask any questions because he won't answer any. We now know that two important people are arriving late tonight. Both suites on the second floor are reserved. Otherwise, I'm not sure what we are supposed to do, so let's wait for instructions."

"Nana, did I tell you that Mr. Carter asked me if I was related to Sandy Wexford?"

"No, when was that?"

"The first time he came, I told him he was my father but I hadn't seen him since I was about nine." Sarah sensed tension, slight but it was there.

"That's odd. He hasn't said anything to me or Bill as far as I know. It must be another Sandy Wexford."

"Mr. Carter said he got the name from my birth certificate but my father's name would be Alexander on that, not Sandy. Maybe your right there's another Sandy Wexford." Sarah paused, "Did you ever hear from him?"

"No, we tried to find him a couple of times." Anna rubbed her hands together and gave a nervous cough, looking away from Sarah.

Sarah's eyebrows almost met in the middle as she watched Anna. "Nana, is there something you are not telling me about my father? Have you heard from him?"

"No, the last time we heard anything was not long after he left and he had found work in London. We thought he would come back. No, nothing since then." Sarah was convinced that Anna knew more than she was saying, the first part was undoubtedly true, but Anna was a poor liar and there was more to the story, which made Sarah even more determined to find her father.

"I suggest you get yourself settled. Amy will need help with housekeeping, checking everything is okay. After the meeting, I will need you to greet the guests and show them to their rooms. Mr. Carter requested dinner as the delegates arrive, so you'll need to show them the dining room."

Sarah kissed Anna. "I'll go and change into my business suit. What time and where are we meeting with Mr. Carter?"

"The Emily Carr dining room at five-thirty. We'll have an early meal." Sarah nodded and went to the penthouse.

The smell of fresh paint greeted her when she opened the door. She had forgotten about the fire until she saw the painted kitchen, new cooker and linoleum on the floor. She wandered through the flat, but nothing else had been affected. Her easel and paints had been moved for cleaning but that was it. She was tired and lay on the bed, she had an hour before meeting the now infamous Mr. Carter.

**

At five-fifteen Sarah walked into the empty dining room. It was strange to sit at the family table without their regular waiter or Balaji to greet them. She ordered a gin and tonic as Anna came in and then Dorothy showed Mr. Carter to the table.

"Good evening. Thank you for meeting with me. We are expecting dignitaries and you will recognize one of them. I must remind you of the Secrecy Act and the documents you signed earlier. This meeting must never get to the press. The Right Honourable Harold McMillan, yes, our Prime Minister, will arrive at about ten this evening. He will require a meal but I have already talked to the chef. The remaining delegates will be arriving between seven and nine. Henry has the list. The hotel is to be locked and no one is to be allowed in or out without my permission and that includes trades people. Do I make myself clear?"

"Yes, closing for repairs after the fire and during our quiet time is easily believed. Just one suggestion, the locals might ask questions if they see too many black limousines around the hotel."

"That has been taken care of, Mrs. Blaine. You'll also notice a van or two belonging to an Eastbourne refurbishing company parked by the service entrance during the day."

"That's good, you thought of everything." Anna clicked her fingers and ordered wine.

Mr. Carter never relaxed the whole time they were eating. He was a master at making nothing conversation, and very good at getting Anna and Sarah to talk about themselves. *Part of his job description,* Sarah thought but his casual conversation prompted Sarah to find out more about her father.

"Mr. Carter, I am curious about why you asked if I knew Sandy Wexford, which I'm sure you already know is my father's name. However, Mrs. Blaine and I were wondering if there was another man of that name. If you saw the name on my birth certificate, it is written as Alexander Wexford." Sarah paused. Mr. Carter actually gave the minutest shuffle in his seat, *I've hit a nerve,* she thought. "I haven't heard from my father in ten years and I would like to find him." Sarah's stare shifted to Anna who was not as adept at hiding her feelings; her expression appeared neutral but pain and shock reflected in her eyes. Sarah frowned, keeping the words silent in her head, *I don't know why this hurts you so much, Nana, and I'm sorry, but I need to know.*

"My job, Miss Wexford, is security, the nation's security, and I need to know a lot about a lot of people and what threats and challenges they may face from inside or outside; threats that might put the Crown in danger. I would have thought it was obvious the connection is nothing more than your surname, Wexford, Sandy is a coincidence that is all." There was no mistaking his words were final. Sarah's sense of triumph was short lived and the conversation reverted to general trivia and was cleverly diverted to Anna and Sarah's life. Sarah stubbornly refused to be drawn in, but Anna talked away.

Mr. Carter listened intently, Sarah thought it was a skill his profession had taught him and by the time they had finished their coffee he had heard Anna's life story, including the pride she had for her brother's secret military service and her life in Canada.

"Charlie Neale," Mr. Carter said, "an intelligence officer with the Royal Canadian Mounted Police." Anna stared wide eyed as her brother's name rolled off his tongue. "I didn't know him during the war, but I met him several years ago. Britain and Canada were consulting on an international case."

"You know Charlie?" Anna's face light up. "I miss him, we were close growing up but his intelligence work seemed to part us."

"I'm afraid our job does that to families. I met his wife and daughter and Charlie has managed to preserve his personal life, I admire him for that. I wish I could have known him better. But friendships don't exist in our business." Sarah had been watching the man closely, and for the first time she had seen a glimpse of humanity and realized the harshness of the job made its operators seem cold. *What kind of person can do such a job?*

Sarah remembered Great Uncle Charlie being kind and fun. She had played with Charlotte when they were kids on the family's rare visits from Canada. Although they were first cousins once removed, a combination of Charlie being younger than Nana and having gotten married late in life because of his military career, Cousin Charlotte was only six years older than Sarah.

She tuned out of the conversation as childhood memories of her Grandfather Alex, Nana's first husband who had died when she was little, popped into her head. It was the day the family had moved to Scotland and Nana and Uncle Charlie were going to Canada. She remembered being afraid Nana wouldn't come back and at the tender age of five she had said, "One day I will live in Canada." It had been said in innocence and forgotten until today. She felt the desire deep inside her heart and she sensed there was more.

"Sarah!" Anna's voice was sharp. "Mr. Carter asked you about Le Papillon Art Exhibition."

"What about it?" Sarah snapped back. She thought but didn't dare say. *Your questions, Mr. Carter, are beginning to be intrusive and annoying and how do you know I was at the exhibition?*

Almost as though he was answering her thought, he said, "It may surprise you, Miss Wexford, but I appreciate fine art and have attended many of Madame's shows. However, I was unable to attend the last one, but someone from my office told me it was a great success."

"It was. Madame finds the most amazing artists. One day she will display my art."

"Undoubtedly. I have seen your work and it is worthy of Madame's attention." He motioned towards the two paintings of Bexhill hanging in the dining room. "Madame needs to be the first to exhibit such talent because one day you will be famous."

"Thank you." Sarah felt her cheeks turn pink, feeling embarrassed but his compliments tempered her annoyance at his intrusion.

"Ladies, I have work to do." Mr. Carter smiled and left the dining room.

"He's quite a complex man." Anna said, "Fancy he knows Charlie, a small world." Anna looked at her watch. "Back to work, the delegates will be here shortly."

**

The conference delegates arrived quietly, ate dinner and returned to their rooms. Neither Sarah nor Anna met the Prime Minister as he entered by the service entrance and ate his meals in his suite and attended the meetings in the conference room next to his suite. Amy got a couple of glimpses when she went to deliver fresh towels and Bill had met him when he first arrived.

Rather than being busy, most of the staff sat around talking, waiting to be called. The kitchen was the exception with meals in the dining room, and the waiters were kept busy with drinks and room service. Mr. Carter was seen wandering around, but he didn't speak with Anna or Sarah again until the last day when the departure arrangements were being made. When the dignitaries actually departed, was anyone's guess, they just weren't there anymore. The remaining attendees discreetly departed in small cars, either alone or in pairs and under cover of darkness.

In contrast, a black limousine pulled up at midnight and picked up Mr. Carter. Anna raised her eyebrows. "No secrecy for you?"

Mr. Carter smiled, climbing into the front passenger seat. "Thank you for your hospitality and discretion." As the car pulled away the light caught two head and shoulder silhouettes through the rear window.

"I'm guessing that was the Prime Minister and his guest," Anna said, closing and locking the front door.

Fourteen

Elusive Men

—❦—

The commuter crowd jostled Sarah as she ran down the steps to the Underground. The platform was crammed as she waited for her train to Kensington. *Bad timing,* she thought, *arriving in London at five-thirty.* But she had waited for James Lytton to return to work before leaving Bexhill; both Anna and Bill were tired and needed some rest. Sarah had talked them into a trip to Hillcrest Hall for a few days, partly for her own benefit so she didn't worry about them. The train screeched to a stop, Sarah hated the piercing noise and rushed off the train. Within a few minutes she was opening the gate to 23 Surrey Street. She'd seen the parlour curtains move as she approached and expected Mrs. D to greet her but it was Johnny who opened the door.

"Miss Sarah, Johnny missed you, and Mum is mad."

Sarah frowned. "Mad, why?"

Before Johnny could answer, Mrs. Debinski appeared from the kitchen. "A man keeps calling for you. He won't leave a name, but three times he's called—woke me up at eleven last night."

"I'm sorry Ms. D., I have no idea who it might be. Have you seen him before?"

"No, it's not that posh feller. But he speaks proper English. Says he's a college friend."

"Perhaps Lizzy knows him."

Johnny answered, "Miss Lizzy not been home either."

"As soon as I know who it is I will tell them to stop bothering you. Good night."

Sarah climbed the stairs, wondering where Lizzy had got too. She suspected, she was at Peter's flat, which would not go down well with Mrs. D, who still considered herself to be a chaperone. Having the place to herself suited Sarah. Who was this man calling on her? As if she didn't have enough to think about between her grandparents, the hotel, the connection between Mr. Carter and her father and she had some explaining to do at college, having taken two extra days. Miss Berkley would be upset. Trying to calm her mind, she went into her little studio and began painting. Her creative mind moved the brush, revealing a woman with a likeness to Anna staring into a seascape. A younger man stood behind her at a distance—a void between them but Sarah felt an emotional connection. She kept painting as though in a trance with an unseen entity moving her brush. She caught a slight hue of pink from the window. It was morning; she'd been painting all night. Yawning, she viewed her night's work. It was Anna in her office, looking out to sea with Sarah's father standing behind her. How she knew what her father looked like today she couldn't tell, but she had no doubt that it was him. Strangely, she felt calm as she walked into the bedroom. She had four hours to get some rest and fell into a deep sleep.

**

As expected, Miss Berkley expressed her disappointment in Sarah's extended absence but did concede her reasons were understandable and she would be forgiven if she caught up. The night's painting had given Sarah placidity and she worked quietly, easily catching up with all the projects and lectures she had missed, giving little thought to her personal life.

That evening she walked to Le Papillon to find out when she was needed, and she wanted to know if Marcus had been around. It had occurred to her that Marcus might be the stranger calling. Once again, Sarah was greeted with disappointment, but Madame was not as understanding as Miss Berkley and threatened to find another assistant. The gallery was busy with early Christmas shoppers, so Sarah redeemed herself by staying to attend to clients.

Madame bristled when a familiar voice called, "Miss Wexford, I was hoping to bump into you tonight."

Madame hustled over and interrupted, "Mr. Carter how nice to see you. I have a new collection you may be interested in."

"Actually, I discovered a new artist that I am interested in, and she is standing right in front of me." Mr. Carter gave Sarah a wry smile.

"And who would that be?"

"Your very own Miss Wexford."

Madame laughed. "She's not an artist of..." Seeing Mr. Carter's annoyance, she stopped smiling.

"I have seen Miss Wexford's work and I want one of her paintings and you would do well to bring her work into the gallery."

Sarah wished she could disappear into one of the paintings, her cheeks were crimson. Madame was obviously angry—Mr. Carter had humiliated her and Sarah sensed she would not be soon forgiven, even though she could think of nothing she had done wrong.

"Well then," she said with pursed lips, "you'd better bring me some of your art pieces and I will be the judge of their suitability. There is no accounting for taste." Her nose in the air, she flipped an arm, almost burning Mr. Carter with her cigarette, perched at the end of a gold cigarette holder. She billowed away in her flowing gown.

"I think I just lost my job," Sarah said.

"When she sees your work, she will see the talent. Madame may be curt, arrogant and pompous, but she's not stupid and she knows talent when she sees it. Do you have any more paintings of Bexhill, like the ones at the Sackville?" Mr. Carter pushed a note into Sarah's hand, whispering, "Look at it later." Sarah nodded. "Bring them in tomorrow evening and I'll come in and purchase what I want. Trust me, Madame will be delighted."

Sarah left the gallery not sure how much she could trust a security man shrouded in secrets, but having the opportunity to show Madame her art was not to be taken lightly. What she couldn't understand was why Madame, an astute art dealer with a talent for recognizing young talented artists, had just dismissed Sarah out of hand; at least Miss Berkley would be pleased. She felt the crumpled paper in her skirt pocket and opened it, stopping under a street light she read, *Your uncle knows where he is.*

She re-read the note, *I don't have an uncle, except Great Uncle Charlie. Is he telling me to go to Canada? Is my father across the Atlantic?* She sighed, the cat and mouse stuff scared her. She had so many questions but didn't need to be told that she would get no answers. She tore the paper into tiny pieces and dropped them into a public litter bin.

Madame took three paintings, two of which Mr. Carter bought and the third one was hung in a corner out of view. Confused by Madame's attitude, Sarah surmised she had not been forgiven Sarah for the humiliation and yet she thought it might be something more. Sarah noted that although She had not asked her for more paintings, she hadn't criticized them. Perhaps Mr. Carter was right and Madame did see her talent, at least she still had a job.

The job was no longer fun, Sarah tip-toed around listening to Madame's constant criticism or complaints. Although she never saw Mr. Carter again, she did notice the third painting had disappeared; whether it had been sold or had just been taken down she didn't know. She had been paid handsomely for the first two, but not for this one, so she thought the latter and decided to quit after the Christmas season.

Miss Berkley had offered her a teaching assistant's position starting in January, which would pay enough to cover the rent, and if she sold some art, it would enable her to save for a trip to Canada—she was convinced she'd find her father there.

Lizzy spent more time at Peter's than she did at home, but

tonight she came bounding up the stairs. Sarah wanted to tell her about the note and Mr. Carter wanting her paintings, but Lizzy's exuberance outweighed Sarah's. Sarah suspected that the romance had blossomed way beyond where it should have, but Lizzy didn't say and Sarah didn't ask. Lizzy had wedding bells ringing in her head and tonight Lizzy flashed a diamond ring in front of Sarah.

Sarah gasped, "Lizzy it is beautiful, a diamond solitaire. It looks gorgeous and suits you so well. I am so exited for you and Peter is the perfect man for you." She gave Lizzy and hug.

"We're meeting Felix and Loraine to celebrate and we'd like you to come too."

"Lizzy, I'd love to but I have an assignment. I'm sorry but why don't I cook dinner for you and Peter on Saturday and we can celebrate then?"

"That sounds like a good idea but are you sure you can't make it tonight?"

"Yes, Miss Berkley is not pleased with me so I have to make an extra effort and I have to have this assignment in tomorrow."

Sarah's reason for declining had more to do with feeling jealous, not of Lizzy, she was truly happy for Lizzy and Peter but she disliked Lorraine and seeing her with Felix gave her a bad, troubled feeling. She knew it was silly but she was afraid she may say something and spoil Lizzy's evening.

That night, Sarah had a visitor. Marcus turned up to reveal he was the elusive caller. Sarah invited him in and showed him up to the flat, much to Mrs. D's disapproval. Instead of being angry with Marcus she welcomed him, feeling defiant, her emotions in a turmoil. She felt mixed up, vulnerable. Marcus, obviously surprised at the welcome, didn't understand what was going on.

"I wasn't sure you would see me," he said, hesitating before making himself comfortable on the sofa.

"I'm curious. You've been badgering Mrs. Debinski while I was in Bexhill and now you are here—it has to be important. Why the change? Two months ago you ignored me at Le Papillon and brushed me off on the train." Sarah snapped at him, "And what's with the fancy clothes?"

"A lot has happened since we went to the farm."

"I think that's an understatement. From commune farm and beatnik friends to black tie and county accent," she snapped again, checking herself with a smile, mellowing as she remembered how good he'd looked. "But you did look handsome in a black tie."

"This is the real me." He paused for a second, "I was born and raised in Liverpool, but my family were not poor. Misguided youth, I guess I wanted to denounce my upper class and boarding school upbringing. My family are snobs and I didn't like that. The scholarship and commune was a great way to reinvent myself. There was no scholarship. My trust fund paid for college." He sighed. "But I did love art and I thought I was talented until I discovered my sculptures were worthless. I cut my family off—actually, my father threw me out. I needed a job. But job interviews didn't go down well with beads and long hair. Some interviewers even took offense when I greeted them with…" Marcus held his right hand up, his fingers in the vee sign, *"Peace man."* His impish grin made Sarah laugh.

"Yes, I can see how that wouldn't work."

"I cleaned up, cut my hair and found a job with an ad agency, drawing housewives with cookers and vacuum cleaners. Not very creative but it pays the bills."

Sarah tried to digest his story. It was plausible, but how could she believe someone who had lied to her for two years? She didn't know what to believe and she wasn't sure she believed *any* of it. But she was happy to see him and surprisingly he had sparked some affection. But she didn't want him to know. Now it was she who was deceiving him.

"I don't know who you are. You aren't the freethinking, no-rules sculptor I dated in college who said he loved me and couldn't live without me. And then you just let me go. That hurt Marcus, and hurt a lot."

"I know. I'm sorry. I made a mistake. I never stopped loving you. I can't stop thinking about you. I want to start over."

Sarah believed he still loved her and she was feeling more love than she had ever felt before. Her anger had dissipated. Gone. It simply wasn't there anymore and she desperately wanted to be loved, especially tonight.

He moved towards her and touched her arm. When she didn't pull away, he moved closer. Sarah stood up and so did Marcus. He wrapped his arm around her shoulder so gently she barely felt it. "Sarah, I love you." His warmth radiated towards her. She tried to step back but was riveted to the spot. Suddenly she wanted to fling her arms around him. Her heart pounded; she was desperate for his embrace, to feel him hold her tight, to shiver as his breath flowed over her neck and down her spine. Her resistance gone, she let her head fall back, enticing him to kiss her throat. His lips tickled and she shuddered as he pressed into a kiss. Pulling her towards him, he moved, brushing his lips against hers. She grabbed his head and kissed him hard, holding her breath as her body ignited. She dropped her hands from his face, linking them around his neck and held him close, not daring to move, afraid he might run away, or was he going to make love to her? She wanted to rip his clothes off and feel his skin against hers; she craved for the warmth, the closeness. As close as they had been in the past to making love, she had never felt such fire or desire. She wanted him to make love, and she was beyond saying no; she ached for him. He stroked her hair and kissed her, she felt him hard against her and she pushed against him. Holding her close he said, "Are you sure?"

"Oh yes," she gasped.

While kissing her lips he lifted her and lay her on the couch and eased next to her, his shirt open. He unbuttoned her blouse and she almost cried out as she felt his skin touch hers. She hardly felt him undress her as he rolled on top of her. Breathing heavily, he gently caressed every inch of her body. She arched her back and cried out clinging to him, tears streaming down her cheeks.

"Why the tears?" Marcus whispered gently wiping her cheek.

"I don't know," she answered, "I'm not sad—they aren't those kind of tears." She thought but didn't say, *You released something that has been pent up inside me for a long time and I'm afraid, afraid of loving you.*

**

"Happy?" he said, kissing her cheek.

She nodded. "Yes. But I'm not sure what happened tonight." She swung her feet to the floor and sat up; suddenly her feelings were in turmoil again. She felt his soothing hand on her back and she relaxed.

"We made love, that's what happened. I love you more than ever, and I think we are together again." He paused, watching for Sarah's reaction.

She leaned against him, soaking up the warmth. "Together again. I think I might be in love with you," she teased.

"I'll take the 'might be' as a yes. Any chance I could stay the night?"

"No, Mrs. D would have a fit. It's time you left. And Marcus…no more secrets." When he didn't answer, she braced herself for more lies. "I mean it, no more lies."

"There is just one you need to know. My real name is not Marcus Perkins. It is Marc, with a c, so not so different, and I like Marcus."

"And your surname is?"

"Perry."

Sarah thought for a minute recognizing the name. "I've met your mother at Hillcrest Hall. She's an American and a friend of Belle Thornton. Belle loved chatting with a fellow American."

"That's why I ran off at graduation, I had only met Lady Thornton once at the house but I was afraid she would recognize me."

"And that's why your parents weren't at the graduation."

"I told them I'd dropped out the year before. My father and I had a terrible row and I walked out. I've never been back."

"How come you and Felix didn't know each other?"

"We have money, through an old established business but we don't move in quite the same society circles as the Thorntons, so I had never met Felix until I met you."

Sarah leaned back on the sofa. "Well, that explains a lot. How did you keep all these stories together?"

"It was easy at college, I was Marcus Perkins, a poor kid on a scholarship with a talent for sculpting. It was after college that things got complicated."

"Any more surprises, Marcus, or should I say Marc?"

"No, and I prefer Marcus," he said, walking to the door.

Sarah let him out of the front door, hearing the usual *tut, tut* from behind Mrs. Debinski's door. Her conscience burned her cheeks as she crept past the parlour and ran up the stairs and straight into her bedroom. She pulled the covers to her chin, still feeling Marcus's warmth, while trying to make sense of everything, particularly the tiny niggle of doubt that Marcus had not told her everything. She discounted it, arguing with herself that his story was quite believable and his reasons, although bizarre, did make sense. Didn't they?

Fifteen

Tides of Change

*C*hristmas had been a lot more fun than Sarah had expected. The Sackville was as festive as in her childhood memories. The enormous Christmas tree in the lobby, heavy with baubles and more twinkling lights than ever before. The choir sang carols every evening for twelve days. She remembered her mother being angry the day she almost knocked over the tree and Albert, the old doorman, comforting her while Woody secured it and then held her on his shoulders to hang the fallen decorations.

It was Brian, the sous-chef's, first Christmas with the Sackville and Bill was in the process of training him to take over the kitchen, so the festive culinary delights were abundant, both in quantity and variety.

Sarah had invited Marcus to join them. Anna was delighted to welcome the new clean-cut Marcus from a good family whose mother was acquainted with Belle. Bill, always the wise one, expressed reservations, doubting a man who had deceived so many people could change so easily.

Lizzy had brought Peter to Bexhill to meet the family and make their engagement official, setting the wedding date for June. Sarah and Marcus helped them celebrate.

Sarah hardly ever heard from Felix and missed the platonic relationship. Lorraine, already insecure about her friendship with

Felix, sensed Sarah's dislike. , She found Sarah a threat and forced Felix to keep his distance and that included the New Year's party with the traditional toast to Grandfather Alex and Sarah's mother. It seemed empty without Felix. Darcy and Belle attended as usual. Sarah had conveniently forgotten to tell Marcus of the Thornton New year tradition. Belle greeted Marcus with caution. She did recognize him, which meant she also knew the history between him and his father, but was diplomatic and said nothing. In fact, Sarah thought Belle was exceptionally quiet and withdrawn; most unusual behaviour for the out-going, fun-loving Belle. Darcy's attentiveness towards Belle was almost protective. Sarah sensed sadness but neither of them revealed their thoughts. Felix had chosen to go to Toronto with Lorraine for Christmas, which implied a serious relationship; one that neither Belle nor Darcy was keen on. Did they fear Felix would abandon Hillcrest like his uncle had? Even Darcy had moved to America and left the estate in the hands of poor management during the Second World War. Would history repeat itself? Sarah didn't think so, Felix's love of the law would keep him in Britain, but only she knew that.

The hotel was doing well. James Lytton had retired before Christmas and joined Jeremy in the Cotswold's. Mr. Grimsby, a highly experienced assistant manager from a large Manchester hotel, took over from James. Sarah thought his name suited him as he always looked grim, but he was excellent at the job and Sarah found it a relief as he took over much of Anna's work. In the kitchen, Brian was gradually taking over from Bill. Having more time to themselves, their health was improving and they planned to spend time over the quiet winter months with Darcy and Belle. Talk of Sarah taking over the hotel was hardly mentioned, and it suited her to ignore it and concentrate on her studies and finding her father.
**

When Sarah returned to London, she decided to write to Great Uncle Charlie asking for help finding her father. She explained that she had met an acquaintance of his who indicated her father might be in Canada. She thought it important to be as vague as Mr. Carter had been. Folding the fine blue paper of the Aerogramme letter, she carefully sealed it. She felt a flutter of excitement at the thought of meeting her father again as she popped the letter in the round, red letterbox. Her feet bounced on the pavement as she walked towards the college.

Today's studies were about her favourite artists, the impressionists, and how they influenced Emily Carr's art. Aware that her style was similar, Sarah had the ability to produce movement in her art; the trees moved and spoke to her as she painted, and she saw the same thing in Emily Carr's western forests.

The urge to visit Canada strengthened every day. Her uncle, her father, Emily Carr, her art, and even Felix's connection drew her across the Atlantic Ocean. She again recalled her five-year-old self promising to take Grandfather Alex's ashes back to Canada. Knowing that her mother had wanted to return to her place of birth, she decided to take her mother's ashes too. Sarah felt a piece of her heart belonged there: the Canadian Rockies, Toronto or anywhere as long as it was on Canadian soil.

Uncle Charlie had been non-committal in his response to her letter, inviting her to visit in the summer and they could talk then.

**

It was a hot June day when Sarah found herself, once again, in the Convocation Hall of the Royal College of Art. Mr. Darwin was handing out the special awards and Sarah was the recipient of the coveted silver medal. It was history repeating as she looked into the crowd; she easily found Anna and Bill standing up, clapping with Darcy and Belle at their side. She heard Marcus whistle amongst the cheers of Lizzy and Peter. She felt a void, Felix was missing. She scanned the back of the hall, hoping that he'd changed his plans and instead of being in Canada with Lorraine, he'd made a surprise appearance. She reprimanded herself for being sentimental; even old friends moved on. She had deliberately neglected to tell Felix that she had her own plans to visit Canada, suspecting that he was in Toronto to ask for Lorraine's hand in marriage. It occurred to her that the Thorntons rarely spoke of Lorraine. Was that why Belle was so sad?

The ceremony over, they moved on to Darcy's club to celebrate.
**

Sarah was feeling the tides of change as she helped Lizzy pack and move her personal belongings to Peter's flat, which boasted new modern teak furniture, so she discarded anything that came from the fifties. Sarah had decided to stay in the flat on her own and was happy to have the old furniture. Old and comfortable suited her taste; material things were not important and finding another place with a studio would not be easy. Her new role as assistant professor, starting in September, meant she could easily afford the rent without a roommate.

Marcus handed Peter the final box to put in his car and Lizzy hugged Sarah. "I'll see you on Friday. I can't believe I'm getting married in five days."

"We'll be there Friday night to help you. I have to pick up my bridesmaid's dress from Jacob's in the morning and then Marcus and I are coming down on the afternoon train."

Sarah saw the parlour curtains move and Johnny's face appeared, waving frantically to Lizzy. As Sarah closed the front door he came out and hugged her. "Miss Sarah, don't go away."

"No, Johnny, I'm staying here. I'm working at the college in September." Johnny's face lit up at the news. "But I am going on holiday to Canada after Lizzy's wedding. I will be away for a while, but I am coming back." Seeing his lip quiver, Sarah quickly added, "I will write you letters," Realizing Johnny didn't read too well, she corrected herself, "How would you like to get picture postcards from Canada?" He nodded and gave Sarah the usual bear hug.

"Sarah," Marcus's voice came from the top of the stairs. "I'm hungry and thirsty, let's go to the pub."

Sarah ran up the stairs, frowning. "That's a good idea, but why so serious?" Marcus shrugged, leaning over to kiss her. "Help me tidy up and then we'll go."

The Fox and Hound, a mere five-minute walk from the flat, was their local, although Sarah only ever went with Marcus. It was pleasantly quiet; the recent Soviet spy scandal had dominated most conversations for the past couple of months. Some of the locals, convinced their neighbours were spies, made for interesting listening. But on Sunday the regulars enjoyed a pint midday, going home at two o'clock for Sunday roast.

Marcus ordered a pint of best bitter, a lager and lime, two beef sandwiches and two bags of crisps—the menu was limited Sunday night.

"It's quiet tonight, so we don't have to listen to ridiculous opinions about spies lurking in the saloon bar," Sarah whispered with a laugh.

Taking a large bite out of his sandwich followed by a gulp of beer, Marcus gave Sarah an odd look, as if to say something but keeping the words in his head.

"Marcus, what's wrong?" Sarah felt her back straighten, her body on guard. She nibbled on her sandwich, waiting for his reply.

He swallowed hard and took another gulp of beer. "I have something to tell you." He stared at his fingers as they traced the pattern on the beer mug, avoiding Sarah's puzzled expression. "I have to go away."

"Why? Are you ending our relationship?"

"No. No, nothing like that. Sarah, I love you; you are the best thing that has ever happened to me. Watching Peter and Lizzy, I couldn't help wishing it was you and I preparing to get married."

Marriage, Sarah thought. *Not in my plans.* "Are you proposing to me?"

"No, but would that be so bad?"

She didn't answer. Marriage had never entered her head; she liked things as they were.

"So…You want to move in with me, now that Lizzy has moved out? That's not going to happen. My grandparents would have a fit, not to mention Mrs. Debinski. Besides I'm looking forward to being alone and…"

"Stop!" Marcus interrupted, hitting his fist on the table. Sarah jumped. "You aren't listening to me." He placed his hand on hers, but she pulled it away. The edge to his voice scared her. Remembering his old pattern of behaviour, she stared at him, seeing the old hurtful beatnik Marcus.

"I have to go away and…" he hesitated and his voice softened to a whisper. "I'm sorry, I didn't mean to shout. I leave tomorrow." He reached for her hand, she let him hold it, hoping his touch would be reassuring. It wasn't.

"I love you Sarah. I don't want to lose you."

"I don't understand. Away: where, for how long, and why?"

"It's complicated, but I have another job. One that requires me to be away for long periods of time." Sarah sensed deceit emerging.

"Another job? What happened to advertising?" She sipped her lager and picked at the crust of her sandwich. Marcus finished his pint and motioned towards Sarah's almost full glass. When she shook her head, he stepped up to the bar and ordered another pint. Stalling, he slurped the thin layer of foam off the top of his beer.

"Well, are you going to tell me what's going on?"

"The company is sending me on a special advertising project for a large corporation. Its an innovative product that has to be kept from the competitors. I had to sign a nondisclosure contract. I can't even tell you what it is about."

"You said a new job and now it's in advertising?" She wondered, *Does Marcus even know how to tell the truth?*

"Oh, well, it's a new job within the company. I wish I could say more but I can't." Marcus sat very still, watching her reaction. "It means I won't make it to Lizzy's wedding."

"What!" Anger bubbled up into her throat. "No. Marcus, this isn't fair. We've been planning this for months. I already bought your train ticket. How am I going to manage on my own? Can't you delay it until next week or after I leave for Canada?"

"It can't be helped. *I have no choice*. Sarah, you've travelled to Bexhill a million times on your own, you'll manage." He attempted to look sorry, but she doubted he was. "I'm sorry to miss the wedding but you will be busy doing bridesmaid stuff—you don't need me. I leave tomorrow."

Marcus was right, she would have little time for him before the wedding, but she had plans for afterwards: going to the beach and hiking up Smugglers Hill. She'd planned to find some stone to ignite his talent, so he could sculpt while she painted. She heard the finality in his voice and something else; regret or sadness, or perhaps shame? She frowned; that last word bothered her.

The anger turned to disappointment; she'd been looking forward to having Marcus at her side during the wedding celebration and now she would be alone. "I'll miss you. Will you write or phone?"

"I'll try, but I'm not good at letter writing and I don't know where I'll be. I want to ask you to wait for me, but that would be unfair." He bent forward and kissed her forehead. "I have no idea when I'll be back."

"I'll be here. I'll be busy teaching and I have big plans for my art, so I'm not going anywhere."

Marcus shuffled and drank a large quantity of beer in one slurp almost choking. "If you don't hear from me, it's because I can't write. I'll walk you back to the flat and then I have to go."

They walked in silence, Sarah took out her key as they arrived at the front door, but Marcus pushed it back into her bag and pulling her close he said, "We'll say our goodbyes here," he paused. "No matter what happens or what you hear, I'll always love you." His voice quivered, "I wish I'd known you a long time ago. It's too late now—I'm trapped." His palms rested on her cheeks and he kissed her with desperate passion, only releasing her when neither could breathe. Breathless he ran his fingers through her curls and held them against his cheek, whispering, "I'm sorry." As he let her go, she saw the light glisten in his moist eyes and regret masked his smile. He turned and walked away.

Sarah stared, waiting for him to turn and wave goodbye, watching him disappear in and out of the yellow pools of the street lights until he reached the end of the road. And then he was gone.

She folded her skirt under her legs and sat on the doorstep. She could still feel his hands in her curls as the warm summer breeze brushed them against her cheek. Buzzing night insects filled the silence; a dog barked in the distance. She wrapped her arms around her legs, resting her chin on her knees and stared into the empty night.

Sixteen

Lizzy's Wedding

❦

S arah leaned back; the velvet headrest felt smooth and comforting as she allowed her body to sway from side to side with the rhythm of the train, staring at the big white box on the luggage rack above her head. The sterile whiteness and sharp corners contrasted the soft blue dress inside. It reflected how she felt: depleted of emotion, afraid a sharp corner might rip open a fissure and expose her gullibility, her soft and vulnerable inner self.

It had surprised her how much Marcus leaving had hurt. He'd done it before, so why the surprise? As an undergrad she had wanted to rebel, or rebel as much as Sarah was able. Dating the long-haired, bearded sculptor, Marcus Perkins, had satisfied that need. At times it felt like love and it had hurt when he walked away the first time, but she soon got over it. Meeting Marcus as Marc Perry had been different, and somewhere along the way she had fallen in love, giving herself to him so completely that she had willingly given him her virginity. Was that why the hurt felt like betrayal—he'd broken her trust? Her throat tightened and she swallowed, trying to force the tears away as she realized he'd manipulated her into trusting the new Marc but in fact he was still the old Marcus. Little acts of deceit she'd hardly noticed before came to mind, including their last conversation at the pub. Nothing he'd said made sense. There was no secret advertising job. She had called the office and was told he'd resigned two months ago and no longer had any association with the company. He'd been lying to her for at least two months. Convinced that Marcus knew full well where he was going, she wondered, *Why the secrecy?* "I'll probably never find out," she whispered to herself. "And despite his lies, I believe he loves me. Will that be enough to bring him back?"

The train jolted to a stop at Reading station and Sarah had to scramble to gather her belongings and catch the train to Bexhill. She squeezed into an already full compartment of excited holidaymakers. The white box seemed enormous on her lap and her suitcase was pressed between her knees. She was glad she'd worn a full skirt; as it was she was showing more petticoat than she would like, but a pencil slim skirt would have shown more than petticoat. There was no possibility of relaxing, and although it was a relatively short journey, by the time she had extricated herself from the compartment she was exhausted and eager to find a friendly face on the platform. Disappointed, she found the grim visage of Mr. Grimsby, who immediately relieved her of her suitcase and holdall, nodded and said, "Welcome home, Miss Wexford. I trust you had a pleasant journey?" He glanced at the train. "Mr. Perry is not with you?"

Sarah clung to her white dress-box and smiled. "No, he had to go away on unexpected business." She felt her cheeks redden at the lie and added, "From London to Reading was fine but the Bexhill train was packed and uncomfortable. I'm glad to be home, Mr. Grimsby."

"We are pleased to have you back. Your grandmother misses you. You bring a spark to the Sackville." The corners of his mouth lifted into a warm smile that reached his eyes and Sarah had a glimpse of caring man. But his words jabbed at the guilt that never completely went away.

Anna stood with Henry under the portico, waving as Mr. Grimsby pulled the car to the curb. Henry took the bags from the trunk. Seeing the white dress-box, Anna said, "Can I see your dress? Henry, take the box into my office."

Sarah wrapped her arms around Anna, happy to feel her love and tenderness. "Nana…" feeling tears welling up she stopped.

Hugging her tightly, Anna said, "What's wrong, sweetheart?"

"Marcus isn't coming. He's gone away and I don't think he's coming back."

Anna took her hand, "Come, let's go to my office. I'll order tea and you can tell me all about it."

"That sounds wonderful, but Lizzy will be waiting for me."

"Lizzy can wait. I need you, or should I say, you need some hugs." Sarah nodded, no longer able to keep the tears back. Being home was like being wrapped in a warm blanket, making her realize how lonely and sad she had been over the last few days.

Balaji knocked on the door and brought them a tray of tea and Sarah's favourite cream filled chocolate éclairs. "Miss Sarah, Chef Bill sent these for you, as an offering of peace for not greeting you," he hesitated, seeing Sarah smile. Balaji's Indian background sometimes made it difficult for him to understand British idiom. "Balaji didn't say that right, but Chef is busy with the wedding preparations."

"Peace offering—you were almost right and I understood you. Please tell him thank you and I'll come down and see him shortly."

"It's good to have you home, Miss." Balaji bowed and left the office.

Sarah and Anna sat together on the office sofa. Sarah described how she was feeling the changes, particularly Lizzy moving out and the most unexpected development, Marcus's sudden and hurtful departure. Anna listened, pulling Sarah close to her until she stopped crying through the hurt.

"You know, Nana, it's like being little again and having you kiss my grazed knee better. You've kissed my bruised heart better." She hugged her and kissed her cheek. "I feel so much better and I'm ready for Lizzy and Peter's wedding." Sarah opened the white box and held the pale blue dress against her. The soft blue chiffon folded around the strapless top and floated into a layered full skirt.

116

"Lizzy has impeccable taste. It is perfect for you, and such a unique design. I guess it helps when you work for a world-renowned fashion designer like Jacob's." Anna felt the soft fabric and glanced at the hem. "It looks a little short for you."

"It's the fashion, Nana. Skirts are getting shorter and it's not as short as the latest Nancy Quan fashions. I'm lucky to have shapely legs, which will be enhanced by the stiletto heels." Sarah laughed, "Me in heels. But it's all for a good cause. I had better get organized and go over to Lizzy's place. I forgot to ask, is everything ready here for the wedding breakfast?"

"Everything is under control. Dorothy has gone beyond the call of duty because she knows Lizzy, and it doesn't hurt that the Elliott's aren't afraid to spend money on their only daughter's wedding. The whole wedding party is staying here tomorrow night. Some have already checked in and several are staying here over the weekend."

"A wedding is always good for business. I need to ask Grandpa if I can borrow the Hillman."

Sara ran down the service stairs to find the kitchen buzzing with staff, many of whom she had never met. A fully booked hotel and a wedding required a lot of food preparation. Sarah gasped when she spotted Bill, in high concentration as he skillfully moved a piping bag full of pale blue icing into tiny delicate flowers on a fine trellis of white icing. He looked up and smiled. "Almost done." Bill made a few swirls and put the icing bag down. "There, finished. Do you like it?"

"Oh, I do. I'm stuck for words. I had no idea you were so talented."

"I learned years ago when I worked at the Royal York in Toronto, but rarely put the skill to use as we've always ordered our specialty cakes from the bakery here in town. Lizzy didn't like the choices the bakery had, so she insisted I make the cake. I think I'll do more—I really enjoyed doing it." Bill moved away from the three-tiered cake and kissed Sarah. "It's good to have you home. Where's Marcus?"

"It's a long story, but he's not coming. I just told Nana and I don't want to talk about it now."

"I'm sorry, honey." He squeezed her shoulders. "What else can I do for you?"

"Can I borrow the Hillman to go to Lizzy's?"

He took the keys from the board and handed them to her. "Off you go. Tell Lizzy and her mum that everything is under control. Mrs. Elliott has been demanding, even more so than most mothers of the bride, and I don't have time for any more discussions or changes."

"I'll keep them distracted." Sarah blew him a kiss as she left the kitchen.

**

Lizzy's household was in chaos. Lizzy was fretting over the length of her veil and her mother wasn't sure the centerpieces were right. Dorothy had called to say that the bandleader was ill and she had hired a new band. Peter's four-year-old niece was throwing a temper tantrum, refusing to be a bridesmaid. Peter's friends were throwing him a bachelor party and he wasn't answering his phone and Mr. Elliott was also at the party.

Sarah walked into the house and ordered everyone into the lounge and asked the maid to bring tea and sandwiches; she suspected no one had eaten in hours and low blood sugar was adding to the stress.

Once the tea arrived, Sarah took each issue and explained that everything was fine. Sarah pointed out to Lizzy that the veil had been designed by Jacob's to go with the dress perfectly. Lizzy agreed. Sarah had seen the centerpieces and they too were perfect. She was able to reassure Mrs. Elliott that Miss Jenkins always had a second band of the highest quality to call upon should the first one not work out, and this particular group played at many of the Sackville functions, and Anna insisted they play for her special New Year's Eve dance. That seemed to satisfy Mrs. Elliott, but the little bridesmaid was still a worry. Other than referring to four-year-olds changing their minds and she was sure it would all work out, Sarah couldn't add much more. Finally, she added that it was unrealistic to try and find the menfolk when they were at a bachelor party.

Sarah helped Lizzy lay out her clothes for the wedding and confirm the hairdressing plans for early morning. She returned to her penthouse, falling asleep immediately.

**

At eleven-forty-five the limousines pulled up at Lizzy's house and the motorcade drove to St Andrew's Church. Everything ran like clockwork. Susie, the four-year-old bridesmaid, took a liking to Sarah and behaved well. Lizzy was stunning on her father's arm, in a long white brocade dress with a unique scooped back, the fabric flowing into a long train mirrored by the veil. Susie walked in front of Sarah at a safe distance from the train and Sarah kept a watchful eye so she didn't step on it. As they approached the altar, she saw Peter and his best man in morning suits. She thought Peter looked handsome but slightly green around the gills. She smiled, thinking he was either nervous or hung-over, or perhaps a little of both.

She took Susie's hand and they straightened Lizzy's train before moving to the side to take the bouquet of white roses mixed with blue forget-me-nots. There was a hush as the vicar approached the couple. Mr. Elliott handed his daughter off to the groom, turned and walked to his seat beside his wife. Everyone in their place, Sarah looked up and almost dropped the bouquet as Felix stepped back from the groom and smiled. She smiled back and gave him a quizzical look.

The best man was supposed to be an old school friend of Peter's who lived in the midlands. Sarah had never met him and Lizzy didn't know him, so they had never discussed him. How had Felix stepped into the role and when did he get back from Canada? She discreetly turned her head, looking for Lorraine in the congregation, but all she saw was a sea of unknown faces. She felt Felix's stare, intense and wanting. Wanting what? Part of her was glad to see him. Her initial instinct was to tell him about Marcus, to feel his support and understanding. But the other part was angry. He hadn't been there when she needed him, and even when he was around, he'd been distant. Yet, as she absorbed his stare, she sensed her old soul-mate.

The vicar said, "You may kiss the bride." Sarah's gaze dropped from Felix to Susie who had started to fidget. She'd been so deep in her own thoughts she had missed the whole ceremony and needed to bring her attention back into the church. The organ boomed out the wedding march and Sarah handed the bouquet back to a beaming Lizzy. With Susie's help she lifted the train and veil and swung them around behind Lizzy as she turned up the aisle. Sarah followed the bride and groom and the best man wheeled into place at her side. She had the strangest feeling, walking down the aisle, side by side with Felix.

Half of the population of Bexhill greeted Lizzy and Peter as they stepped out of the church. Confetti showered over them as they stopped to talk to well-wishers.

Sarah and Felix found themselves alone in the back seat of a limousine waiting for the rest of the wedding party, who eventually filled the waiting cars and the motorcade drove slowly to The New Sackville Hotel. Sarah was the first to speak, "When did you get back from Canada?"

"Early yesterday morning. I had planned to come back to prepare for a big trial and Peter asked me to step in as best man."

"What happened to the school friend?"

"I don't know, Peter didn't say." He took a breath and hesitated. "Is Marcus here?"

"No, he's gone away."

"Gone away. What does that mean?"

"It's a long story. Did Lorraine come with you?"

"No, she has a lot of catching up to do with family after being away for a year. As soon as the trial is over, I'll go back for a while."

"I'm leaving for Toronto next week. I want to find my father and I had a tip that he was in Canada and my great uncle might know where he is."

Felix raised his eyebrows. "Why? I've never heard you speak of your father. No one talks about him."

"That's the point; everyone ignores the fact that I even have a father. I think about him every day but I've always been afraid to say anything. It seemed a taboo subject around my grandparents and I don't know why."

"I would think Anna and Bill can't forgive him for abandoning you. Isn't that reason enough?"

Sarah nodded her head slightly to one side. "Maybe, but I think it's more than that. His name was mentioned at the James Bond conference."

Felix laughed. "James Bond Conference?"

"Oh, sorry." Sarah giggled. "We hosted a government conference that was all hush-hush and we jokingly called it the James Bond Conference. Mr. Carter, the organizer, mentioned my father's name but then covered it up. And then later he said he knew my uncle and implied I should talk to him."

"You're talking in riddles. Should I take this seriously?"

"Not you as well? Felix this is serious; I want to find my father. Is that so difficult to understand?"

"No, it's not and I'll help you. If I had known, I would have offered sooner. As a solicitor I know the places to look for information that lay people might not be aware of. We also have private detectives we can call on."

"That would be wonderful. I was so intent on keeping this from Anna and Bill that I had never thought of asking you." Sarah was filled with gratitude; sharing this burden was huge. She had her friend and soul-mate back. She squeezed his hand, whispering, "Thank you."

Seventeen

Sarah in Canada

arah's white knuckles clung to the arm-rest as the British Overseas Airways Boeing 707 jet landed at Toronto International Airport. She had mixed feelings about flying. Anna had wanted her to sail, but that would have taken too long. Felix had confidently recommended flying—he did it all the time. During the flight she was treated as well as any special hotel guest by smart, friendly air hostesses who came rushing to her side every time she pressed the call button. The meals were excellent and there was as much to drink as she wanted, but the take-off and landing were a touch scary. Relieved and excited to be safely on Canadian soil, she watched the airport buildings appear in the morning sunshine as they taxied to the terminal.

Slightly nervous, she answered the customs officer's questions, declaring she had gifts for the family. She neglected to declare her Grandfather Alex and her mother's ashes; she wasn't sure she was supposed to have dead people in her suitcase.

Emerging from the customs hall, Uncle Charlie, Beth and cousin Charlotte scooped her up in hugs and asked a million questions as they drove into Toronto, eventually arriving at 72 Forest Road. It was a lovely, welcoming house with a large oak tree in the middle of the front lawn and pretty flowers beds around it. The front door had a stained-glass panel that reflected the light. Stepping inside, Sarah was once again overwhelmed with déjà vu. Although she had never been in her uncle's house before, she heard her mother's voice, "Welcome to my favourite place." She turned to see who was talking, all the time knowing the voice was in her head.

"I feel as though I've been here before. Is the house haunted?"

"I'm not sure it's haunted, but this used to be Nana's house," Uncle Charlie said. "Aunt Beth and I bought it from Nana and Grandpa Alex when they moved back to England. Your mother grew up here. I think she was about fifteen and not happy at being dragged away from her friends to live a foreign country."

"Nana told me the story. I wasn't expecting to feel her so close."

"Come, let's take your things upstairs to the guest room. You're right next to Charlotte." Aunt Beth squeezed her shoulders. "It's lovely to have you here."

"Thank you."

Charlotte beamed. "I am looking forward to having company. School finished last week, so I can show you around. Being a school teacher has the advantage of long summer holidays."

**

After a good night's sleep, Sarah came down for breakfast rather late. She hadn't taken into account the five-hour time difference.

"Good morning," Charlotte said, handing Sarah a cup of coffee. "I thought we'd stay around the house today. Mum and Dad are out until dinnertime. Mum belongs to all kinds of clubs and does volunteer work. And Dad, well he's supposed to be retired, but he still does work for the RCMP; always hush hush, but then I can never remember a time when his work wasn't shrouded in secrecy—you get used to it."

"I'm surprised at how tired I am. Taking the day to unpack and get over the jet lag is a good idea." Sarah wanted to ask about Uncle Charlie's work but she wasn't quite ready to tell Charlotte her reasons for being there. She liked Charlotte and they had got along well when they were kids, but she wanted to make sure she could be trusted. Sarah had told no one except Felix about searching for her father.

"Mum said you wanted to go to the West Coast and research Emily Carr the painter?"

"I love her art and model some of my own art on her style. I'd like to know a bit more about the person and the forests she painted. Nana loves her art too, but thinks she was a starving artist and died in poverty. She's afraid I'll have the same fate," Sarah said with a laugh. "My art is already selling and I'm teaching at the college in September, so that's not going to happen. There are times I think it's a ploy to get me back to run the hotel." Sarah grinned and shrugged her shoulders. "But that's another story." Charlotte ignored the comment but Sarah felt her empathy. "Are you still up for coming with me to Vancouver?"

"Oh yes, I have never been to Vancouver. I started looking into Emily Carr's history and she is a fascinating person and artist. I even read some of her books. We can start planning today if you like?"

By dinnertime, the trip to Vancouver was settled and they planned to leave the following week. Sarah was exhausted and she still hadn't unpacked, so after dinner she excused herself and retired to her room. She was relieved that Uncle Charlie had not mentioned her father in front of Aunt Beth or Charlotte, but disappointed he'd made no attempt to acknowledge why she was there. Perhaps he'd forgotten, or he knew nothing after all. As the thoughts went through her mind, she heard footsteps in the hall and a gentle tap on the door. "May I come in?" Uncle Charlie popped his head around the door.

"Yes, of course. We were so busy planning our trip that I never got unpacked." Sarah stared expectantly at Uncle Charlie.

"I know you want to find your father, but it's not a good idea." Sarah felt her heart drop into her stomach. She was about to speak but Charlie put his hand up. "Hear me out first." She nodded and sat heavily on the bed, her heart racing.

"Some time ago, I did meet up with your father. All I can tell you is that he is well, or was when I saw him. I can't say much, but he is in a similar line of work as me."

"He's in the secret service?" Sarah frowned. "That's why Mr. Carter asked me if I knew him. But why did he tell me to contact you?"

"I'm not sure, but he broke protocol even mentioning it to you, which is troubling. I know Michael Carter—we've worked together on international business."

"Uncle Charlie, I miss my father and I know from my memories that he's a good man. My grandparents never speak of him, as though he's done something wrong and they don't want me to know about it. I want to find him and if you won't help me I'll find another way." Sarah felt like stamping her feet. Her disappointment had turned to anger; Uncle Charlie was not going to help her after all. She thought of Felix, who had promised to do some digging. She decided she had a better chance with Felix than Uncle Charlie.

Almost as though he had read her thoughts he replied, "It is complicated and I would prefer that you let it go. I don't want you to get hurt, nor do I want you to get into trouble."

"Trouble! What do you mean?"

Uncle Charlie didn't answer, twisting his mouth in thought. Taking a deep breath, he said, "Okay, I will make some inquiries. The fact that Mr. Carter told you to contact me tells me there might be a way. I will do my best but I can't make any promises. And for now, it has to stay between us. Do you understand?"

Sarah nodded her compliance. "Does that mean you will help me."

"Yes, but you have to be patient. Now I'll let you get on with your unpacking."

Her half-unpacked suitcase lay on the bed and she lay beside it staring at the ceiling, and instead of sifting through her belongings she sifted through the conversation, looking for nuances and body language that would tell her more than Uncle Charlie's words had revealed.

**

Her inner clock, now on Canadian time, woke her early the next morning and she ran down for breakfast, hoping to catch her uncle, although she wondered, why the rush as nothing would have changed since the night before. Aunt Beth and Charlotte greeted her with coffee and thick pancakes smothered in butter and maple syrup, a true Canadian experience. It was far more food than Sarah was used to, but as the day was to be spent touring Toronto, it was ideal.

**

"Wow! Nana told me about Lake Ontario being as massive as an ocean. She wasn't kidding," Sarah said as Charlotte motioned for her to sit on the beach. Sarah felt a shudder, remembering Nana's story of sitting on the beach with grandfather Alex and her mother when she was a little girl. She had a strong desire to paint the scene and she knew that this was where she would sprinkle their ashes. Should she tell Charlotte or come back on her own? There were few people in her life that she felt a deep connection with: her grandparents, Felix and now Charlotte. She noticed she didn't have to question Charlotte's friendship; she just knew it was there.

They both stared at a dot on the lake, a ship moving along the horizon on the far side of the invisible American border. "Charlotte, I have something to tell you. It might seem a bit odd."

Charlotte turned and looked at her. "If it's about your father, my father has told me that he's helping you find him. But he also said we are not to talk about it."

Stunned, Sarah whipped her head around to face Charlotte. "He told you? But if you know, why can't we talk about it?" Sarah wanted to talk about it. It felt good to know someone else understood.

"Ears are everywhere. I've grown up with this secret stuff. Neither Mum nor I ever know what's going on. He'll let us know when we can talk. Leave it to Dad—if there's anything to find, he'll find it."

"I trust you and Uncle Charlie and I'm so glad you know about it. But actually, that wasn't what I was going to say." Sarah paused, "This may sound morbid. Nana saved Grandpa Alex and my mother's ashes, and many years ago I promised to bring them back to Canada.

I've done that, and I want to lay them to rest here in Lake Ontario."

Charlotte's eyes widened, a look of disgust on her face. "Where are these ashes?"

"In my suitcase. I was afraid customs might open my suitcase." Sarah laughed, hoping Charlotte would join in.

There was an awkward pause and then Charlotte burst out laughing. "I'd loved to see the custom's officer's reaction. I don't know what ashes look, like, but you're right, it is a bit morbid."

"I don't know either as they are sealed in urns, but I think its just ash."

"I'm hungry. Let's go eat and discuss how we are going to disperse these ashes." Charlotte led the way to a small diner-style restaurant overlooking the lake.

"It's as I imagined it," Sarah said, sitting at a small table and not taking her eyes off the scene. The late afternoon sun glowed in the west as it began its slow decent into the horizon. "The sun and sky is quite different to the sunset in Bexhill. I have to paint this."

"Why don't you?" Charlotte said.

"Would you mind if I made a quick sketch?" Sarah took out a sketch book from her satchel and began illustrating the scene. Charlotte watched Sarah's hands and eyes take in the image and replicate it on the paper. Sarah turned to Charlotte and sketched her sitting in the window of the restaurant.

"Wow, that's amazing. We have to make sure you have time to sketch when we get to Vancouver. I will read all Emily Carr's books while you paint."

**

Two days later, Sarah and Charlotte placed the urns in Sarah's holdall and took the tram down to Lakeshore. As they walked along the beach, she cradled the bag in her arms. She felt sad and was glad for Charlotte's arm around her shoulders. They found a little sheltered inlet. Sarah removed her sandals and walked into the lake, loosening the top of each urn. She released the ashes and the north wind blew them out into the lake. Expecting to feel sad and tearful, she was surprised to feel happy and peaceful. She closed her eyes and felt her heart shimmer as her mother's smiling face floated by, and then her grandfather, whose face she'd long forgotten, appeared clear and loving. She listened to the wind and could have sworn she heard it whisper, "Thank you."

She heard Charlotte's voice calling, "Are you all right?" Sarah turned and waved and walked back to the beach.

"I'm fine. I kept my promise."

Eighteen

Surprises

"*L*orraine and Felix!" Sarah repeated louder than she intended. "Why so surprised?" Charlotte paused with a perplexed expression. "Lorraine's a friend. We met at teacher's college and we teach at the same school. We both applied for the exchange program. When it was awarded to Lorraine, I suggested she look you up."

"I didn't know that. I thought it was a coincidence that she came from Toronto. She *did not* look me up. She found Felix first, so I met her through him." Sarah hoped that Charlotte hadn't noticed the tightness in her voice. Her own reaction to Lorraine mystified her. She seemed like a nice person and Lizzy got along with her, in fact they were quite friendly, but Sarah had never liked her. Perhaps the feeling was mutual; maybe that's why she hadn't mentioned Charlotte.

"Felix arrived yesterday to finish his holiday, and as we are leaving tomorrow I invited them to dinner tonight. Lorraine thinks he came back to propose," Charlotte giggled. "And I agree. I thought you'd be happy to see Felix?"

Sarah took a breath to calm herself. "I'm always happy to see Felix—second only to Lizzy, he's my oldest and closest friend. I don't think his parents will be happy about a proposal. You know Felix is heir to the Hillcrest Hall estate and he will be the Earl of Hillcrest, an English gentleman. And he will soon be a QC, Queens Counsel; that's a very privileged position."

"I know what QC means. Are you implying Lorraine's not good enough for him?" Charlotte looked upset and Sarah realized she was being a snob.

"No, I didn't mean that. I'm sorry, it came out all wrong. I have known Felix's family all my life and I know his father has what might be considered unrealistic expectations and Lorraine might not realize what she's getting into. His mother is American, so she will be more accepting, although she has been critical in the past about Felix's girlfriends. He's a bit if a playboy you know."

"I think Lorraine understands. She's only met the Thorntons a couple of times but she told me she sensed their disapproval." Charlotte glanced in the mirror over the fireplace and patted her wavy hair. "I need to get tidied up. No need to change, it's a casual dinner."

Sarah felt uneasy and went into the kitchen to help Aunt Beth with the dinner preparations. Ignoring the doorbell, she continued to fuss in the kitchen.

"Is everything all right, Sarah?"

"Of course, Aunt Beth. I just thought you could do with some help."

"I'm fine, almost finished, so why don't you go join the guests?"

Sarah walked into the living room and Felix greeted her with a hug, somewhat tighter than usual as he whispered in her ear, "I have news about your father." He held her at arms length and said, "It's good to see you again."

Sarah went to greet Lorraine who extended her arm, leaving no doubt that she was keeping Sarah at a distance, and her cold, limp handshake confirmed Sarah's suspicions. *I'm not imagining it,* she thought. *Lorraine does not like me. Well, Lorraine, the feeling is quite mutual.*

Sarah picked at her dinner, too anxious to eat, wondering how she could talk to Felix alone; he'd given her several glances during dinner. As everyone finished dessert, Uncle Charlie suggested they have coffee outside on the patio. Toronto was in the middle of a heat wave. The steamy heat was tempered indoors by air conditioning and the evening breeze had cooled enough that it was now pleasant to sit outdoors. Uncle Charlie led the way through the patio doors. It was dark out, so she couldn't see the flowers that surrounded the patio, but their perfume greeted Sarah's sense of smell as she breathed in the night air.

"Excuse the darkness, but the light will attract the bugs." Uncle Charlie looked upwards. "With a nice breeze like tonight and a little moonlight we can hopefully keep the pesky little things away. I'll fetch the coffee."

Sarah found herself alone with Felix. "What a beautiful garden. I looked at this earlier today and tried to think of my mother playing when she was little."

Felix took her arm. "Let's take a walk around."

Sarah laughed. "It's not a whole estate, it's a suburban back yard."

"I know, but I have something to tell you."

"My father?" Sarah walked with him over the lawn. "What did you find out?"

"It might not be what you're expecting. Are you sure you want to know?"

"I'm a big girl, I can take it." But Sarah wasn't sure that she could—she had fantasized about this wonderful man for years.

"He moved to London and worked for Dover Engineering for a short time, but was fired after getting arrested. From what I can tell from police records he lived in a boarding house and had several run-ins with the police, mostly for being drunk and disorderly. It's a bit sketchy, but it appears that he became very ill. I found a hospital admittance record, most likely because of the drinking, but I couldn't confirm that. It seems he was sent from the hospital to a nursing home to dry out. Again, the records are sketchy and inconclusive and I have yet to talk to the matron. Then he disappeared for a few years and re-appeared briefly about three years ago as an engineering consultant on a renovation project at St. Ermin's Hotel in London."

Sarah's eyes lit up. "So you found him!"

"Not exactly." Felix moved his head from side to side. "The engineering company had dodgy records and went belly up after a bad accident when someone was killed. Sarah, there are indications that person might have been your father."

Sarah's heart sank. *No, not after all this time,* she thought. *Is that the secret Nana is keeping—is that why they never speak of him?*

Aunt Beth's voice came from the patio. "You'll get eaten alive walking on the grass. Coffee and liqueurs would be more pleasant."

"Just looking at the flowers. You did a wonderful job this year." Felix leaned in to Sarah and whispered, "I can't find a death certificate. But he's certainly disappeared again."

"So, there is hope?"

"Maybe. I'll keep looking."

Lorraine appeared silhouetted in the doorway. Felix called to her, "Come and look at Beth's garden."

"I'm happy on the bugless patio," Lorraine said, watching Sarah squish a bloody mosquito and slap her leg where another was landing.

"I see what you mean about being eaten alive," Sarah said.

"They seem to like *posh* British blood," Lorraine joked. Sarah didn't like the sarcasm and took offense but said nothing, still reeling from Felix's news.

Felix turned towards Sarah as he reached the patio, his expression gentle with empathy. She wanted to talk to him some more, to feel his support and kindness, to hear him say he understood her disappointment. Memories of her drunken father in the penthouse brought back the fear she hadn't felt since she'd asked to move into Nana's suite. Her nine-year-old mind had thought she had abandoned him and that's why he'd abandoned her in turn; it was all her fault he'd moved away. If he had died before she could say sorry, she didn't know what she would do. Felix had said there was hope. She had to be patient.

Uncle Charlie seemed to have a sixth sense that she needed support and took Sarah's arm. Did he know what Felix had just told her? She sat down in a lawn chair.

"Tell me what do you two have planned for your adventure out west?" Sarah didn't answer as she tried to switch her thoughts, aware that she needed to be sociable.

"Sarah wants to explore the old forests and follow Emily Carr's footsteps," Charlotte said.

Talking about her passion was easy for Sarah and it immediately took her mind off her father. "I studied the artist and her work fascinates me. I'm told I have a similar style. My grandfather was an inspector on CP rail, and he took Nana on a trip to the west coast, years ago. She tells wonderful stories of the mountains and meeting a friend of Emily Carr's in a cafe in Vancouver, where she first spotted her art. You know the dining room at the hotel is called the Emily Carr Room and houses Nana's collection of her paintings. I think I'm following a lot of footsteps. I hope Charlotte won't be bored while I'm sketching. I get a bit carried away sometimes."

"I have a stack of books to read, and maybe Sarah can teach me to paint." Charlotte clapped, trying to catch a bug. "The bugs are getting bad. I'm ready to go inside."

Felix glanced at Lorraine. "We'll be on our way. You two have a big day tomorrow. Have a great trip and send postcards. I'll be back in London when you return." He took Lorraine's hand and they left by the back gate.

**

Uncle Charlie pulled up to Union Station and hailed a porter. The little group hurried behind him onto the platform for The Canadian, an apt name for a train that travelled the entire country from coast to coast. The massive locomotive towered above them and Sarah put her hands to her ears as they passed the diesel engine, sensing its impatience to get going. She couldn't remember ever being so excited.

Uncle Charlie smiled. "You think this is loud, you should have heard the steam engines; they were twice the size of the British steam engines. The Canadian is a lot of weight to pull through the Rocky Mountains."

"I'm so excited." Sarah could barely stand still.

Uncle Charlie smiled, saying, "You are so much like your grand-mother. Anna, had the same grin when she was excited. We called it the Cheshire cat grin. You've also inherited her independent and adventurous streak. As kids we talked about traveling to India like our uncle." He pointed at Sarah's blue pendant. "I think his inspiration helped her through some tough times. Let it help you." He gave her a hug. "Things will work out. Felix told me what he'd discovered. Leave it to us—we'll find him. Now, go and enjoy your holiday."

"Look after her, Charlotte." Charlie hugged his daughter.

Sarah and Charlotte found their seats and waved as the train began to move from the platform, gathering speed as it left Union Station and settling into a rhythm as suburban Toronto flashed by.

"I feel as though I might burst, I'm so excited."

"Me too. Now I know how the kids feel when we're getting ready for a field trip." They both giggled.

Sarah pulled her sketch book from her satchel. "I want to sketch the platform scene while it's still fresh in my mind. I think I'll sketch a journal of our trip."

"I'll read while you sketch. Shall I read *To Kill A Mockingbird?* I've never heard of the author, an American. It's supposed to be really good." Charlotte pulled out another book from her bag, "Or Ian Fleming's *For your Eyes Only?* My dad laughs at the James Bond stories and assures me it is nothing like real life. But short stories might be better for my concentration."

Sarah's eyes widened with dismay. "Is Uncle Charlie a spy?"

"No, but he did work in the secret service. But I honestly have no idea what he did."

"We had a British Secret Service conference at the hotel last November and we nick-named it the James Bond conference. It was one of those guys that told me to contact your dad about my father. Very strange."

"They are strange." Charlotte hesitated, "Changing the subject, I probably shouldn't ask this, but is there anything going on between you and Felix?"

"Going on! What do you mean?"

"I couldn't help noticing you and Felix having a tête-à-tête in the garden last night."

"Tête-à-tête," Sarah chuckled, "Charlotte that sounds like something out of *Pride and Prejudice.*" Charlotte didn't smile, prompting Sarah to add, "No, there is nothing going on. Felix offered to help find my father and he had some news. Not great news—he's disappeared again and may not be alive. I was upset."

"I'm sorry about your father. And that explains things, but Lorraine thinks you have a thing for Felix."

"I figured she didn't like me, and the feeling is mutual. Rest assured, there is nothing but friendship between us. Felix is eight years older than me. He took care of me when I visited the estate; he's like a big brother. At times he still treats me like a little girl, which I find annoying."

"Are you sure that's all it is? I see the way he looks at you, and the glances across the dinner table last night were more than brotherly love."

"How do I convince you he's a close friend and nothing more? I'm in love with Marcus. I'm not sure I can ever love anyone else. But, like my father, he left—gone, disappeared." Unbidden tears suddenly burned Sarah's eyes.

"Marcus. Is he the beatnik? Aunt Anna wrote to my dad about him."

"He'd changed. The beatnik thing was an act, a rebellion. It turned out that he's from a wealthy family and did eventually get Nana's approval." Sarah stared out of the window, willing the tears to go away.

Charlotte patted her hand. "I'm hungry. Let's go to the dining car."

Nineteen

The Canadian and Totem Poles

*T*he flatness of the Prairies had, at first, been a challenge to Sarah's artistic skills. Finding passion in the flat, unbroken landscape, enormous skies and the occasional dot of a farmstead had not been easy. But she found beauty in the intense colours of the sun, the yellows of the swaying crops and a startling blue sky. The train barreled its way through infinity and Sarah began to think there was no end to the sameness and exchanged her sketch book for a copy of Emily Carr's autobiography, *Growing Pains.*

Sensing a slower rhythm to the train, she lifted her eyes and glanced towards the window. A group of buildings rose up from the prairie and the city of Calgary appeared in the shadow of the Rocky Mountains.

"Charlotte look; the mountains and finally habitation."

Charlotte closed her book. "Let's go to the observation car." Climbing the circular staircase, Sarah felt as though she was embarking on something new. A pleasant young waiter greeted them as they stepped into the domed observation area on the second floor of the bar car. Sarah stood motionless; her first view of the Rockies took her breath away.

The waiter smiled. "This way ladies." He showed them to a table at the very front. "What can I get you to drink?"

Awestruck, Sarah sat down and pulled out her sketch book. The late afternoon sun enhanced the skyline, throwing shadows over the mountains and the City of Calgary nestled beneath them. The mountains appeared to be growing in size as the train drew closer. "I've never seen anything like it. The light is amazing and to have the city, prairie and mountains in one scene is..." Sarah paused, realizing that she had spoken aloud. She eyed the smiling waiter, "Gin and tonic with lemon for me please." Charlotte ordered a rye and ginger.

The car filled up quickly. The mood was celebratory as passengers chatted happily while taking in their surroundings. Sarah and Charlotte chose to stay in their seats when they reached Calgary. Afraid they would lose their prize spot if they vacated the table to go to the dining room, they ordered sandwiches and another drink. The train was shunted onto a side track and acquired a second large locomotive for the journey through the Rockies.

It was almost dark when the train entered Kicking Horse Pass. The energy from the mountains almost consumed Sarah. She leaned back and looked up through the dome and involuntarily placed her hand on the blue pendant around her neck. She saw Anna smiling and an older gentleman standing behind her. His words came as clear as day: "Follow your dreams and don't let anyone destroy them." The scene was so vivid that she blinked and rubbed her eyes. Was she dreaming? Was her mind playing tricks? She remembered the story from Nana's account of her trip across Canada.

Charlotte tapped her shoulder. "I'm going to bed. You're in another world. Will you be all right?"

"I'm fine, but I want to stay here for a while."

Sarah had no idea what time it was, and time didn't matter. The moon had risen above the mountains and as the train wound around a gentle curve it filled the dome car with brilliant white light; so close she felt like reaching out to touch it. The mountain energy filled her with hope and strength. The moonlight glinted on the snow-covered mountaintops; an iridescent white glow contrasted the darkness of deep crevices. She felt the train labour, tired but determined, as it pushed through the mountains. She felt the same toil as she pushed through life. The shimmering white mountaintops filled her with the same joy she felt through her art, with its promises and dreams. The dark crevices seemed to be hiding things she wanted to deny. The deepest of them harboured her guilt for abandoning her father, for disappointing her grandparents and mourning lost love.

"Sorry to disturb you, miss, but the lounge is closing." Sarah spun around, startled and angry, about to yell her indignation at this intruder. She glanced around the empty car, realizing the intruder was the waiter.

"Oh dear, I'm sorry. I got caught up in the mountains."

"Many people do. You're welcome to stay but the bar is closed until morning." He gave Sarah a kind smile. "We serve coffee and pastries from six in the morning."

Sarah didn't feel comfortable staying alone and gathered up her sketch pad and pencils and flung her satchel over her shoulder. "Thank you and good night," she said as she descended the circular stairs and returned to the compartment.

Charlotte was sound asleep. Sarah tried to navigate the tiny space in the dark, but finally turned on the light rather than risk falling as she climbed into the top bunk. No longer able to see the mountains or the moon, she tried to unravel her feelings; the slow rhythm seemed to form the words, "Follow your dreams," and lulled her into sleep.

The whooshing blind snapped into place and Charlotte's cheery voice woke Sarah. "Good morning. Just look at those mountains."

Sarah scrambled down the ladder and they both strained their necks to see up, up to the top of the mountains.

"The waiter told me they serve coffee and pastries in the dome car," Sarah said, pulling on some slacks and a blouse. "Let's try and get our same spot."

A different waiter greeted them at the top of the stairs and showed them to a table, the front table already being occupied by an elderly couple. The waiter poured coffee and offered a tray of French croissants: chocolate, almond, apricot and strawberry. Sarah had never seen such a variety but declined, sipping her coffee and opening her satchel. As she flipped the pages of her sketch book she said, "Wow, where did that come from?" She stared at a scene from last night. She gave a slight shudder, seeing a faint shadow of two faces that she instinctively recognized.

Charlotte frowned. "You were sketching that last night when I left for bed. Those shadows look like a man and a woman. Did you do that on purpose?"

"No." Sarah pointed, "That's Nana when she was young and next to her is Great-Great Uncle Bertie." She paused, "I don't remember sketching any of this."

"You were off in your own little world last night. What's going on?"

"The moon and mountains triggered thoughts and memories; decisions I have to make. I have so much to sort out."

"Can I help?"

"I wish you could, but I have to do this on my own. And for now I want to enjoy the mountains and exploring the west coast."

**

The Canadian chugged into Vancouver on time and in pouring rain. Collecting their bags, the porter took them to the taxi rank and within fifteen minutes they had checked into The Cottage Hotel, an appropriate name for the small but quaint hotel that would be their home for the next two weeks.

Arthur and Barbara Green owned the hotel, and the couple reminded Sarah of Anna and Bill. The hotel was considerably more modest and informal than the Sackville, but had a homey feel to it. Knowing Sarah's connection to the Sackville, the Greens gave her and Charlotte special attention, insisting the kinship warranted first names. The fact that Arthur had inherited the hotel from his father did represent a kinship to Sarah, but the similarity ended there. There was no doubting that Arthur loved his work and his whole life had been dedicated to the comfort and entertainment of hotel guests.

Barbara was a native of Victoria on Vancouver Island and her interests were nature and local history. She had laid claim to having Tlingit and Haida Indian blood in her veins after Sarah had expressed an interest in the Indian villages on the West Coast. Sarah thought this questionable, as upon hearing Sarah's accent when she greeted her at the at the reception desk, Barbara described strong ties to British ancestry, and her pasty completion, mousey hair and blue eyes were definitely Anglo-Saxon. Regardless, the couple had an immense knowledge of British Columbia, which was perfect for Sarah's purposes.

The young bellboy was ordered to take their baggage to their room while Barbara showed them into a small dining room of six uniform, square, white-clothed tables for four. The hotel only served breakfast and dinner, but for these special guests an afternoon tea had been prepared.

Sitting at a table near the window, which Sarah suspected was the best table in the house, she turned to Charlotte and asked, "So, what do you think?"

"I like it. Good choice, cousin. Barbara seems to have an interesting mixture of ancestry."

Sarah grinned. "You noticed too. And I haven't mentioned my interest in Emily Carr yet—perhaps she's related." They giggled as Arthur placed a large teapot on the table with Barbara on his heels, carrying plates of cucumber sandwiches and homemade cakes.

"Did I hear you mention Emily Carr? I was born in Victoria on the very same street that the Carr family lived." This was a statement confirmed by a fast bob of Barbara's head snapping forward. Sarah thought she might burst as she muffled erupting giggles. Charlotte had a coughing fit, unable to stop herself laughing. It also had the effect of distracting Barbara, who patted Charlotte on the back and ordered Arthur to fetch a glass of water.

Sucking in an extremely deep breath, Sarah calmed herself by allowing the air to escape slowly before speaking. "I too am an artist and I have a special interest in Emily Carr, as a person as well as for her art. In fact, that is why we are here in Vancouver." Barbara listened intently as Sarah explained the Emily Carr Dining Room and Anna's connection to the artist.

To Sarah's surprise, Barbara pulled up a chair and poured herself a cup of tea. "I dabble with a brush myself, but this place takes up most of my time." She leaned in and whispered, "I think it was Emily Carr's influence."

"Oh really." Sarah said, swallowing giggles but sensing an opportunity to find out about the family. "How well did you know the Carr family?"

"I remember the Carr sisters. There were five of them—both parents had died—and the eldest sister, Clara, took care of them. Emily was away a lot, and rumour had it that she was rather strange and didn't get along with her sisters, except for Alice. I remember seeing this old, eccentric looking woman sitting in the garden reading with a little dog on her knee and a monkey on her shoulder and more dogs around her wicker chair. My mother said she used to put the monkey in a pram and go shopping." Barbara paused, "I don't remember that. She was staying with Alice, recuperating after an illness—a bad heart I think. She died shortly after that. I was a teenager and my mother dragged me to the funeral." Barbara raised her eyebrows. "The respectful thing to do. My father kept nudging me throughout the service, whispering and motioning towards two men in the front. 'That is Mr. Harris, a famous artist, and Mr. Dil...something, who wrote books.' I had no interest in either art or books so I had no idea why these people were important. Maybe they mean something to you."

"Lawren Harris was a fellow artist who influenced Carr's art and was a member of the famous Group of Seven, and I think you might mean Mr. Ira Dilworth who published her books. Both were close friends of Emily Carr's."

Barbara shrugged. "Perhaps. Anyway, her art is in the Vancouver Art Gallery and the house she grew up in is still standing but in disrepair—no one lives there. Now I must get back to work. Arthur might know more. Dinner is served at six sharp and breakfast between eight and nine." Proudly tapping the table, she continued, "And this will be your table for the duration of your stay."

Twenty

Whispering Trees

T he next morning, Sarah and Charlotte headed for the Vancouver Art Gallery. Although the gallery visit was worthwhile and the few Emily Carr paintings on display were beautiful, the limited size of the exhibition was disappointing. Not quite as enthusiastic about art as Sarah, Charlotte became bored and left to find a tea shop. Sarah stared at a canvas with one artist's eye to another; the totem poles were magnificent. She closed her eyes trying to feel the artist but the sterile environment of the gallery blocked the energy. "I have to experience the scene and land first hand," she said aloud.

"Are you talking to me?" Charlotte said, returning from tea.

"No, I was thinking aloud. I need to visit these places."

"I'm sure Arthur could tell us how to do that. A boat I would imagine. I like the idea of a boat ride along the coast."

Returning to the hotel late that afternoon, Sarah found Arthur at the desk. "Arthur, do you know the places where Emily Carr painted and even lived at times?"

"The easiest place is Stanley Park, just down the road from here. You could walk it."

"Of course, the famous Stanley Park trees." This suggestion satisfied Sarah's longing to paint the larger than life pines and cedars.

"She spent a lot of time along the coast and in Prince Rupert. There used to be a local cruise that Emily Carr took on occasions, but one of the big cruise lines took it over. It sails along the coast of Alaska into Ketchikan, Juneau and Sitka where you will find settlements with longhouses and totem poles. It takes about a week and it's a bit pricey." Arthur paused and rubbed his chin, "There is the mail boat, which travels in and out of the inlets on the BC coast just north of here and into the Queen Charlotte Islands. But Vancouver Island would be the closest. The ferry will take you to the island and there are always fishermen willing to take tourists along the coast. I'll see what I can do for you."

While Arthur searched for a fisherman willing to play tour guide, she packed her sketch books and paint into her satchel and tucked two folding stools under her arm. With Charlotte carrying her easel, they set off for Stanley Park.

The fresh, green, earthy smell alerted Sarah to something different, something more than trees.

"Ah, do you smell the green?"

Charlotte looked at her sniffing the air with amusement. "No, how do you smell green? I see a mass of green and I feel like a dwarf. Look at the size of these trees."

Sarah reached out and touched the bark. The sanguine vibration of its centuries-old anchored roots touched each cell of Sarah's body and mind. *These trees are as alive as I am. Now I know why Emily Carr painted these forests.* She leaned her head back and let her eyes climb to the top of a red cedar, where bits of blue sky and shafts of sunlight tried to pierce their way to the forest floor.

Charlotte stood opposite, staring into a hollow tree, the opening larger than a house; she called "Hello," and laughed at the sound as it echoed. The noise broke the peace and calmness. Calling softly so as not to make the sound worse Sarah said, "Charlotte, not so loud!"

"What,"

"I'm sorry, but the trees are alive. I find the noise offensive," Sarah

145

glanced up, not sure what to say next.

"Really, Sarah, this is a tree. A magnificent tree and a magnificent forest but a tree all the same." She laughed again. "I don't expect them to grow legs and walk about the forest, holding hands."

"Spiritually they do," Sarah said, placing her stool and easel on an area of flat forest floor. Charlotte's flippant attitude had annoyed and disappointed her. Perhaps unrealistically, Sarah had assumed Charlotte would feel the same way she did. Sarah felt alone and suddenly she missed home—missed Anna, the one person she knew who understood Emily Carr's trees.

Charlotte sat on her tiny stool, wobbling on a tree root and brushing the fan of ferns from her legs, her lips pursed, pretending to read.

Sarah's anger dissipated. "I didn't mean to speak that way. I thought you understood."

"I'm sorry for laughing, but I don't see what you see." She stood up from her stool and touched the tree. "Sorry tree."

Sarah smiled, "I know it is a bit odd, but I appreciate you trying." It was unrealistic to ask Charlotte to understand the emotional the connection with trees and forests. "I'm sorry Charlotte, I do get carried away. I'm the one that likes the silence, not the trees. I think you've had enough, lets go back to the hotel."

⁎⁎

Arthur could hardly contain his excitement and ordered the bellboy to take Sarah's art stuff to their room before ushering them into the dining room. Barbara joined them with tea and cakes.

"We have arranged, well Barbara ..."

Barbara interrupted, "My Haida blood comes in useful; through my second cousins, one of the Haida elders actually remembers Emily Carr."

Arthur continued, "As soon as we have the meeting confirmed, I will book the ferry to Nanaimo and you will be taken by boat to the Queen Charlotte Islands. It will require two over night stays."

A silly grin spread over Sarah's face and her insides felt like it was

Christmas Eve. "Thank you, this is more than I could have imagined. When will you know?"

"A couple of days perhaps."

Barbara joined them for tea and prattled on about her Haida ancestry. Sarah was still not convinced, but if the connection took her to someone who knew Emily Carr, she would not question it.

Sarah patted Charlotte's arm, "This is so exciting." She hesitated, seeing Charlotte's expression; the afternoon tiff had upset her. "Charlotte, what's wrong?"

"Nothing; just tired. I think I'll go and rest for a while."

"Your friend is not so keen," Barbara said. "Excuse me, I have to start dinner.

Sarah looked across at Arthur. "We had a bit of an argument this afternoon. Charlotte doesn't understand the forest as I do. It's an unusual understanding, seen through the eye of an artist. My grandmother gets it because she understands Emily Carr. It's unfortunate we can't have the same understanding about the hotel."

Arthur frowned. "The hotel?"

"Like you, I am heir to a hotel; except I don't want it."

"There was a time when I didn't want this." Arthur spread his arms. "I was an angry young man when I was your age. I fought in the war and wanted to make the Canadian Air Force my career. My father was furious and kicked me out. I didn't care and stayed in the forces for fifteen years. I reluctantly came home to help out when my father had a heart attack. I never told my father that I loved the business, but I think he knew—and here I am."

"My story is similar. I actually like the hotel business, but I love art. And I'm good; one day I want to be famous and see my work hanging in art galleries. Strangely, I suspect my grandmother knows this, but she has a need to pass her dream on. It should have gone to my mother, who died, and I'm a sort of substitute."

"Do as I did; pursue your art and take up the hotel later."

"I don't have the luxury of time—maybe five years or less. They are nearly seventy and ready to retire now."

"Take those years to paint and prosper. Fill the art galleries. You have an amazing spirit and you will do the right thing, and so will your grandmother." She stared at him, puzzled. He smiled and added, "Your grandmother has to let you fly away and trusts that you will come back. And you have to embrace the freedom without guilt and fly back home knowing the decision is not yours alone. When the time comes, the decision will be the right one for you both."

Suddenly Sarah felt close to tears. The guilt lifted and she knew Arthur was right. She bent forward and kissed his forehead. "Thank you."

He laughed, calling after her as she headed to the stairs. "Better not let Barbara catch you."

Charlotte was lying on the bed, her eyes closed, but Sarah could tell she wasn't asleep. "Are you going to tell me what's wrong?"

"I don't want to go on this trip with you. I don't want to upset you, but I'm not interested in forests, trees and Indians or totem poles. I want shops and concrete. There I've said it."

"If it's the argument today, I'm sorry." Sarah sat on the bed. "But it's not, is it?"

"No. Would you mind if I went shopping tomorrow? I don't want to go back to Stanley Park."

"I don't mind at all. I prefer to be alone with the trees. What about Vancouver Island?"

"I've been thinking about that. I would like to go to Vancouver Island, but not to the Indian thing. How would you feel if we got the ferry to Nanaimo together and then you can meet your person and I'll take the bus to Victoria? I'll stay at the Empress Hotel and explore the shops, then you can meet me there when you're done."

"That is a great solution."

Charlotte and Sarah were happy to be friends again, and having planned separate activities for the following day, they retired early

The following morning Sarah crept down stairs before anyone was up. Her easel tucked under her arm and satchel over her shoulder, she headed to Stanley Park. The morning dew was heavy in the grass and a soft white mist lingered on the forest floor and hung over the tree tops, making the trees appear to be suspended and ghost like. She listened to the trees whisper and the birds chatter. A chipmunk sat up and stared at this human disturbing his quiet morning. She sat on a large tree root and began sketching. As the sun moved from the horizon, changing the light and colours on the forest floor, the trees, leaves and brush, each sketch looked different. The sun now high in the sky, Sarah moved towards the water and sketched the driftwood on the beach. Stretching her cramped hands, she lay back in the sand and watched the clouds move behind the forest. The sun was getting low in the sky, it was time to meet Charlotte, have dinner and get ready for the trip to Nanaimo.

**

Jimmie, a Haida Indian fisherman and tourist guide met the girls at the Nanaimo ferry terminal. Charlotte took the bus to Victoria and Sarah climbed into Jimmie's old truck and set off for Alert Bay, situated on an island off the northern shore of Vancouver Island.

Arthur had pointed out that Sarah's thoughts of tracing Emily Carr's footsteps along the vast British Columbia and Alaska coast were unrealistic and she had settled on Alert Bay. Once on the road, or to be precise the dirt track, Sarah understood the word remote.

European diseases had decimated the Haida population and small pockets of broken, rotten totem poles and wooden shacks dotted the landscape. Jimmie stopped the truck frequently, allowing her to sketch. Often overwhelmed by an extreme sense of grief and hopelessness, tears spotted her sketch pad. She wondered how different these scenes had been thirty years ago when Emily Carr sketched them.

It was a short ferry ride to Alert Bay; the pier bustled with fisherman as the ferry docked. Everyone greeted Jimmie as they walked up the only street through town. They passed a large wooden structure, a longhouse, with intricate and meaningful symbols painted on it. It now served as a community hall, but had once housed much of the village. Her neck ached from looking up at the totem poles, some new and brightly coloured, others grey and crumbling.

Jimmie pushed open the door of the general store and sat at a counter and ordered coffee. He then pointed to the only table in the corner and said something to an elderly man in a language she didn't understand before introducing him as Joe Smallest. Joe gave her a toothless grin. She had never met anyone so old; his wrinkles had wrinkles. His small, thin stature could have been that of a child, which was perhaps where his name came from, but his all-knowing eyes were full of wisdom. He waved a gnarled hand towards the chair across the table.

"You have her spirit." He glanced at Sarah's sketch book that she had laid on the table. "You don't laugh like Klee Wyck." Sarah wondered if he was looking for a name to describe her, she knew Klee Wyck meant 'laughing one', the name the local people had given Emily Carr. Sarah sat silently still as Joe studied her. In another setting it might have felt intrusive. Instinctively, she knew it was his way of getting to know her. His intrusion comforted and reassured her and she relaxed. He opened her sketch book, he slowly nodded his head and grinned widely, repeating, "You have her spirit. But you have too much grief and sadness. You will bear more grief...sometime soon." Deep creases furrowed across his forehead. "Many troubles for someone so young. Be patient; you are strong like Klee Wyck. Troubles will pass."

Joe took her into another world, reminiscing about the village life of thirty or forty years ago. He had been a wise man when he met Emily Carr, the crazy lady, and her dog Billie.

Finally, he said, "Sarah understand like Klee Wyck."

Sarah smiled. "Yes, I think I do."

Joe Smallest's connection with Sarah had touched her creative soul and awakened a burning desire to fulfill her artists dream.

Jimmie had business to attend to and left Sarah to sketch. Having filled one sketch book she took a new one from her satchel. She sketched the totems poles in proportion to the surroundings and the longhouse. Examining the intricate carvings, she sketched portions of the poles to get the detail of the faces, patterns and animals. Knowing they were significant to the Haida, she planned to ask Jimmie to explain them on their way back.

**

Sarah arrived at The Empress Hotel late the following evening. She was not sorry to enjoy a little luxury, a sharp contrast to the remoteness of Alert Bay that lacked even the basic necessities. Charlotte positively bubbled upon Sarah's return; shopping had lifted her sombre mood.

With only two days left, they compromised, and Charlotte agreed to accompany Sarah to Goldstream Park if she agreed to spend the last day shopping in Victoria. Sarah was delighted with this arrangement, and much to Charlotte's surprise she treated the trip to Goldstream Park as a tourist visit and left her easel and paints at the hotel. Sarah enthusiastically explained to Charlotte that Emily Carr had lived in her caravan called The Elephant and that her reason for wanting to visit was because it was a time and place where Emily had been happiest and the most prolific with her forest art. Sarah didn't need to paint; she wanted to experience the place. It turned out to be a beautiful park and the highlight of the day was eating dinner and watching the sunset from a delightful bistro overlooking the water.

As Charlotte had enjoyed the park, so Sarah enjoyed the shopping. She picked out a few special gifts to take back to England and they rounded off their last day with a very English afternoon tea at The Empress Hotel. Sarah had noted that most of Victoria was more English than England.

**

Uncle Charlie met them at Union Station, looking pale and grave. Charlotte immediately ran to him. "What is wrong? Is it mother, or are you ill?"

"We are fine. Let's get your bags in the car and we'll talk about it when we get home."

Sarah stayed quiet. She didn't need to be told something was wrong in Bexhill. Aunt Beth was waiting for them in the living room and sat Sarah next to her, putting her arm around her shoulders.

Uncle Charlie cleared his throat. "We had a phone call yesterday from Anna. Bill has taken ill and is in hospital."

Sarah felt her heart drop into her stomach. "What's wrong?"

"It might be his heart, and he is gravely ill. I have booked you a flight to London tomorrow. I told Anna we would call when you got back."

"I'd like to call now." Sarah said, picking up the phone. I know it is late, but Nana will be waiting.

"Nana, it's Sarah." Everyone in the room held their breath as they waited for Sarah to respond.

"He's stable then? Now they think it's a stroke. Can he talk?"

Another pause as Sarah listened.

"How are you holding up? I'll be home tomorrow. Send Mr. Grimsby to pick me up from the station. I love you, Nana. I'll be home soon."

Sarah looked up at the faces. "He had a stroke, but he is conscious and can talk. The doctors don't know the extent of the damage yet." Close to tears, Sarah felt fear grip her heart. "I need to keep busy," She gave a nervous giggle, "I'll unpack so I can pack."

Twenty-One

Futures in Jeopardy

⁓✧⁓

*S*he was grateful that Uncle Charlie had booked her in first class and the stewardess seemed to understand that Sarah needed quiet. Her mind burned with a million thoughts and her insides were tied up in knots of fear: fear for Grandpa Bill, fear for Nana and fear for her own future. She reclined her seat, hoping she could sleep, but the engine drone magnified her thoughts into chaos—nothing was clear.

The plane jolted as it hit the runway at London Heathrow and it seemed to take hours before the cabin doors opened. She ran to grab a porter and sighed with relief when her suitcase popped onto the carousel first. She tipped the porter handsomely to find the fastest cab to get her to Paddington Station.

The cab weaved through London traffic and down side streets; the porter had done well with his choice of cabbies. The platform at Paddington was empty except for a guard and a few porters loading luggage. She hoped her suitcase had made it to the baggage compartment as she sat down and felt the train move. Exhausted, she fell asleep and was woken by the conductor asking for her ticket. She handed him a ten-shilling note and waited for the change and ticket.

Mr. Grimsby greeted her at Bexhill station. "Mrs. Blaine is in

Eastbourne at the hospital. I am to take you there immediately." Sarah was filled with dread at his even grimmer than usual appearance.

"Is there any news?" she asked tentatively.

"I am told Mr. Blaine is stable." Mr. Grimsby loaded the luggage into the boot. "I'll take you to the hospital. Mrs. Blaine drove the Hillman this morning. I'm needed at the hotel." They drove to Eastbourne in silence.

Mr. Grimsby opened the big glass hospital doors for Sarah, releasing the sterile hospital smell, a combination of healing and death. She felt a shudder in her spine and for a fleeting second wanted to run away.

"He's in intensive care; third floor, west wing." Mr. Grimsby pointed to a bank of lifts, giving her a weak smile and she saw his normally guarded kindness and caring.

She smiled back. "Thank you."

Sister knew who she was as soon as she stepped out of the lift. "Miss Wexford, I'm pleased you are here. Can I speak with you before you see Mr. Blaine?"

"How is my grandfather?" she asked anxiously.

Sister took Sarah's arm and led her into a little, screened-off sitting area. "Mr. Blaine is very ill. He had a stroke, which he is recovering from quite well." Sarah breathed a sigh of relief, but sensed Sister had more to say. "But his heart is extremely weak. He's had a bad heart for some while."

"The coughing," Sarah said. "I knew there was something wrong. I should have done something."

"Coughing is a sign of cardiac problems." Sister frowned. "It isn't your fault or Mrs. Blaine's—she too is worried she should have prevented it. Which brings me to my reason for speaking with you. Your grandmother is putting on a brave face, but I am concerned about her own health. She is in a great deal of pain from the rheumatism, and I don't think she has eaten or slept for three days. Can you persuade her to take something for the pain and get some rest?"

"I'll try, but you may have noticed she is stubborn." Sarah paused, not knowing how to ask the next question. "What's the prognosis?"

Sister looked away from Sarah, "You'll have to ask the doctor."

Fighting back tears, Sarah continued, "You have to have an opinion."

"From my nursing experience: fifty-fifty. He has a strong will to live. I can't say anymore. I'll ask the doctor to speak with you. Here, let me take you to the ward."

The passageway was silent and Sarah walked on tip-toe so her heels wouldn't click on the tile floor. Anna stood at the doorway to a private room lined with windows to the hallway so the staff could keep an eye on the patients within. She opened her arms and held Sarah tightly. "It's okay, Nana. I'm here." That was all she could say as they cried on each other's shoulders. Holding hands, they moved to the bed.

Bill opened his eyes, smiled and said, "Sarah... Aren't you supposed to be in... Canada?" His voice was raspy; the sentence had exhausted him.

"Well, I'm back. How are you feeling?" She stared at his ashen complexion. The greyness had spread from his face to his bald head, shoulders and arms. Any visible portions of his body looked grey and wrinkled. *When did you get so old?* she thought. *I never noticed.* She glanced at Anna, wincing as her knees bent to lower herself into a chair. *You too, Nana.* She looked away, feeling a new batch of warm tears on her cheeks.

"Hey...no tears. I can't kiss them away right now." Bill coughed and Sarah bent down to kiss him.

"I'll kiss you instead." She rubbed her hands across her face. "Is that better?" He nodded and closed his eyes.

An efficient-looking nurse strode up to the bed. Placing her fingers on his wrist, she lifted her upside-down watch with the other hand and said, "Mr. Blaine is tired. He needs to rest. I suggest you go to the cafeteria and have a cup of tea. Sister said to tell you the doctor

will see you this afternoon when he's finished rounds."
**

Receiving the news from the doctor felt like being on a roller-coaster ride. At first, he said the stroke had been milder than they'd originally thought, so there was a good chance he'd recover from it. But then he followed up with the bad news that Bill's heart was extremely weak and he could have a heart attack at any time. Sarah held Anna's hand and felt her nails dig in at the news. Maybe the doctor sensed their disappointment because he then added that there had been inroads into heart research. Although the recovery would initially mean a long hospital stay, if Bill modified his lifestyle and with help from some new drugs, he could live for several more years. Sarah couldn't help wondering if the latter statement was true or had been said to appease them. Feeling Anna relax, she decided it didn't matter at the moment. The doctor concluded with the best news yet: that if he continued to improve, Bill would be moved from intensive care to a ward in the next day or two. Sarah saw Anna actually smile, and she agreed to go home and get some rest.

Returning to the Sackville, Sarah and Anna were surprised and pleased to find Darcy and Belle waiting to see them. Their visit would be short as it was tourist season and they didn't usually leave the estate in the summer. Darcy was anxious for news about Bill and arranged to take Anna back to the hospital that evening. Sarah was pleased at Belle's support and Anna was delighted to see her old friend. Listening to her advice, she went to her suite to rest and Sarah, who hadn't slept since leaving Toronto, crawled up to the penthouse and slept until dinner.

Sarah couldn't remember the last time she'd eaten and went into the dining room to find Belle at the family table. "It's just us two?" Sarah asked as she sat down.

"Yes, Darcy and Anna went to the hospital for evening visiting hours."

"How does Nana seem?" Sara asked.

"She looked much better than when we arrived. She had slept and eaten and had a bit of colour back in her face."

"Good, she needs to take care of herself. I have been so caught up in my own life that I hadn't realized how old they are getting." Sarah's lips trembled.

"Life changes so quickly. One minute everything is fine and then everything turns upside down." Belle sighed, fiddling with her napkin.

"Is everything all right, Belle?"

"I have some good news and some iffy news and I'm not sure which is which."

"That sound more like a riddle than news." Sarah tried to laugh, relieving the tension.

"Felix has been called to the bar, so he is very excited. At long last, he'll be a barrister. Darcy doesn't know he wants his silk."

"It's Felix's dream. We've talked about it. I am so happy for him. He knows Darcy wants him on the estate. It's the same as Nana wanting me here, and it looks as though that will be sooner rather than later."

"You two know each other better than I realized. I'm not sure my next news will be as welcome." Belle leaned her head to one side. "Felix and Lorraine are officially engaged. Felix wouldn't make the announcement until he'd told you."

Sarah held her breath. Although it was not a surprise, she felt betrayed. "My cousin Charlotte is a friend of Lorraine's and she thought a ring was coming soon. Felix and I are close, but it's platonic. We've known each other for a long time; he's always been my hero." She stopped short of saying she was happy for him, because she wasn't.

"Is there anyone in your life?" Belle asked, keeping her eyes on Sarah.

"No, I don't trust men anymore. I gave Marcus all the love I had and he left me, not once but twice. For what, I don't even know."

"Darcy is not happy. He's afraid Lorraine will whisk Felix off to Canada."

Sarah shook her head. "That won't happen. Not because of Lorraine or Hillcrest Hall, but because his dream is to be a QC. Darcy might not like it now, but his legal career is what will save Felix for the estate."

"I'd never thought of that, but you're right." Belle hesitated, fidgeting with her napkin again. "I'm not sure Lorraine is right for him—for the estate. But then who am I to talk? Lady Thornton was very upset when Darcy married me, an American, instead of a society debutante. He had no time for those ladies and treated them badly."

"Like father, like son." Sarah glanced at Belle and quickly added, "From what Nana has told me of Lady Thornton, I can imagine her reaction."

"A wise observation. I mean about father and son. Playboys," Belle said drifting into thought.

"Ah food," Sarah said thankful for the interruption as Balaji placed a plate of roast beef and Yorkshire pudding on the table. The meal acted as a sleeping draft on Sarah's still jet-lagged body. Yawning, she said good night to Belle and retired.

**

By the beginning of August, Bill was well enough to come home under Anna and Sarah's strict supervision along with daily doctor visits. He had made a remarkable recovery, with only a slight limitation to the movement of his right arm. In mid-August, the doctor allowed him to work in the kitchen for two hours a day, which made him use his arm and helped him recover even faster.

Sarah had not so much as touched a paintbrush since she had arrived home. While Anna had been at the hospital, Sarah had stayed home to run the hotel and hire staff. Brian was promoted to executive chef and a new sous-chef was hired. Anna had completely forgotten that Amy Peterson, the head housekeeper, was to retire at the end of the summer, so it was left to Sarah to find a replacement. None of the current maids were experienced enough to promote beyond head maid, so an outside search was needed. Mr. Grimsby, a relatively young man in his forties, took on more responsibility and Sarah found him exceptionally supportive. Dorothy Jenkins loved her work and had expressed no interest in retiring. Her job was her life and Sarah thought she might work until she was a hundred.

Today everything in the hotel was running smoothly and Anna and Amy were interviewing housekeepers, so Sarah snuck off to her studio. She unpacked her satchel and portfolio from the trip to western Canada, sorting the sketches and paintings. She put several aside to work on now and other's she'd work on in London. She thought about London, college and Felix.

Felix had not come to see her as Belle had thought he would, sending a letter instead. The engagement was announced in the society papers and the wedding was planned for the following spring. She felt a little sad as she suspected that her friendship with him would end after his marriage, but she dashed it from her thoughts. She didn't like how it made her feel—sad and jealous. On a positive note, Charlotte was to be a bridesmaid and would be spending Easter with her after the wedding. She was anxious to get back to her own little flat and start her new life as a junior professor. She wanted to share her love of art and she even wondered if Madame at Le Papillon would be interested in her West Coast art. *That might be a bit too ambitious,* she thought.

Sarah quickly became engrossed in painting Alert Bay. The face of Joe, the wrinkled old man with his toothless grin appeared in front of her. Had he predicted Grandpa Bill's illness? And what else had he predicted: her success as an artist, her connection to Klee Wyck?

Leaving the painting on the easel to dry, she embraced how wonderful each brush stroke made her feel and found herself planning her painting sessions. Last year during the summer, she had painted in the morning and worked in the hotel in the afternoon; she would reverse that as it was important for her to be around in the morning, but she'd make it clear to the staff that she would not be available in the afternoons.

If Bill continued to improve, she planned to return to London next week to begin preparing her classes for the Michaelmas term. Despite Bill's speedy recovery, he still coughed and often got short of breath. A part of her feared for him, but Anna was convinced that all Bill needed was tender loving care.

She heard a tap on the door and a voice saying, "Can I come in?"

Sarah ran to the door, Bill stood out of breath and proud that he'd climbed the stairs.

"Grandpa, are you supposed to be climbing stairs?"

"Doc said to try a few at a time."

"I don't think he meant a whole flight. But come in and see my paintings; I just finished one for Nana for the dining room."

"Sarah, it is beautiful. You are so very clever. I know your Nana wants you at the hotel, but don't give this up."

"Where did this come from?"

"I had a lot of time to think, lying in that hospital bed. I made the journey up the stairs so I can talk to you. I don't know how much longer I'm going to live..." He put his hand to Sarah's lips as she opened her mouth to object. "Sh... hear me out. My heart is not going to last much longer and when I'm gone I don't want you giving up your life for the Sackville. When Nana and I started working here, Mr. Kendrick owned the hotel and it ran well with a general manager. I had my reasons for choosing a man like Mr. Grimsby. He's a solid man with a good head for business—he can run the hotel without you or Anna. I want you to take care of Nana, but promise me you won't give up your art."

"I'm not sure I can do both. It's not just the art or the hotel, I have a job to consider. I'm going back to London next week and I'll be busy teaching classes at the college, so I won't be able to just drop everything and come home if you need me. It will be Christmas holidays before I'm home again."

"How can I reassure you? Promise me you will not give up your art." Sarah nodded, "I promise."

Twenty-Two

All About Art

*J*ohnny ran down the path and his large body buried Sarah in an enormous hug. "Miss Sarah, back home." Sara tried not to cringe, feeling the wet kisses on her head and the odour from under his arm.

"I'm pleased to see you too," she muffled from under his armpit. "Johnny, let me go." Taking a gasp of fresh air, she added, "Be a good boy and carry my suitcase upstairs."

"Where's Miss Lizzy?"

"Remember, Miss Lizzy got married and she lives with her husband now."

"Oh, I forgot."

Mrs. Debinski stood at the open door. "He's never stopped talking about you since you left. He was so worried you wouldn't come back. It's nice to have you home." Sarah smiled, noting the difference in Mrs. D's tone—she appeared to be genuinely happy to see her.

"I'm back. It's been an interesting summer." Sarah climbed the stairs to her flat feeling liberated; this was her space and to her surprise it felt like home. She walked from room to room opening the windows and patting the furniture. Entering her box-room studio she pulled the drape from the easel, a blank canvas stared at her. "We can't have that," she said, tapping the canvas affectionately. She dragged her portfolio and satchel into the studio and laid out her brushes and water colour palette. The first sketch she pulled from her bag was of new and old Haida totem poles. She pinned it to the frame of the easel, closed her eyes and recalled the shapes and colours, the stories and myths of the totem figures. She could hear the silence of the forest behind them, the groan of the old crumbling colourless totem poles. And she began to paint.

**

Sarah gave a cat-like stretch, opening her eyes upon hearing a familiar voice. "Sarah, are you here?"

"Lizzy!" Sarah jumped out of bed. "Oh, it's good to see you. How are you? How is married life?"

"I'm well, how about you? I heard about Grandpa Bill, how is he doing? I have so much to tell you. I'll make some tea."

"Sorry, no tea or milk. I got back yesterday afternoon and started painting. I forgot about food. Go take a look in the studio while I freshen up. My best work yet," Sarah called from the bedroom. "Haida totem poles. Needs a bit of touch up, but I'm pleased with it so far."

"I'm speechless. I've never seen anything like it. It's beautiful. Have you thought of going to Le Papillon? I'm sure Madame would like this."

"Thanks, but I'm not sure about Madame. She kicked me out. Shall we go out for breakfast? I want to hear all about married life."

Lizzy laughed, "How about a late lunch? It's one-thirty."

"I didn't realize it was that late. As you can see, I was painting until dawn. I couldn't stop. Why aren't you working today?"

"You really are in another world. It's Saturday. Peter had to work today—some big case he's working on with Felix. That's how I knew you were back."

"How does Felix know I'm back? I haven't spoken to him. His mother told me he was engaged."

"I wondered if he'd told you. How do you feel about it?"

162

"I don't like her, but it's his choice. Sorry, I know you're friends."

"Not really. Its only because Peter works with Felix. I liked her when we first met, but she's become very snooty; Peter didn't like her from the start. He suspects she's after the money and wants the title of Lady more than she wants Felix."

"Interesting. I hadn't thought of it that way."

"That doesn't surprise me. You are jealous of Lorraine. Felix means more to you than you will admit."

"No, I'm not," Sarah felt herself pout. "I saw her in Canada. My cousin Charlotte is her friend and they teach at the same school. She was positively rude to me. Charlotte is to be bridesmaid."

"She asked me too."

"I guess I'm the wicked witch. She didn't ask me."

"She is threatened by you. She doesn't understand your friendship with Felix. If she'd had her way, they would be getting married now rather than in the spring. But there is one thing Lorraine can't compete with, and that's the law. I know, because I know how Peter feels. Now that they are barristers, their careers come first."

"I doubt Lorraine could ever understand his love for the law." Sarah grinned, thinking, *And his ambition to be a QC. Maybe that will be her undoing.*

"Well, my friend, that is a wicked grin. Speaking of wicked, have you heard from Marcus? I still can't believe he would walk out on you like that." Lizzy gave her a sympathetic look. "I thought after…you know, he would have asked you to marry him." Lizzy was the only person she had told that they had made love.

"Not a word, and I don't really care anymore. I think I'm doomed to spinsterhood."

"Never. I think you will meet the love of your life. He will be an advocate for your art, an art collector and a gentleman. Come, I'm parched. Let's go get a cup of tea."

"Dear Lizzy, always the dreamer." But Sarah had a strange sensation, an intuition, and she wondered if there was some truth in Lizzy's comment. Brushing the thought aside, she laughed and said, "And you forgot to mention he has to be rich and handsome, with a title of course. How about a duke? I like the sound of Duchess Sarah. Put that in your pipe and smoke it, Miss Lorraine." They burst into giggles, linked arms and walked to the coffee shop.

＊＊

Sarah spent the mornings at the college preparing for her classes and the afternoons painting. She had decided to approach Madame with her new art, which meant she had to have some sample pieces and sketches of proposed paintings to show her. She thought about Emily Carr and how her local community had rejected her. Was this going to happen to Sarah? Her relationship with Madame was already rocky. Should she approach a different gallery? Her mother and grandmother both had more tenacity than Sarah, *But,* she thought, *it must be in my blood. And I want to prove to Madame that my art belongs in Le Papillon Gallery. I can do this.*

The day she called, Madame was not available, no surprise there, but the receptionist booked her an appointment and told her to bring samples of her art. Surprised at how easy it was, she realized the receptionist was new and didn't know either Sarah or the history between her and Madame and she waited for the call to say the appointment was cancelled.

As she was sitting on the floor packing canvases into her portfolio bag, the phone rang and her heart sank. This was it; Madame had seen her name and the appointment was cancelled.

"Hello."

"Sarah, it's Felix. How are you?"

"Felix, I'm sorry I can't talk now. I am just getting ready for an appointment."

"Anywhere interesting?"

"No, I really do have to go. Bye." She hung up, her heart racing and wondering why she hadn't told him where she was going. Perhaps she was afraid she'd be rejected. If no one knew where she was, no one need know she'd been turned down. She didn't want Felix to know she was a failure.

She pulled the zipper around the portfolio and took a deep breath saying, "I can do this."

The engraved glass doors to Le Papillon were heavier and stiffer than she remembered. The receptionist greeted her with a friendly smile.

"Miss Wexford, Madame is waiting for you."

Sarah squeaked, "Thank you."

Madame sat at her desk and gave Sarah a frosty smile. "I didn't expect to hear from you again. Do you want your job back? As you can see, I have a competent receptionist who doesn't have ideas of grandeur. Are you still painting?"

Sarah had the urge to run out of the office and she questioned her wisdom at coming, but decided to ignore Madame's sarcasm.

"Good afternoon, Madame. I hope you are keeping well?" She didn't wait for an answer, "I have been studying art in Canada over the summer. The native art of Emily Carr to be precise. I've discovered that I have a similar style and I've brought some samples, with a view of showing them in your gallery."

"Oh, you have, have you?" The corner of her mouth lifted in a sneer, perhaps intended to be a smile, but Sarah doubted that. "The only reason I agreed to see you was because I have had some requests for your work. Sometimes people's tastes are… Well, let's say not as cultured as mine."

Anger at Madame's snide remarks had replaced Sarah's trepidation, and far from being shy, she was having trouble holding her tongue.

"Are you implying that my work is not cultured? If I recall, one of your patrons, Mr. Carter, was very taken with my art."

"Show me what you have." A slight pink flushed her cheeks as she wafted her hands towards the portfolio bag and pointed to an empty easel. Sarah took out a painting of Stanley Park, "I call this one *Whispering Trees*," she said, placing it on the easel. She stepped to one side. Hearing Madame draw a sharp breath, Sarah smiled—her talent confirmed.

Sarah waited, holding the Haida painting in her hand while Madame absorbed the trees. Madame muttered under her breath, unaware the words were audible. "Exquisite. Such emotion, the skill is…"

Sensing disbelief, Sarah interrupted, "Before you ask: this is all my work." She turned the Haida painting towards Madame. "I have more, and some sketches that I have to work on, but I could have enough for a show by the spring." She couldn't believe her own ears, realizing she had just asked Madame for an exhibition.

"Maybe I'll keep these two for the gallery." She glanced from painting to painting, "If and only if I get enough interest from my clients, I might consider a show. We'll see." She pushed her nose in the air and sat back with a cat-like satisfaction on her face.

Why can't you admit my paintings are good? I could slap you, for being a bitch to me. Sarah felt her cheeks flush even thinking of such a word, but the woman deserved it. *Take a deep breath—don't react.*

"I'm afraid both canvasses are spoken for," Sarah lied. "I can have something similar in a couple of weeks that the gallery could purchase, and I do have a small one of Alert Bay. But it will depend on you, Madame. Can I assume an exhibition? And if so, we will need a contract."

"Really!" Madame's eyebrows lifted to her hairline. "You always did have to high opinion of yourself. As I said we'll see." Her lips pursed, beads of sweat shone on her nose, tiny red veins popped unhealthily on her cheeks and her breath was short and shallow as she patted her chest.

Sarah picked up her portfolio and lay it open on the floor, carefully placing the canvas in it. She was shaking, sensing Madame's anger. No longer sneering, she was about to have a temper tantrum. Familiar with Madame's 'turns', Sarah wanted to leave.

"Good day, Madame," Sarah said, moving as fast as her portfolio allowed. Escape was all she could think about. *How could she have been stupid enough to think that Madame would offer her a solo exhibition and accept her as a contemporary? I don't understand. Why is she ignoring my art, she knows it's good and yet continues to deny it. It does not make sense.* As she charged towards the glass doors, they suddenly opened and she almost fell onto the pavement. An arm caught her and her bag fell to the ground. "Oh no!" she cried out, feeling tears burning in anger as she bent down.

"Miss Wexford, are you all right?" Sarah stopped, afraid to look up. Embarrassment coloured her cheeks. She knew that voice; it was Mr. Carter. "You look upset."

Sarah stood up straight and patted her unruly hair. "Oh, I just met with Madame. I don't understand why she hates me."

"I don't think she hates you but I don't understand why she doesn't sell your art. The reason I'm here is to find out if she has any more of your work."

"No, she doesn't at the moment but she did offer to take two pieces. I really wanted a solo exhibition but she's making it difficult."

"What's in there?" Mr. Carter pointed to her portfolio.

"Two paintings of the west coast of Canada. I studied Emily Carr this summer."

"Can I see them? I'm not familiar with the artist."

Sarah looked around. "Not here. I'm not a street vendor and I'm not going back in there." Hesitating she said, "Come round to my flat. I have a small studio set up there. It will have to be after five as I'm on my way back to college to teach a class this afternoon."

"Are you sure?"

"Don't get any ideas." Sarah realized how the invitation might sound. "Believe me, nothing gets past my landlady. I'm quite safe but…", she raised an eyebrow and giggled, "you might not be."

Mr. Carter stepped into the gallery. "I'll see you later, I know where you live."

Sarah smiled, *How does he know?* Remembering his occupation, *Of course he knows where I live.* The latter brought her father to mind. Leaving Toronto so quickly, she had not been told anything, Great Uncle Charlie had promised to talk to her when they returned from out west, but she had forgotten in her rush to get home to Bexhill. Getting to know Mr. Carter through her art might also shed some light on her father's whereabouts.

She hurried down the street. Not having time to drop off her portfolio at home, she lugged it to the college. Already late for class and she bumped headlong into Mr. Darwin, the principal, who frowned and asked, "Why so rushed, Miss Wexford?"

"I'm sorry, Mr. Darwin, I'm running late for class. I was at Le Papillon Gallery." She held up her portfolio.

"Let me see." Observing her hesitation, he added, "Your class will wait, Miss Wexford." He peered inside without removing the paintings. "Emily Carr. I always sensed your talent was different, even as a student. "Come to my office after class and bring the paintings."

"Yes, sir. I studied her work this summer."

Sarah couldn't concentrate to teach properly, so she sent the students into the grounds to sketch trees. All she could think about was her own *Whispering Trees*. Madame had upset her, but as a result of being there she had bumped into both Mr. Carter and Mr. Darwin. She finished the class at four sharp and headed to the principal's office.

Mr. Darwin took the paintings and admired them. "Miss Wexford, I don't think you understand. These are brilliant!"

"Thank you, sir, but Le Papillon Gallery doesn't agree."

"Well, Madame is a fool, she lets her own past disappointments cloud her judgment." He glanced away from the paintings. "She's jealous."

Sarah searched for words. She didn't quite know whether to answer and decided to stay quiet.

"With your permission, I would like to contact the London Art

Gallery on your behalf. Do you have more of these?"

"I'm working on them now. And these two may be spoken for; I'm meeting someone today who is interested." *That's twice today I've said they are spoken for, what's wrong with me? I could use the money.*

"I don't need any right now. I'm not promising anything and it will take a few weeks. Keep painting, and when the time comes we'll put some samples together. Do you think you could have some ready for our student exhibition at Christmas?"

"Yes, sir. I'd be honoured."

He gave her a strange, almost sympathetic look and said, "Madame *is* aware of your talent and she will offer you a show. Be cautious and if she offers you a contract, inspect it carefully. If you are comfortable, bring it to me I'll check it for you. Fairness is not one of Le Papillon's attributes."

Sarah glanced at her watch. "Thank you, sir. I really have to go."

"Whoever is buying those is a lucky man. My advice is to hang on to them until you have more completed paintings."

Twenty-Three

Art and Spies

Sarah found Mr. Carter pacing up and down the garden path and Mrs. Debinski peering through the curtain.

"I'm sorry, the principal called me to his office after class."

"That sounds ominous—it takes me back to my school days, being summoned by the headmaster and usually meant real trouble, even six of the best."

Sarah laughed, "Oh no, it wasn't bad. He wanted to talk about my art. He had some interesting things to say about Le Papillon Gallery. Come on in. I think we'll be accosted by Mrs. D—short for Debinski. She's been watching you."

The front door opened and Mrs. D's face showed a mixture of so many emotions that Sarah couldn't read her. "This gentleman has been pacing up and down here for half an hour."

"Really, I'm only five minutes late." Sarah gave him an amused look, "Mr. Carter has come to view my paintings."

Sarah led the way up the stairs, hearing Mrs. Debinski say "I hope you behave like a gentleman, Mr. Carter. I'll be watching." He nodded, stifling a laugh.

Sarah closed her flat door and showed him into her small studio. Placing the canvasses on easels and the chest of drawers, she opened the drawers containing her sketches. "I'll leave you to look and I'll make some tea or would you rather have a cocktail?" They agreed on dry martinis.

Sarah made sure the bedroom door was tightly closed and busied herself tidying the sitting room. She placed the cocktail shaker, olives and two glasses on the table and waited.

"I find the *Whispering Trees* piece stunning. I'd like to buy it, and to commission some paintings from your sketches." He lifted the shaker. "Shall I pour?" Sarah nodded. "I probably should ask if you promised anything to Le Papillon."

"Oh, she was noncommittal. Mr. Darwin called her a fool and said something about disappointments but didn't elaborate."

"Perhaps if I tell you the story behind Madame or Miss Cecilia Jones—her real name—you will understand. I have known Cecilia for fifteen years. She was a student at the Royal College of Art, although I didn't know her until later, after she opened the gallery. Cecilia was a talented artist, not unlike yourself, and was expected to receive an award. But she received an honourable mention instead. Rumour had it that she slashed the winner's art. She denied it and accused another artist, which later turned out to be true. A bitter and vengeful Cecilia dropped out of college and never painted again. Fifteen years ago, she bought the gallery and made quite a success of it. She never forgave the college and my guess is that she sees herself in you; had she stayed at college she would have been a successful artist. Watching your success has unleashed fifteen years of pent up rage and she's jealous."

"That explains a lot. How sad, she could have been a great artist and bitterness has eaten her away," Sarah said thoughtfully.

Handing her a tumbler, Mr. Carter sat next to her on the sofa. They clinked glasses. "Here's to your success. Do you know how talented you are?"

Sarah smiled and nodded. "Yes, I know I'm good."

"And that, my dear, is exactly what I mean. Good does not describe your art; even excellent is an understatement." He leaned one arm along the back of the sofa, and turning towards her, he gently pushed a strand of curls off her face.

"Mr. Carter, I will have a swollen head with all these compliments." She tried to ignore his touch but his fingers on her cheek had sent delightful shivers in her neck.

"Michael. Call me Michael. May I call you Sarah?"

"Sarah sounds good...Michael." They observed each other. Sarah saw a kind, considerate man. Good looking but unassuming; neat suits but someone you could easily forget or pass in a crowd. *I like him,* she thought. *He's older than me.* She briefly thought of young, thoughtless and demanding Marcus. *I prefer mature men.*

He stared again, "I liked you the first day I met you, but Marc was in the way. Perhaps I can get to know you better now that he's on assi...gone away." Seeing her puzzled look, he added, "I'm assuming he's not around anymore."

"He walked out on me for a second time in June. I haven't heard from him since. But how did you know his name was Marc or that he'd gone away?"

"I didn't. But he's not here, so I assumed. Can I take you for dinner?"

Sarah wasn't sure if he'd cleverly changed the subject or genuinely wanted to go out for dinner, but not having eaten for most of the day, she decided on the latter.

"I'll go change." She quickly changed from her favourite artsy clothes into a more conventional blue sleeveless dress with full skirt and high heels.

Admiring her outfit, Michael said, "I think we'll dine where there is a dance floor. I know just the place."

He drove through Kensington past Harrods and stopped at a small but sophisticated restaurant. The maître d' greeted him by name and they were shown to a discrete table. Sarah couldn't help wondering if the seclusion was business, romance or just coincidence. A quartet finished playing a waltz and dancers wandered back to the small, round tables with white table cloths and glowing candles that surrounded the shiny wooden dance floor.

Michael ordered two dry martinis and asked for the menu as the quartet began playing a foxtrot. He extended his arm and said, "Shall we dance?"

Sarah hesitated; she loved dancing but was out of practice. She need not have worried as Michael was an excellent dancer and whisked her confidently around the floor. By the time the music stopped she was quite out of breath and glad to sit down and sip the waiting martini. Michael looked at the menu and ordered for both of them. Shrimp cocktail served with a white wine to start, followed by roast duck and a different wine.

"The sauce is exquisite. Grandpa Bill would love this for the Sackville," Sarah said.

"The chef here is excellent, but he guards his recipes with his life. It is refreshing to be out with someone who appreciates good food."

"Being raised in a high-class hotel does give me an edge. Except when I was really small, when Mum and Dad and I lived in Edinburgh, ordinary family food has never been part of my diet." Sarah stopped talking; her parents flashed before her—her mother gone, her father out of sight, invisible. *Did Michael know where he was or what had happened to him? The note he had given her and his association with Uncle Charlie: did that mean anything?*

"Is something wrong? You've gone very quiet?" Michael refilled her wine glass.

"Thinking of my parents always makes me a little sad." *I should ask him about my father. Why am I afraid it will spoil the evening? I hardly know this man; he doesn't mean anything to me. Well, not much.*

"I can understand. My parents abandoned me to boarding school when I was five or six because I was a nuisance. As far as I know they are alive, but they might as well be dead. I haven't seen them since I left school and went my own way, fifteen years ago."

"I can't image what it's like to be alone." Sarah felt sorry for him, seeing for the first time his vulnerability. His sorrow was deeper than her own. "I'm grateful that my grandparents have been the most wonderful parents to me."

"One of the masters at school, Mr. Beecham, took me under his wing. He invited me to his house during holidays when my parents were too busy to have me home, so I didn't have to stay at school alone. He was very good to me. He died two years ago. I still miss him."

"I still miss my mother and…" She looked him straight in the eye, "and my father."

"I thought Charlie Neale would help you."

"I did ask him and he seemed to know something, but I had to leave when Grandpa Bill had a stroke. I found out nothing."

"I hear a waltz—let's dance." He had dismissed the subject of her father. Annoyed, she stood up and wobbled slightly. *Too much wine,* she thought and nestled her head in his shoulder. *Definitely too much wine, but this feels so good.* He held her close and whispered, "This has been a wonderful evening. Can we do it again?" She didn't answer, his gentle breath on her neck went rippling into her spine. She wanted to stay annoyed, but she couldn't.

"I think it's time I took you home." He kissed her as the music came to an end and she didn't resist. They drove in silence. As he pulled up to the curb, Michael took her hand and smiled. "Be patient. I'll see what I can find out about your father." He held her close as they walked up to the front door. "I'll come by tomorrow so we can talk about the paintings."

"Okay." She kissed him goodnight and crept by Mrs. D's door, surprised no one was watching. Mrs. D had pinned a note on her door that read, *Mrs. Blaine called from Bexhill. Not urgent but please call when you get home.* Anxiety tightened her stomach, had something happened to Grandpa Bill? She looked at her watch 1 a.m., if it wasn't urgent it was too late to call. She'd call first thing.

Sarah slept fitfully. Waking from strange dreams, a mixture of Bexhill and Michael Carter, her father and the room spinning out of control. As soon as she heard Johnny up and about, he always rose early in the mornings, she ran downstairs and phoned Bexhill. It rang a long time and by the time Anna answered, Sarah was in a panic. "Nana, what's wrong? I called as soon as I could."

"Sarah, we are fine. I said it wasn't urgent. Where were you last night?"

"I went out for dinner with Michael Carter; you remember him from the James Bond conference. I bumped into him at the art gallery and he's interested in buying some paintings."

Anna replied, "A date or business?"

"Nana, business of course." Sarah crossed her fingers, Nana always knew when she was lying and it had definitely been a date.

"It sounds more like a date to me. Be careful, Sarah. You know he's British Secret Service: they live dangerous lives, even get killed, and are apt to disappear without a trace."

What a strange thing to say, Sarah thought, but didn't reply. "How is Grandpa Bill?"

"He's fine, but I called to tell you we're coming up to London in two weeks to see a specialist. The appointment is at two o'clock Friday, October 6th. We'll come up on the early train and stay at the Thornton's townhouse for the weekend. They are at Hillcrest, but we hope to see you."

"I can arrange for someone to take my classes that day and I'll meet you at the station."

"That would be really nice. I'd like you to be there. The doctor thinks this specialist will help his heart get stronger."

"I have to get ready for work, but I'll call you later I'm looking forward to seeing you, and it's good news about this specialist, right?" Sarah hung up the phone but wasn't sure if the news was good or not.

She dragged herself into work. There was no doubt in her mind that she had a hangover, and the lack of sleep made her feel worse. Mr. Darwin had asked to see her, but she didn't trust her stomach. She thought she might be sick at any minute and asked his secretary

175

to delay the appointment until tomorrow. His secretary took one look at her, called a cab and sent her home. Sarah was relieved that Mrs. Debinski was out shopping when she arrived home and went straight to bed.

The jangle of the old pull bell on the front door persisted in her dream until she opened her eyes and realized the noise was real. Mrs. D was talking to a man. The clock said seven o'clock: she had slept for five hours. Her stomach had settled and she felt better. *The voice*, Sarah thought, and leaped out of bed. It was Michael. "Keep him talking, Mrs. D," she giggled. "Likely more instructions about calling on a young lady." Pulling a sweater over her head, she walked to the bathroom and gathered her unruly hair into a frizzy ponytail. Finally, she adjusted her cotton skirt and opened the flat door.

Mrs. D stood in front of the stairs wagging her finger at Michael, quoting the no gentleman callers rule. Sarah noted that in all the time she and Lizzy had been there, she had never enforced the rule beyond raising an eyebrow. The night Marcus had made love to her came to mind; she determined Mrs. D knew more about that night than she was saying and was not going to let it happen again. *I can hardly explain that to Michael.*

"Thank you, Mrs. D, I didn't hear the doorbell. Mic...Mr. Carter is not a gentleman caller, he has come to pick up his paintings; this is business."

Michael pushed by her and thumped up the stairs; a man not used to being ordered around. Whatever Mrs. D had said to him had struck a chord.

"I'm sorry, Michael, she's just looking out for me. A promise she made my grandmother when I was a student. I usually get the door, but I wasn't feeling well and had fallen asleep. I forgot you were coming. Sorry."

"She really is irritating." As he calmed down, his face showed concern and he asked, "What's wrong, you're not feeling well?" He gently stroked her face and kissed her cheek. "What can I do to make you feel better?"

Michael was different from other men; older and calmer. Sarah liked his kindness and protectiveness, and she felt different towards him. She wanted to be looked after, and that puzzled her. She had a sense of being starved of warm-hearted tenderness and Michael fed that void.

"I'm fine, really. A hangover from last night, that's all. I'm not used to drinking cocktails, and all that wine and rich food. I had a disturbing message from Nana, which didn't help. It turned out to be a false alarm, but all of it resulted in no sleep. I must have looked pretty bad, as they sent me home from college. I just had a good sleep and I'm fine now."

"You look pale. Are you sure you're feeling okay?" Sarah nodded. "I'll be more mindful next time we go out. If there is a next time?" He pulled her towards him and his fingers twisted around a ringlet that had escaped from the ponytail. The warmth of his hand touched her cheek and she leaned in, waiting for the security and comfort of his arms as he kissed her. She wasn't disappointed. Returning the kiss, she felt his body press into her and she melted. She wanted this man to make love to her, but she knew it was wrong and pulled back, taking a deep breath. "No, Michael. It's too soon." He didn't argue, but rested his forehead on hers and said, "I know. We're moving too fast. You do something to me that most women can't. You are young and bubbly, bright and artistic, kind and generous. I've never met anyone as lovely as you before."

"Oh, Mr. Carter, you do but make me blush," Sarah said, teasing and faking a swoon. "I don't think Jane Austen or Charlotte Bronte could string more complimentary words together in one sentence." He laughed and grabbed her and pulled her closer, "Should I be Mr. Rochester or Mr. Darcy? Whichever one, I will sweep you off your feet, Miss Sarah Wexford." He stopped talking. Sarah nestled into his arms, closing her eyes. She felt safe. He rested his head on hers and whispered, "I'm falling in love with you." And then silence.

Twenty-Four

All Sorts of Love

Sarah didn't care that she could hardly see her hand in front of her face. One of those dense London fogs had descended on the city, but she felt full of sunshine as she ran to the Underground station. Michael was in love with her and she might be in love with him. If feeling good, happy and safe with someone meant you were in love, then, she thought, *I'm in love.*

She arrived early for class and went directly to Mr. Darwin's office. His secretary, Mrs. Pitt, a war widow and a loyal, efficient employee, sat at her desk arranging his day.

"Miss Wexford, how nice to see you, and looking much better than yesterday. How are you feeling?"

"Much better. Whatever it was, I slept for hours and felt fine when I woke up. Thank you for helping me yesterday. I wanted to let you know that if Mr. Darwin wanted to see me, I'm here."

Mrs. Pitt glanced at her watch and said, "His first appointment just cancelled because of the fog. He's in his office. I'll ask him if he'll see you now."

She beckoned to Sarah from the door and closed it behind her.

"Good Morning, Miss Wexford." Mr. Darwin motioned towards the chair by his desk. "I have some very exciting news for you. My colleague at the London Art Gallery is a great fan of Emily Carr's west coast art. I had difficulty convincing him that one of my assistant profs was as good if not better than Emily Carr. The only way I can persuade him is to show him your work. Is that possible?"

"Well, yes and no. I only have two completed, and I just sold the *Whispering Trees*, but I think I can borrow it back. I still have the *Haida Long House with Totem Poles*. How many does he need to see?"

"Those two would be a good start, but be prepared to do more. I would like two or three for the College Christmas Exhibition."

"I'll try, but that's quite an order. It generally takes me several weeks to paint one, and I have my students to consider."

"I'll assign you an assistant to do your prep work."

"That would help. You'll let me know when to bring the paintings?" Mr. Darwin nodded.

The rest of the day seemed to pass slowly, and when a senior student arrived to help with her lesson prep in the afternoon, she quickly gave her instructions and left early. She wanted to get in touch with Michael; she needed the painting back at least until she could paint another one. Happy to have an excuse to see him again, she waited until she got home before calling him, hoping Mrs. D was out, but the sitting room door creaked open as she dialed.

Michael answered. "Michael, I had some good news from the college today. But I need to borrow *Whispering Trees*. The London Art Gallery doesn't believe I can paint like Emily Carr." She laughed. "I can't really talk right now."

Michael replied, "Mrs. D is eavesdropping no doubt. I'll come and pick you up in an hour." Sarah replaced the receiver and went upstairs.

When Michael arrived, they decided to take both paintings to her office at the college, followed by dinner at the Coffee Shop; not Michael's style, but Sarah decided that Michael needed to get used to a simpler life if they were to spend more time together, and she wasn't ready to face any alcohol today.

**

Sarah and Michael met every day for the next month, either at lunchtime or in the evening. Mrs. D finally stopped accosting him at the door and accepted he was there to stay. Sarah found herself torn between spending time with Michael and painting. The problem was solved when Michael announced he had to go away on business. He was vague about his return date and Sarah sensed some of the old Mr. Carter before he had become Michael. She didn't need to be told it was an MI6 assignment and didn't ask any questions. He told her he loved her and would be back, and then said, "In my job I have to do things I'm not always proud of. If you hear things, try to ignore them." Before she could answer, he kissed her and disappeared, leaving her guessing what he meant and wondering if he would return.

Michael's departure plunged her into old doubts, making her question even the college principal. He had kept her paintings in his office but she hadn't heard a word about the London Art Gallery. Were the delays a ploy to get hold of her art? She reminded herself that Mr. Darwin was principal of the best art college in the Britain. If she couldn't trust him, who could she trust? Having an assistant freed up her time to paint, and she was enjoying it. Painting took her into another world—her own world—and she loved it and didn't miss Michael so much.

Spending so much time with him, she had neglected her friends. She hadn't seen Lizzy for weeks and Felix hadn't called. Now that she thought about it, she was the one not calling him. She hadn't even been to Bexhill, too afraid of discovering she was needed at the hotel. Nana phoned regularly and said everything was fine, but she would say that whether it was or not, and Sarah didn't want to know. Guilt finally won and Sarah packed a suitcase and decided to make a surprise visit to Bexhill.

The train rumbled into Bexhill Central and Sarah automatically scanned the platform. Today there was no one to meet her and she had a flash of loneliness, seeing a little girl standing on the platform holding her mother's hand, not understanding why her father was still at home. Home being Edinburgh at that time. It wasn't her father's fault he wasn't there; her mother didn't want him there. The familiar feeling of guilt overwhelmed her; she too had pushed him away, not wanting him to be there. She had to find him, say she was sorry. Why is he so difficult to find? Did Uncle Charlie know anything?

She took another look around the platform and laughed at herself—no one knew she was coming so how could they meet her? "It's about time you stood on your own feet," she muttered, hailing a cab. "The New Sackville Hotel please."

"Miss Sarah, I didn't know you were expected," Henry said, opening the cab door.

"I'm not," she replied, walking across the lobby to Anna's office. She tapped on the door, "Surprise!"

"Oh my goodness, Sarah." Anna hugged her tightly. "I am really happy to see you. It has been a day of surprises. Darcy, Belle and Felix arrived unexpectedly this morning."

"Felix! What's he doing here?"

"I don't know. It might have something to do with the wedding. I haven't talked to Belle yet. We'll see them at dinner." Anna hugged Sarah again. "I'm so happy you're here."

"Nana, what's wrong?" Sarah frowned, seeing Anna's thin and colourless face. Deep lines crossed her forehead, her eyes glistened on the brink of crying.

"I'm worried about Bill, he's not doing well. That London specialist told him he couldn't work and gave him some pills. He's no energy, he gets out of breath walking across the room. The doctor just keeps saying he needs rest. I'm so scared."

Sarah took Anna in her arms. "I'm sorry, Nana. The specialist didn't help?"

"For a while, but this last week he's not been well. He hates being idle, but the work in the kitchen is too much. He went to lay down. Go and talk to him."

"I'll call in on my way to the penthouse. I need to get changed and then I'll come and help you."

"Thank you, sweetheart."

Sarah knocked tentatively on the door of suite 305, trying not to think of the worst, as she suspected Nana was already doing. Darcy opened it. "Sarah, what a surprise, and how lovely to see you."

"It seems we are full of surprises today. What brings you to Bexhill?"

"We were worried about Bill and needed some neutral space to talk to Felix. Have you seen him?"

"That sounds ominous. And no, I only just arrived and talked to Nana. She's worried about Grandpa Bill, so I'm here to see for myself."

Darcy shook his head from side to side and whispered, "Not good, Sarah," as a voice from the lounge called, "Is that Sarah's voice? Stop talking about me and let me see her." Bill gave a raspy laugh.

"Grandpa, what's this I hear about you not being well?" Sarah sat at his side and hugged him, holding on as long and as tight as she could to hide the shock of seeing his deathly grey complexion and almost lifeless body. She wondered how he was managing to stay sitting up. He tapped her back, "Hey, that's enough of that, the old ticker is giving me a bit of bother, but I'll soon be okay."

Sarah let him go and smiled. "Of course you will."

"Now, Sarah, tell me why you are here and what you've been up to."

"I'm here because I was tired of London and wanted to surprise you. What have I been doing? Mostly painting."

Darcy interrupted, "I'll leave you two to chat and go find Belle. We'll see you at dinner."

Bill shook his head, "I can't make it, it's too far to walk. Come and have a nightcap later." Darcy nodded and left.

"Grandpa, would you like to come down for dinner? If it's just the walk, why don't we get you a wheelchair and I'll wheel you down?"

"Me in a wheel chair!" He shook his head and then paused. "You know, it would be nice to join everyone for dinner."

"I have to go change and help Nana. I want you to have a rest. I will find a wheelchair and we will surprise Nana and bring you down to the dining room. And look at that, you have some colour in your cheeks. I think you're bored, Grandpa." She kissed his forehead. "Put your feet up and I'll get a blanket and tuck you in. I'll see you later."

Sarah wearily climbed the stairs to the penthouse, suffocating in guilt. Whatever had made her come home this weekend—divine intervention, intuition or coincidence—she was grateful. She really needed to be here. She flopped on her couch, gathering her thoughts. The state of Nana and Grandpa was overwhelming. She needed to come home more often or, dreading the thought, permanently? She could paint here, but she'd lose her contacts. She buried her face in her hands, close to tears. A voice inside her said, *Grow up, Sarah.* She took a very deep breath and decided she would do what she could this weekend and come home every weekend if necessary.

On her way downstairs, she tip-toed in to check on Bill, who was sleeping. She needed to keep moving and took the stairs instead of the lift. "What's this?" she said, bending to pick up a discarded scrap of paper and noted little dust balls near the skirting board and hair and dirt on the carpet.

Frowning, she knocked and went into Mr. Grimsby's office. "Mr. Grimsby, how is the new housekeeper working out?"

"Miss Wexford, I didn't know you were home. Mrs. Henderson seems to have settled in well."

"I hate to be picky, but it has been a while since the staircase was vacuumed. I hope that isn't a reflection of the rest of the hotel."

"I haven't had any complaints. I'll see it's done right away. Are you staying long?"

"Just the weekend, but you will be seeing more of me until Mr. Blaine's health has improved."

**

Anna sat at her desk, staring out of the window, blinking and adjusting her glasses, hoping it would remove the blurring. She hadn't told anyone about her declining eye sight. She rubbed her eyes, trying to read the contract Dorothy had asked her to check over. It was no good, she couldn't read the numbers and took a magnifying glass from her desk drawer. Last week she had written the wrong amounts on two cheques; thankfully both merchants were long time suppliers to the hotel and honest enough to return the cheques with the extra zeros. It could have cost the hotel hundreds of pounds. Hearing Sarah's voice, she quickly pushed the glass back in her drawer.

"Grandpa is sleeping. I talked to Darcy for a while. What's wrong with Felix?"

Anna shrugged, "Can you look over these contracts for me while I check with Balaji how many bookings we have tonight."

"No problem. The usual, making sure the inclusions and exclusions are correct and the numbers match?"

"Yes, thank you," Anna said leaving the office.

Sarah lifted the papers, looking for the file and frowning. *Nana must be worried. Her desk is a mess, which is not like her at all.* She opened the drawer. Seeing the magnifying glass, she wondered where it had come from. Mr. Grimsby put his head around the door, "I'm off, Miss Wexford. The maid is vacuuming the carpet now."

"Oh good. Have a good weekend," Sarah said, continuing to read the contract.

She gathered up the papers and placed them in folders for filing. Surprised that many of the folders were not in alphabetical order, she re-filed them. *I'll have to speak to Dorothy about that,* she thought, locking the cabinet and leaving the office to see Dan, the night doorman.

"Dan, where do you keep the wheelchairs for guests?"

"In the luggage room. Can I get one for you?"

"Yes please. I've persuaded Mr. Blaine to use one to come down for dinner tonight." Seeing Anna come out of the dining room, she whispered, "I want it to be a surprise."

"Okay, I'll take it up. She won't question me; we have a gentleman on the second floor who uses one occasionally. Go talk to Mrs. Blaine and I'll take one up there for you."

"Nana, are you going in to dinner?"

"Yes, the Thorntons are waiting."

"I'll be there in a few minutes."

Sarah went upstairs to find Bill already sitting in the wheelchair. "Dan helped me and I'm ready for dinner."

"Let's go surprise everyone," Sarah said, pushing the chair into the lift.

Balaji greeted them and quickly moved chairs to accommodate the wheelchair at the table next to Anna, who jumped up, taking the wheelchair from Sarah. Happy to see them both light up, she took her place next to Felix, who leaned in towards her and said, "It's good to see you. Where've you been and how's the new boyfriend?"

"He's away and I am painting for an exhibition at the college—some exciting things going on. What's going on with you? Your father indicated there were some problems."

"The usual. I can't talk here. I have some exciting news too—the cause of the problem."

Sarah nodded knowingly. "Come up to the penthouse after dinner, we won't be disturbed there." Felix reached under the table for her hand and squeezed it, his gentle blue eyes searching for her smile as she squeezed back. She realized how much she missed his warmth and reassurance. She always felt understood with Felix.

The dinner passed quickly, like old times. Bill had colour in his face once more. Sarah thought perhaps part of the problem was not getting around. He was one of those people who needed to keep busy. If Bill was happy, so was Anna. Whatever was going on between Felix and his parents, she was soon to find out. Anna insisted on wheeling Bill back to their suite.

Twenty-Five

Solutions and More Problems

" his is the first time I've been to your penthouse and I like it," Felix said as he poured two brandies and handed one to Sarah, who was sitting on the couch. She leaned across him to turn on the table lamp. He kissed her head. "I love your red curls—I've always loved them. I remember when you were little and came to the Hillcrest Hall your curls bounced as you ran to greet me."

Sarah laughed. "Those were fun days. Life has become so serious; the penalty for growing up. So, are you going to tell me what's going on? Your father said you were here to talk on neutral ground."

"Nothing much to tell that you don't already know really. After I was called to the bar they were so happy about my success that I finally told them that my ultimate goal was silk. Mother was okay with it but a bit reserved, probably because she suspected father's reaction. He was so angry he marched out of the drawing room, this was at Hillcrest, and wouldn't speak to me. I was equally angry and drove back to London. We've hardly spoken since. Hence the reference to neutral ground."

"Has neutral ground helped?"

"Somewhat. Mother is the mediator and we are speaking to each other." Felix frowned. "I should perhaps back up. About a month ago, the senior partners asked to see me to find out if I was interested in silk. Sarah, this is huge: senior partners, all QCs themselves, do not ask those questions unless they intend to groom you for the position.

"The partners know I'm heir to Hillcrest, which could be an advantage, but also a problem if I abandon the law for Hillcrest. They want to know where my loyalties lie. And that is an issue. I have no choice but to become the next Earl of Hillcrest, but that could be fifteen years or more. Plenty of time to practice law as a QC, and if necessary I could do both. I convinced the partners, and as a result I am working with the senior partners on some big cases."

"First of all, this is great news. Congratulations, Felix, I am thrilled for you. So, what's the problem?"

"I am not sure who—father won't tell me—but someone told him that I had chosen the law over Hillcrest. He didn't believe them, perhaps because I hadn't discussed my ambition. When I announced my plan to become a QC, it must have confirmed the gossip and that's why he lost his temper. He's convinced I will walk away from the estate like his brother. I sometimes think having my uncle's name is a curse. I'm not my uncle and I would never do such a thing. However, while I have the opportunity, I want to practice criminal law. Is that so unreasonable?"

"No, your father is the unreasonable one. He can't see past your uncle's disloyalty to the family and that's what he sees in you, even though it isn't true. Does he want you to give up the law altogether?"

Felix nodded, "He wants me back at Hillcrest and, Sarah, I can't do that right now." She saw the agony in his eyes and taught lips. "And then there is Lorraine."

"Other than being your fiancée, what does Lorraine have to do with this?"

"Lorraine agrees with my father; she wants me to return to Hillcrest. She hates the law, says it takes up too much of my time. Which is true. If I'm on a big case I can't drop everything and fly to Toronto. She isn't like you—she has no understanding of my passion for the law, but she has plenty of passion for Hillcrest. Sometimes I wonder if she loves Hillcrest more than me." He put his arm around Sarah, "I need more Sarahs in my life."

"I probably shouldn't be saying this, but have you considered Lorraine might be more interested in the prestige of becoming Lady Thornton than being your wife?"

"Sarah, that's not fair. I know you don't like her, but she's not like that." Felix paused and Sarah hid a grin. She had planted some doubt; he would think about her comment. "I wish you two could get along," Felix added.

"I've tried, but she doesn't like me." Wanting to change the subject, Sarah suggested, "Let's have some music. Can you stand Pat Boone, Paul Anka or Elvis? Most of these are from before college." She opened the record player and stacked all three LPs to play automatically.

Felix took her lead and dropped the subject. "How's the job going at college? And you mentioned exhibitions?"

Sarah told him about the college and Mr. Darwin's request for her art and how Madame had asked for a couple of her paintings but not an exhibition yet.

Felix looked her in the eye. "You mentioned Michael had gone away. I don't know what you see in that man. You know he's MI6. Sarah, you deserve better than that."

"I like him and we get along well. He's an art collector—it's nice to be with someone who appreciates my work."

"Is this serious?"

Sarah shrugged her shoulders. "Could be. I'm far more excited about the college exhibition, but I'm afraid this place may pre-empt it."

"You have the same problems as me. Your art is going well, but I see how things are in the hotel, and judging by Bill's health and Anna's declining abilities, your decision will come before mine."

Sarah stopped tapping her feet as the song "Diana" came to an end. The record player dropped another LP record onto the turntable

"Love Letters in the Sand" began to play. She instinctively moved closer to Felix as Pat Boone crooned and she sang along.

"I'm afraid you're right and I don't know what to do. I thought I had more time. Mr. Grimsby is working out well, but the new housekeeper is not like Amy. The main staircase had not been vacuumed. That would never have happened when Amy was here."

"Mother mentioned the bathrooms weren't as clean as usual. I can't say I notice these things, but I did have to phone down for more towels."

"Nana would never have tolerated the smallest speck of dust but she doesn't seem to notice. I think she's too worried about Bill. I will talk to housekeeping tomorrow. Amy really liked this woman and her references were impeccable; I did wonder why she was moving from a London hotel to here. I'll hire a new housekeeper if necessary. It's hard to keep an eye on things from London. I'll start coming home every weekend for a while. If I can get the right staff in, it should run itself. Do you think I can do both?"

"I've never known you give up on anything. I'd give it a try. I'm going to try both. At least we'll have each other's support," Felix said.

"Good. And on that note, Felix, I'm kicking you out. I need to get some sleep. I'll see you tomorrow before I leave, or are you heading out early?"

"I have to be in London Monday morning. I thought I'd leave after an early dinner. Sarah, why don't you drive in with me instead of taking the train?"

"Thanks, I'd like that." She paused, "Felix, did you ever find anything more about my father?"

Felix put his head to one side, frowning. "Where did that come from? No, nothing, but then I haven't really looked. I thought Charlie knew something."

"He does, but is reluctant to help. I think it has something to do with the secret service. I left Toronto so quickly that I never had chance to talk to him. I need to know if my father is still alive. I want to see him."

"Secret service? That doesn't sound like the man I remember. If he's to be found, we'll find him."

**

Sarah woke early, before it was light, and went to the reception desk. She took the keys to three unoccupied rooms to check on their cleanliness and to her disappointment they all needed attention. Next, she checked the linen: it was clean but the cupboards were messy. Taking the service stairs, she went directly to the staff-dining hall. The night staff was finishing their shift and the day staff had started to arrive. She told everyone to stay as she needed to talk to them. The kitchen appeared to be clean and organized, so she left its staff to their work. Sarah had assumed it was Mrs. Henderson's day off and proceeded with a general staff meeting focussed on tidiness and then let everyone except the chamber maids leave or get on with their duties. She was in the middle of listing the complaints and explaining what each maid was assigned to do when Mrs. Henderson arrived. Sarah asked her to order some coffee and wait in the housekeeper's office. Two of the young maids looked terrified, and Sarah realized something was wrong. After a few questions and a lot of tears, she discovered Mrs. Henderson was not an easy person. After reassuring the maids that things would change, they went off to do their work.

Sarah leaned on the big wooden table and buried her hands in her face. Could things get any worse? *Well,* she thought, *at least there will be a cup of coffee waiting.* Sarah walked in to find a straight-backed, pursed-lipped Mrs. Henderson and no coffee.

"Mrs. Henderson, did you order coffee?"

"I am not a maid and you are not my boss." She flipped her head with satisfaction.

In spite of Sarah's red hair, she rarely lost her temper, but at this she thought she might explode and needed some air. "Excuse me." She left the office and went into the kitchen and asked a waiter to bring some coffee. Taking an extremely deep breath, she returned to the office.

"Mrs. Henderson, I *am* your boss. I am part owner of this hotel and while Mrs. Blaine is taking care of Mr. Blaine, you will be dealing with me." She stopped when the coffee arrived. "And I have no problem fetching coffee. Would you like some?" A red-faced Mrs. Henderson refused. "I have received several complaints from guests about the housekeeping. I had to ask Mr. Grimsby to have a maid vacuum the main staircase on Friday. There are towels missing from the bathrooms and complaints that the bathrooms are not clean."

"I'll talk to the maids, I'm sure its an exception."

"No, it's not." Sarah picked up the three keys in front of her. "I checked each of these rooms this morning and none are fit for our guests."

"I'll have the maids see to it right away."

"It's already done. You are not managing your staff. Bullying does not work. Teach them and help them and inspect their work. What do you do all day?" Sarah looked around the untidy office, newspapers were scattered among magazines and unfinished crossword puzzles. "Start by tidying this up, and I want to see a cleaning plan for each maid. If I have one more complaint, I will fire you." Sarah didn't wait for an answer and left the room, closing the door carefully, restraining the urge to slam it hard. She went directly to Anna's office, not quite sure what she was going to say.

Opening the door, she was delighted to see Bill in his wheelchair sitting at the table with Anna having breakfast. Anna took a third cup and began to pour coffee, except she poured too much and it spilled into the saucer.

"Sarah, what's wrong?" Anna said, getting a clean saucer.

"Mrs. Henderson!" Sarah relayed the morning's events.

"She certainly isn't Amy Peterson. I miss Amy," Anna said. "I wonder if I could persuade Amy to come in a couple of mornings a week to work with Mrs. Henderson?"

"We could try, but I doubt Mrs. Henderson would take kindly to having Amy around." *But,* Sarah thought, *if she didn't like it, perhaps she would leave.*

"Nana, we needed a new head housekeeper."

"I'll talk to Amy first. If that doesn't work you can advertise in London."

Bill had quietly listened. He nodded towards Sarah. "I like Nana's idea. I'd like to see what's going on in the kitchen. Sarah, would you wheel me around the outside of the hotel and into the service entrance so I can check? I can't get down the stairs."

"I can do that, but you are not to overdo it. I'll arrange for the bellboy to take you to kitchen for an hour every morning. Would you like that?"

"If I know what's going on, I won't worry."
**

Sarah spent the rest of the day inspecting and organizing the staff. Mr. Grimsby was told to be more observant and as general manager he was put in charge of supervising Mrs. Henderson. The staff in general had become complacent and this worried Sarah; she knew it wouldn't be long before the complaints escalated into hotel vacancies and she couldn't understand why Anna was not doing anything. Something was not right. Sarah was also surprised that Dorothy hadn't noticed. She'd have to call her tomorrow and ask her to take on more responsibility.

Felix was waiting for her at six and they ate dinner with both of their families. Bill looked much better but Anna was not at her best. *What am I missing?It will have to wait until next weekend,* Sarah thought.

Felix brought his Jaguar to the front entrance and Sarah climbed in, tired and happy she didn't have to take the train. They drove most of the way in silence—a comfortable silence that they both appreciated.

As they approached London Sarah asked, "Any progress with your father?"

"I think so. He still doesn't understand why I'm not at Hillcrest, but I have convinced him that Hillcrest is important to me and that I will be ready to take over when the time comes. And you?"

"I'm worried. I should be there, but I've done my best to put things in order. Mrs. Henderson is not a good housekeeper. I gave her a good talking too—we'll see. I'm pleased to see Grandpa Bill is doing much better, but I am concerned about Nana. There's something not right. I'll go back next weekend. Felix, keep in touch. I need you right now."

The car slowed down, they were at Sarah's flat. Felix moved a strand of hair and gently wiped the moisture from the corner of her eye. "It will work out, and I'm always here for you. I need you just as much." He took her hand in his, leaned over and kissed her. Neither pulled away.

Twenty-Six

Sarah Does it All

S arah hadn't seen Felix since the kiss—the kiss that had thrown her into complete confusion, a kiss she couldn't forget. As if she didn't have enough to feel guilty about. Was she being disloyal to Michael? And what about Lorraine? What was Felix thinking? He was practically a married man—suddenly she felt like the other woman.

She stared at the painting on her easel, hardly remembering painting it. Emotion tightened her throat. She saw a storm blowing in from the sea: angry waves throwing sea spray in the air, about to roll over shadows of people, and dark green trees fighting the wind that blew heavy clouds apart, allowing a single beam of sunlight to break through into the sea. And the Sackville Hotel a backdrop to the whole painting, waiting to be engulfed in an enormous cresting wave.

The symbolism scared her. Was the storm her anger? Her father's face came and went in the sea spray. The shadows would surely drown and as the sea released the crest of the wave, the hotel would disappear. She alone stood in the midst of the wavering trees, fighting the wind. She parted the clouds and released a beam of sunlight and inside the beam she saw Felix.

She sat back on her stool, knowing this was the most powerful painting she had ever created, and only she understood it. Afraid of it, she took it off the easel and placed it facing the wall in her studio and tried to forget it. Thankful that she had a train to catch to Bexhill, she gathered her things and caught the Underground to Paddington Station.

The Friday night train to Reading was busy and she sat squished in the centre of the compartment, wishing everyone would be quiet so she could think. Relieved that the Bexhill train was almost empty, she found a compartment to herself. Not many people went to seaside towns in late November. Mr. Grimsby met her at the station.

"Sorry to bring you out so late on a Friday night."

"I don't mind, Miss Wexford. I use the time to check on Mrs. Henderson and catch up on paperwork."

"How is she doing?"

"Better, but I think it's Mrs. Peterson's influence. I'm not sure what will happen when she leaves."

"I agree with you and I am grateful that you are giving us your time. We need a good general manager who really cares about the hotel. We were spoiled with James Lytton; he had been here so long. His were big boots to fill. I am pleased with your performance and I would like to see you take on full responsibility now that Mr. and Mrs. Blaine are not able to cope. I will raise your salary accordingly. I'm afraid you may find some interference from Mrs. Blaine, but I need you to take over. I can't keep coming down every weekend."

"Thank you. I found it difficult at first and didn't want to overstep my authority. Mrs. Blaine wants to do it all herself. Will you speak to her?"

"Mrs. Blaine has to trust you, and that will take time. Mr. Grimsby, I think we can work together. Mrs. Henderson, I'm not sure. She may have to go. I'll give her until after New Year and if there is no commitment, I will hire a new housekeeper. In the meantime I'd like you to monitor her work and attitude towards the staff." He nodded, pulling the Rover under the portico.

Dan opened the car door. "Good evening, Miss Wexford. Mr. and Mrs. Blaine are waiting for you in the dining room."

Sarah stood at in the dining room doorway and smiled. Anna and Bill looked like their old selves. Bill waved and she went to the table, feeling suddenly hungry. Anna's colour was better but she still seemed anxious. Bill was well enough to walk with a cane and no wheelchair. He was doing the menus from their suite and visiting the kitchen twice a day. Sarah decided Bill's problem had been inactivity. Now she had to make sure he didn't overdo it and figure out what was wrong with Anna.

By the time Sarah left on Sunday, she was quite comfortable leaving Mr. Grimsby, Dorothy and Mrs. Henderson—with Amy in charge of her—to run the hotel in her absence. The college exhibition was only three weeks away and she had end of term exams and papers to mark and several paintings to complete. She hoped things would run smoothly until Christmas when she would be home for the holidays.

**

The students were excited but tense when she walked into class on Monday morning. They were always excited, but today's assignment would not only contribute to their end of term marks but also towards their overall marks for the year, hence their anxiety. She wanted to see them blossom with their own styles.

"Good morning everyone. Today's examination title is Storms. I want to see you explore emotions on the canvas. It can be nature, as in seascapes or landscapes, or an event or a personality reflecting emotion. You may choose the title, so long as it includes the word storm. Before you start, feel the storm and allow you creative minds to interpret the title." You have four hours to complete your work." She glanced at her watch. Please start now."

She was aware that her own painting called *Beyond the Storm* had inspired this theme. Her mind drifted back to Friday. *Beyond the Storm* had stirred such emotion she had not dared move the canvas—it still faced the wall in her studio. What was she afraid of? The power of the painting or the power it evoked within her. Feeling her throat tighten and her breath shorten, she had her answer. She wandered through the classroom between the easels nodding approval at the exceptionally talented and grinning at the not so talented. A soft tap on the door got her attention. The porter waved an envelope and she opened the door, whispering thank you as she took the letter.

She sat at her desk staring at the letter, the familiar butterfly motif in the corner and the words Le Papillon Gallery of Art.

Dear Miss Wexford,

It is with great pleasure that Le Papillon Gallery of Art would like to invite you to present your paintings, including the Canadian West Coast art.
Please contact Mr. Sebastian, the gallery manager, to schedule an appointment at your convenience so that we may discuss details.

Yours truly,
Mr. D. Sebastian
General Manager
Le Papillon Gallery of Art

Sarah read the letter several times. Finally, an exhibition. She had butterflies in her stomach thinking of the implications of such a show. A tiny twinge of concern crept in as she remembered the trauma of her last encounter with Madame and Mr. Darwin's warnings regarding fairness at Le Papillon. *I'll show Mr. Darwin the letter. I trust his opinion and it will give me an excuse to ask about the London Gallery.*

The rest of the session she spent working on the term papers. At one o'clock, she said, "Put your brushes down and if you haven't already done so, sign you work and then step aside." She glanced at the anxious faces as she walked through the easels. "Good work, all of you. Now I'd like to see some smiles. Every canvas here today has passed—to what degree will show in your final marks, but I can assure you that nobody in this class needs to worry. Off you go and enjoy the afternoon."

As Sarah followed the students along the corridor towards Mrs. Pitt's office, she bumped into Mr. Darwin.

"Miss Wexford, how did the examination go today?"

"Very well, thank you. I have a talented group of students. Mr. Darwin, I wondered if you have a minute? I've had a request from Le Papillon." She handed him the letter.

"Madame had no choice; your reputation precedes you my dear. Make the appointment with Mr. Sebastian. He is a nice man and he'll treat you well. When they offer you a contract, bring it to me before you sign it. Speaking of exhibitions, my colleague from the London Gallery will be attending our Christmas exhibition. Miss Berkley is in charge of submissions. Please contact her and make sure you have your best for them to view. Now, if you will excuse me I'm late for a meeting." He smiled, looked over his shoulder and added, "Well done, Miss Wexford."

Sarah called, "Thank you." She felt like doing a jig and actually twirled in the hallway; seeing odd stares from the passing students she restrained herself and went into the staff room for tea. The empty teapot told her it had been a busy lunchtime, but everyone had gone back to class. As she picked up the phone the tea lady brought a fresh pot and poured a cup for Sarah as she began to dial Le Papillon. Watching each number rotate in what seemed like slow motion, she listened to the *ring, ring,* afraid she would lose her nerve if they didn't answer quickly. An effeminate male voice answered, identifying himself as Mr. Sebastian, and an appointment was made for the following week. Excited, Sarah wanted to share her good news and tried to call Felix, but he was in conference. She tried Lizzy at work but was told she was not feeling well and had gone home. Sarah immediately called her home number but there was no answer.

She returned to her classroom, wondering what Lizzy was up to. It wasn't out of the ordinary for Lizzy to take off and go up to Bond Street to shop, but saying she was unwell was unusual. Maybe she was sleeping. Sarah began to grade the canvasses from the morning's exam.

**

Mrs. Debinski gave Sarah *the look* as she ran downstairs to answer the front door. Felix had phoned earlier to apologize for not taking her call. He and Peter were working on a big case involving treason. What he was really saying was that he didn't have time for her right now, so she didn't bother to tell him her news. No sooner had she gone back upstairs than the phone rang again. An excited Lizzy said she was coming over. The final straw for Mrs. Debinski was Lizzy arriving at the door. Sarah made a cursory attempt to apologize for disturbing Mrs. D's evening and the girls went up stairs.

"I'm going to have a baby!" Lizzy announced as soon as the door closed.

"Oh Lizzy, that is wonderful news. How exciting. What does Peter think of being a daddy?"

"He doesn't know. I only found today. I had to leave work this morning. I've felt so poorly, I thought there was something wrong with me. This morning my stomach was so bad, I couldn't work. I kept running to the bathroom to be sick. They sent me home and I went straight to the surgery to see the doctor."

"I wondered where you were. I called the office and your home."

"At first, he thought I might have food poisoning and pressed around my tummy. And then examined me—not a very pleasant exam," Lizzy hesitated, pointing to her lower body. "Down there. And then he said I was pregnant and was suffering from morning sickness. Something to do with changing hormones and it usually stops at around three months. He thinks I'm close to that now, so I should feel better soon."

"When's the baby due?"

"He thinks the end of May or early June. He said he'd be more specific when he sees me again in a month. I am so excited. I can't wait to tell Peter."

"A baby! This is exciting. What would you like a boy or a girl?" Sarah asked.

"I'd like a little girl but I'm sure Peter would like a boy. Don't most men?"

"I expect they want a boy to carry on the family name. Little girls are cute. I will buy Lizzy junior her first frilly dress."

Lizzy laughed at Sarah's reference to Lizzy junior. "I don't think I want her to have my name, I always thought I'd call my daughter..." Lizzy giggled, "that sounds weird and wonderful, *my daughter*. What do you think of the name Kaitlin?"

"I do like it, it's unusual. What about a boy's name? "

"I have no idea, maybe I'll let Peter pick the boys name." Lizzy looked at her watch. "Gosh, look at the time. Peter will be wondering where I am."

"I think they are working late tonight. I just spoke with Felix he said they were working on a really big case involving treason."

"You're right, Peter told me last night. It involves MI6. Peter's being extremely secretive and has implied someone we know is involved."

"What!" Sarah heart almost stopped. "Do you think its Michael?"

"I doubt it. Didn't you say Michael was on assignment?"

"He is, but he was weird before he left." Sarah remembered his parting words and repeated them to Lizzy. "In my job I have to do things I'm not always proud of. If you hear things, try to ignore them."

"I don't think he meant treason. I'll see if Peter will give me a hint."

"Cheer up." Lizzy smiled, "What was it you were calling me about?"

"Oh, your baby news is far more interesting than mine. I am so pleased for you and Peter. Are you happy?"

"I am over the moon happy. You've known me a long time and this is what I've always wanted a good marriage and a family, and good friends of course." Lizzy gave Sarah a hug. "You will be Aunt Sarah."

"Thank you, I would like that. You are my best friend, Lizzy. You know that, right?"

"Yes, I do. But I won't be if you don't tell me your news."

"Le Papillon has invited me to their annual exhibition next year. I have an appointment to meet with Mr. Sebastian next week."

"I'm not surprised, you deserve this. Madame's problem has always been jealousy because of her past but that has nothing to do with you. She allowed a disappointment to rule her life. You are not like that."

"I want to show you something." Sarah led Lizzy to the studio and she picked up *Beyond the Storm* and placed it on the easel, stepping back as the power of the painting hit her. She realized it revealed all her inner emotions and as she looked at it again, she was ready to face them all.

Lizzy gasped, her hand on her mouth as she stared. "It is the best you have ever painted. You can't sell it, it's too good. And definitely not to for Le Papillon. But people need to see it."

"Maybe the London Art Gallery. What do you think?" Sarah stood back watching for Lizzy's reaction.

"Excellent idea. Won't they be at the college's Christmas exhibition? I'd show it there—on display but not for sale." Lizzy yawned, "Another side effect of expecting a baby. I'm always tired. The doctor said I should take naps. That's a little difficult when you work. He suggested I quit, but I think I'd like to keep working. I'll be fine as soon as the sickness passes."

"Would you like me to drive you home?"

"No, I'm fine to drive. But I do want to be home when Peter gets in. I am so excited to tell him the news."

As Sarah closed the front door, Johnny came out of Mrs. D's siting room looking serious.

"What's wrong?"

"Mum mad with you with all your phone calls."

"Oh dear, it has been a busy night."

Mrs. Debinski came out of the sitting room and placed a little table at the bottom of the stairs. "I'm moving the phone here. I don't get calls at night, so from now on if the phone rings in the evening you can answer it, and if you're not home people will have to call back. Same with the door: if you're expecting someone, you answer it."

"I'm happy to do that Mrs. D and I'm sorry for the interruptions tonight. I wonder if the GPO would put an extension in my flat? I will inquire."

"That will cost money. Just answer the phone."

"All right. But there is lots of good news tonight. I've been asked to do an art show at Le Papillon and Lizzy's news is the best of all, she is expecting a baby."

Mrs. D's eyes lit up and a smile spread from ear to ear. "A baby, that is good news. Auntie D has a nice ring to it."

Johnny began clapping, "Baby, baby." He put his head to one side, "Where is Miss Lizzy getting the baby from?"

"I'll let your mum answer that. Good night."

Twenty-Seven

Royal College of Art's Annual Exhibition

*S*ubmerged in her own goals and triumphs, six weeks had gone by since her last visit to Bexhill. She stared at the telephone as she replaced the receiver. Dorothy Jenkins had called to say that Anna had taken another fall, this time at the bottom of the stairs. Thankfully, she was only shaken up and not hurt, but she refused to see the doctor. Dorothy went on to say that her writing and instructions were not making sense. She was quiet and at times unresponsive. Dorothy had not actually used the words "losing her mind" but Sarah had to agree that her behaviour was much more than the forgetfulness of old age. The call confirmed Sarah's worst fear; something was wrong with Anna. *I don't know what I'd do without Nana, she's always been my rock. This could be serious.*

Sarah picked up the receiver again and asked the college operator to put her through to the Sackville hotel, explaining it was urgent and she would pay for the call.

"Mrs. Robertson, this is Miss Wexford. Put me through to Mrs. Blaine, please." Sarah expected to wait, but Anna picked up the phone immediately.

"Sarah, is something wrong? It's not like you to call during the day."

"Nothing's wrong, Nana. But Dorothy just told me you had a fall. Are you all right?"

"I told her not to bother you. I'm fine. I just missed the bottom step. No broken bones, just a bruise on my knee, which the rheumatism doesn't like. Aspirin will take care of that. How are you? Are you ready for the exhibition?"

"I'm well, Nana. I'm nervous about the exhibition but everything is ready. Mr. Darwin loves the *Beyond the Storm* painting; I wish you could see it. We open tomorrow, so it's going to be a hectic couple of days. Are you sure you're all right?"

"Sarah, I'm fine. Stop worrying. I have to go; Mr. Grimsby is waiting to see me. Some problems with Mrs. Henderson. Not good timing as we are booked up for a Christmas party."

"I'll be home in a couple of days. Please be careful—no more falls."

"We wish you good luck, darling. We'll be thinking about you. Belle said she and Darcy were going to be in London, so I expect they will visit the exhibition. Grandpa Bill's right here and he's giving you the thumbs up. We'll see you next week."

Stepping aside from the phone, Sarah felt better. Anna sounded fine, but then her calls always did sound fine. How was she able to cover up on the phone but not in person?

Sarah could not settle down. She was pacing her classroom; with no students to teach and the exam papers all graded, she had nothing to do except plan next term's classes, and her brain would not focus on the future. She went to the convocation hall to help Miss Berkley finish the setup. Entering the hall, Sarah gave an involuntary gasped at her own painting, *Beyond the Storm*. It had been placed front and centre as the main feature.

Miss Berkley approached her and said, "When the artist is over-whelmed I know it's an exceptional piece of art." She put her arm around Sarah's shoulders. "Remember what I said to you on graduation day?" Sarah nodded, still not able to speak. "This is what I meant. This will hang in a famous gallery, mark my words, Miss Sarah Wexford. Now, I could do with some help."

Finding her voice, Sarah said, "Thanks, Miss Berkley, you inspired and encouraged me more than you will ever know." She hesitated but quickly moved on before Miss Berkley could speak. "I would love to help, it might calm my nerves."

**

Sleep eluded Sarah well into the night. Her mind would not rest, and when she did fall asleep her dreams were of disappearing paintings, accusing people, and the worst one, a sense of darkness and death, woke her up. She sat bolt upright in her bed, her heart pounding, thankful to be awake and knowing they were only dreams. But she found it hard to shake off the darkness of the last dream. It was still dark outside but a respectable six o'clock, so she made coffee and stared at her wardrobe. "What shall I wear?" Her formal business suits were at Bexhill and she hadn't thought to bring one back for the exhibition. Her taste in clothes was casual: longish wool skirts, embroidered blouses and warm jumpers for cold days and loafers for her feet. Artsy but not acceptable for this occasion. She spotted one pair of black high heels and she did have some stockings. That was a start, and at the far end of the wardrobe were the dresses and skirts she rarely wore. She saw the blue dress she had worn on her first date with Michael. Holding the dress up, she said, "Perfect." For a brief second, she wondered about Michael and wished he could be here and see his *Whispering Trees* on display. He loved art and would appreciate the exhibition. The dress had a matching bolero style jacket, which she could not remember ever wearing, but it was a fashionable outfit, suitable for a famous artist. She giggled, "I guess that's me." She glanced at the clock; somehow she had managed to fritter away two hours.

Wriggling into the Playtex girdle, she cursed, remembering why she never wore such garments. But she needed the suspenders to attach her stockings and it did give her a nice smooth line. Staring into the mirror, she tried to get the brush through her red curls. *Bobby pins*, she thought, remembering how Connie, Lady Thornton's maid, had managed to pin her hair into curls on top of her head.

"Not bad," she said gently pulling some wisps of curls around her face. She opened her dressing table drawer and took out the blue pendant and fastened it around her neck saying, "Well, Great Uncle Bertie, it is my turn to follow my dreams. Work your magic."

Sarah took one last look in the mirror and nodded her approval. She was glad she didn't have to wrestle with the Underground as Lizzy had offered to drive her. The *toot-toot* from outside told her she was waiting. Lizzy was dressed in the latest fashion; a loose-fitting coat hid her growing tummy and she had a cute matching hat. Sarah had never thought about a hat.

"You look lovely, Sarah. I've never seen that outfit before. Is it new?"

"No, I wear the dress sometimes, but this is the first time I've worn the jacket. I like your coat, that *is* new."

"I'm so glad loose-fitting coats are fashionable—I'm putting on weight. My boss has already said she expects me to quit work as soon as I'm showing."

"That doesn't seem fair."

"I'm in the slim, thin fashion industry. Weight gain, even in pregnancy, is a sin. On the bright side, the morning sickness has passed. Let's stop talking about me. Today is your day and you look fabulous. Are you nervous?"

"A little. My painting, the one I showed you, is in the centre of the hall—the first painting people see when they walk in. Miss Berkley told me last nigh that I'm famous. I'm not sure I'm ready for this. Thanks for coming with me, it means a lot."

"Hey, I'm your best friend. I'll always stick by your side," Lizzy giggled, "You can pay me back by babysitting my son or daughter."

"That's' a promise."

**

Come on, let's see what's happening. It's open to invited guests only this morning, so it'll be quiet," Sarah said, pushing the big oak doors open into the lobby. They took their coats off in the cloakroom and walked towards the Convocation Hall. Sarah stopped as she saw about twenty people standing around *Beyond the Storm*. Mr. Darwin beckoned to her and she grabbed Lizzy's hand and pulled her along with her. Mr. Darwin took her elbow and guided her to the front of the painting.

"Gentlemen, I would like to present Miss Sarah Wexford, the creator of this fine painting and one of our most talented emerging artists. Miss Wexford is a graduate of the college and this autumn she joined our staff." Sarah wasn't sure what to do, except smile. Lizzy had stepped back as the cameras started flashing. She looked at Mr. Darwin, "Sir! What's going on?"

"The press is invited to take pictures for the arts magazines before the dealers or public showings."

The group moved around the exhibition and Lizzy moved to her side as Miss Berkley joined them. "I'm sorry, I should have warned you about the press. Mr. Darwin doesn't like them wandering around once the guests arrive so they come early. I'm pleased they took photographs of you."

"It was a bit of a surprise. Miss Berkley, I'd like you to meet my best friend, Mrs. Lizzy Langford. Lizzy studied fashion here."

"Hello. I remember you, Lizzy Elliot. You two were always together through college. Didn't you go to Jacob's Fashions?"

"Yes, and I still work for them."

"I asked Lizzy to come along for support and I'm glad I did."

"The doors don't officially open until noon. Did Mr. Darwin ask you to come early?"

"Mr. Darwin said ten o'clock. I didn't question the time."

Miss Berkley nodded. "We have a cafe set up where you can get hot drinks and biscuits. I'll come and fetch you if the press wants an interview."

"Interview?" Sarah gulped and almost choked on air.

Miss Berkley smiled, "I told you that you would be famous. Take a deep breath and you will be fine. Now I must go and join the group."

The cafe turned out to be a cordoned off piece of the lobby with small round tables and chairs. They ordered tea and biscuits. Lizzy munched hungrily on the biscuits and Sarah stared into her tea, excited and scared. Lizzy touched her hand. "Are you going to be all right?"

"It's a bit overwhelming and kind of exciting. Do you know if Felix is coming? Nana said she thought Belle and Darcy would be here."

"I'm not sure. Peter was working today. That case they are working on is very complicated and the security level is so high that Peter is afraid to say anything to me. I'm used to him not being able to discuss clients, but this is different."

"I haven't seen Felix for a while. I'd like to know who it is that's involved in the case that we are supposed to know. I hope it's not Michael."

Miss Berkley tapped Sarah on the shoulder, the press is leaving, but the reporter from *Artist Now* magazine would like to talk to you."

Sarah actually enjoyed the interview. She was asked what inspired her art and she was able to tell them about Emily Carr and her trip to the Pacific Coast of Canada.

The doors were officially opened at noon and people flocked in. Sarah noticed there was always a group of people around her paintings, and she answered many questions about the other pieces of West Coast art. Few British people knew Emily Carr's work and Sarah liked talking about her art and the artists she'd worked with and the Haida Indians and native people. Suddenly, she felt her spine tingle and a warm breath on her neck. "How's my favourite artist?" She swung round to find Felix standing behind her. She wanted to give him a hug, but thankfully thought better of it as she saw Lorraine walking towards them with Belle. He put his hand on her shoulder and squeezed slightly, "Lorraine arrived unexpectedly. She's staying at Hillcrest Hall."

Lorraine put her hand out to Sarah who politely shook the same insipid limp hand she had been offered in the past. "What a surprise.

I'm assuming you are here for Christmas?" Sarah said, being as sweet as she could. Felix excused himself and joined his father talking to art collectors and critics. Sarah watched them for a moment, noticing the father son tension had disappeared. Miss Berkley asked her to meet some people and Lizzy entertained Lorraine and Belle.

Standing in front of *Beyond the Storm,* she spoke with Mr. Darwin's colleague from the London Art gallery. "Robin has been talking about your paintings for some time. Young lady, I had no idea. This one is exceptional."

"Thank you, sir. It is my favourite and my best work so far."

He shook his head, "I can only imagine what you might create in ten, twenty, thirty years time. You are a cute little filly" Sarah felt her cheeks redden. "Your modesty becomes you, my dear." He winked and Sarah took a step backwards, bumping into Darcy.

"Sarah, I'm sorry. Are you alright?" He turned to the man. "Sir William, how are you? Still collecting art?"

"Lord Thornton, I am well and I trust you and your family are too. Robin was telling me about this young lady's art and I am hoping this will go in the London Gallery."

"Sarah is indeed a talented artist. I have known her for most of her life. Mr. and Mrs. Blaine, Sarah's grandparents, are old friends."

Sarah smiled, seeing Sir William back away and was pleased Darcy had stepped in.

Darcy whispered, "He's a womanizer—never be alone with him. But he's an incredibly knowledgeable and influential man in the art world."

"Thank you for rescuing me."

"Glad I was here. What are you doing after the show? Do you have to stay or can we take you for dinner later?"

"I don't have to stay. But I'm with Lizzy and she might have to leave."

Lizzy had told Belle and Lorraine her news, so the women were engrossed in baby talk and delighted that they could continue on during dinner.

Belle and Darcy were proud of Sarah and delighted with Lizzy and Peter's news and turned dinner into be a double celebration. They must have sensed Sarah's apprehension at dinner as they sat one on each side of her. Lizzy, Peter and Lorraine were totally immersed in wedding and baby talk. Sarah noted that Felix seemed to be on the outside, more interested in smiling across the table. An act that she was pretty sure had not escaped Lorraine.

Sarah declined a nightcap at the townhouse and Darcy sent her home in the Rolls. As Harris opened the door for her, Mrs. D was at her window post, Sarah smiled.

"Miss Sarah, you look lovely tonight. And congratulations, I hear the exhibition went well."

"Thank you, Harris." He doffed his cap and Sarah put her key in the door. She flung her shoes off before climbing the stairs; her feet hurt and now she needed to get the wretched girdle off so she could breath. She flopped on the bed, completely overwhelmed; happy and excited—the evening events all seemed a blur.

The exhibition was to continue tomorrow and she wasn't sure she could handle another day. One thing she wanted more than anything was her friend Felix. She knew her art was good but the response had been enormous and far surpassed anything she could possibly have expected, excited and scared at the same time she wondered what it all meant. Felix would make sense of it all. And she couldn't deny she was curious about Lorraine's sudden visit. It was obvious to her that Belle was not welcoming of the visit and Felix didn't seem overjoyed either, but that could be due to his work schedule.

Twenty-Eight

Solving the Sackville Problems

Sarah woke late. Stretching, she was relieved it was Sunday and she could relax. Her back and legs ached from two days of standing at the exhibition. Her head felt as if it might explode with all the information and questions. She smiled at her own success at being able to mingle and talk to art collectors and admirers as though she'd been doing it for years and without either Felix or Lizzy's support. In fact, she thought she managed better being alone than constantly looking for approval. "About time," she whispered to herself.

Felix had gone to Hillcrest to spend time with Lorraine, and why shouldn't he? They were engaged, she reminded herself. But they were not the same loving couple she had seen a few months ago. "And why does that bother you?" she said aloud, answering her own question. "Because I don't want to see Felix get hurt." She moved her focus to other interesting events.

Madame and Mr. Sebastian had stared at *Beyond the Storm* for ten minutes or more and said nothing. Sarah watched from a distance. It was an odd scene. All indications suggested that Mr. Sebastian had a leaning towards homosexuality, until she had seen Madame slowly and carefully entwine her fingers in his and he had held her hand, giving her a subtle affectionate glance; familiar gestures that suggested Madame and Mr. Sebastian were lovers. *Interesting,* she thought. *I had better wander over and thank them for coming.*

"Madame, Mr. Sebastian, how lovely to see you. I hope you are enjoying the exhibition." Sarah smiled and Madame smiled back but stayed silent.

"Oh, oh it is magnificent, exquisite, such depth." Mr. Sebastian's compliments were accompanied by flourishing gestures of adoration for both Sarah and the painting, making Sarah blush. As though on cue, Lizzy and Peter walked into the hall and things became even more interesting. Madame's face drained so white that even the copious amounts of rouge on her cheeks paled when Peter joined the group. Mr. Sebastian addressed Madame by her first name, Cecilia, and whispered something. They immediately excused themselves and left the building. Sarah looked to Peter for an explanation but he brushed it off as confidential legal business. After a quick visit, they too left, with Lizzy promising to call Sarah later.

She shuddered, thinking of Sir William, who had been skulking around her several times, possibly trying to find an opportunity to pinch her bottom, and she found herself playing cat and mouse around the gallery. Aware of his influence, she hadn't dared be blunt and tell the creep to get lost. Seeing the group at the painting he had announced that it was not for sale. Sarah bristled at the words afraid that Sir William wanted to buy it not for the London Gallery but for his private collection. She approached the group.

"Sir William is correct, the *Beyond the Storm* is not for sale at this time." She glanced at Sir William. "I would like to see this painting exhibited where the public can enjoy it. Don't you agree, Sir William?"

"Splendid idea."

As the crowd thinned out, Sarah bid everyone good night and went to her flat to pack some things for Bexhill; a week tomorrow would be Christmas Day. Tomorrow she had a meeting at the college in the morning then she was off for three weeks. *Not much of a holiday,* she thought, *working at the Sackville.* But it would be a change of pace and time to spend with Nana. Perhaps a longer stay would reveal Dorothy's concerns.

**

Tuesday morning, Sarah joined Anna and Bill for breakfast. Having decided to take the hotel business seriously, mornings were a good time to catch up on the staff, bookings, guests and parties. It also meant she could be selfish and get in a few hours of painting in the afternoons.

"How did the art show go?" Anna asked.

"As far as I know, really well. I won't know if I sold any paintings until I get back in January. But the interest in my paintings was overwhelming, particularly as the purpose of the annual exhibition is really to show off the student talent. I think the buyers and collectors come more as a social event."

Bill stood up to pour more coffee and Sarah was pleased to see that he walked without a cane and generally looked well.

"Bill is back in the kitchen part-time. Chef Brian is taking over and doing well. We promoted him to executive chef and Bill monitors when necessary." Anna laughed, "And sometimes when it's not necessary." Anna squeezed his hand. Sarah loved it when she saw the affection they had for each other.

"Dinner was excellent last night, so I had a feeling you were back. But I think Chef Brian has learned to cook to your high standards, Grandpa Bill. What about housekeeping?"

Anna sighed. "Not so good. Mrs. Henderson alienates her staff—the maids are in tears half the time and angry the other half. Unless Amy is here, the rooms are only adequate, and guests are always calling down for clean towels. I wish Amy would come back full time."

"Nana, Amy wants to retire. Where is she now?"

"Getting ready for a family Christmas. She and Sam host the whole family; I've lost count of how many grandchildren she has now." Anna got up, rubbing her knee. She moved to her desk and picked up a photo. "She gave me this lovely family photo before she left on Friday. I remember Amy as a tiny laundry maid, the first maid I set eyes on when I came here. She was thirteen, an orphan and the hardest working maid, even back then." Anna gazed off into space. "I miss her. I miss James and the others. I miss the old times." She stared in silence, a slight smile on her lips. Suddenly, she took a deep breath. "What were we talking about?"

Bill answered, "Mrs. Henderson. We should have fired her weeks ago."

Anna ignored Bill and said, "Sarah, I'll have to ask you to deal with Mrs. Henderson; she won't listen to me."

"Oh, I'll deal with her alright. I don't understand—I hired her and her references were good. Nana, can you pass me her file?"

Sarah had noticed the lapse of concentration, or was it just thinking of old times? Watching her at the filing cabinet was more worrying; she seemed to have forgotten what she was looking for. Bill jumped up, found the file and passed it to Sarah.

Studying the file, she noticed the documented complaints from Amy and Mr. Grimsby. She scanned her application and the letter of reference.

"There are enough complaints to fire her. She just doesn't seem to learn." Sarah looked at her watch, "See you two later. I'm going to meet with Mrs. Henderson and the maids."

**

The story from the maids matched what Anna had told Sarah. She noticed that Lily, the head maid, seemed to be taking control. Mrs. Henderson was nowhere to be found, and it was 8:30.

"Lily, can I speak with you?" Sarah took the master keys and unlocked the door to Mrs. Henderson's sitting room.

Lily stood back. "Nobody is allowed in there, Miss Wexford."

"Why not?" Sarah gasped; the mess was terrible. Newspapers were piled up to overflowing and half-finished crossword puzzles, dirty cups, plates and glasses were strewn everywhere. Sarah bent down to pick up some papers and immediately deduced the problem as she gathered betting slips off the floor. Mrs. Henderson had a gambling problem.

"What are you doing in my sitting room?" Mrs. Henderson's voice boomed. "Lily, get out."

Lily's eyes widened with fear. Sarah touched her arm to reassure her but she jumped away. "Lily, you are not in trouble; don't be afraid. I need to talk to Mrs. Henderson. We can finish our conversation later. I would like you to go back to your duties and I'll meet with you in Mrs. Blaine's office at ten o'clock."

Lily's reaction shook Sara. Lily was not reassured, and wouldn't be while Mrs. Henderson was in the picture. She turned to the pompous woman standing with pursed lips and folded arms.

"You can wipe that look off your face, Mrs. Henderson. How come you are arriving an hour late for work and in your coat and hat? It is a requirement of your employment that you live on the premises with one day off per week, which I believe is Saturday."

"I went for a walk because I have a headache."

"Not good enough. I'd suggest we sit down and talk about this, but there is nowhere to sit—this room is a disgrace. The last time I was here I asked you to clean it up."

"I can keep my room however I want. I don't need young snippets like you telling me what to do." Her last words quivered as she threw her head back, sticking her nose in the air.

"Young or not, you report to me." Sarah threw the betting slips on the table. "You have a gambling problem."

"No, I don't. Those belong to a friend." Taken off guard, she swayed slightly. Her fingers held the edge of the table; defiance turned to anguish.

"You need help. Are you in debt? Do you owe money to anyone?" Mrs. Henderson didn't answer. "I'm sorry. I have no choice but to let you go. I've looked at your file. I've talked to Mr. Grimsby and Mrs. Blaine and they have given you several chances. It seems you hid your gambling when Mrs. Peterson was here but take advantage when she's not."

"Please, Miss Wexford give me another chance." Tears brimmed on her eyelids and her face revealed a sad, frightened woman. Sarah thought that was perhaps the real Mrs. Henderson.

Sarah shook her head. "This has happened before, hasn't it? I only just noticed it in your letter of reference: 'Works well when she's here.' I didn't pay any attention to it. Perhaps you are a good housekeeper when you work. I can't be here all the time, so I need someone reliable that can take charge. Please pack your things and I'll have Mrs. Robertson make up your pay for the rest of this week and an extra week in lieu of notice. No reference. I suggest you try another line of work. Do you have family you can go to?"

"I have a sister in London. She might take me in for a while." Sarah looked at her with surprise. Her attitude was compliant, almost as though she had expected the outcome.

"I advise you not to gamble away your pay and get some help. Once you are packed, Mr. Grimsby will bring you your wages and escort you off the premises."

Sarah walked out of the room and up to the lobby. She felt terrible. She wondered how many times her sister had taken her in and would she this time? Sarah knew she would gamble her last pay and probably finish up on the streets of London. It wasn't a good feeling, but she had no choice.

Dorothy and Mrs. Robertson were in conversation about an upcoming party when Sarah arrived in the lobby and Mr. Grimsby happened to be at the reception desk.

"Just the people I want to see. I have terminated Mrs. Henderson effective immediately. She is packing her things now. Mrs. Robertson, make up her wages, what she is owed plus an extra week. Mr. Grimsby, I would like you to give her the envelope and make sure she leaves the premises. She will be catching the London train."

Mr. Grimsby spoke first, "I'm glad to see that one go."

216

"Long overdue, but I'm wondering how we will manage. We are fully booked over Christmas," Dorothy added.

"Mrs. Henderson didn't do much anyway, except upset the maids. Lily has a good head on her shoulders and I think she will encourage the young maids. I'll help where I can. Mr. Grimsby, can you ask Woody to clean out the housekeeper's sitting room? It is a terrible mess. Excuse me, I need to tell Mrs. Blaine."

Sarah tapped on Anna's door and opened it quietly. Anna was standing by the window staring into the horizon. "Calm, grey days like this often mean a storm is brewing," she said without turning to look at Sarah.

"Nana, I might just have caused a bit of a storm."

"Oh, what did you do?"

"I fired Mrs. Henderson. She is packing as we speak. I know I should have consulted you, but the opportunity was there and I took it. Did I do the right thing?"

"It needed to be done. I should have done it weeks ago. Amy kept telling me there was something wrong with her. I've never been good at the firing thing."

"There was something wrong; she has a gambling problem. I found betting slips in her sitting room, which is a disgusting mess. I sent Woody to clean out all the papers and junk."

"Gambling, that's easy to hide. What are we going to do for a housekeeper?" Anna said with a sigh.

"I'll help out. Can we hire an extra maid for Christmas? I'll put Lily in charge for now. She is young but has a lot of potential and seems mature. How old is she?" Sarah couldn't help comparing Lily to herself, it had not escaped her that the staff respected her mostly as Mrs. Blaine's granddaughter but not as the boss. Was she putting Lily in the same position?

"If I remember, she's older than you. I don't think age has anything to do with ability. Lily is capable; I was the same age as you when I took over during the Great War. Lily deserves a chance; give her a

217

trial period while you are here and I'm sure we could persuade Amy to train her during the winter months. Hiring an outsider is always risky. Mrs. Henderson proved that. And Sarah, you handled this very well. I'm not so good at it these days."

Sarah thought she saw another opening to find out if Anna had a problem she would admit to. "What's wrong, Nana? You don't seem yourself."

"Nothing, I'm just getting old and I don't like it. It's getting more difficult to deal with the hotel problems. All my treasured staff have gone and I have no one to rely on except my Bill, and his health worries me. There's Dorothy, of course, who is only a couple of years younger than me. And you, but you're in London most of the time."

"I don't think Dorothy is going anywhere soon. Mr. Grimsby may not be James, but he's an excellent general manager. Chef Brian has the kitchen and dining room running smoothly. I can't be here all the time. I work in London. I have students and a college that rely on me. I promise I'll do whatever I can from London." Sarah thought about telling Anna she would consider coming back to Bexhill at the end of the college year, but she wasn't sure that was true.

She opened her mouth to continue, but realizing she was only making excuses, she stopped. Anna stared out to sea again. "Nana, are you going to tell me what's bothering you?"

"Nothing's bothering me. Go on, I'm listening."

"I have three weeks to help you get things sorted out. Christmas will be a success, it always is. And afterwards we will have lots of time together."

Anna had moved to her desk and sat down, smiling, "I'm looking forward to time together. Perhaps we could take a day off and go to Eastbourne for the Boxing Day sales."

"I'd like that, Nana. I could do with some new shoes and I'd like one of those new loose-fitting coats. Lizzy has one. Nana, I almost forgot to tell you, Lizzy and Peter are expecting a baby. We could pick up a present for the baby."

Twenty-Nine

Christmas 1962 - Ringing in 1963

*T*he New Sackville Hotel glistened and sang with Christmas cheer. Robust, joyous Christmas carols rang out from the lobby. Sarah and Anna joined the guests to celebrate Christmas Eve. Colourful presents overflowed from under the ten-foot-tall tree. The tradition of a present for each guest had been going on for fifteen or more years. Isabelle had started it. Sarah glanced at her grandmother and realized that the tradition had become a tribute to her lost daughter.

Anna glanced at the time and wished everyone a Happy Christmas. "We had better get downstairs; the staff will be waiting." Another tradition was that the staff had their own Christmas tree and every member of staff got a personal present from Anna and Bill. This year, Sarah noticed two things different: the labels were typed, not handwritten, confirming Sarah's thought that things were getting too difficult for Anna, and her name had been added at the side of Anna and Bill's.

Bill led his kitchen crew into the crowded staff dining room and Sarah suggested that Lily, as acting head housekeeper, help hand out the presents. She impressed Sarah as she managed the situation with confidence and the staff seemed to accept her new position without resentment. *I think you will do very nicely, Mrs. Midwinter.*

Housekeepers were always known as Mrs., whether or not they were married, a tradition from the manor houses and estates of high society. Sarah considered the tradition a bit archaic, but it served the purpose of raising Lily's authority. The title of Mrs. always seemed more respectable. Sarah wondered if she should change from Miss then remembered her mother was Mrs. Wexford.

**

New Year's Eve day, Sarah kept busy checking on the tables, the menu and anything else she could find to avoid Felix and Lorraine. The Thorntons had arrived the day before. They always stayed for several days over New Year's and usually Sarah enjoyed their visits, but the addition of Lorraine, who seemed to have taken on the role of Lady Thornton in waiting, was more than she could handle.

Having successfully avoided the Thorntons and her family all day, she sat at her dressing table in her bedroom, conjuring up an excuse not to attend the dinner, dance and New Year toasts, but knowing it was not an option. The thought of watching Felix kiss Lorraine Happy New Year made her feel sick as she remembered the kiss that should never have happened in Felix's car. She stared at her reflection, "Sarah, what are you thinking? Felix is engaged to be married. Whether or not you like Lorraine is immaterial, and it would behoove you to try and like her, as she is going to be your oldest and dearest friend's wife. Do you want to lose him altogether?" Resolving to be pleasant to Lorraine and enjoy the evening, she took an emerald green, full-length strapless evening gown from her wardrobe and smiled. The tight-fitting bodice showed off her trim figure and bared her creamy, sensual shoulders, to say nothing of how the emerald green reflected her hazel eyes. She piled her hair on top of her head; sophisticated, with soft wisps of red curls around her face heightening the sensuality. She chuckled. "Who could resist? I'll be very pleasant tonight." Dinner was seven-thirty and Sarah decided to be fashionably late.

As she entered the Emily Carr Dining Room, heads turned to watch this beautiful young woman with flaming red hair and bewitching hazel eyes dressed in a gown the colour of the Irish countryside glide to the VIP table. Sarah's lips twitched with a smile as Felix's mouth dropped open and Lorraine kicked him under the table. *Mission accomplished, now I'll be nice to Lorraine.* Balaji pulled out the chair between Bill and Darcy and she sat down, pretending not to notice the looks of admiration. Bill leaned towards her and whispered, "Quite the entrance. I think you made your point."

"And what point would that be, Grandpa?" She whispered back with a grin and kissed his cheek.

"I think you know," he whispered and then spoke normally. "My darling Sarah, you look beautiful. I am so proud of you."

Anna nodded. "Me too. Your mother could wear emerald green and tonight you look just like your her."

"Thanks Nana. It's because of you two, stepping in for Mum that has made me who I am. I'll always be grateful." Sarah felt overwhelmed with gratitude and love. Close to tears she added, "Let's celebrate and eat!"

The table returned to general chatter as the meal was served. Sarah patted Bill's hand to reassure him not to worry about the meal. He didn't really like being on the "other side" as he would say. Tonight was Chef Brian's first New Year's dinner, and a fine dinner it was. The quartet played soft music in the background while the waiters served the main course.

Suddenly, Lorraine beckoned Balaji to the table. "My meal is quite cold." Bill frowned looking at all the plates and all were steaming including Lorraine's. Balaji called Eddie to the table, whispered something and the meal was removed. Balaji gave Bill a worried look. "My apologies, Miss Howser."

"I would think so. Make sure it is hot." Lorraine's face turned red as every table within earshot stared at her.

Bill excused himself, following Eddie into the kitchen. Chef Brian stopped what he was doing and frowned at Bill. "Is something wrong,

Chef?"

"A complaint at my table that the food was not hot." Bill took the plate from Eddie and looked puzzled. "This plate is hot. Just make up another plate as hot as you can and as fast as you can. I'm not sure what this lady's problem is."

Bill returned to the table followed by Eddie holding the plate with a white serving cloth and placed it in front of Lorraine. Felix leaned towards her and whispered, "What was that all about?" Lorraine ignored him and gave Eddie a sweet smile, saying, "Thank you so much, that was kind of you." Everyone kept their heads down and the table fell into a tense silence.

Anna always requested there be a timely break before desert for those who wished to have a smoke and let their meals digest.

The quartet was replaced by a dance band and guests tapped their feet to the sounds of Glen Miller. Bill took Anna's hand and moved to the dance floor. The guests clapped as they spun around in a waltz, inviting everyone to join them. Halfway through the dance, Anna sat down and Bill took Sarah's hand on to the now crowded dance floor, followed by Felix and Lorraine. Sarah could feel Felix's eyes on her back and she smiled, waiting for him to ask her to dance. The music stopped and he returned Lorraine to the table; before Sarah could sit down and before Lorraine could object, he scooped Sarah onto the dance floor.

"Sarah, you look more beautiful tonight than I ever remember. I want to dance with you all evening."

"Stop teasing. You are not being fair to Lorraine and she does not look happy. Why did she complain about the food? That really upset Grandpa Bill."

"I don't know, but she's been bossing everyone around. I'm not sure things are going to work out. She's changed and…" Felix stopped. Sarah waited and listened. He said nothing more until the music came to an end. "I miss my best friend. I wish we could talk." He tightened his arm around her back and brushed his cheek against

222

hers. Sarah lifted her head and as Felix tried to smile, she saw regret, even sorrow beneath it.

"Maybe later, Lorraine is already on her feet claiming the next dance." Sarah moved back to her seat.

The evening passed quickly and the not so hot meal seemed to be forgotten as the table laughed and danced. The waiter prepared the traditional whisky and champagne toast and at five minutes before midnight, Anna, Bill and Sarah stood by the bandleader. Anna made her usual speech and toasted Alex and Isabelle. Sarah was filled with a strange feeling as the roar went up "To Alex and Isabelle," followed by, "Happy New Year." Shivers rippled down her spine as she raised her glass. Instinctively she sensed this was the last time she would make this toast.

**

The day after New Year's Day the ladies planned a shopping trip to Eastbourne. Lorraine declined, saying she and Felix had plans. Sarah, Anna and Belle sighed with relief.

Harris drove them into Eastbourne in the Rolls so they could chat in the back. The subject of Lorraine had been avoided since New Year's Eve dinner, mostly because there wasn't an opportunity to comment without Lorraine hearing.

Anna took a deep breath, "I'm going to ask the question: What is going on with Lorraine?"

Belle shook her head. "I don't know, but she arrived at Hillcrest unannounced. Even Felix didn't know she was coming. She said she wanted to spend Christmas with Felix and get to know his family. It has been a difficult visit and I have no idea when she's returning to Canada."

"What do you mean difficult?" Anna asked. Sarah had decided to just listen.

"She's taken it upon herself to order the staff about. She's pretty much taken over my maid, Connie, and Harris is being diplomatic but I can see his exasperation. Cook threatened to quit unless I forbade her to go to the kitchen. I spent some time with her explaining how staff are treated and the ins and outs of estate living. She's a school teacher, so I wouldn't expect her to know, but she won't be taught."

"So, that's what that outburst at dinner was all about. What are you going to do?"

"I don't know. Both Darcy and Felix have tried to explain to her how to treat staff, but she ignores us all. The part that worries me is she has no respect for Felix and frankly doesn't care about him. I doubt she loves him; she's in love with being lady of the manor. It isn't going to end well and I'm afraid Felix is going to get hurt."

"Can you talk to Felix?"

"I'm reluctant. Felix knows his father doesn't think Lorraine is good enough for him or the estate. I'm trying to be neutral and not interfere. I remember how Darcy's mother was with me; she did not approve of me, a commoner and American. I don't want to be unkind to Lorraine. I keep saying this is my son's choice not mine."

Anna laughed. "I remember Lady Thornton literally dismissing you, and at the time I thought Darcy was dating you just to upset his mother."

"I think at first there was some truth in that, but we fell in love and our love has been passionate ever since." Harris pulled the car to a halt outside the Grand Hotel. Belle glanced at Sarah. "No more talk of Lorraine. Let's enjoy our day shopping. Harris, pick us up here at five, please."

Sarah found the coat she was looking for in a pale green. Anna found her a small hat to match, which Sarah refused when she saw the price. "Nana, you missed a zero, its £20 not £2."

By four o'clock they each had several carrier bags in their hands and bags and parcels tucked under their arms. The doorman at the Grand relieved them of the parcels on their way to the lounge for afternoon tea. Anna picked up the menu, pointed at something and smiled at the waiter. He gave her an odd look and Sarah leaned over to see what she had ordered. "Nana, that's a party order of champagne and hors d'oeuvre. I think we want afternoon tea." The waiter smiled and nodded.

It suddenly occurred to Sarah what was wrong with Anna; she couldn't see. "Nana, you need new glasses. You can't see properly."

"I'm okay. It's numbers that are difficult." It all became clear to Sarah: the messy filing system, the price tickets, pouring tea until it overflowed the cup, and now the menu.

"I might as well tell you two. I'm going blind. I can't read any more, I haven't been able to decipher numbers in months and now..." she looked at Sarah, "I can hardly see you. Everything is blurred."

"Dorothy tried to tell me there was something wrong. She couldn't make sense of your notes. She thought you were having difficulty remembering and planning. She didn't know you couldn't see."

"I've passed as much as I can over to Mr. Grimsby and Dorothy. I dictate what I can to Mrs. Robertson."

"What does Dr. Gregory say?"

"I haven't told him," Anna replied wiping tears. "I'm really afraid. I'm almost blind. I haven't told Bill either. I'm surprised he hasn't guessed. I haven't read a book in over a year."

Sarah took Anna's hand. "First we must tell Bill and then we'll get you an appointment with Dr. Gregory."

Belle wrapped her arm around her shoulder and added, "We can get you in privately. Darcy knows a good eye doctor in Harley Street. Anna, they can do all kinds of operations on eyes now. I'm sure something can be done to save your sight. You must be so worried. It's going to be okay."

"I have been so afraid to tell you, and now I am very glad I did."
**

On their return to the Sackville, an extremely distraught Felix was pacing the lobby. He and Lorraine had had a big fight and Lorraine had marched off in a temper and had not returned to the hotel. Bill had loaned him the Hillman, but he couldn't find her anywhere. Belle managed to calm Felix. Everyone was sure she would turn up soon, but by eight that night there was still no sign of Lorraine, and without voicing it, people were beginning to think something had happened to her and Darcy called the police. She was found in a small hotel, three streets over. Felix picked her up and brought her back to the Sackville. She went to her room with Felix close on her heels, apologizing.

Anna and Belle, while relieved that she had come to no harm, were convinced the whole thing was a ploy to make Felix feel guilty. And it had worked. The following day, Felix returned to London, leaving Lorraine to return to Hillcrest with Darcy and Belle. He promised to go to Hillcrest that Saturday. Lorraine was still sulking over the argument and stayed in her room until Harris picked up her bags. Sarah was happy to see her go and felt sorry for Belle. True to her word, before they left Bexhill, Belle had made arrangements for Anna to see the eye specialist the following week.

The New Year's hotel guests were mostly gone by the end of the week, so the part-time staff went on their way and the permanent staff relaxed a little. Sarah managed to get some painting done. She wanted to complete the last Bexhill seascape for the dining room. The first, *Ladies Spinning Parasols* hung in the dining room. The second one, *Bexhill Summer at the Beach*, needed some finishing touches, but right now she was working on the last one, *A Bexhill Winter Storm*. Sarah wasn't sure why storms evoked such passion in her. This latest painting had moved her in the same way that *Beyond the Storm* had and she felt her internal turmoil spread onto the canvas. She didn't know what it was, just that it was there. It fragmented into thoughts about Felix, about Nana's eyes, the success of her painting in London, her gratitude to her grandparents and duty to the Sackville, her love for Marcus seemed to hang on and a different kind of love for Michael crept in, but there was nothing she could specifically define. Tomorrow they would know more about Anna's eyes.

Thirty

Sarah is Famous

~⚬✿⚬~

B ill insisted they take a taxi from Paddington. Anna said it wasn't necessary, but as much as she tried she couldn't hide the pain in her knees and she twisted her hands nervously. Harley Street looked like any other London street, rows of houses painted white at street level and brick above, black iron railings around the basements and tiny balconies. Charladies vigorously polished the shiny brass name plates. Mr. W. H. Turner's plate caught the sunlight, making it easy to find. Bill pushed the equally polished brass doorbell labeled "Patients and Visitors". A nurse opened the door and smiled, ushering them into a comfortable waiting room, furnished and decorated like a drawing room. It was nothing like any doctor's surgery Sarah had ever been in before.

The nurse took Anna into a small anteroom. Sarah jumped up but the nurse motioned for her to stay seated. Bill and Sarah stared at the door where Anna had disappeared. It was quiet. The nurse appeared from another door with a tray of tea and biscuits.

Sarah asked, "Where is Mrs. Blaine? She's very nervous. Can't I be with her?"

The nurse smiled her nurse's smile, which annoyed Sarah. "Mrs. Blaine is with the doctor now. It will take about half an hour for him to complete his examination. When he is ready, I will come and

227

call you and he will talk to you." She smiled reassuringly. "She's in good hands." This time Sarah did feel reassured. She took Bill's hand. "She's going to be okay, Grandpa."

"Would you like me to pour your tea, Miss Blaine?"

"Oh, no thank you. I can manage. I am Mrs. Blaine's granddaughter but my name is Sarah Wexford. Thank you for the tea."

"Excuse me, but are you Sarah Wexford the famous artist?"

"Yes, I am an artist. But I'm not sure about being famous."

"Mr. Turner and I, I'm his wife, attended the Royal College of Art's Christmas show. I'm really taken with your art." A shrill phone rang from the reception area. "Excuse me, I have to get that."

Bill squeezed her hand. "How about that, someone recognized you." Sarah couldn't stop grinning; it felt so good to be famous.

By the time they had drunk the tea, they heard an intercom and the nurse, escorted them into the surgeon's office. Sarah gave Anna a worried glance but then saw that she was smiling.

"Please take a seat. I have just explained to Mrs. Blaine that she has cataracts in both eyes. It is a film that grows gradually over the lens. As it gets larger over many years, it impedes and blurs vision. Mrs. Blaine's cataracts are both very advanced, which is actually a good thing. There is no treatment for cataracts except surgery to remove the lens and replace it with an artificial lens, and we have to wait until the cataract is large enough before we can remove it. In Mrs. Blaine's, case we can remove them right away. We will do one eye at a time, with about a one to two-month break, allowing the first surgery to heal before doing the second one."

Sarah spoke cautiously, "Will she be able to see normally after the surgery?"

"Most certainly. Patients tell me the clarity of vision is like a miracle, even with just the one eye."

"When can you do the surgery?" Bill asked.

"I can book Mrs. Blaine into the clinic next week as a private patient. Under National Health I'm afraid there is a long waiting list."

Bill didn't hesitate. "Private is no problem, Mr. Turner." Bill turned to Anna. "As soon as possible, right dear?" Anna nodded, smiling from ear to ear.

As they climbed into the taxi, Anna said, "I'm not going blind! That is such a relief."

"I couldn't work out what was wrong," Bill said, rubbing his chin.

"You knew. I thought I'd hidden it from you, Bill. I thought Sarah would figure out something was wrong, but not you."

"I knew something was wrong, but you wouldn't tell me. Dorothy thought you were going senile; falling off the stairs, none of your notes made sense to anyone, spilling tea. I want you to promise me if anything else happens you will tell me."

"I will. I wasn't being fair to you. I'm sorry."

The train was on time for a change and Bill had left the Hillman at the station, so they were home in time for dinner with the good news.

Sarah took a walk to Amy's house. She hadn't had chance to tell Amy that Mrs. Henderson had been fired and Lily was acting housekeeper. With today's good news, Anna would be back at work in a couple of months, but she needed Amy's help. Amy agreed to come in three mornings a week until April, after that she and Sam would be at the caravan. Sarah thanked her, grateful for her help, and joined Anna and Bill for dinner to give them the good news.

Intending to paint, Sarah went up to the penthouse after dinner to put the finishing touches to the storm and beach paintings, but exhaustion took over and it was early morning before the paintings were finished. She planned to give them to Anna before going back to London. She smiled, knowing that after the surgery Anna would be able to see them properly.

**

Sunday traveling on British rail could be a nightmare due to track repairs and maintenance, and today the train was two hours late getting into Paddington. Sarah hopped a taxi, not wanting to face the Underground. Johnny was waiting and she wondered how he managed to always know when she was coming home. Mrs. D told her he stood and waited, patient and excited. He ran out to the taxi and took her suitcase. She gave him a bear hug and two boxes of chocolates from the hotel, one for him and one for Mrs. D. She said goodnight and sat in her sitting room appreciating the quiet. It had been a hectic two weeks and this coming week would also be frenzied in a different way. Anna was having surgery on Tuesday and would be in the clinic for a few days, and college started Monday, although classes didn't start until Wednesday. She was hoping for good news from Mr. Darwin about the London Gallery. Just thinking about it made her tired. And then the phone rang; she waited, thinking it couldn't be for her as she'd only just got back, but Mrs. D's irritated voice yelled up the stairs, "Phone's for you, Sarah."

"Hello, Felix. What's wrong?"

"I need to see you." The tremor in his voice scared Sarah.

"Can we go out to eat. I haven't had dinner."

Felix arrived in ten minutes and they walked to the cafe to eat.

"Lorraine disappeared again. It appears she's gone back to Canada."

"You look worried," Sarah said.

"After the fight at Bexhill, she went back to Hillcrest with Mum and Dad. She had a fight with Harris about the car. I'm not clear on what happened, but whatever it was, my father was so angry he told her it was not her place to order the staff about and asked her to apologize to Harris. She called me in tears. I told her I would go to Hillcrest as promised on Saturday. She hung up on me. When I got to Hillcrest, she had gone and left this note."

Dear Felix,

It is obvious your family does not want me, and you are too busy to care, so I am going back to Canada. If you love me, you will come to Canada so we can talk. And I want an apology from your father. If not, the engagement is over.

Lorraine

"I asked my dad what had happened. He said Lorraine had tried to take over the household. Father told her in no uncertain terms that as a guest it was not her place to order staff around. She had a temper tantrum and left."

"Oh Felix, I'm so sorry. What are you going to do?"

"I'm not going to Canada. I couldn't even if I wanted to. The trial starts tomorrow and she knows that. I'm breaking off the engagement. I couldn't marry her now. I guess my dad was right. I don't understand what happened to her. She was so nice when I met her; we had fun together. Now she won't even go out with Peter and Lizzy. She said they were too ordinary and we should only mix with the right people. I loved the woman I met, not whoever she is now."

Sarah ordered two shepherd's pies and a bottle of red wine. She stayed quiet, listening but making no comment.

"Mum is very upset. She has always treated the staff well. Dad often said she was too lenient with the servants. He's old school, but even he is appalled at the way Lorraine threw her weight about. Connie almost quit, she was so rude to her. Sarah, you don't treat staff like that. She may not have been raised with servants, but it's human decency."

The waiter popped the cork and poured the wine. Sarah took a large gulp, and was grateful when the dinner plate was placed in front of her; she was hungry. Felix had obviously not eaten either and ate between words and wine. As he finished, he said, "I guess it's over."

Sarah looked at him, her face full of sympathy and said, "I'm sorry, Felix. You must feel awful. I know it hurts. Maybe she'll think about it and apologize. Would you take her back after if she was sorry?"

"No. She isn't the right person for me. Why am I so upset?"

"You're hurt. She deceived you. Falling in love with someone and then having them change into someone else is painful. I know how it feels, Marcus did the same to me. It probably doesn't help much, but I don't think you've loved Lorraine for some time."

"You are right, Sarah. You are always right. I don't know what I'd do without you." He leaned over and pecked her cheek.

She patted his hand. "I'll always be there for you. It will get better with time."

"I know. It never occurred to me how Marcus hurt you. It's pretty nasty when the people you love change."

"Speaking of Marcus Perkins also known as Marc Perry, he's turned up on a witness list. The trail is getting complicated. Every time Peter or I think we have everything ready, something else comes up."

Sarah didn't want to be reminded of Marcus. Part of her loved him and it was a hopeless kind of love. Her comparison with Lorraine being one person and turning into someone else was correct. She felt sorry for Felix and could feel his hurt. Thoughts of Marcus suddenly made her think of Michael. That was a different kind of love—dependable. Or was he?

"Hey, penny for them. Sorry, I've been talking my head off. How are things with you? Mum called to say Bill would be staying at the townhouse while Anna is at the clinic for eye surgery."

"Tuesday morning." Sarah yawned.

Felix patted her arm. "You're tired. Time I went home."

"I'm truly sorry about Lorraine, but you have to make those decisions for yourself."

She waved goodnight, relieved there was no one behind Mrs. D's curtains. She climbed the stairs thinking of Felix and walked into her little studio. Her art usually gave her comfort, but not tonight. She flopped on the bed, willing sleep to silence her thoughts. Felix's hurt had filled her with memories of Marcus and Michael that she had struggled to lock away. And the mystery surrounding her father seemed impenetrable—a mystery she wanted to unlock but nobody else did.

**

The first day of college after the holidays, whether a student or teacher, always felt exciting. It reminded Sarah of elementary school. She appreciated the time to get ready; classes didn't start for two days. Chatter in the staff room was loud with much laughter and sharing. Mr. Darwin joined the staff and made an informal speech to welcome everyone back after the holidays and wish them a good spring term. He asked Sarah and Miss Berkley to come up to the front.

"As you old timers know," he laughed, "I like to announce the winners of the Christmas Exhibition contest before the students return. Today I have two announcements both, of which concern Miss Wexford, and one for Miss Berkley. The winning student is Robert Leclaire, Miss Wexford's student, and Miss Berkley's student Gillian West is runner up." Applause filled the staff room. The honour fell on the prof as much as the student, and it was unusual for a first-year prof to win such an honour. Anna herself had been a recipient of this prize under Miss Berkley. Sarah glanced at her fellow professors and saw several unsmiling faces who were not applauding her success. She surmised that some of the "old timers" as Mr. Darwin put it, were not happy, believing their experience and students were more deserving. She wondered if Mr. Darwin played favourites and she felt uncomfortable.

"I have another exciting announcement to make. Miss Wexford's painting *Beyond the Storm* has been bought by the London Gallery for their emerging artists section." Applause rang in Sarah's ears as she felt the heat in her cheeks, not sure if it was pure excitement or the fuss that embarrassed her. Mr. Darwin presented her with an envelope containing a cheque for £250.

"Thank you. I couldn't have done it without your help, Mr. Darwin and Miss Berkley's constant guidance and the support of my colleagues. I am so grateful to the college and all of you. Thank you."

"Well deserved, Miss Wexford." Mr. Darwin bowed his head slightly. "If you'll excuse me, I'll leave you all get on with your class preparation. Miss Wexford, come by my office later today."

The buzz of congratulations from her colleagues was making her feel lightheaded. She thought she might faint and sat down, asking someone to get her a glass of water. She gave a nervous smile, "I don't know what to say. It doesn't seem real. Wow!"

Miss Berkley handed her a glass. "Just enjoy the success. There will be more."

Sarah wanted to call Anna and tell her, but they were on their way to London. Anna had to check into the clinic the night before surgery. She would have to wait and drop by the clinic later. She wanted to call Felix, but he was in court. She picked up the staff room phone and called Lizzy at work but was told she didn't work there anymore. She called her house and Lizzy answered.

"I just called Jacob's and they said you didn't work there anymore. Are you all right, is the baby okay. What happened?"

"Both the baby and me are fine. They told me I had gained too much weight—too much Christmas pudding," Lizzy gave a weak laugh. "Because I was pregnant they were terminating my employment with two weeks pay. I kind of expected it, but not so soon. Why are you calling? You don't usually call from college. Is Anna all right?"

"Anna's fine, she has surgery tomorrow. I'm sorry, Lizzy. They shouldn't be able to fire you because you're expecting a baby. That is terrible. I will never buy another Jacobs dress again."

"Sarah," Lizzy giggled. "You've never bought a Jacob's dress, except the bridesmaids dress. But thank you, I needed that."

"Why didn't you call me?"

"It only happened yesterday and I didn't feel like talking last night. Peter was home so he took me out for dinner to cheer me up. I've been looking at nursery designs and I went out this morning and bought material to make a crib set."

"What colour? I have a great idea: why don't I paint a nursery rhyme mural on the nursery wall?"

"That would be amazing. I feel better all ready. Come by on Saturday or Sunday."

"I will. I have to go now."

"Sarah, don't go. What did you call me about?"

"I almost forgot. The London Gallery bought my painting. Okay, brace yourself…for £250."

"Wow! That is wonderful news. What are you going to buy with the money? New clothes—*not* Jacob's—or furniture? Mum's cast-offs are a bit dated."

"Trust you to ask that question. I'll put it in the bank. I thought I could contribute towards Nana's eye surgery. Grandpa says they have the money, but it's terribly expensive. The timing is good. I can't stay on the phone. We'll get together this week."

"Come over for dinner one night. I'll ask Peter what night he can be home early. The trial started this morning so he and Felix will be working late some nights. Shall I invite Felix? Peter told me about Lorraine."

"Dinner would be nice. I'll bring some sketches over for the nursery wall. Felix needs cheering up, so yes invite him too. I have to go, but I'll call you later."

Thirty-One

Treason and Trickery

*A*nna sat up in bed, grinning her Cheshire cat grin from ear to ear. The doctor looked into her eyes, nodded and said, "It's healing nicely."

Anna pointed to the rather bad painting of swans on the wall. "I can see every detail. Thank you! I am so excited, I feel like celebrating."

"My job is rewarding; cataracts surgery always has positive results. I'm afraid the dressing has to stay on for a couple more days. And Mrs. Blaine, no celebrating just yet. You need to stay still and rest and let the eye heal."

The nurse came in and covered up Anna's good eye, making her vision blurry again as her other eye still had a cataract. She couldn't believe the difference and put her hand up to the eye patch, wanting to rip it off. The nurse must have seen the movement, or perhaps was used to patients doing just that, because she patted Anna's hand and said, "The doctor keeps the patch on to avoid infection. Be patient, Mrs. Blaine. Infections are nasty and can do irreparable damage to the eye." Anna put her hand down.

Sarah knocked and put her head around the door. "Are you up to visitors?"

"Yes, yes, come in, Sarah. The nurse has just finished."

"You look so well," Sarah said with surprise. "I thought you'd be…I'm not sure what I thought."

"I feel fine. When they changed the dressing I could see. I could see that picture. I can't wait to get this patch off."

Sarah smiled. It had been a while since she had seen Anna so animated. "Where's Grandpa Bill?"

"He was here earlier. I sent him to get some rest. He's looking pale and tired. I worry about his heart."

"Nana, stop worrying. The best thing you can do is get better. You two are a pair, the way you worry about each other. Grandpa Bill is fine. He probably just didn't sleep worrying about you. But now that he knows the operation was a success he can relax. When can you go home?"

"The doctor says a few more days."

Sarah looked at her watch. "I have a class at two o'clock so I can't stay long. I can't come tonight as I have to meet Madame at Le Papillon Gallery." Anna raised an eyebrow. "Yes," Sarah nodded, "it was a surprise to me too. She called and left a message at the college demanding I meet her at seven tonight."

"It's all right, Grandpa Bill will be here tonight."

"I'll pop by tomorrow afternoon after class and see how you're doing." Sarah bent over and kissed Anna.

It was a relief to see Nana looking her old self, Sarah thought as she walked to the Underground. She had to admit that was only part of the relief; the other part was that Anna could keep running the Sackville, allowing Sarah to delay indefinitely her decision about returning to Bexhill. She could focus on her art. *Being famous is going to take some getting used to,* she thought and then smiled to herself, *but I kind of like it.* The train was fast at mid-day and Sarah walked into the college with time to spare before class.

**

As she pulled the heavy glass doors of Le Papillon Gallery of Art, a peculiar sensation hit her. It felt physical and yet it couldn't be. The receptionist looked pale. Her smile not at all convincing, she said, "Good evening, Miss Wexford. Mr. Sebastian and Madame are waiting for you."

Sarah looked into the gallery, Madame lay on the rich burgundy brocade chaise-lunge, the only piece of furniture on the floor, fanning herself with a sheaf of papers. Mr. Sebastian handed her a glass that looked like water, but Sarah thought it might be gin or vodka. It was his words that caught her attention. "Cecilia, I'm sure we can resolve this out of court." Whatever *this* was, it sounded personal and serious. No one ever used Madame's real name; few people even knew she had a real name. Another man, familiar to Sarah but she couldn't place him, stood with his back to her. As he turned to speak to Mr. Sebastian, Sarah gasped, losing her balance. Barely staying upright, her handbag dropped to the floor. Michael Carter came rushing to her aid.

"Sarah," he said, holding her by the shoulders. She sensed his indecision in his grip; whether he should embrace her or not. Speechless, she thought, *What's he doing here?*

"Its good to see you again." His smile told her he really wanted to kiss her.

Finally, Sarah found her voice, "I'm so surprised. I've been waiting to hear from you and gave you up for dead."

He leaned into her shoulder and whispered, "I tried to call. Mrs. D said you were out. I have some good news and some bad. But first, finish your business here. I'll wait outside in the car." He pushed away and cheerfully added, "Madame tells me she is hosting a show for you. I shall look forward to it. I'll speak to you later, Madame. Now if you will excuse me, I have to run."

Mr. Sebastian helped Madame up from her reclining pose and directed Sarah into the office. Her heart had stopped beating out of her chest as a result of Michael's sudden appearance, but her senses were still on guard. Madame's grey complexion with a slight flush on her cheeks indicated she was not well.

"Miss Wexford," Mr. Sebastian said, "we only have four months before the spring show and Madame would like to know how many paintings you will exhibit, and we have not agreed on the finer points of the contract."

"Contract? I haven't seen the contract."

Madame sat straight up in her chair, the paper rustling in her shaking hand. Sarah glanced at her face and saw fear. It couldn't be the contract, so what was it? She placed the paper on the desk and said, "Its only a case of signing. But I need to know how many pieces you will be displaying."

Sarah had no intention of accepting it as it was. The debate over the contract went on for some time. She soon realized that Mr. Darwin's caution was well founded.

"I will need to read and understand the contract before I sign. If that is not to your liking, Madame, then there will be no exhibition." Sarah made a motion to stand. She was quite prepared to walk away and stifled a grin, knowing that little Miss Wexford, young talented artist, had grown up. She had accepted her role as an up-and-coming famous artist. She no longer feared Madame, but she recognized fear. Something had terrorized Madame.

"Please," Mr. Sebastian's tone pleaded as he moved next to Madame and placed a hand on her shoulder. "Don't do anything hasty. I'm sure we can allow you some time to review the contract." He glanced at Madame who gave a not very convincing nod.

Sarah picked up the contract. "I will return it tomorrow when my class finishes. It will be signed if it's acceptable or have requests for changes if needed."

Madame opened her mouth and Mr. Sebastian gripped her shoulder and spoke for her, "Thank you. We'll look forward to seeing you tomorrow. Shall we say four-thirty?"

"I'll see you then," Sarah replied and walked out of the gallery, quite forgetting that Michael was waiting for her.

Michael tapped her shoulder. "Did you forget me already?"

Sarah clutched her chest, her heart racing. "Oh Michael, you scared me. It's rather tense in there. Anyway, what are you doing here? I haven't heard from you in months and you suddenly appear at Le Papillon."

"Can I take you for dinner? I have a lot to tell you."

"I'm not dressed for dinner, so somewhere casual."

"I know just the place."

The restaurant was more like a greasy spoon, with Formica tables, metal-framed chairs, and a waitress chewing gum. Michael quickly explained, "You did say casual and the food is amazing. The owner and cook is Italian and I swear you'll never taste better spaghetti and meatballs anywhere."

"It's clean, I'll say that. And I am hungry."

Sarah couldn't take her eyes off the masticating jaw of the waitress as she wrote down their order for spaghetti and then placed a jug of red wine in the middle of the table with two tumblers.

Michael smiled, "Perhaps not the standard of the Sackville, but it's good. Try it."

Sarah took a tentative sip. "Wow! It really is good. I like it. How did you find this place?"

"It's close to the office and a good place to meet people or hang out with colleagues without being observed." Sarah followed his gaze to a table occupied by two black-suited men.

"Oh, I see. Its a spy hang-out."

"Shush Sarah, not so loud. But yes, something like that."

"Are you going to tell me what's going on? Speaking of which, what is going on at Le Papillon?"

"Cecilia is mixed up with some shady foreign art deals."

"That doesn't surprise me. She sold one of my paintings and I never got paid."

"Its a little more serious than that. Sarah, you know I can't say anything."

"Are you saying the British Secret Service is involved?"

"Perhaps, along with many other things."

"I am about to sign a contract with them for their show and a solo exhibition for me. I don't want to get involved with anything illegal, or the nation's secrets."

"You already are involved, by association with Marc Perry, your father, Madame and me, and not forgetting Felix being one of the barristers for the trial."

"What!" Sarah felt her heart jump into her throat at the mention of Marc, knowing it was Marcus. At the mention of her father she thought she'd misheard.

Michael took both of her hands in his. "I'm so sorry to dump all that on you in one sentence. I wasn't thinking. I thought you knew the trial was about MI6 and treason. But then Felix would not have been able to discuss it with you."

"I knew Felix was involved in a trial about MI6 but no details." Michael moved to the chair next to her and put his arm around her. She felt his warmth; she always felt safe with Michael, but right now she wasn't sure of anything. *Why would he say those things? Did he say, 'your father'? I can't remember.* Her thoughts bounced around her head. The waitress plonked two steaming plates in the middle of the table. Sarah looked up and Michael kissed her cheek. "Are you going to be alright?"

Sarah took a long, deep breath and nodded, picked up her glass and swallowed the contents in one gulp. Refilling it from the jug, she said, "Did you say my father?"

"I told you I had some good news and bad. I know where your father is. The bad news is we're not sure how to get him back to England."

"Please. Stop talking in riddles."

"I'll start at the beginning. How much do you know about your father?"

"Not much, except that after mother died he drank heavily and left me with my grandparents. Felix traced him through some run-ins with the law and at some point, he finished up in nursing home, presumably to dry out. The last time anyone heard about him he was working at a hotel in London."

Michael moved back to the other side of the table and started eating his spaghetti. Having downed two glasses of wine on an empty stomach Sarah's head was spinning. She pulled the other plate towards her and began eating, waiting for Michael to begin the story.

"It was St Ermin's." He looked up from his meal, "It's a known meeting place for the British Intelligence. Your father was recruited because of his exceptional engineering skills and no lifestyle ties."

"You mean no wife or family. How could he dismiss me so easily?"

"He knew you were taken care of and he wasn't capable. I doubt he had any idea what he was getting into. At first he was asked to decipher some schematics here at headquarters."

"How do you know all this if its secret."

"Because I trained him. That's why I knew his real name."

"The James Bond conference at Bexhill that was when you asked me if we were related. You called him Sandy. Had you taken the name from my birth certificate you would have called him Alexander."

"You're right, I slipped up." Michael began laughing. "Did you really call us the James Bond conference? I wish it was that glamorous."

Sarah was enjoying the spaghetti. Michael had a knack of relaxing her, but she still didn't know the full story. She wanted to know more.

"There's a lot you are not telling me."

"There's a lot I can't tell you. Not only to protect Britain but also to keep the press away. Since the sensational trial of the Portland Spy Ring last year, the press is unrelenting, putting operatives and the country in danger. These are not Hollywood films; double agents like George Blake are not James Bond and they are real men committing treason by selling secrets to the Soviets or other enemies.

"Your father was assigned to a different group and was sent to Europe. I don't know exactly where. We never know where we are going on assignment or what we are doing. The information comes to us on an as-needed basis and it is never discussed with other agents unless the assignment requires two people, which is rare. Your father's assignment did involve a second person. Your early assessment was correct; we are intelligence officers. Operatives. We don't often use the term spy."

"You were his partner. You know where he is." Sarah felt excited, she had never come this close.

"No, I wasn't his partner. I wish I had been. Things would have been different."

Sarah felt exasperated. "I don't understand you."

"Please just listen. The work is dangerous and breaking the law is not uncommon, but if anything goes wrong we are on our own. Identity is key. You never operate under your own name or your own life. No one knows who you are and the firm will not come to your aid. As far as the firm is concerned, you do not exist. However, we do help each other and there are rare occasions when the firm gets involved. More often than not it is at a direct order from the Prime Minister's Office, and that is what happened in your father's case."

The restaurant door slammed shut and a couple walked in and sat at the next table. Michael neither said nor did anything that Sarah noticed, but instinctively she was aware they knew each other and Michael's demeanour changed. She wondered if he was one of his contacts.

He whispered, "We need to go, and don't say a word." Sarah didn't argue, although she regretted having to leave half of her dinner.

As the car door closed, she asked, "What was that all about?"

"I can't answer, but I may have been followed."

Sarah turned to look through the back window. She didn't feel safe any more. Her heart pounded in her chest and suddenly she was scared. Michael's face was intent on the road and whatever was going through his head seemed oblivious to her fear. He drove slowly at first and then sped up, driving down side streets, stopping and

starting, the whites of his eyes bright in the lights as he glanced in
the rear-view mirror. Finally, he drove down a deserted street and
through the entrance of a park. Sarah could see the outline of several
parked cars. Michael pulled up among them. *Lovers Lane,* she thought.
What is he thinking?

Michael took a deep breath. "I had to make sure we weren't being
followed and I can assure you we're not. Anyone seeing us will think
we are enjoying Lover's Lane." Michael leaned over and placed his
hands tenderly around her face. "I am sorry for frightening you, but
more than anything in the world I want to protect you." He kissed her
and Sarah kissed him, feeling safe again until he embraced her and
she sensed something desperate, or was it just awkwardness with the
stick shift between them? She had the urge to crawl on his lap and
let him protect her and yet he was at the centre of all the chaos.

"Are you going to tell me where my father is?"

"You may not like what I have to say."

"Just tell me!"

"He was captured three years ago and accused of a bogus crime
and is in a jail cell awaiting trial. Remember I said he was working
with another operative? We now know he was set up by his partner.
Someone who had been in the service since public school. One of
our best and most trusted operatives turned double agent, working
for the Soviets."

Stunned at the news, Sarah stared into the darkness, imagining her
father locked in a dark cell. Her last memory of him was misery as he
drank hopelessly to ease his grief and she imagined the same hopeless
misery as he sat in a foreign jail cell. Tears ran down her cheeks.
Michael held her tight and whispered, "I'm sorry. The government is
trying to get him released through diplomatic channels. If that doesn't
work the secret service have their ways." He wiped her cheeks. "There
is something I don't understand. Your father listed your grandparents
as his next of kin. Although they would have no details, they where
aware that he was working for the government and the government

would have informed them of his capture."

"They never said a word. My father's name was never mentioned. How could they not tell me?" Sarah pulled away from Michael as anger burned her throat.

"If it's any consolation, I think they wanted to protect you. You would have been only ten or eleven at the time."

"I was an adult when he was captured. They could have told me then."

"I can't answer that. I think you've had enough for one day. I'm taking you home."

Thirty-Two

Secrets and Truths

S arah slept little that night. Vague images of her father floated in and out of her head. She tried to concentrate hard to remember his features, but was only able to recall his touch and gentle soothing voice. Frustrated, she smacked her hand on her forehead as if it would jog her memory. Anger bubbled inside her. She had so many questions and no answers. Who was the double-crossing partner? Why hadn't Nana told her they knew about her father? Perhaps they didn't know and Michael was lying to her. But he had no reason to lie, or did he? He hadn't told her everything, of that she was certain. How did Le Papillon and Marcus fit in? Felix had said Marcus had turned up on a witness list.

Le Papillon, she thought, *I have to sign the contract today.*

Sarah abandoned sleep and boiled some milk and made a milky instant coffee, smiling as she heard Grandpa Bill saying, "That's not coffee, it's hot flavoured milk." This morning, the hot drink calmed her. She needed a clear head and took Madame's contract from her handbag and began reading. The legal jargon made no sense, filled with clauses and addendum's that contradicted the clauses. She placed the contract back in her bag and ran a hot bath, deciding to leave early and meet Mr. Darwin.

**

Sarah hadn't realized just how early she was until she found the main doors of the college locked, which was not surprising as it was barely light out. She sat on the steps, taking in the pink glow on the clouds as the sun rose somewhere behind the concrete buildings. She listened to the quiet—a rare thing in busy London. It was only a matter of time before the bustle would start and the craziness of running from here to there and for what purpose no one seemed to know or care. "What is my purpose?" she said, staring at the sky. "I want the peace of those pink clouds." She yearned for the quietness of her easel, her escape from reality. Was it normal to be mixed up with secret service chameleon men, switching from one life to another? Felix being the exception, but was he a lie too? Dishonest art galleries, grandparents that kept secrets—as angry as she was with Anna and Bill, Bexhill seemed the most normal part of her life. Did that mean she should give up London?

"Good morning, Miss Wexford. You are an early bird today." Mr. Darwin bounded up the steps.

Sarah stood up quickly, trying to shift her focus to Mr. Darwin. "Good morning. I'm a little early," she stated the obvious, feeling slightly embarrassed. "I came early to talk to you. Madame has given me a contract for the art show."

Pulling a key ring from his pocket, he unlocked the front door and a security guard greeted them. Seeing who it was, he waved them on.

Mr. Darwin studied the contract while Sarah sat in an overstuffed brown leather chair surveying the masculine office. Wood and leather were contrasted by a variety of paintings, sculptures and interesting mock-ups of industrial designs.

He looked straight at her. "You can't sign this. She's asking for exclusivity for all your future art and the commission structure is too complicated. I suggest you get legal advice and draw up your own contract."

"She wants it back today."

"What she wants is for you to sign this so she can control you, and

247

I can assure you she will do that. There are other galleries that would be happy to invite you to exhibit. The choice is yours, but if it was me, I would walk away. At the very least you must get legal advice and change the contract."

Sarah thanked him and went into the staff room to call Felix, but no one answered the phone. She tried his private line but there was still no answer. She read the contract again and wondered if being exclusive was such a bad thing. Le Papillon was the prime gallery in London and well connected to some impressive art dealers. Securing an exhibition with Le Papillon had always been her dream. It would simplify her life. She could return to Bexhill, paint and run the hotel. Afraid she might make a wrong decision, she needed to talk to someone. Picking up the phone again, she dialed Michael's old number and was told it was disconnected. *Of course it is*, she thought. It hadn't occurred to her to ask him where he was staying since his return. People like Michael had no fixed numbers or address.

She called Lizzy who immediately described a glamorous picture of champagne receptions and wealthy art dealers scrambling for Sarah's art. Although Lizzy was not practical and had no head for business, she loved money and gave Sarah a lecture about being specific on the price of her art and only offering a small percentage to Madame.

Feeling confident, Sarah went into her classroom having decided to accept the contract with a clarified fee structure. She should wait for Felix, but she rationalized he was too busy and he might complicate things, and she really wanted this exhibition.

After morning classes, Sarah took the Underground to Piccadilly and went to see Anna. Her anger over her father had dissipated somewhat. She was still mad, but confronting Anna at the hospital didn't seem right. Sister greeted her in the corridor. "Miss Wexford, your grandmother is an exceptional patient. I've never seen anyone heal so quickly."

"That is good news. Nana is tough. She had to be. I suspect she wants to get home. What does the doctor say?"

"He is very pleased. I think he will discharge her early."

"Thank you, Sister." Sarah walked into Anna's room.

"Nana, you're out of bed and you look well. How do you feel?" Sarah sat on the arm of the chair and kissed her. "Where's Grandpa Bill?"

"He went to get some tea. I can go home tomorrow. As nice as they are here, I'm bored out of my mind."

A nurse entered carrying a tea tray, with Bill on her heels. Sarah got up and hugged Bill who sat where Sarah had been sitting. As she stared at the two of them, her heart filled with love. She frowned as resentment stirred inside her, even though she knew that whatever they had done, they'd done it with her best interest at heart. But, how could they have deliberately kept news about her father from her for all those years?

"Sarah! What's wrong?" Sarah shook her head. "Sarah, I know that look and something is wrong." Anna said.

"I don't want to talk about it now." Annoyed with herself for having let Anna see her distress, she changed the subject, trying to sound cheery. "Le Papillon has offered me an exhibition. I'm signing the contract tonight."

"Wonderful! Did you have Felix look at the contract?" Bill said, "You can't be too careful these days."

"No, he wasn't in the office. I showed it to Mr. Darwin this morning."

"And what did he say?" Anna gave Sarah *the look*. "I know how much you want this, but please don't compromise. Do you have it with you?"

"It's fine, really." As she said the words, she knew it wasn't fine. Anna had ignited the doubt she had attempted to push away.

Anne put her hand out. "Please, Sarah. Let me take a look?"

Sarah took the envelope from her handbag. "Mr. Darwin suggested I ask for clarification of the fees." The room fell silent and Sarah was wishing she had kept quiet. She blurted out, "Michael is back in town."

Her attempt to distract them didn't work. *Probably a good thing,* she thought.

Anna looked up. "You can't sign this! I'm surprised you would even think of signing it. You've seen enough contracts at the hotel. I taught you what to look for and what has to be clear. There is nothing for you in this." Anna flipped the paper under her nose. "Le Papillon is asking to own you forever." Anna ripped the contract in half and then quarters.

"Nana, please! Having an exhibition at Le Papillon has been my dream for years." Sarah couldn't hold back the tears. So much and happened in the last twenty-four hours and now Anna was angry with her.

"Are you going to take this opportunity away from me like you took my father away?" Even before she finished the sentence she regretted her words. "I'm sorry; so sorry. I shouldn't have said that."

Bill moved close to Anna, shock on both of their faces. Bill spoke, "What do you know about your father?"

"Like I said, Michael is back in town. He thought I knew that my father had been jailed Europe. He said you were listed as next of kin and you would have been notified of his capture." Sarah brushed her cheeks and glanced at Anna. "I'm sorry, Nana. It has been a difficult day."

Bill guided Anna back to the bed and motioned for Sarah to sit in the chair. "Nana and I thought long and hard about telling you about your father. He did contact us, but asked us not to tell you. That was before he joined MI6. We were notified when he was captured. It was around the time you graduated and we didn't want to spoil your success and one day led into another. I think we both hoped Sandy would be set free and we could tell you he was coming home."

"Michael tells me he had a partner who was turned, resulting in his capture. He also said they were trying to get his release through diplomatic channels. I don't think Michael is being completely honest. Keeping secrets and telling lies is his way of life."

"Come here," Anna reached over and took Sarah's hand. "Sit." Sarah sat on the edge of the bed. "We should have told you. Your father went to pieces when your mother died. He began drinking heavily and lost his job. He loved you very much but couldn't take care of you and did the next best thing and left you with us. I think he felt he was better out of your life all together."

"I see that now. But all my life I couldn't understand why you never talked about him. I wanted to know about him."

"I think we were afraid for you. Afraid he might die and it would be easier if you forgot him. I'm sorry; we were wrong."

Sarah nodded, "Do you think he will come home?"

"Nobody knows what will happen. But we will let you know if we hear from the government."

Sarah waved the torn up contract in the air. "You're right. I will not sign my life away. I will ask Felix for his advice and tell Madame that if she wants my art it will be on my terms."

"Good girl. I know how much it means to you. If it is right for you, it will come together. If not, something else will come along."

Sarah glanced at her watch. "I have a class in half-an-hour, I'm afraid I have to go. I love you both. I'll come home on Friday and we can talk some more. No more secrets, agreed?"

Anna and Bill replied in unison, "Agreed."

**

Sarah telephoned Mr. Sebastian, deciding he was less volatile than Madame. He surprised her by suggesting she should take as long as she needed. There was hesitation in his voice, enough to make Sarah wonder if he wanted to say more. Instead, he added that seeking legal advice was a wise decision. She smiled as she looked at the torn pages in her hand—Nana always knew best.

She had called Felix several times, and finally left a message with his secretary. That night, she called Lizzy who filled her in on a few trial details. Peter said there was a publicity ban because it involved the British Secret Service and national security.

Thirty-Three

True Colours

⟨ornament⟩

By the end of March, Felix, still immersed in the treason trial, had not been much help to Sarah regarding the Le Papillon contract; in fact he'd suggested she approach a different gallery. Sarah, fixated on Le Papillon, reluctantly accepted that she had missed the opportunity for a solo exhibition, but if she acted quickly she could to be included in Le Papillion's Annual Exhibition. The decision made, she headed to the gallery to speak to Mr. Sebastian. As she turned the corner she had a strange feeling and a shudder slipped down her spine.

Police cars lined the street in front of the gallery and the glass doors were wide open, like jaws devouring and spitting out people. The cars were at all angles, having obviously arrived in a hurry. An occupied gurney was being wheeled to an ambulance. She stared, rooted to the pavement, not able to retreat or move forward. She saw a man being led to a police car in handcuffs. He turned as though he sensed her stare and her hand flew up to her mouth. Gasping, she said, "Oh my God, that's Marcus." Fear released her feet and she began running and didn't stop until she reached home. She ran up the stairs not wanting to be greeted by Johnny or Mr. D. She sat in her room shaking. Even from a distance she had felt evil coming from Marcus. Something terrible had happened. Who was on that gurney? She wanted to call

Michael, but had no number to call.

She needed Felix. She felt vulnerable and frightened. Listening for movement downstairs, she heard nothing at all. Johnny and Mrs. D were out. She ran downstairs and called Felix. She didn't wait to be told he was busy and yelled into the phone that it was an emergency. Within seconds she heard Felix's voice, "Sarah whatever is the matter? Are you hurt?"

"No, I'm frightened. Something terrible has happened at Le Papillon." She related the scene.

"I'm coming over. Please stay where you are."

Sarah paced the floor, trying to figure out what she had seen and why had it upset her so much. She had a very bad feeling and cursed her intuition. The image of the gurney was fresh in her mind. Had the sheet been over the occupant's face? If it was, the person was dead. *No, it was at his neck. His,* she thought, *it was a man. How do I know that and who was it?* An uncontrolled shiver filled her as the image of Marcus flashed in front of her. She jumped as the doorbell rang and leapt down the stairs two at a time. She opened the door and threw her arms around Felix.

He held her tight. "Hey, it's okay. I'm here." He held the back of her head to his shoulder and leaned his head against hers. "Why so upset? Were you at the gallery when it happened?"

Sarah pulled away. "When what happened? I was on the street, going to meet with Mr. Sebastian. I ran home when I saw the police."

"Let's go upstairs. I have a lot to tell you."

Felix poured whisky and made Sarah drink it in one gulp. The burn in her throat calmed her. "What about all the secrecy?"

"The trial was suspended today. Based on a witness's testimony, it appears that the wrong person may have been charged. It will be all over the news by tomorrow. Some secrets might be preserved, but most of the information will be in the early morning editions."

"What does Le Papillon have to do with the trial?"

"A great deal. Le Papillon was not just an art gallery, although that part was genuine, as was its reputation as a leading gallery. However, Cecilia Jones has been accused of art fraud. Few people were aware of its other function: a meeting place for the secret service, but it appears more popular with Soviets and double agents. I couldn't tell you at the time, but that was my reason for stalling about the contract."

"Did Nana know?"

"No, she knew how much you wanted the exhibition, and she also knew it was a very bad contract and that is why she contacted me. They were looking out for you, like they always do."

"How come you spoke to Anna and not me? Never mind, I know the answer. So, what happened tonight? I don't understand how you could have known about it before I called."

"Because Michael Carter called me from the gallery about two hours ago. He had something to tell me. We were to meet later tonight, but he was shot before he could tell me."

Sarah's blood ran cold as she said, "It was Michael on the gurney at Le Papillon. That's why I sensed the familiarity. And Marcus was the shooter."

Felix nodded and placed his arm around her. "Sarah, Michael didn't make it. He died on the way to the hospital. I'm sorry; I know you were dating."

Sarah thought for a moment. "Not really. I was fond of Michael. It was more than friendship, but not love. He had a way of making me feel safe; kind of odd, considering his occupation. He was a lot older than me. A father figure, perhaps. But I think he was in love. I had the sense he was putting MI6 behind him. I also thought he was going to propose."

Felix sat up straight. "Would you have accepted?"

"No. Why, would it have bothered you?"

Felix sighed. "It always bothers me when you date other men. I'm selfish, I want you all to myself."

"But Felix, we've always been friends." Sarah felt a spark of

254

inexplicable excitement. "I've never thought of us as anything but friends. You are like the big brother I never had."

"I think that's why I don't like to see you with other men; none of them are good enough for you. The one that bothered me the most was Marcus, and as it turns out, I had cause for concern. Sarah, Marcus is an evil man. He shot Michael because he testified against him in court. Michael had more truths to tell but Marcus silenced him."

Sarah wasn't sure of her feelings. She was sad that Michael was dead and felt grief for Marcus; shock and sadness for a man she had loved. It didn't seem right to shed tears over Marcus and yet feel no tears for Michael—a friend who would be sadly missed.

She was melting into Felix's arms and it wouldn't be the first time she had found herself suppressing feelings. He bent his head and kissed her forehead. "Are you all right? I didn't mean to upset you."

"I'm fine. Sad about Michael, he didn't deserve to die. He was a nice person. Marcus, I don't understand. I loved him once. He wasn't evil then. What do you think happened?"

"I don't think Marcus had a chance. His parents never cared about him. He was raised at a boarding school, and he was recruited while still in school."

"Recruited for what?"

"The Secret Service recruits young society men, just out of school, and moulds them into agents."

"Michael told me about that, he was recruited from school but he had a teacher who mentored and cared for him. He turned out to be pretty decent."

"Young teenage boys are impressionable, looking for excitement. And those without family to guide them think of the service as family."

"So, Marcus was already on a mission when I met him in college? The whole beatnik thing was one of his disguises, an identity. He was convincing. He had a whole made up life that included friends like Dave and Jenny at the commune, who had supposedly known him since childhood. What a fool I've been. That's why he tried to ignore me when I saw him dressed as a businessman. We went out together for two years; his life seemed so normal." Sarah felt her throat tightening. "How could I have been so blind? All that time he was working as a spy. Why was he spying on me?"

"Because you were Sandy Wexford's daughter."

"And Michael, was he spying on me too? He asked me about my father. It seems everyone knows about my father but me."

"No, at that time Michael was looking for a quiet place for the meeting. Marcus suggested the Sackville." Felix gently twisted her curls around his fingers. "There's more. Marcus was working as a double agent. It's because of Marcus that your father was captured." Felix held her tighter. "I'm afraid he has always been evil. He covered it well."

"Marcus was my father's partner, wasn't he?"

Felix nodded, "Yes. Because of the betrayal, the government will negotiate his freedom."

Sarah wanted to believe Felix. "I don't know what to think anymore. It's like a bad dream."

"I know what you mean. I became a barrister to put criminals behind bars. Who would have known my first big case would be right out of an Ian Fleming novel?" He shook his head. "And it's going to get worse. It makes me think that life minding the estate at Hillcrest Hall is not such a bad idea after all."

She turned her head upwards and smiled, the empathy shared by both of them brought a peaceful calm. Felix leaned towards her and she felt his warm lips on hers. At first, she wanted to resist. Her brain wanted to accuse him of taking advantage of her vulnerability, but what she felt was passion, love, and something much bigger than both of them. She embraced his kisses, making the whole ugly world disappear. In that moment nobody needed to tell them that their relationship had changed.

**

Felix crept down the stairs before daybreak and silently twisted the front door handle with on eye on Mrs. D's bedroom door. Sarah wanted to giggle as she blew him a kiss from her flat door and waited until she heard his car start, grateful that they had not been discovered. She curled up on the sofa and wrapped a blanket around herself, wondering if the events of the past twenty-four hours were real, a dream or nightmare; Marcus being the nightmare and Felix the dream, with Michael somewhere in the middle.

Last night, she had realized that Michael had been a father figure, that's why she had always felt safe with him. But knowing her real father was still alive and, dare she think, maybe coming home, she only felt mournful for a friend who had lived with danger every day—Michael's death was not entirely unexpected, only the circumstances.

Where was her father? Michael had said he was in jail. Was anyone really trying to get his release?

Felix, she thought, and smiled. He'd always been her brotherly protector, at least that is what she had made herself think. But looking back, she had always loved him. She remembered the first time she set eyes on him at Hillcrest; she had only been eight years old. It was Easter she had helped her mother with the Easter Parade at the hotel. Later that afternoon, Harris came to pick them up in the big black Rolls Royce to take them to Hillcrest. Aunt Belle had left the French doors open so she could play in the garden. She literally ran into a tall, handsome teenager. He had smiled at her and in a very deep voice, at least it sounded deep to Sarah, had said, "My name is Felix. You must be Sarah. My mother asked me to show you around the estate." Was that when the perception of brotherly love started? It would be logical. Had she known as a little girl how much she loved him, or did it grow over the years, becoming an unlikely or forbidden love? Perhaps, somewhere in her subconscious, loving a bad boy like Marcus had filled a void that she didn't even know existed.

She hugged a cushion to her chest and rested her face on it, recalling another wonderful memory of her father: the weekend he came back from Scotland. She closed her eyes and heard him laughing and saw her mother's face glowing with love and happiness.

"I want to hear you laugh again, Dad. It's time you came home." Exhausted, she slipped into a deep sleep.

Thirty-Four

Summer 1963

⟨⟨⟨☙⟩⟩⟩

*L*e Papillon Gallery of Art closed in May. The scandal surrounding Madame, now known as Cecilia Jones, of art fraud, murder and double agents, putting the nation's safety at risk kept clients far away from the big etched doors. Although there was a kernel of truth in most of the newspaper stories, much of the information was classified and the courts had ordered a publication ban, giving the press an opportunity to speculate and make up what they didn't know.

The popularity of James Bond fired up all kinds of crazy stories. Fortunately, none included Sarah. She hated to admit it, but had the show of her dreams gone ahead, her name would have been associated with the gallery.

Anna and Bill, still listed as next of kin, were informed of Sandy's condition and were told by the authorities that everything was being done to procure his released—to Sarah it seemed like they were doing nothing. She hated that the information came second-hand from her grandparents. Felix reassured her that it was better that way; the more distance between her and the situation the better. He explained how governments worked, how things were being done behind the scenes. Diplomatic bargaining took time. Foreign regimes didn't care that they had the wrong man, and the double agent responsible for their prisoner's capture was allegedly responsible for a number of treasonous crimes. Marcus was sitting in a humane British jail, being treated as innocent within the British justice system, while Sandy was being treated as guilty, with no chance of trial and being beaten and tortured to reveal government secrets he did not have.

Sarah believed Marcus had the information that would get her father released; all she needed was permission to talk to him. There was a time when Marcus had loved her and she was convinced he would confide in her and divulge the secrets that would result in her father's immediate release. It took Felix some time to persuade her that this was a bad idea. Even if she did get permission to visit Marcus, which was doubtful, she would be swarmed by reporters wanting to know who she was and her connection to the story. Sarah agreed to let the government to do their job and reluctantly accepted that it could take years.

**

The only people, who knew that Felix and Sarah had declared their love for each other were Lizzy and Peter, and they were sworn to secrecy. Their already tight friendship covered it well. But had anyone been looking closely, they would have seen fingers gently entwining, subtle touches and eye contact that told all. It was Sarah's choice to keep quiet. Having made two mistakes in love, she didn't want to make a third. Felix had agreed that they must be certain; the break-up with Lorraine had been painful.

Sarah breathed a sigh of relief as life settled into a normal pattern. Anna had fully recovered from eye surgery and was her old self, taking charge at the Sackville. The hotel experienced a good spring season and Sarah was comfortable leaving the hotel business where it belonged, with her grandparents and a well-trained staff. Occasionally she thought about the inevitable, but for at least one more season she could concentrate on her life. The summer term was always the busiest and most rewarding as the academic year came to a close. First, the curriculum had to be finished, examinations and papers marked and art projects completed and adjudicated. And then Sarah had some decisions to make about her artwork, Felix and her father.

Le Papillon had been an unexpected blow to her plans, but Nana always used to say, "When one door closes, another one opens,"she thought as the morning train barreled through the London Underground tunnels. She always found it comforting but odd being alone in a crowded train. She glanced at the other travelers, all deep in their own thoughts, planning their days or futures. *What does my future look like?* She sensed she was on the cusp of something, but what? In spite of, or maybe because of, Le Papillon closing, her paintings were selling as fast as she could paint and her reputation as an emerging artist was moving as fast as this train. Aware that Mr. Darwin considered her his prodigy, she had many advantages. *Can I make a living off my painting?* She had allowed the college to assume that she would return for the Michaelmas term, but in truth, she wanted to paint full time. The train screeched to a stop, shaking her out of her thoughts. As she jumped onto the platform, reality hit her. What if, like the train, her art suddenly came to a screeching halt? People were fickle and trends changed. What if an artist more talented and trendy appeared? As she stepped into the college foyer, she thought, *No, it's too early to go it alone. Without the support of the college, I could be on the street or back at the Sackville.*

"Good morning, Miss Wexford," Miss Berkley greeted her as she approached the staff room. "There is a message for you from Felix Thornton. He said it is important and to call immediately as he'll be in court all day." She smiled. "He seems to call you often. A new boyfriend? A solicitor, you need to hold on to that one."

Sarah felt her cheeks colour. "Barrister, actually, and he's an old friend." She wondered why she still didn't admit that they were much more than friends. "Thank you." Sarah glanced at Miss Berkley, her eyebrows raised with a knowing smile.

"Felix, you called. Is something wrong?"

"No, I wanted to let you know that Peter just phoned to say he wouldn't be in today. Lizzy started in labour during the night. The doctor and midwife were with her and the birth is expected any time. Calm, cool and collected Peter was talking so fast I could barely understand him. He's terribly nervous and anxious, I wish I was there to give him a stiff Scotch, but I have to take over his case in court today."

"Gosh, I'm nervous too. Did he say everything was okay? I know Lizzy wanted a home birth, but if things don't go well she needs to get to the hospital."

"The doctor has reassured Peter things are going well. Mrs. Elliot arrived while I was talking to him, which is good. I won't be able to call until after court."

"I'll call after my first class and if there is any news, I'll leave a message on your private line. Can we meet tonight?"

"I'd like that. I'll pick you up at six and we can have an early dinner and go and visit the new baby. I'm surprised and I'm really excited. One day it will be our turn."

"See you at six. I have to go or I'll be late for class." Sarah wasn't sure she liked the last phrase. Motherhood had never crossed her mind. Even marriage was way in her distant future. Lizzy's goal had always been to get married, have children and keep house, but Sarah wanted none of that. Her ambition was to excel at art. As much as she tried to avoid it, there had always been a cloud of doubt surrounding her art. Felix's comment had introduced another hurdle to avoid—babies.

The first class of the day had not gone well. Sarah snapped at the students as visions of nappies and babies flashed in her mind. She realized her unusual behaviour was affecting her class and finished it early to call Lizzy. Mrs. Elliott answered the phone. Lizzy had given birth to a baby boy, Nicholas Peter, 8 pounds 1 ounce, a healthy weight for a newborn. Both mother and baby were well and resting. Sarah made arrangements to visit and called to leave a message for Felix. Putting the receiver back in the cradle, she smiled, the irritation gone as she thought about being a pseudo aunt. Aunt Sarah had a nice ring to it. Lizzy had asked her to be godmother and Peter wanted Felix as godfather. She hoped that being a godparent would quell any aspirations of becoming a father sooner than Sarah wanted. She went into her next class with a different attitude.

**

Johnny greeted her at the door to show off his new blue suspenders; Mrs. D was always after him to pull up his trousers. He spent several minutes explaining to Sarah how they worked. Mrs. D put her head around the kitchen door. "Any news on the baby?"

"Yes, Lizzy had a baby boy this morning." Sarah wondered if it was a coincidence or if she had a sixth sense.

"I had a feeling she'd have it today. Here, give her this." Mrs. D pushed a soft parcel into Sarah's hand. "I knit some baby booties to match the matinee coat you asked me to knit her."

"Thank you, I'm sure she'll love it. I wrapped the matinee coat up and Felix and I are going to see her tonight."

Johnny beamed. "Can I come and see the baby?"

"Not today. The baby needs to stay quiet and Miss Lizzy needs to rest. Perhaps when Miss Lizzy is up and about she'll come and visit and then your mum can see the baby too." Sarah gave him a big hug. Knowing he would be disappointed, she had stuck a Cadbury's chocolate bar, his favourite, into her pocket. He glanced at his mum for approval and went off to the kitchen happily breaking chunks off the chocolate bar.

Before Sarah got upstairs, Felix knocked on the front door and Sarah opened it. "You two will be next." Sarah shook her head as she opened the door.

Felix kissed Sarah and then saw Mrs. D. "Hello Mrs. Debinski. How are you?"

"I knew it, you two will be next."

Not understanding Mrs. D's comment, Felix gave Sarah a puzzled look.

Sarah ignored Felix and said, "Good night, Mrs. D. Thank you for the booties, I'm sure she'll love them." She grabbed Felix by the hand and ran upstairs.

"What was that all about?"

"I think Mrs. D has figured out we are more than friends. Of course, kissing me as you walk in the door was a big clue."

"I didn't realize she was there. But don't you think it's time we told the world? I love you, Sarah, and I want everyone to know." Felix frowned. Holding her hands, he added, "What's happened? I see hesitation."

"I love you more than I ever thought I could love anyone. But I'm not ready to settle down and do the baby thing." Sarah held her breath, waiting for his response.

"Baby thing! Sarah, we're not even married yet. It's bad enough being the heir to Hillcrest and having my father prattling on about making sure he has a grandson."

"But when you told me Lizzy was in labour, you said we would be next."

"Well, I guess we are, but not for many years." He smiled tenderly. "Sarah, you are adorable and I love you so much." He pulled her towards him and kissed her. "I do want to marry you, but I'm not ready for the baby thing either." Felix wrapped his arms around her, kissing her neck and hugging the breath from her. Love oozed out of every cell in her body; the love she felt for Felix just grew every day and she wanted to spend every minute with him. She rested her head on his chest, his heart beating in her ear synchronized with her own heart.

She lifted her chin and said, "Marriage without the baby thing, at least for a couple of years, or more, sounds perfect. I think being godparents will suffice for now."

**

It soon became common knowledge that Sarah and Felix were a couple, and no one was surprised. The only people who didn't know were Anna and Bill, and Darcy and Belle. Busy with the summer season at the hotel and estate, neither couple had been to London since Anna's recovery. Delighted to have the summer to paint alone in her little London studio, Sarah had promised to visit in late August. She knew that Felix was reluctant to tell his parents as they would push for a wedding date, hoping to get him back to Hillcrest.

Sarah gazed at the painting as she put the finishing touches to the trees, the *Whispering Trees* picture, which had once been Michael's had become a catalyst for variations of forest paintings. The Canadian pine forests were the most popular, and she never tired of painting them. Each time she saw something different and each painting was unique. Felix was in the sitting room watching TV and preparing a brief. Sarah tip-toed in and put her hands on his eyes, kissing his head. "I leave for Bexhill tomorrow night. Why don't you come with me for the weekend?"

"I'd love to, but I have this murder case to prepare and Peter's not much good at the moment. To say he was sleep deprived would be putting it mildly. Baby Nicholas has colic."

"I know, Lizzy sounds distraught. I suggested she go to her mother's with the baby for a few days while I'm there."

"An excellent idea, Peter can get some sleep and help me. I need Peter's help on this one. I thought the MI6 case was complicated, but this is worse."

"Felix, I know you are busy and I hate to ask again but have you heard any more? I was wondering if you'd heard anything about my dad."

"No. In fact, it's gone silent. That could mean something is happening..." Felix paused and Sarah picked up the conversation, "Or it could mean they want to forget about it."

Felix nodded. "It surprised me when they took the case to another firm and it surprised me even more when the senior partners didn't object. Peter and I have nothing to do with it anymore. I can't say I'm sorry, the kind of work I have now is what I want. But I will ask about your dad." He leaned over and pulled her onto the sofa. Sarah playfully dabbed her paint stained finger on his nose. "Unless you want to be covered in paint, I suggest you let me go and wash my hands."

Thirty-Five

Troubles in Bexhill

*S*arah's artistic accomplishments over the summer had brought in a tidy income. A letter had been burning a hole in her pocket since yesterday. She hadn't wanted Felix to see it last night and then she'd forgotten about it. The return address had Mr. Sebastian's name on it. He had moved to another gallery and approached her about buying her art. He assured her that he'd had no involvement with the scandals at Le Papillon. Now, safely settled in the train compartment, she opened the letter.

Dear Miss Wexford,

I hope this letter finds you well. I recently took up the position of art director for Justin's Art Collection and Gallery. Mr. Justin has asked me to contact you with regard to a solo exhibition of your Canadian West Coast art collection.
At your convenience please contact me at the gallery to meet with Mr. Justin to discuss details.

Yours Truly
Keith Sebastian
Art Director

She almost screamed in delight, kissing the letter and saying, "Thank you." The woman sitting in the opposite corner of the compartment peered over the top of *The Daily Telegraph* and eyed Sarah quizzically. Sheepishly, Sarah said, "I'm not crazy. I just had some very good news." The woman smiled and returned to her newspaper.

Sarah's heart pounded as she read the letter a second time. *Finally I made it, a solo exhibition.* For the remainder of the journey, she composed her reply to Mr. Sebastian, deciding to meet with him as soon as she returned from Bexhill, which didn't give much time as she needed to prepare her classes before the term started. *Serves you right for procrastinating,* Sarah thought, a little annoyed with herself for being indecisive about whether she would return to teach. She had ultimately decided to do one more year so she could be sure of her future as an artist and her future with Felix—a lot could happen in a year.

Unrealistically, they had assumed their day-to-day lives would continue unchanged, but suddenly they were talking of settling down and marriage. Sarah didn't feel like a bride and they never talked of wedding plans or where they would live, they just wanted to be together. The train jolted to a halt at Bexhill station.

Sarah breathed in the fresh sea air as Mr. Grimsby drove along the Promenade. Such a change from London's grime and the thick fogs that were increasing in thickness and frequency. Bexhill bustled with holidaymakers.

"The Promenade looks busy this evening. Has this been a good summer, Mr. Grimsby?"

"It has, Miss Sarah. It seems the Continent has lost some of its appeal for people's holidays this year."

Anna stood under the portico, beaming as Henry opened the car door.

"Oh, its so good to have you home." Anna hugged Sarah tightly.

"Its good to be home. Where's Grandpa Bill?"

"In the kitchen. He'll be up shortly. Are you hungry?"

"Starving."

"I haven't eaten. I was waiting for you, and Bill will join us."

Balaji bowed slightly as they walked into the Emily Carr Dining Room. "Welcome home, Miss Sarah."

Sarah glanced around the room. "It never changes—I love this room. The Emily Carr paintings are more beautiful every time I look at them. I see you rearranged my paintings of Bexhill. I like it. Nana, I have some good news. Justin's Art Collection and Gallery wants to give me a solo exhibition." Sarah pulled the letter from her pocket.

"This is good news." Anna read the letter. "Are you sure about Mr. Sebastian? Wasn't he involved with Madame? If you know what I mean."

"Nana," Sarah whispered, "Mr. Sebastian is a homosexual. Nothing happened between them. Their relationship was just for appearances." Sarah raised her eyebrows and her voice. "And he assures me he had no involvement with the secret service scandal. I believe him."

"I trust your judgment. I am pleased for you. I know how much you want this."

"Speaking of the secret service, have you heard any more about Dad?"

Anna shook her head, "No, the last we heard the government was working on his release, but it could take years." Anna's eyes filled with empathy. She squeezed Sarah's hand. "I promise, we will tell you as soon as we hear. No more secrets. Does Felix know anything?"

"Another firm has taken over the new trial, so he doesn't know much, but he promised to find out what he could."

Sarah was wondering if this was a good time to mention the change in their relationship when the service door swung open. A thin man in a chef's outfit walked haltingly towards the table. Their waiter, Eddie, pulled out a chair. Sarah put her hand over her mouth to muffle a gasp. The man was Bill Blaine. He could have been a stick figure he was so thin. His face was so translucent that she imagined seeing through him. Anna laid her hand on Sarah's arm and whispered, "Not a word. We'll talk later."

Bill took a big gasp of breath and held his arms out. "Don't I get a hug and kiss from my favourite granddaughter?" Sarah jumped up, her arms wrapped endlessly around his bony shoulders. She was afraid to hug too tight in case she hurt him. "Grandpa, you only have one granddaughter." She laughed and held him at arms length. "You are much too thin. Working too hard no doubt."

"I like to keep busy," he spoke slowly. "Today is Chef's day off, so I am a bit tired." He stopped talking to take in another breath. "Look at your Nana. Doesn't she look good?" Bill held Anna's shoulders and kissed her forehead. "She's ten years younger since the eye surgery." He dropped into the chair beside Anna and kissed her again. "I could marry her all over again."

Sarah laughed and said, "Are you two going to embarrass me?" Should she tell them about Felix? The laughing had given him some colour, but it showed the deep crevices of a too-thin face.

"I agree, Nana, you do look ten years younger. How is your sight?"

"Perfect. Couldn't be better. Now let's eat."

Sarah and Anna ate well. Bill picked at his food, claiming to have been nibbling in the kitchen. Sarah watched his chest move up and down as he struggled to get his breath.

"Well, ladies, I've had a busy day and I need some sleep." He kissed them both goodnight.

Sarah watched him leave the dining room. "How ill is he?" she snapped at Anna. "And why didn't you tell me? I've been enjoying my life in London, not knowing Grandpa Bill was so poorly."

"He made me promise not to say anything to you. With all the stuff that was going on in London, you didn't need to worry about Grandpa Bill. It isn't as bad as it looks. Today was a bad day because Chef was off and so he was working in the kitchen all day. He usually only does a couple of hours light work; paperwork and the menus. He'll be better tomorrow."

"What's wrong? Has he been to the doctor?"

"His heart is enlarged." Anna smiled. "He always did have a big heart. Dr. Gregory is treating him and he's seen a specialist in Brighton."

Sarah felt her own heart beat in panic. "How are they treating it? Is he going to get better?"

"He has some tablets to control his blood pressure and breathing and he's to get rest—lots of it." Anna paused, "Sarah, I don't know what to do. He won't take it seriously. He forgets to take his tablets, works in the kitchen like he did today and rest…well he doesn't. He loves reading, so I signed him up to a book club. He gets two or three books delivered by post every month, but he reads so fast, it doesn't keep him sitting for long. I can remind him about his tablets but I can't stop him in the kitchen." Anna removed her spectacles and wiped her eyes with the napkin. "Can you talk to him? I'm so afraid of losing him."

"Nana, don't cry. I'm here. We'll sort something out between us." Sarah put her arm around Anna and looked up to see Balaji approaching the table. She shook her head and he stepped back, frowning with concern.

"Oh dear, that's not like me to make a public display. I'm sorry." She brushed the tears away and put her spectacles on. "I don't want to talk in our suite. Bill is sleeping. Let's go to my office."

"We could go to the penthouse. It's comfortable there."

"My knees won't like the stairs, sweetheart, and Grandpa Bill made our favourite spice cake for sweet. I'll have Balaji bring us coffee and cake."

Anna beckoned Balaji and gave him instructions. Sarah walked behind her to the office. She couldn't help but notice Anna's pronounced rolling limp. Balaji followed with the tray.

As he placed the tray on the table he paused. "I know, none of Balaji's business, but are you quite well, Mrs. Blaine?"

Anna smiled, Balaji was an excellent maître d' because he cared about people; he'd been at the Sackville for fifteen years and also cared about the family. "I am well. Thank you, Balaji. I apologize for my emotional display in the dining room."

"Please, no apology necessary. Balaji worry about you and Mr. Blaine."

"Thank you, but there is no need to worry." Balaji bowed slightly, aware that he was being dismissed and closed the office door behind him.

"I must be more careful around the staff." Anna said.

"Balaji understands and he is not a gossip." Sarah handed Anna some cake and poured the coffee. "Is there anything you can add about Grandpa's heart condition?"

"The specialist said his heart is damaged and there is always a risk of another stroke or heart attack. He can reduce the risk by taking his tablets and resting quietly. But if he over-exerts himself, then it isn't a question of if but when..." Anna stopped and took a lace hanky from her pocket to dry her tear-soaked eyes. Clearing her throat, she added, "He also suggested easy walks would strengthen his heart. Your grandfather thinks running around the hotel kitchen is as good as an easy walk."

"Nana, I'm sorry I snapped at you. I was just so shocked. I'll help you with Grandpa Bill. I'll talk to him and take him for a walk every day."

"I'm sorry darling, I should have warned you. It will be a tremendous help for me if you take care of Grandpa and talk some sense into him. I am busy with the hotel." Anna grinned. "Our best season for several years. Now, I need to get to bed."

**

Two days later, Sarah managed to persuade Bill to walk along the Promenade. Breathing heavily at first, Sarah made him sit on a bench. She cuddled up to him like she used to do as a child. They gazed at the sea in silence. She rested her head against his chest; his erratic heartbeat scared her, but after a while it slowed down and settled, as did his breathing.

"Grandpa Bill, why won't you do as the doctors say? You are hurting Nana."

"I'm afraid that if I stop I will die. I don't mean to hurt anyone."

"I think you have that all wrong. If you do as your told, you will feel better and live a lot longer. You cannot work in the kitchen. What normally happens when the chef has a day off?"

"The sous-chef takes over, but he's new and inexperienced, so I do it."

"If you and Chef Brian trained the new sous-chef, he can cope. You do not need to be there. Do you?"

"I have to be sure the food is up to standard. I can't walk away. I'm scared; for me, the hotel and most of all for Nana. Who is going to keep an eye on the kitchen and dining room if I'm not there? Nana has enough to do with the hotel guests."

"Listen to yourself, Grandpa. The kitchen and dining room staff are well trained. You practically cloned Brian, he's so much like you. But he's twenty years younger with lots of energy and brilliant ideas—he deserves to take over. Balaji is the best maitre d' you've ever had; the dining room runs smoothly all the time. Nana doesn't need to run the hotel and worry about you. You are not being fair." Sarah stopped, seeing a smile cross his face. "What is it?"

"Balaji is good, I won't deny it. But the best maître d' I ever worked with was your Grandfather Alex. He was impulsive and as annoying as heck, but he ran the best dining room. He charmed the guests, especially the ladies, and between he and Nana they ran this hotel before and after Great War, and Nana ran it alone during the war. The general manager was a terrible man." Seeing his hesitation Sarah said, "I know about Mr. Pickles, you don't need to protect me."

Bill shook his head. "You know your grandmother was not much older than you at that time. You talk about me training my staff; I think Nana did a good job training you. Look at what you have accomplished in twenty-two years. I couldn't be prouder."

"I think you are changing the subject. Please promise me you will stop working in the kitchen. Paperwork, menus and limited supervising is allowed when you are feeling well enough—nothing more."

Sarah waited for his promise and stayed silent. She gazed at the blue sky and listened to the seagulls screech as they wheeled around searching for tidbits left behind by picnicking sunbathers.

"All right, I promise. I'll take up reading again. Nana signed me up for a book club."

"She told me, but she thinks you've read all the books. But you haven't, have you? When are you going to start?"

"Today. Will you sit with me?"

"Of course. Are you ready to head back? I'll pick up my sketch pad and sketch while you read."

**

Every day, Sarah and Bill walked a little further along the Promenade and read and sketched for a couple of hours. Sarah was pleased with Bill's progress. His colour was better and his breathing steadier. She kept him away from the kitchen for nearly a week, except when his advice was needed.

Sarah had work to do. She had stayed in Bexhill longer than she intended. She had paintings to finish and college work to prepare.

She bought Anna a walking stick, hoping the support would ease the pain in her knees. After expressing indignation, she agreed to try *the stick* as she called it, and walked with Bill every morning. Surprisingly, the walking helped Anna's knees and she stopped objecting and began enjoying the walks.

Relieved that she had jumped another hurdle, Sarah returned to London and started the Michaelmas term and signed the contract with Justin's Art. But far from being relaxed, Sarah felt anxious as though she was in a constant race against time. She kept telling herself everything was fine in Bexhill, but deep down she knew it wasn't. Her heart pounded if she was called to the phone during class. She held her breath until she heard Anna's usual cheery voice every time she called Mrs. D's.

It was the end of September before Sarah accepted that Anna and Bill were doing fine, and that was partly because of Felix's reassurance and partly because Darcy and Belle had persuaded Anna and Bill to take a break and spend a couple of weeks at Hillcrest.

Thirty-Six

Anna and Bill Make Decisions

*A*nna hated it when Sarah went back to London and missed her more each time. This time it was worse, and she had shed a tear. In fact, she had been shedding a lot of tears recently. She had not been entirely honest with Sarah about Bill's health, although knowing how astute Sarah was, Anna thought she had probably guessed. Dr. Gregory had been quite blunt: Bill was living on borrowed time. Although his recovery from the stroke had been remarkable, the heart consultant had determined that Bill had suffered at least one, if not more, small undetected heart attacks, causing irreparable damage. The next one would be his last. Bill appeared to be living in denial. Anna carried the burden alone and her heart was breaking.

Things were already changing. She stood in her office at 5:30 a.m., waiting for the sun to rise. The horizon glowed, hiding the rising sun. The sea undulated in the semi-darkness and the plankton glowed on the waves as they rolled onto the beach. She had made many decisions gazing at this scene, and there were more to contemplate. She turned to acknowledge a tap on the door. "Come in, Chef." Chef Brian entered with a tray of coffee and toast. Bill was too tired this morning and had stayed in bed. Every morning, she rolled over in bed and kissed his forehead, dreading the day it felt cold.

"Good morning, Mrs. Blaine." Anna saw Chef searching her face.

"He's all right. Just tired this morning. I persuaded him to get some more rest."

"It perhaps isn't my place to say, but I think Chef is looking better these days. He does listen to me when I tell him to get out of the kitchen," Chef laughed. "Not too graciously, but he understands. Miss Sarah had a big impact on him."

"I'm pleased that he is listening to you in the kitchen, but he tries to take over on your days off, like yesterday. It's hard for him not to be involved. Since Sarah's visit, he is paying attention, and yes, he is looking a little better."

"I must get back to the kitchen. Miss Jenkins left me a note last night to say the Donaldson Luncheon party has grown from twenty to thirty people."

"Goodness, that is a big difference and short notice; the luncheon is today right? Do you have enough food?"

"It's a bit of a scramble, but the butcher owes me a favour. We'll manage. Remember, I was taught by the best. Have a good day, Mrs. Blaine." He smiled again and left the office.

Anna sighed, saying aloud, "At least I have reliable staff. But I do miss the old staff, especially James and Amy. Lily is coping well as head housekeeper. I think it's time I told her that the job is hers permanently."

A voice came from the door, "Talking to yourself again?" Anna spun round. "Bill, I thought you were resting." She studied him carefully and was pleased to see he looked well. Not his old self, but much better. "I've decided to give Lily Amy's job. She managed the summer well and I can't find anyone any better. Amy trained her, so she's easy to work with. Do you think she is too young?"

"No, I don't. She is mature for her age and I think if you talked to Amy she would help when needed. Brian tells me they have a big luncheon today. I think I might help a bit."

Anna gave him a stern look. "Just because you are feeling better doesn't mean you have to go to work. Brian doesn't need your help. I was talking to him this morning. If you feel up to it, why don't we take a drive into Eastbourne and have lunch at The Grand? I need cheering up. I miss Sarah."

"I know what you're up to, trying to get me out of the hotel so I'm not tempted to help." Bill pecked her cheek. "You're right, and I agree that a trip to Eastbourne would be nice."

"Do you think she'll come back and take over the Sackville? I thought if we let her go to art school she would get it out of her system, meet a nice man, and they would come back to Bexhill. I always felt she had talent, but I never dreamt she was brilliant, with so many art opportunities."

"Anna darling, I think we have to accept that she's not going to take over. As far as marriage is concerned, her choice in men has not been good, and unless she isn't telling us something, there isn't anyone on the horizon. She's passionate about her art career and we have to support her. The hotel was our dream, and if Isabelle had lived things would be different."

"What do we do? I love the hotel, but I'm tired and I want to spend time with you."

Bill stared at her seriously, the aqua in his eyes seemed to penetrate her gaze. "I know you think I'm at death's door, but I'm not. I've got a lot of living to do. I need you to stop worrying. Whatever time we have, let's enjoy it together. You gave me a lecture about Brian being able to cope without me and I am going to give you the same lecture. You trained all the staff and the hotel is running smoothly. Mr. Grimsby and the others can manage without you. We are being unfair to expect Sarah to come back, but there is another option."

"Easy now. I'm getting used to leaving the staff in charge. I'm not sure I can handle anything else." Anna gave a nervous laugh.

"We could sell. I know you had an inquiry from Holiday Hotels."

"How did you know?

"I saw the letter on your desk."

"I destroyed it. Insulting, that's what it was. How could they even think we would consider becoming a cheap, no-service hotel?"

"Did they mention money?"

"No. The letter said they were looking at hotel property in Bexhill or Hastings." Shocked at Bill's response, Anna added, "Bill, you wouldn't consider it, would you? What if we have it all wrong and Sarah does want to take over? We've never really asked her outright, and don't forget she is part owner. She loves her studio in the penthouse."

"You're right. We've made assumptions and never really asked her."

Anna stared at the red sky reflecting on the sea. "Red sky at night shepherd's delight, red sky in the morning shepherd's warning. We're going to get a storm today." She felt Bill's arms circle her waist and his breath on her neck. "I think we should begin by stepping back and letting the staff take the reins. "If Sarah can see that the hotel runs smoothly with an absentee owner, she might want to come home." She grinned. "A famous artist might even help promote the hotel."

Bill rested his chin on Anna's head. "You never give up, do you? But I agree we need to spend time away from here. A trip to Eastbourne today, and let's plan a trip to Hillcrest Hall at the end of the month."

"I'll call Belle today."

"I'd like to take a drive up to Rugby for old time's sake. We could stay at the Kings Head Inn, if it still has guest rooms."

Anna didn't answer. She had mixed memories of Rugby, most of them unhappy. Alex had fallen ill and died at the King's Head, Isabelle went to pieces and moved with Sandy and Sarah to Scotland, and Bill had abandoned her, leaving her in the depths of loneliness. Rugby was not a place she wanted to re-visit.

Bill didn't notice her silence and continued, "If the hotel survives when we take small trips, we could go for longer ones."

"Canada." Bill took a wheezy breath. "I'd love to go back for a visit before..." he paused, "We could stay with Charlie and Beth." He started coughing and moved away from Anna to sit on the sofa.

Canadian memories are better, she thought, although the memory of her miserable conniving mother-in-law did flash before her. A trip to visit Charlie and Beth sounded tempting. "It looks to me like we're talking retirement," Anna said, trying to smile. She'd heard the wheeze and now the cough. *Chatting has exhausted him,* she thought. *How is he going to manage a trip anywhere?*

"Did you take your tablets this morning?"

Bill shook his head. "I forgot."

"If you want to do any of these things, you have to be diligent with your pills. I'll get them for you. Stay here."

**

Anna had no idea how difficult it would be to limit her work to a few short hours a day. Bill and the hotel were her life, and if Bill was to live, she had to keep him out of the kitchen. They read books, a pastime they had enjoyed together in their early days at the Sackville. They walked along the Promenade and on good days they stopped for tea at the Pavilion. They went to the Fisherman's Nook for beer and mussels. Anna accepted that their lives had found a new normal, but she couldn't shake a niggling doubt in the back of her mind.

Then, one day while they sat at the Pavilion having tea on the terrace, it hit her like a fist in her stomach: Bill was taking her down memory lane. He strolled to the railing, looked out to sea and said, "I remember the first day we had tea. I was standing at this railing wondering how I could ask you out, not knowing you were sitting at the table behind me." He sat at the table. "Remember, the wind caught the waiter's tray, almost spilling hot tea over you? The commotion made me turn. I couldn't believe my luck when you invited me to join you. That was one of the best days of my life. The other even better day was watching you walk down the gangway off the ship; the day I proposed."

Bill's rash statement, "I'm not at death's door," was a lie. He wasn't getting better, he was preparing to say goodbye, aware that when the time came it would be sudden. Anna vowed to stop worrying about the hotel and live every day with Bill. She found it comforting, and scarily deceiving, that despite his condition, Bill actually looked well at the moment. And they were looking forward to two weeks at Hillcrest with Darcy and Belle.

**

Anna's promise to stop worrying about the hotel was short lived. When they arrived back from Hillcrest, Amy was waiting for in her office.

"Anna, I'm sorry but Lily has done a bunk."

Anna frowned. "What do you mean? I just promoted her to head housekeeper."

"I had a frantic call from Mr. Grimsby to say that there had been a complaint about the cleanliness of one of the guest rooms and 'e couldn't find Lily. Young Susie told 'im Lily had run off to Gretna Green with her boyfriend to get married."

"Is she coming back?"

"I doubt it, her room is empty, not as much as a scarf or stocking left behind. Would you want 'er back?"

"I guess not. I didn't have much luck looking for a housekeeper last time. Amy, can you fill in for awhile?"

"I can give you a couple more days but that's all. Sam and I are going to 'is sister's. We all chipped in and rented one of them villas in Spain."

"That sounds nice. Do you know anyone here in Bexhill that would like to work here?"

"Not really, but I'll ask around. I 'ave to go, Sam's waiting for me. I'll come early tomorrow and get the maids started." Amy paused, adding, "They're all young, Anna you'll 'ave to watch 'em."

"Thanks Amy. See you tomorrow."

Anna leaned back in her chair. "So much for leaving the staff in charge," she said to herself and wondered what Bill had found in the kitchen. She stared at the pile of mail on her desk. It was going to take time to get through that. She would have to work at least half days if not full time to catch up, and she had to watch the chambermaids, advertise and interview housekeepers. She was secretly pleased to have an excuse to work; sitting around reading when there were things to do was frustrating. Surely Bill would understand that she had to work for a while. She wondered how to convince him to stay out of the kitchen. Unlike Lily, who was young, inexperienced and in love—a fact that might have dissuaded Anna from promoting her had she known—Chef Brian was an experienced chef and ran his kitchen well.

Overwhelmed, Anna looked at her desk and decided to start fresh in the morning and went to find Bill in their suite. He lay on the couch watching television. An addition Anna had fought against, preferring reading and conversation but it did keep Bill quiet watching news and football and she did enjoy Coronation Street. She sat next to him and lifted his head to rest it on her lap and stroked his forehead. He felt clammy and looked tired. The journey had exhausted him.

"How was the kitchen? Did they manage while you were away?"

"I didn't go down. I came straight upstairs. I'm not feeling well. Brian can manage. I'll check in the morning."

"Lily quit. Eloped with her boyfriend. Amy took over but she can't stay. I have to find a new housekeeper."

"I am surprised." Bill turned to look at Anna. "Sorry that didn't work out. Did you know she was courting?" Anna shook her head.

"If I had I might not have promoted her. Bill, are you sure you're just tired? You feel sweaty. I think you should sit up; you're breathing funny."

Bill sat up and put his arm around her. "I'm fine." He rubbed his fist on his chest. "Just very tired."

Thirty-Seven

Sadness and Joy

S till holding the receiver to her ear, Sarah disconnected the call with her finger and waited for the dial tone, immediately dialing Felix's flat. He answered on the first ring. "Felix, Nana just called. Grandpa Bill has had a heart attack…" Sarah gasped through sobs, tears streaming down her face.

"I'll be there in ten minutes. Pack a bag and we'll drive there tonight." Mrs. Debinski, came out of her sitting room and took the receiver from Sarah's hand, placed it on the cradle and held Sarah in her arms. Johnny hugged her, crying with her. When Felix arrived, they were in a huddle in the hallway, Mrs. Debinski stepped back and let Felix take over.

"Come, let's get a your things." He mouthed a thank you to Mrs. D. "Did Anna say how he was?"

"Just that Dr. Gregory was sitting with him and had told her to telephone me to get to Bexhill quickly." Sarah didn't need to say anything more.

Felix broke all the speed limits, grateful for the Jaguar's power as they hurtled to Bexhill. Sarah stared at the darkness in silence. Felix held her hand as he saw her tears glisten in the oncoming headlights. As they passed the old Cooden Military Camp she wiped her face and took a breath. "I'd better stop these tears. I need to be strong for

Nana."

"You'll be fine. I'm here. I'm not going anywhere. I love you."

"I love you too. I'm glad you're here. Thanks." His kindness set off more tears.

The portico lights shone into the car and Dan the night doorman opened the door for Sarah. His face pale and grim, he said, "Mrs. Blaine and Dr. Gregory are with Mr. Blaine in their suite, Miss Sarah."

Sarah stood outside Suite 305 and tried to prepare herself. *Was he still alive? Had he waited for her?* Felix, saw her hesitation, brushed her cheek and put his arm around her. "You'll be fine. Here, take my hand."

She opened the door and called, "Nana, we're here."

Anna came out of the bedroom, her cheeks white, her eyes red and her chin trembling. She said, "He's hanging on for you." Sarah rushed into the bedroom and Anna clung to Felix.

Bill sat propped up with pillows, every breath a gasp. If he hadn't spoken, Sarah would have thought him a ghost. "Sarah...my sweet Sarah..." He began coughing.

Dr. Gregory stepped forward and put a mask over his mouth and explained, "The oxygen helps him breath. Give him a minute. You can talk to him, but he's too weak to reply at the moment."

Sarah climbed on the bed and held his hand until he opened his eyes. He tried to remove the mask, Dr. Gregory helped him. "Sarah, do you remember what I said about following your dreams?" One sentence and he was gasping again. The mask went back on.

"I do Grandpa Bill." She knew he was talking about choosing art over the hotel. "My dream is already coming true. I am successful. I'm featured in the London Art Gallery and Justin's is preparing an international show."

"I'm proud of you." He closed his eyes. Sarah glanced at Dr. Gregory.

"He needs to rest for awhile." He looked from Anna to Sarah. "Make some tea and relax in the sitting room while he sleeps. I'll come and get you when he wakes."

Sarah went into the little-used kitchen and made tea and coffee and Felix poured himself a brandy, offering one to Sarah. She shook her head.

"Perhaps Dr. Gregory might like a brandy or a coffee?"

"I'll ask." Felix went into the bedroom. Dr. Gregory declined the drink but asked Felix to stay as Bill had been asking for him. Bill opened his eyes and pulled the mask away. "Felix, I don't have much longer but you need to know... Sarah loves you." He took a breath. "I want you to promise me you'll marry her and take care of her. Don't let her take over the hotel..." Another breath, "Art..." The coughing drew Dr. Gregory back into the room.

Felix said to the doctor, "I need to tell him something."

"Bill, I love Sarah and we plan to marry. We just hadn't found the right time to tell you." Bill stopped coughing, smiled and said, "I knew...I saw the same look in your eyes that I had for Anna, but I let someone take her away..." He stopped to breath in more oxygen. "One more thing...look after Anna for me...this place is too much for her."

"Of course. Anna is family." Felix's voice croaked, a tear rolled down to his chin.

Bill's fingers touched Felix's hand as he whispered, "Thank you.... I'd like Sarah and Anna...to come here."

Anna lay beside him and Sarah held his hand all night.

Bill died as the sun was rising.

**

Two lonely figures in black dresses, their fingers linked together as they walked silently down the aisle behind the coffin. Each wore a black veil to hide the streaming tears. The scene familiar to both; memories of loved ones lost. Anna turned slightly, glancing towards Sarah. Sarah squeezed Anna's hand, oblivious to the surrounding mourners. St. Andrew's church was full, the doors left open as the crowd spilled into the street.

Anna had closed the hotel for the funeral to allow the staff to attend. As she and Sarah walked into the silent lobby, she heard Bill's voice. *"Don't cry too long. Celebrate my life, my love for you."*

"This quiet won't do. Bill would be so upset to see us crying and miserable, tip-toeing around the hotel."

"Nana, it's all right. It's quiet because no one is here. The staff are coming back from the funeral. The place will soon be full of people. Charlie, Felix, Darcy and Belle are right behind us. Let's go and freshen up." Anna nodded and followed Sarah.

When Anna and Sarah stepped back into the lobby it was full of people. The staff were already serving drinks and hors d'oeuvres.

"I want to be with family first," Anna said, moving towards Charlie and her sister Lou. Charlie had come alone as Beth and Charlotte couldn't make it in time. Sarah hugged Great Aunt Lou, who looked very old. Although her husband Robert had died several years ago, his abusive drinking had damaged her irreparably and she hid away on the farm with her youngest son, Simon, who took care of her and the farm. Anna was pleased but surprised that Lou had made the journey. She glanced at Robbie, her eldest, and figured he had persuaded his mum to come.

Sarah sidled up to Felix and felt his warm hand on her back. She appreciated the comfort. Belle and Darcy were always included in the family group and it occurred to Sarah that in fact they would soon be family, they just didn't know it yet.

Anna was talking to Julia Castillo, who had flown in from Alabama. She was no longer Julia Castillo; having moved on from bad memories in Chicago, she had married a rancher and settled happily in her hometown in southern USA.

Sarah asked the waiter to fetch her a brandy and she sat on an unoccupied sofa, in awe of the number of people. Some she recognized, like Mr. Darwin, Miss Berkley and Mr. Sebastian and several of her college colleagues. And to her surprise she saw Mrs. Debinski and Johnny. *How did they get here?* she wondered. Lizzy sat beside her, gave her a hug and patted her arm—they sat in silence. Aware of what all this meant to Sarah's life, no words were necessary. Friends understood.

All of a sudden, Anna's voice screamed over the babbling group. "Sophie!" Sarah jumped up and ran to Anna, stopping when she saw the smiling faces.

Anna repeated, "Sophie Romano." Tears filled their eyes and the room went still. James Lytton and his boyfriend Jeremy stood with Amy and Sam, and watched the scene unfold. Sarah wasn't sure who Sophie was. She looked about Nana's age and quite beautiful, and she obviously knew James and Amy. Sarah figured she must be an old staff member.

She felt a tap on her shoulder and turned around, she couldn't believe her eyes. Already close to tears, she wailed, "Aunt Florence, Uncle Wilfred, I didn't expect you to come down from Scotland." She hugged Florence and bent down to kiss Wilfred in the wheelchair. Wilfred tapped his leg. "Gammy legs don't work too well."

Hearing Sarah yell, Felix was at her side. "Felix, I want you to meet two of the most wonderful people. Great Aunt Florence is Grandpa Alex's younger sister and my mum used to call Wilfred her pretend grandfather when she was a little girl. We lived in the same neighborhood in Scotland when I was very young." Childhood memories of Scotland flashed before her, mostly of her father; happy at first and then profound sadness.

The afternoon continued along the same tone as people from far and wide came to pay their respects. Sarah anxiously glanced at Anna. She looked pale and tired. It was time the guests departed, but so many old acquaintances were being rekindled she thought it could go on for some time.

"Nana, would you like to take a rest?"

Anna nodded, "But I can't leave all these guests."

"Yes, you can. They will understand. Charlie can be host and Belle and Darcy won't mind entertaining everyone."

"Bill would have been so happy to see so many old friends. Although as the crowd grew, he would probably be hiding in a corner or heading back to his kitchen by now, telling me there were too many people and too much noise." She tried to smile but the thought brought more tears.

Sarah and Anna made their apologies and said goodbye then took the lift to the third floor. Anna lay on the bed and fell asleep almost immediately.

Sarah wasn't sure if leaving the mourners was for her benefit or Anna's, but she too had had enough of crowds and called the kitchen to make arrangements for dinner to be sent up to the suite for the immediate family members plus the Thorntons. The rest of the guests would eat in the dining room. She knew that this small group would respect Anna's privacy. Felix came up to check on them.

Dinner in Anna's suite was not only a wise decision, but turned out to be pleasant for everyone. Balaji delivered and served the dinner, and rather than it being a sombre occasion, it was a time of reflecting on the past, particularly Bill's past, and the tight knit family were able to share. Sarah, intrigued by Nana's reaction to Sophie, decided to ask who she was.

"Nana, who is Sophie Romano?"

"Sophie was my roommate when I first started working at the Sackville. We didn't get along so well in the beginning but we became close friends. When I was courting Alex, she was courting Bill. We were a foursome; we went to the beach, to the pictures. Bill taught Sophie to play chess and she was good and I was jealous. When I married Alex, Sophie thought Bill would propose, but he ran away instead. Sophie hated me at that time because she knew Bill loved me. She quit her job here to be a nurse in the Great War. I haven't seen Sophie since maybe 1915 or 16 and yet I recognized her right away. She lives in Derby where she grew up. I hope we can meet and catch up."

"Wow, that's quite a story. Something Bill said to me the night he died is making sense now." Felix paused, *Is this the right place or time to tell them about Sarah and me?*

"What did he say?" Anna said curious.

"I have to ask Sarah something. I'm not sure it is an appropriate time."

Sarah smiled and said, "I think it is a perfect time, we're all together and I think we could do with some cheerful news. Grandpa Bill would approve."

Felix went quite red and cleared his throat several times. He took Sarah's hand and they stood in the middle of the sitting room.

"As you know, Sarah and I have known each other since we were kids, best friends, but a few months ago that all changed. We discovered we loved each other in a romantic way and I asked Sarah to marry me and she said yes…" The group started congratulations and questions. Felix held his hand up. "But, hold on there's more. We both have careers and didn't want to get married just yet, that's why we kept it to ourselves."

Tears trickled down Anna's face. "I'm so happy, and Bill would be have been too."

"I told Bill the night he died because he asked me to marry Sarah. He said, I had the same look in my eyes that he had for Anna, but he let her go …or words to that effect. I told him that Sarah and I loved each other and we planned to marry but we'd never got around to telling anyone. He said I'd made him very happy and…" Felix looked towards Anna, "He said I had to take care of you too Anna."

Between tears, Anna replied, "Bill was heartbroken when I married Alex, but he was always a friend. On his deathbed, Alex told Bill he had always known that Bill loved me and Alex made Bill promise to marry me and look after me. It nearly didn't happen. A long story for another time, but I'm so glad it did."

Darcy shook his son's hand, "You have made me so happy, son. And Sarah, I couldn't ask for a better daughter."

Belle beamed through happy tears, first hugging Sarah, then Anna, then her son.

"I'm so glad you told us tonight. I know Bill is still with us and he always hated tears and sadness. He's at peace and happy that we ended this sad day on such a happy note. Thank you."

**

Sarah stayed with Anna for another week, longer than she'd intended, but when Charlie announced he had to return to Canada, Anna had cried so much that Sarah couldn't leave her. Julia offered to stay. It was an opportunity to introduce her rancher husband to southern England. Although Anna and Julia were old friends from a train trip in Canada, Julia had befriended Bill in Chicago; a time in Bill's life Anna knew little about. Belle planned to come back to Bexhill after she'd finished closing up the store and cafe at Hillcrest. Sarah returned to London and her classes, feeling comfortable that at least for the next few weeks Anna would manage. After that, Sarah wasn't sure, and she was afraid to think about Christmas. If she was honest, Anna's future scared her. The devotion between Anna and Bill was rare. As independent a woman as Anna had been in her younger days, Sarah feared she wouldn't cope without Bill. Perhaps she should resign from college and return to Bexhill, at the end of term?

Thirty-Eight

Exhaustion Takes Over

Mrs. Debinski and Johnny met her at the door. Sarah hadn't realized what a fusspot Mrs. D had become, or maybe her severe exterior had always been a cover-up. She certainly showed much warmth, caring and love for Johnny. Sarah learned that they had caught the train to come to the funeral and instead of staying the night, they had returned on the evening train.

"Mrs. D, you should have stayed at the hotel. I'm sorry I didn't spend time with you. But it meant a lot to me that you and Johnny came."

"Oh, no, we couldn't have stayed. Johnny and I wouldn't fit in. You and Miss Lizzy have been kind to us; me and Johnny. Accepting him and the like. You gave him the courage to go out and mix with people. I won't forget that. So, when you needed us, we were there." Mrs. D patted her hair and changed the subject. "I put a pint of milk and loaf of bread in your cupboard. It's not a gift, you owe me one shilling and thrupence. I thought you might be wanting a cup of tea. Leaving in such a hurry, the milk had turned."

Sarah smiled at her duplicity and wondered why she had to cover up her kindness. Some hurt in her past, no doubt. She opened her handbag and handed a Cadbury's Chocolate bar to Johnny. "I nearly forgot, this is for you, Johnny, and Mrs. D, that's for the milk and bread. Thank you."

Mrs. D took the money. "You look a bit peaky. You need to get to bed early and I've got things to attend to."

Johnny gave her a bear hug. She patted his back and turned to hug Mrs. D, who brushed her away. "None of that soft stuff. Keep it for Johnny."

Sarah felt as though she had lead boots on as she climbed the stairs. Tiredness overwhelmed her, the past two weeks had been hard and she had some thinking to do. Nana was okay for now. Too tired to think, she lay down on the bed and closed her eyes.

"Hillcrest!" Sarah shouted and sat bolt upright. She wasn't just marrying Felix, she was marrying the next Lord Thornton and eventually she would be Lady Thornton. Was this what she wanted? Suddenly, decisions about her future, already difficult, had become extremely complicated. She concentrated on the word, *eventually*. This gave her time, or did it?

Sarah slept fitfully, resulting in her waking up late and arriving at college unprepared for class. How could this happen? She felt disengaged, as though her life was spinning out of control and moving on without her. Could she be losing it? She couldn't think as she rushed into the lecture hall and stood speechless in front of the lectern.

A sea of faces stared at her, puzzled and concerned. She heard a voice, Miss Berkley stood at her side, her hand cupping Sarah's elbow. "Miss Wexford, come with me." The voice sounded hollow and distorted, the buzzing in her ears shut the world out. She didn't have to think anymore.

Sarah opened her eyes, wondering what had just happened. She felt a scratchy wool blanket on her legs and arms. She recognized the staff room sofa, but she didn't remember lying down. She heard whispering, but couldn't make out what they were saying. In spite of the blanket, she felt cold and shivered. A smiling young woman in white pulled the blanket up to her chin and took her wrist, gazing at the nurse's watch pinned to her chest. She asked, "How are we feeling?"

"I don't know," Sarah squeaked and cleared her throat. Miss Berkley was perched on the edge of the sofa. Sarah looked at her, "I'm not myself…" Tears pricked the back of her eyes. *No, I mustn't weep. Not here at college.* "What happened?"

"You are the only person I know who can faint standing up." Miss Berkley chuckled. "A worried student fetched me and I brought you to the staff room and called Nurse Green."

"I remember feeling spaced out. I'm okay now, I must get back to class."

Nurse Green put her hand firmly on Sarah's shoulder. "Not so fast. You need to rest." She turned to Miss Berkley, adding, "Miss Wexford should go home and see her doctor before returning. Is there anyone we can call?"

"I'm fine. I've just returned from a stressful time at home and I have a lot on my mind. Things just caught up with me, that's all." The thought of going home appealed to Sarah, she did feel strange. "I'll just go home today. My fiancé will pick me up. If I'm no better tomorrow, I'll call the doctor." Satisfied with Sarah's response, Nurse Green wrote down Felix's telephone number and returned to her office to call.

"Fiancé?" Miss Berkley repeated.

Sarah sat up and removed the itchy blanket. "Yes, I thought if I said fiancé Nurse Green would believe I was being looked after. Actually, it's the first time I've said fiancé. It's not common knowledge; please keep this between us."

"Of course. Who's the lucky man?"

"Felix Thornton."

"A barrister and an earl in waiting. I'm impressed."

"That's part of my problem. On top of the hotel, my grandmother, and my career…" Sarah paused, "When Grandpa died, everything changed. Nothing is the same." The lunchtime bell drowned any more conversation with Miss Berkley as the teachers flooded the staff room for their break. Upon seeing Sarah, many of her colleagues expressed their condolences. Her already pale face turned to parchment. Miss Berkley explained that Sarah wasn't feeling well and motioned for the staff to give her some space. Sarah felt her head spinning again and then a familiar hand took her arm. Felix wrapped his arm around her. Holding her tightly so she wouldn't fall, he practically carried her to the car.

Felix tapped on Mrs. Debinski's door. "Mrs. D, Sarah had a fainting spell at work and I have just brought her home and put her to bed. Would you be kind enough to check in on her? I'll be back later, but I have to be in court this afternoon."

"I told her she looked peaky last night. It's all too much for her. Leave it to me, I'll look after her."

Sarah lay in bed staring at the ceiling, with Mrs. D feeling her forehead and tucking the blankets around her and pulling the curtains. She remembered her mother doing that when she had measles. Eventually her eyes too heavy to keep open and she began to dream. Her mother's hand stroked her cheek and she smiled, but as she smiled back her mother was cross, pointing to a piece of paper with disapproval. Nana appeared from nowhere and snatched the paper, wagging her finger at her mother. Sarah called out in her sleep, "Stop." She felt a cool cloth on her head. The dream frightened her. She remembered her mother arguing about her art. Her mother said it was no good and that she needed to learn the business. Was her mother right? It seemed that Nana had changed her mind over the years. Although she'd encouraged her, she considered it just a hobby. Mrs. D patted her hand and gently whispered, "Shush, my dear. You're safe; go back to sleep." The words soothed her and Sarah drifted back into a deep sleep.

The next time she woke, the room was dark and quiet and the chink in the curtains showed an artificial yellow light. The dream remained vivid in her mind and brought back vague memories of her mother and grandmother arguing. How long had she been sleeping? She listened hard and heard footsteps on the stairs.

"Hello. You're awake." Felix sat on the bed and brushed loose curls from her face. "Feeling better?"

"Much better. What happened?"

"I'm not a doctor, but I would say exhaustion. You passed out at college and gave Miss Berkley quite a fright. I think you should see the doctor."

"I'm all right. Sleep is what I needed. There's so much to think about. Felix, I'm not sure I want to get married."

"Where did that come from?"

"How can I manage the hotel, my career and Hillcrest?"

"Slow down there, little lady. We won't be taking over at Hillcrest for years. My dad is only in his mid sixties, Mum's younger, and they're in excellent health. You know how I feel about giving up the law. Trust me, we have years before we become Lord and Lady Thornton."

"It doesn't seem real. I'm marrying you, not Hillcrest, but last night it hit me that I was marrying the heir to Hillcrest. I had never thought of you that way."

"Me neither." Felix laughed, "I'm like my Uncle Felix; he hated the estate. I can't say I hate it, but if it wasn't my birthright I wouldn't choose it. My dad loved it, even as a boy. He told me they used to call him Little Lord Thornton even though it wasn't his birthright until Uncle Felix died. We don't have to rush getting married, but I do want to be with you and marriage would make it easier, and make an honest woman of you."

"Its not marriage, it's the title. Knowing it will be many more years makes me feel better."

"Are you hungry? Mrs. D made us dinner. I'm not sure what it is, but it smells delicious. I'll set the table while you get dressed."

Sarah pulled on trousers and a jumper, tied her hair into a ponytail and sat at the table. The smell from the kitchen fueled her appetite as Felix carried two steaming plates to the table.

"Now this is a real home-cooked meal. I'm hiring her as my housekeeper. I almost forgot, guess who I had a letter from?"

Sarah shook her head, "Who?"

"Lorraine. I can't make out what she wants, but knowing Lorraine, she wants something." Felix gave a wry smile. "I don't know what I saw in her. You two are so different. She couldn't wait to be Lady Thornton, and for you it was an afterthought." Felix kissed her forehead. "Stop frowning, I can handle her. I owe her nothing. But she mentioned you and wished us all the best, which I found strange."

"Charlotte. Uncle Charlie would have told Charlotte we were engaged. Charlotte teaches at the same school as Lorraine."

"Oh, she won't be happy about that. She was jealous of our friendship. Actually, she didn't believe me when I said we were only friends. Seems she was right." Felix reached for her hand. "She can't use her manipulating ways across the ocean."

"I wouldn't be too sure. I will write and tell Charlotte not to discuss our plans with her."

**

Mrs. D insisted Sarah go to the doctor before she returned to college. The doctor assured Sarah the fainting was caused by stress and exhaustion and advised her to stay off work for the remainder of the week. She informed Mrs. D and Felix that the doctor had given her the okay to return to work—she just omitted to say when, and neither asked.

She returned to the college early the following morning to do some catching up. There was a message waiting for her from Anna. Knowing she would be worried, she immediately dialed the hotel.

"Nana, is everything alright?"

"Where were you? I called yesterday and Mrs. D said you weren't home."

"Sorry, Nana, I didn't get your message. How are you? Is everything okay at the hotel?"

"Yes, I miss you, that's all. Julia went up to London for a few days. She'll be back by the weekend."

"Did Belle say when she was coming? I don't want you to be alone, but I can't come down. I have a lot of work to do, Nana. I'm not sure when I'll be home. I'll try in a couple of weeks. I'll see if Felix will come and then we can drive down."

"I'm excited about you and Felix, it's hard to believe you'll be the next Lady Thornton. I remember the day I met Darcy's mother. She was a very imposing lady who scared me to death."

"It is hard to believe and it scares me. Nana, I can't chat now. I came in early this morning to prepare my class. I'll call in a couple of days." As she hung up, the loneliness in Anna's voice seemed to linger. Maybe she should go this weekend, but she had exams to prepare and art assignments to administer, not to mention two commissioned art pieces that had to be finished before Christmas. *I'll call her on Friday.*

The bell jangled as she dismissed the class, grateful that she had a spare period after lunch. She would have loved a cup of tea, but she felt woozy. She put her head on her desk, afraid she might faint again.

"Are you all right, Miss Wexford?"

"Miss Berkley, yes, just tired and I have so much to do."

"Did you see the doctor? Is he okay with you coming back to work?"

Sarah nodded, not wanting to lie because she wasn't good at it. "He said it was nothing to worry about and to take it easy for a couple of days."

Miss Berkley frowned and paused, "You look pale." Sarah sensed she didn't quite believe her explanation. "Don't you have an assistant?"

"No, not this term."

"I'll find a student to help you."

"Thank you, that would be marvelous."

"I'll let you know by Monday. Now come and get yourself some lunch." Sarah stood up. The dizziness, thankfully, had passed and she went to the staff room, which was buzzing with shock and sadness—the US President, Kennedy, had been assassinated the night before. It wasn't that she didn't care, but she just couldn't take on any more drama and made tea, escaping back to her classroom.

She had intended to stay late after class, but afraid she might have another dizzy spell, she hailed a cab and went home. Johnny greeted her at the door with a hug and handed her a blue airmail letter from Canada.

"Thanks Johnny. It's from my cousin Charlotte. She lives in Canada. Do you want to come up and have a cup of tea?"

"Yes. Mummy at Women's Institute tonight. Johnny not like being alone. Can I see your paintings?"

Sarah made tea and Johnny went into her studio, he picked up a sketch book and some charcoal, Sarah couldn't believe her eyes as she watched him sketch. "Johnny, when did you learn to do that? It's very good."

"Sorry, Johnny didn't mean to touch your things."

"Its alright I don't mind. You can have the sketch book and charcoal. Who taught you?"

"You. Johnny like to watch you." Sarah realized all the times he had sat quietly in her studio, he was learning. The front door banged. "Mummy's home. See you later alligator." He gave a sly grin. Bill Haley's song was his favourite.

"In a while crocodile." They both laughed as Johnny ran down the stairs.

Sarah slit the three sides of the aerogramme and carefully unfolded the thin blue paper.

Dear Sarah

I am so sorry I was not able to come to Uncle Bill's funeral. Dad told me all about it and I am so sad for you and Aunt Anna; I know you'll miss him terribly.

I understand your paintings are causing quite a stir in the art community. Your name is often associated with Emily Carr. I tell everyone that we travelled to B.C. together and I was with you when you when you were inspired to paint Whispering Trees. You are famous here too, and I'm so proud to be your cousin. School is going well. I was promoted to Vice Principal this fall, so I'm kept pretty busy, as I still teach but now have a lot of other responsibilities and I enjoy every minute. I even manage to find time for a boyfriend. He's a professor at the university. I think it might be serious, but it is too early to tell.

How's college with you? Dad mentioned you might have to quit teaching to run the hotel if Aunt Anna can't manage alone. How do you feel about that? From our conversations when you were here I had the impression that the hotel business was not for you. Any news on your father's release? I asked Dad, but he didn't know anything.

Sarah stopped reading, the reminder about her father made her feel guilty, or was it the hotel? Had Uncle Charlie made an assumption, or had Anna said something to him? The next paragraph took her attention away from the hotel.

I've saved the best for the last. I have some juicy news about Lorraine. She came back to school, not happy I may add, and then took sick leave towards the end of the school year. I didn't think much about it until I heard on the grapevine that she had a baby. Rumour has it that she and the baby's father are to be married. I don't know why they didn't marry before and announce a premature baby. Isn't that the way it's done? Anyway, she's back to teaching, so I don't know where the baby is; with a nanny probably. She hardly speaks to me, so what I've heard is hearsay. She still looks stunning and I didn't notice any weight gain. I guess some people are just lucky. I took great pleasure in telling her about you and Felix. Oh, I forgot to congratulate you.

*I knew you two loved each other. I think Lorraine did too. When
is the wedding? Make sure it's during school holidays so I can
come.*

She read the last paragraph again and grinned saying, "Well, Miss
Social-Climbing Lorraine, I'm happy about your upcoming nuptials.
You didn't get your Lord, so who's the unlucky man? I can't say I
wish you well, but at least you'll leave Felix alone. So why did you
write to him?" Sarah yawned, too tired to think.

Thirty-Nine

Christmas 1963

⚬⚭⚬

T he Royal College of Art's annual Christmas exhibition for exceptional students was underway. Three of Sarah's students were exhibiting, which reflected well on her teaching abilities, but Mr. Darwin had been disappointed that she had only exhibited two of her own paintings. She had rationalized it by saying the exhibition was for students, knowing full well that the big draw was Sarah Wexford's Canadian West Coast art. Had she not approached one of her clients to show his commissioned piece, she would only have had one, which she had neglected to tell Mr. Darwin. She was reminded that there was still one commissioned piece of art to complete. Panic hit her stomach; she only had two days to finish it.

The Convocation Hall was hot and loud with so many people. Sarah nodded and tried to pay attention to the conversation she was part of, but her head was spinning. She excused herself and went to the lady's room. These dizzy spells were becoming more frequent. *Stress,* she thought. *As soon as I get home for the holidays I'll be fine.* She splashed cold water on her face and touched up her makeup. Feeling better, she went back to the exhibition just as Felix arrived. She grabbed his hand, happy to have an escort for the evening. He glanced at her quizzically. She smiled and whispered, "I miss you. Are your parents coming?"

"No, Christmas at Hillcrest is going well. More visitors than they've ever had before. Mum did a fabulous job of decorating this year. Sometimes her American roots are dazzling. Hillcrest Hall is a cross between an old-fashioned Dickens Christmas and flashy American glitz, but it works. Why don't you take Anna to see it? You can take notes for when you take over."

"Me! I thought you said it would be years before we took over Hillcrest."

"It is. I'm teasing."

"Well don't. I'm not ready for all that."

"I'm sorry." Felix kissed her cheek.

"Enough of that, you two love birds." Sarah swung around to find Miss Berkley grinning at them. "Mr. Darwin is looking for you, Miss Wexford. Excuse us Mr. Thornton."

Mr. Darwin was standing in front of her paintings, talking to Mr. Justin.

"Miss Wexford, it is nice to see you again. I was asking if these paintings are for sale?"

She pointed to the painting she had called *Gatherings*, a Canadian coastal scene with a Haida long house. "I'm afraid this one is sold, but the windy forest scene, *Winds of Time*, is for sale."

"Um…I really like this one. Do you have any others? I'm looking for my private collection."

"I don't have anything at the moment."

"I'll take the *Winds of Time* and I want one just like *Gatherings*, say by March? At that time, you can show me what you have for the autumn show."

"Thank you. Mr. Justin, you do realize that my paintings are unique. I can paint something similar to *Gatherings* but it won't be identical."

"It has to be similar, totem poles, long house and the coast."

"It will have all those elements and be unique." Mr. Justin nodded dismissively. Sarah hated it when people dismissed her like that, but two sales were worth the insult. She returned to join Felix, who was talking to an art critic who was an acquaintance of his father's. Darcy had quite a reputation for collecting rare art and as Sarah listened to Felix it was apparent that he had an interest in modern art, something she had never been aware of until today. Felix took her arm and they spent the evening talking to students and guests. As the crowds thinned, they said goodbye and went for dinner.

Sarah worked day and night to finish the canvas. The painting was a Christmas present from Lord Cardish to his wife, one of Belle's friends. She felt uncomfortable because it wasn't her best work. She really needed more time. She reminded herself that her perfectionism was often unrealistic. Felix had assured her it was beautiful and any flaws, if there were any, would not be noticed. Lord Cardish's chauffeur pulled up to the house to pick up the painting just as Felix arrived to take her to Bexhill.

"That was much too close," she said to Felix as he loaded the car.

"You've had a lot of distractions in the last few months and you made it with a day to spare, Christmas Eve isn't until tomorrow," he said, laughing with a hint of sarcasm.

"It was due three weeks ago. I think your mother spoke to Lord Cardish because he was understanding."

"Time to relax. You look tired. Not much sleep I'll bet? You can sleep in the car."

Sarah was asleep before they had driven out of London and didn't open her eyes until Eastbourne. Felix patted her hand. "You slept all the way. Do you feel better? We're almost there."

Henry opened the massive lobby door. "Welcome home, Miss Sarah." The lobby was filled with Christmas lights and garlands, and the tree stretched up to the ceiling, the chandelier reflecting the prisms of light on the staircase. Colourful parcels were piled under the tree, and yet Sarah felt no Christmas joy. She looked for Anna, wondering why she hadn't greeted them like she usually did.

"Nana!" she called walking into her office. Sarah's heart sank to see

303

a thin, frail old lady standing by the window staring out to sea.

"Sarah, "Anna rushed over and hugged her so tightly she could hardly breathe. "I didn't hear you come in. I'm so happy to see you. Here, give me another hug. Where's Felix?"

"I'm right here, mother-in-law-to-be. May I call you that?"

Anna laughed, "Well, that depends son-in-law-to-be. If we keep this up we'll be tongue tied before the night's out." They all laughed. "You can call me Nana or Anna. I'll stick to Felix."

"You must be hungry, or do you want a drink?"

"Both," Sarah and Felix said in unison.

"We'll go into the dining room. But before we do, I have some news for you. Good news, I hope." Anna took a buff envelope with Her Majesty's Service written across the top in bold black letters and unfolded a white letter. "Your father has been released from jail and taken to a military hospital where he'll spend the next five to seven days."

Sarah stood perfectly still, afraid to speak in case she had not heard correctly. Her fear wrapped around the word hospital. Releasing her tongue, she said, "How is he? Did they say why he was in hospital? When will he be home?"

Felix put his arm around her shoulders. "He's in hospital so the doctor can give him a thorough examination before he is debriefed by senior officers. That is normal practice."

"Can we go and see him?"

"The authorities won't let him speak to anyone until the process is complete. Try and be patient. I anticipate with the Christmas holidays it will be next week before we hear any more. I'll call my office and see if they've heard anything. You and Anna go in for dinner."

Balaji greeted them. "How nice to see you in the dining room, Mrs. Blaine, and welcome home, Miss Sarah. Sarah liked the familiar greeting from Balaji, but it wasn't the same. Grandpa Bill was missing and Anna felt it too. Obviously she didn't eat in the dining room very often.

"I miss him," Sarah said, squeezing Anna's hand.

"Me too, everything reminds me of him. Sometimes I see the baize door open and imagine Bill smiling, rushing in, apologizing for being late. I miss him so much. Some days are so long I think they'll never end."

"I'm sorry, Nana. How can I help?"

"You can't, child. Time will heal. I keep busy. Let's enjoy our first evening together. We get precious few these days."

Felix arrived at the table. "We're in luck. I thought everybody would be gone for Christmas, but I used my charm and gleaned a little more information from an unsuspectingly helpful clerk." He raised his eyebrows, "She's new and keen and told me more than she should have. This is what I was told. Sandy Wexford was released four days ago. He is in hospital, probably in Belgium of all places. He is reported to be in good health, all things considered and currently in the debriefing process."

Sarah relaxed, feeling excited that soon her father would be home. Suddenly hungry, she dittoed Felix's order of steak and red wine. Darcy and Belle arrived unexpectedly early, making dinner a festive occasion.

**

Christmas Eve afternoon, Sarah tried to be upbeat as she and Anna went downstairs to wish the staff Happy Christmas. The staff tree was in their dining room, loaded with presents, but the mood was sombre. Bill had been well liked among all the staff. Chef was doing a great job, but he wasn't Bill. The new housekeeper was a severe, cold woman and the young maids were afraid of her. The atmosphere was not good; Sarah could not remember it ever being this bad. The staff were worried for Anna. She had to do something.

She heard the choir warming up in the lobby. Christmas carols around the tree had become a Sackville tradition—perhaps the staff would enjoy a sing-a-long? Sarah beckoned to Balaji and whispered,

"Balaji, go upstairs and ask the choir to come down here, please. And ask Eddie to pour everyone a glass of sherry."

Sarah tapped her glass. "Hello everyone, Mrs. Blaine and I would like to wish you a Happy Christmas. We miss Chef Bill; it's hard for us all. But one thing I'm certain of is that he would have been quite upset to see so many long faces, especially at Christmas. So please, put a smile on your face and raise your glass to Chef Bill."

"Chef Bill."

Anna and Sarah handed the presents out, each personally labeled and chosen carefully. The room filled with rustling paper and gasps of pleasure and a buzz of conversation.

"I thought you might like some cheerful music, so I have invited the choir to come join us to sing some of your favourite carols. Mrs. Blaine and I will look after your stations for twenty minutes. Please go ahead and ask for your favourite songs."

Sarah helped Anna up the steps. "I don't come down here often, my knees creak on the stairs. Whatever gave you the idea to toast Bill?"

"I had to do something, everyone was so sad. We might be sad, but our guests are expecting fun and celebration," Sarah said as the choir and staff belted out "Good King Wenceslas". "I think that did the trick."

Anna smiled, "Dorothy did something very similar after your mother died. The staff were sad and worried about me and Bill. Dorothy recognized it. We met with the staff and reassured them that everything was fine."

"Nana, how's the new housekeeper working out? She seems a bit severe. I think the maids are afraid of her."

"I don't really know. Mr. Grimsby seems to like her and Dorothy hasn't complained." Anna grinned. "I was terrified of Mrs. Banks when I started here. It keeps the maids on their toes."

"Maybe," Sarah said thoughtfully, she didn't like the fact that Anna seemed unaware of what was going on in housekeeping. "Are we fully booked for the holidays?"

"I think so. Ask Mr. Grimsby."

"And winter conferences? January is usually slow, but what's it like in February?"

"Why all the questions? Dorothy takes care of all that."

"Just wondering how business is going. You always had these things at your fingertips."

Anna gave a shrug, "It seems busy enough."

Now back upstairs, the choirmaster tapped his baton and the choir sang "God Rest Ye Merry Gentlemen" followed by "Rudolf the Red-Nosed Reindeer" and guests and staff couldn't help but sing along. It lifted everyone's spirits.

Anna insisted the family have their private breakfast in her suite to open their gifts. This had been Bill's idea so he could have family time before the big day in the kitchen. Sarah was afraid it would be too upsetting, but Anna insisted.

Sarah remembered the big trolley of food being wheeled in and her mother helping Nana serve breakfast. She had had to wait until after breakfast before she could open her presents and then the pleasure of sitting on the floor with her father. She was happy he had been found and released, but she wished he could be home this Christmas and not stuck in some sterile hospital. She had mixed feelings about the celebration. Darcy, Belle and Felix were considered family. Otherwise it would be just Anna and Sarah.

Christmas morning traditions went ahead. She missed Grandpa Bill and her father. Anna handed out the colourful parcels. Sarah sat on the floor and checked under the tree and all the labels, but there was nothing from Felix. She unwrapped a silk blouse from Belle and a silver locket from Nana. She looked up to see Felix staring at down at her and then he suddenly knelt on the floor next her and whispered, "Will you marry me? "He opened a blue velvet box and a sapphire and diamond ring almost popped out of it. The room fell silent as everyone held their breath waiting for the answer.

"Yes, I'll marry you." Felix placed the ring on her finger.

**

Felix and Sarah's engagement brought celebration to a Christmas that was tinged with sadness. Even Anna had smiles. Felix returned to the city after Boxing Day to work on an upcoming trial; he would be back for New Year's Eve. Sarah took the time to check on the staff, corporate bookings and the kitchen. What she found made her nervous. The Christmas bookings were down from last year, and unless Dorothy had corporate bookings she had not entered in the calendar, those bookings were down by fifty percent. The New Sackville was looking tired and in need of renovations to keep up with the times. A coat of paint and a new lobby carpet would give the place a lift. Sarah searched the accounts looking for capital money and discovered there was none. The operating account was in the black, but there wasn't much of a buffer for the upcoming slow season.

"Mr. Grimsby," Sarah said, tapping on his office door. "Do you have a minute?"

"Of course, come in." He motioned to a leather chair opposite his desk, his eyes glanced at the ledger in Sarah's hand. "I see you are checking up on the ledger."

"Not checking up, just seeing how much money we have. I think it's time we had a new lobby carpet and a coat of paint. However, I do have some concerns, but numbers are not my thing."

"What would you like to know?"

"Where is the account for capital expenses?"

"There isn't one. Mr. Blaine instructed me to move it to the operating account last year. He didn't want to worry Mrs. Blaine and told me to keep it between us. It was around the time she had eye surgery and I took over all the accounts—they needed a lot of work."

"I understand." Sarah pointed to the open ledger. "We are in the black again and it looks as though we have recovered, at least the operating account has, but there isn't much profit as we head into the slow season."

"You are correct." Mr. Grimsby was a man of few words. Sarah realized the world was black and white to him. He knew his job well and did everything by the book. But he lacked James's personal touch.

"What are you doing about increasing revenue?"

"Me, nothing. It is my job to keep the books straight and the hotel running. I did speak to Miss Jenkins about the corporate bookings and the early projections indicate we will break even."

"Mr. Grimsby, as general manager it is your responsibility to make sure the hotel is profitable, and from what I see today, it is not."

Sarah found his attitude condescending and suspected he didn't like being spoken to by a woman young enough to be his daughter. And, being honest, there wasn't much more he could do.

"What about cutting costs?"

"I know my job, Miss Wexford. Cutting costs is how I pulled us out of the red." Mr. Grimsby's face tightened, colouring slightly, but he maintained his decorum.

Sarah realized that upsetting Mr. Grimsby was a bad move and lightened her tone, "In your professional opinion is there anything else we should be doing or not doing to increase the hotel revenue?"

"Off season, we should be reducing payroll, but Mrs. Brigg won't hear of it and insists she needs the maids for a thorough cleaning off season."

"We always used to reduce staff in January. I'll speak to Mrs. Blaine and Mrs. Brigg. You work with Mrs. Brigg. Is she a good housekeeper?"

"She's adequate."

Sarah wondered what adequate meant and it didn't fill her with confidence. "Thank you for your help. I will meet with you later this week to discuss the staffing for January."

Sarah went immediately to the staff dining room to find Mrs. Brigg, who was taking a tea break. Sarah suspected she took a lot of tea breaks.

"May I join you?"

"Suit yourself." Mrs. Brigg gave a shrug.

"I need a list of all your staff and their duties so I can determine who will be laid off in January."

"You can't do that. I need them."

"No, you don't. Mrs. Peterson always managed with half her staff of maids during the off season and the hotel was spotless. Please have the list in Mr. Grimsby's office tomorrow morning. And I suggest you get back to work, we have a full house for New Year's Eve." Sarah didn't wait to see her expression but she heard the chair slam against the table. She didn't care. Mrs. Brigg rubbed her the wrong way.

Chef came out of the kitchen. "I heard something bang."

"Mrs. Brigg isn't happy,"

"She rarely is happy. She's a cold woman." Chef gave a wry smile.

"How are things in the kitchen?" Sarah asked.

"Couldn't be better. Dining room sales are up by fifteen percent over last year. We turned people away for Christmas dinner."

"That's the best news I've heard today. At least I know the kitchen is in good hands."

"Chef Bill taught me well. Is there anything I can do for you?"

"No, just making sure everything is in order." Sarah moved to the service stairs.

Sarah couldn't explain where she had found the courage to confront Mr. Grimsby and Mrs. Brigg, except Anna wasn't capable at the moment and she needed these people to do their job because *she* did not want to run the hotel. She knew that there were three key elements: management, housekeeping and good food. Chef Brian was not a problem, but the other two were.

310

Forty

Independence

⚜

The New Year's celebration was even more tenuous than Christmas. Sarah saw a cloud forming over Anna as the joy of the engagement dissipated. She dressed early, joining Anna in her suite for a cocktail only to find Anna sitting at her dressing table, tears flowing quietly onto her petticoat. She glanced through the mirror as Sarah walked into the bedroom.

"I can't do it. Sarah, I can't do it." Sarah sat on the corner of the stool, gently rubbing Anna's back. "Shush, it's all right. I'm here. What can't you do?" Sarah handed her a lace hanky.

"I can't make the toast…but I promised Alex." She sobbed into the handkerchief. "Then I included Isabelle because she was so close to her father. Now, I have to add Bill. I can't do it. I've lost everyone but you; the reminder is too much."

"Grandpa Alex would understand. He would never want you to suffer like this, and neither would my mum or Grandpa Bill."

"But it was a tradition, a remembrance." Anna wiped her eyes. "There is no one left here at the Sackville that remembers your Grandpa Alex or your mum for that matter. The tradition started at the Kings Head Inn in Rugby. We started it for the locals who loved Alex to the very end."

"Why don't we have a private toast before dinner with just family?

Darcy wants to make an official engagement announcement at the ball tonight and I think that will suit everyone."

Anna sniffed and wiped her face. "That will do nicely, and I hope Alex won't mind. I don't know what I'd do without you." Sarah gave her a squeeze. Anna stared at her red, swollen face. "Now, what can I do about this?"

"Cold water and lots of make up. Um…and a dry petticoat," Sarah said, laughing.

The transformation complete, Sarah in a short bronze strapless dress, which had the effect of lighting up her red hair, and Anna wore a blue silk full-length gown. They sat at the family table as Darcy and Belle walked in.

Sarah frowned. "Where's Felix?"

"He's only just left London, so he'll be late. He said to go ahead without him." Sarah looked at Darcy's face; he was hiding something and Belle looked as confused as Sarah felt.

Anna didn't seem to notice Felix was missing and made the announcement. "Sarah and I have decided not to give the usual toast at midnight. I've lost too many loved ones. But in their memory, I would like to make a toast to Alex, Isabelle and Bill." She raised her glass. "To loved ones lost and remembered." The group repeated the toast. Anna sat back in her chair and smiled with satisfaction as Sarah nodded across the table.

She leaned in to Belle and whispered, "What's going on with Felix? He said he'd be finished by noon."

"I don't know, but I think Darcy does. He had a weird phone conversation with Felix this morning about taking someone to London Airport. Darcy brushed it off as being an important client and said Felix would be late for dinner. I thought it odd as I know Darcy wants to announce your engagement tonight. He said not to worry; he'd here by then. He doesn't seem worried, so I don't think it's anything bad."

"Have you thought about setting a date for the wedding? Felix said you would live in London after you're married. Darcy will give you the London townhouse, which makes sense as you both work in London and we hardly use it these days."

"No date yet, but I was thinking either August, an outside wedding at Hillcrest, or during the Christmas break. As you know, Nana and Grandpa Bill married on Christmas Day, and Felix tells me Hillcrest sparkles. His words were, "A cross between an old-fashioned Dickens Christmas and American glitz.""

"He did, did he?" Belle chuckled. "I think he's right. A Christmas wedding would be lovely. What do you think, Anna?"

"Christmas and a wedding at Hillcrest. I like the idea."

Sarah breathed a sigh of relief, she hadn't known she was anxious, but setting the wedding date a year from now seemed to lift a burden off her shoulders.

Balaji whispered something in Darcy's ear and he jumped up and rushed to the entrance. Sarah saw Felix standing by the doorway beckoning to his father, and they disappeared. Darcy returned and asked Balaji to add a table setting and chair to the table. He then nodded to Felix.

"Darcy, what is going on?" Belle demanded, but was ignored.

"Sarah, we have a surprise for you." Sarah turned. Felix walked into the dining room with his arm around a small, extremely thin man with grey hair and a tuxedo two sizes too big. Sarah's heart stopped. Could it be? Was it? Did she remember? And then the man smiled and she knew it was her father. She stood up and ran, although she felt as though her limbs were moving in slow motion.

"Dad, is it really you?" She took his frail body in her arms.

Between gasps and tears she heard him say, "My little Sarah, I never expected to see you again." He held her at arms length, brushing away a fountain of tears. "You look just like your mother. Beautiful, so beautiful."

Sarah led him to the table and glanced towards Felix. "How long have you known?"

"I didn't until yesterday. I made inquiries and was told he was being flown to England. I called in a favour and arranged to pick him up at Heathrow."

"Thank you. You have made New Year's Eve 1963 very special, my darling Felix."

**

Two days later, Sarah, Sandy and Anna were having breakfast in Anna's office, reading *The Daily Telegraph* headlines that announced Felix and Sarah's engagement and Sandy Wexford's release. Of course the stories were linked together, making them far more sensational than they really were.

"It looks as though we are famous at last. Perhaps this will help bookings," Anna said.

"I think it might. What do you think, Dad?" Sarah got a thrill every time she said the word Dad.

"I had no idea I would come back to such fanfare." She glanced at her father's pale, drawn face. Although he said little, Sarah had the feeling he was struggling with demons. She reminded herself he had just spent three years being tortured in a foreign jail. Anxiety strained his face and the slightest noise made him flinch. Even the penthouse brought back memories of Isabelle and he chose to stay in Anna's second bedroom. He needed someone to take care of him and Anna did that well, taking her mind off her own grief and loneliness.

Belle and Darcy had returned to Hillcrest and Felix was back in London. Most holiday guests had checked out and the hotel was quiet.

Sarah met with Mr. Grimsby, who had made up slips and wages for four maids and two kitchen maids, and all part-time staff had been terminated until the spring. She asked Mr. Grimsby to keep Mrs. Brigg on her toes. She made it clear to him that Mrs. Blaine would be looking after her father and that Mr. Grimsby was in charge of the hotel. If he had any issues he was to call her. He actually smiled and Sarah thought he was looking forward to the responsibility and implementing his authority. Dorothy confided that she had two more corporations interested in conferences, and Chef Brian welcomed the challenge of finding ways to pare down his food costs.

Sarah hugged her father and Anna. Henry drove her to the station and she relaxed in a compartment to herself. Tired but confident that the hotel was running smoothly, she was proud that she had proven she could run the hotel. However, for now she wanted to concentrate on college and art, and spending time with Felix. As the train rolled into Paddington station and jolted to a stop, she wondered if things could run too smoothly. She shook her head, admitting that it wasn't often things fell into place and she considered herself overdue for an uncomplicated life.

Felix took her bags and drove her home. She declined dinner for an early night in her own little flat. Mrs. D and Johnny greeted her as usual. She dug in her coat pocket and gave Johnny a Cadbury's chocolate bar and then handed money to Mrs. D, knowing there would be a loaf of bread and pint of milk in her cupboard. She climbed the stairs and went straight to bed.

Sarah woke up screaming from a nightmare. All she remembered was feeling terrified as Felix was being dragged away. Every time she closed her eyes the same scene came back and she gave up on sleeping. She wrapped her woolen dressing gown around her and made tea. Tucking her legs underneath her on the sofa, she curled her hands around the warm cup. Still cold, she lit the gas fire, hoping there were enough shillings in the gas metre. She wanted to call Felix but it was only four-thirty. The tea and fire warmed her up and she went into the studio and began painting one of her favourite scenes, the Haida longhouse. Mr. Justin was not among the most patient of people. She thought it wouldn't hurt to get a head start.

She painted until the sun came up, which in January was at eight and late for Sarah. Feeling a chill, she figured the gas had run out and she had given Mrs. D her last shilling. This also meant she couldn't have a bath. She washed in cold water and shivered, pulling on a warm jumper. The thought of living in the Thornton's townhouse started looking pretty good. It occurred to her that the house was staffed and she probably wouldn't have to run her own bath and would have all the hot steamy water she wanted—such luxury.

A car honked its horn and she pulled back the curtains. Felix waved up to her. She threw on her coat, grabbed her bags and ran downstairs, looking forward to the car heater and a morning kiss from Felix.

"What have I done to deserve such service?" Sarah asked, kissing his cheek.

He held her tight and kissed her on the mouth, taking her breath away. "I don't think we had one nice kiss all Christmas. And I miss you."

"I think you're right." Sarah replied pulling him into another kiss. "I could do this all day."

"Me too, but we both have to work. I have to work tonight, so now is the only time I can see you," he said, driving towards the college. He kissed her again as she opened the car door. Hearing whistles, she blushed and said, "Not a good idea in front of the students. Bye."

An announcement in *The Daily Telegraph* meant that the whole world, including teachers and students, knew that Sarah Wexford was engaged to be married. Sarah had not given this a thought until droves of students started whistling and her colleagues shook her hand. Overwhelmed, she could feel panic rising and it was Miss Berkley that came to her rescue. "Congratulations, Miss Wexford." Mr. Darwin shook her hand. "I had no idea."

No idea of what? she thought but didn't say. "Felix and I have known each other since childhood."

"So, when is the day? I expect you'll be leaving us," Mr. Darwin added.

"Not until next Christmas, but no date yet. And I have no intention of leaving, either before or after I'm married. We plan to stay in London."

"But isn't he an earl?"

"Not until his father dies, and Lord Darcy Thornton is fit and healthy. Felix is committed to the law and I'm committed to art and college for a good many years."

Mr. Darwin coloured. "Of course, how foolish of me. But that is good news for the college. Excuse me, I have things to attend to."

Sarah and Miss Berkley stifled a giggle. "I'll walk you to the staff room. I think everyone wants to see you. I read that your father has come home too. How did that feel?"

"It was…I can't describe it. I was only nine or so when he left, but I recognized his smile. He's thin and weak after a terrible ordeal. Nana is looking after him, which is good for her too."

"Can I see your ring?" Miss Berkley asked as Sarah stepped into the staff room. Suddenly she was surrounded. She had admired the ring greatly, but seeing the envious looks and gasps, she realized the admiration was for the shimmer and sparkle of a very expensive piece of jewelry. She had never thought of it that way; it was Felix's love she saw in the glimmering sapphire and diamonds. She was beginning to feel lightheaded and all she wanted to do was get to class. The bell rang and the staff scattered and Sarah walked into a class of cooing and whistling students.

"She banged her fist on the desk and the room went silent.

"Your seats please, ladies and gentlemen." Sarah told her students what she had told Mr. Darwin and taught the class. The students asked the odd inappropriate question that she refused to answer, but eventually settled down to normal. As she dismissed the class for the day, Mr. Darwin sent for her.

"Miss Wexford, I was talking to Mr. Justin this afternoon and he wants to know when his Haida painting will be ready. I should warn you he thought it would be ready by now."

"Why would he think that? I don't recall giving him a date. I only started it last night. I'll try for the end of January. I can't rush things or I don't do my best work."

"Mr. Justin is an impatient man. I have the college's reputation to consider, Miss Wexford."

Irritated by the implication, she retorted, "Then he should be contacting me without involving the college. He has my number."

Walking to the Underground, she wondered where this new assertive behaviour was coming from. First the hotel staff, now the college. She quite liked it. She felt liberated. Was she becoming one of those feminist women? She hoped not. She liked her independence, but not in a harsh way.

Forty-One

Shattered Dreams

hen Sarah decided to walk to the college on the morning of January 23rd, 1964, she had no idea that it would be the worst day of her life. She nodded good morning to a group of students huddled around the college entrance listening to the Beatles on a portable radio. Her interest in pop music was limited, but "I Want to Hold Your Hand", the Beatles hit song, did have a nice lilt to it and she found herself humming as she entered her classroom. She picked up several envelopes, more mail than usual, and glanced at the address on the first one: Justin's Art Collection and Gallery. She sighed. He was becoming difficult. The painting was finished and would be delivered after class today. Assuming the contents of the letter, she didn't open it. She was anxious to open the letter that bore the Cardish family crest.

Dear Miss Wexford
I am sorry to inform you that the painting I purchased for Lady
Cardish arrived damaged and my wife wishes to return it.

Damaged? How could it be her fault it was damaged? She wasn't one hundred percent happy with it and wished she hadn't rushed it, but it wasn't damaged. *That's it.* She realized the paint hadn't set and it had smudged when the chauffeur put it in the car. She felt terrible. This had never happened before and just the thought that someone was unhappy with her work made her feel sick. She reassured herself that it would be all right because it could be easily fixed; oils could be painted over. She glanced at her watch. She had time to telephone and went to the staff room.

Lord Cardish came to the phone, but before she could explain, he accused her of selling substandard art and called her a disgrace to the art community. When he asked her what she was going to do about, it she offered to re-do the painting. Instead of calming him, he began another rant. All Sarah heard was his anger until she heard the name Mr. Justin and that her painting would be returned as they had purchased a different piece of art from Justin's Art Gallery.

Sarah rushed back to the classroom to open the letter from Justin's. The first thing she noticed was that it had been signed by Mr. Sebastian, which she thought was a good omen, but the words in the letter made her drop into her chair. Mr. Justin was withdrawing his support and canceling her art exhibition. She read aloud.

Due to Mr. Justin's disappointment at not receiving his Haida art and some disturbing statements from a valued client...

She sat staring into space, nodding at the students' greetings as they began to take their seats. The next thing she knew, Mr. Darwin was standing by her desk ordering the students to wait outside and close the door.

"I've received a disturbing letter from Mr. Justin. I told you he was impatient. And that's not all, Lord Cardish is threatening to pull his donation from the college."

"I told Mr. Justin I would have his painting for the end of January. It is the 23rd and the painting is finished. I've received letters from both and I do not understand what is going on."

"I suggest you sort it out or you will be without a job." He opened the classroom door and marched out as the students filed in.

She tried to smile through halted tears and focus on the swimming faces as her stomach churned. She thought she might retch right there in the classroom. Taking and holding a deep breath, she managed to say good morning and distribute the day's lessons before asking a student to fetch her a glass of water, afraid she would faint if she stood up. She sipped on the water and somehow managed to teach most of the day.

At lunch break, she called Felix. He sounded busy but said he needed to see her and would pick her up at four. His voice sounded upset. Sarah wondered if the day could get any worse.

He drove straight to her flat, saying nothing. She wondered if he'd heard about her art issues, but he shook his head, frowned and made no comment.

Once in the flat, he made sure the door was closed tight and handed a manila envelope to Sarah. "I received this today. Lorraine is accusing me of fathering her child and abandoning them. If I don't agree to marry her, she will go to the press and ruin my legal career and damage your reputation with threats of other legal proceedings. She conveniently doesn't mention what proceedings. I'm assuming financial compensation."

Stunned, Sarah stared at the envelope, the third today that could ruin her. "My art career is already shattered." Fighting back tears, she thought of Charlotte's letter and how she had thought Lorraine was out of her life forever, not knowing Felix was the father of her child. Could it be a mistake? She realized Felix had not denied it. Had he known when he proposed to her? Her tears turned to anger.

"You slept with her? You knew she was pregnant when you proposed to me?"

Felix looked more stunned than Sarah felt. "No, I didn't know. And yes, I slept with her, but we were careful. Remember, we were planning to marry. It was long before you and I got together."

"It couldn't be that long, how old is the baby?"

"I don't know, but we weren't dating. You were seeing Michael, or Marcus, or somebody. You're no saint you know." Felix lashed out, and although he didn't know it, he had hit her hard where it hurt. She thought about how much she had loved Marcus the night they made love, and she wasn't ashamed to admit she enjoyed it. Did Felix feel the same way about Lorraine?

"What do you intend to do? You can't marry two women." She regretted the question. Did this mean the end of their relationship?

"I'm marrying you. I'll pay her off or do what she asked, but I'm not marrying her."

"What about the child? Your son or daughter." Sarah felt as though she was painting herself into a corner and out of a marriage.

Felix didn't answer the question. "I discussed it with Peter at the office. He doesn't trust Lorraine and said we need proof. He's looking into it."

Felix paced the room. She felt off balance watching him, in fact she didn't feel well. "Why don't you go and see Peter now and talk this through. You need legal counsel. I can't help you. I'm not feeling well. I've had a terrible day."

Felix stared at her. "You're not going to walk out on me, are you?"

"How can I answer that? You've just told me your ex-finance has had your child and wants to marry you. Things are not exactly normal." She walked to the door and held it open. "Good night, Felix." He bent to kiss her and she moved away. The hurt in his eyes haunted her all evening.

She lay on the bed, staring at the ceiling, seeing that hurt. Her stomach hurt and her throat was sore. She thought of her beautiful art and Felix, the two most important things in her life and they were gone. How could she stay at the college teaching when she was no good? Felix felt tainted. Would she ever know how much he loved Lorraine? Even if Lorraine and the child went away, she could never look at Felix the same way again. She looked at the ring on her finger; it seemed dull, as though the life had been sucked out of it. She slid it off her finger and placed it in the blue velvet box.

She wanted to call Lizzy. She needed to talk, but she'd sent Felix to their house to talk to Peter. Sarah took an airmail letter from her desk and started to write to Charlotte. She told her Felix was Lorraine's husband-to-be and the child was his. It seemed to give her some peace being able to scribble her thoughts. She told her about Mr. Justin and Lord Cardish. As she wrote, the tears plopped onto the thin blue paper, but she kept writing until all three sides were full. She sealed it and decided to walk to the post box; the air would do her good.

When she returned, there was a car outside and Lizzy ran towards her. "I tried to call you and when you didn't answer I was worried."

"I went to post a letter, but I'm so glad you're here." Lizzy hugged her and the tears started again. "I've lost Felix and my career is ruined." Lizzy and Sarah sat up talking until the early hours. When Lizzy had to leave to feed the baby, Sarah crawled back into bed, but it seemed like only minutes before the alarm went off. Terrified of going to the college, she found things to do and decided to send Mr. Justin's painting to the gallery. She wrote him a note and arranged for it to be picked up. She wrote a cheque for Lord Cardish refunding his money, and posted it on her way to the Underground. There was nothing more she could do but go to work. She stayed in her classroom all day and spoke to no one. She dismissed her class early so she could leave without bumping into any staff. It was Friday so she had the weekend to gather herself together. Lizzy had promised to come by with baby Nicholas on Saturday morning. She'd left a message for Felix to tell him not to come by. She needed to think about things and would be in touch when she was ready.

**

There is nothing like a chubby, smiling baby to make adults coo and play and forget they're adults. Sarah adored Nicholas, but she couldn't help wondering what Felix's baby looked like and who would coo and play with him or her.

"Stop that," Lizzy said. "I know your wondering what Felix's baby looks like. Well, Peter thinks it's a hoax."

"Come on, how would she do that? Charlotte told me Lorraine had a baby. It's common knowledge at the school in Toronto. Admittedly, we've no proof that it's Felix's child, but there's a high probability." Sarah paused, "And Felix didn't deny it, which is proof to me." Sarah's chin began to quiver. She couldn't remember feeling so wretched.

"Hey! Things will work out."

"Not his time. I think it's over. I took my ring off last night."

"Sarah, come back to my house and stay the night. Peter's working today and Felix won't be around. He went to Hillcrest to talk to his father."

Sarah's cheeks were wet again; it seemed the tears never ended. "Darcy will be angry. He hated Lorraine and practically threw her out. I guess he'll have to accept her now. He has an heir in waiting."

"Don't give up so easily. You never trusted Lorraine and there's a lot we don't know. Sarah, I can't leave you like this and I have to get home for Nicholas's nap."

"Thanks, but I want to be alone. I have to make sense of all this."

"Call me later. I left some shopping in the kitchen. I guessed you hadn't picked up any food. And I made a steak pie; just heat it up in the oven. You have to eat."

"I will." Lizzy hugged her friend and kissed Nicholas. Mrs. D and Johnny were waiting at the bottom of the stairs. Sarah smiled, knowing it would a while before Lizzy would get home.

Nicholas started crying and Lizzy was making her exit when a man came to the door with a large parcel for Sarah. Johnny took it up stairs.

"It's Lord Cardish returning the painting." She waved to Lizzy and unpacked the painting. She was right, the painting had smudged. She shook her head and said, "Lesson learned." She propped it up by the wall and a sheet of paper dropped on the floor. Unfolding the paper, she realized the handwriting wasn't the same.

Dear Miss Wexford,

It appears the painting was damaged during transit. I do like the painting and I am a big fan of your art. I'm proud to have this in my collection. Is there a way you can fix the damage? If so, please contact me.
My husband, was very upset, fueled by Mr. Sebastian suggesting you had fallen from grace in the art world. I can't imagine this is true, but either way, I would like the painting.

Yours sincerely,
Lady Cardish

Sarah wasn't sure whether to laugh or cry. In spite of the damage, Lady Cardish liked the paining and wanted it fixed. But why would Mr. Sebastian say such a thing? Sarah immediately wrote back, apologizing and explaining what had happened and that she would be able to paint over it. The painting would be ready by next Saturday, after it had thoroughly dried, and she would have it delivered.

Happy to have a second chance, Sarah put the painting on the easel and not only fixed the damaged parts but finished it in the way that she had originally intended. Now she was satisfied, and in fact, it was one of her better forest paintings.

The weekend passed quickly and she dreaded going in to the college. Keeping to herself, she only spoke to students and avoided the staff, especially Miss Berkley and Mr. Darwin. Going home to her flat was lonely. She missed Felix and wondered if there were any developments but she was too stubborn to ask. That night, Mr. Grimsby phoned to say that he was concerned about Mr. Wexford. Nothing serious, but he suggested she come home at the weekend. As an afterthought, he added that there was no improvement in Mrs. Brigg. *A weekend at Bexhill is exactly what I need.* For the first time, she welcomed hotel issues over art and the college. It would be nice to get up in the morning and not dread meeting people. There were problems at the hotel, but she was in control of solving them. A change of scene and different problems would be good.

She drudged through the week and gave her students an extra assignment and caught the early train, telling no one but Lizzy.

Forty-Two

The Demon Drink

⟨⟨⟨✦⟩⟩⟩

*T*he wind howled along the empty platform; few people visited Bexhill in the winter. Sarah's footsteps sounded hollow and thick, grey sleet covered the pavement. She hailed the only car in the taxi rank, wishing she'd told Mr. Grimsby to pick her up. The taxi crawled along the Promenade as waves crashed over the sea wall, the wipers struggling to remove the heavy sleet and now the seawater from the windshield. Glad to be home, she wanted to hug Henry when he opened the taxi door.

"Miss Sarah!" he said. Sarah smiled, she had intended her visit to be a surprise. "I'll take care of your bags and the taxi. Mrs. Blaine is in the dining room."

"Thank you, Henry." Sarah checked her watch: four-thirty. Tea time.

Sarah's heart pained to see Anna in the empty dining room, sitting alone and lost at the big round table with no family left to keep her company. She was notably thinner and dark circles rimmed her eyes. Seeing her approach the table, she jumped up and took Sarah in her arms as a broad grin spread from ear to ear. "What a surprise."

Sarah clung to Anna, feeling her love. She felt ten years old. Nana always made things better. She was afraid to let go, and then the tears came. Anna held her tight, gently patting her back and whispering,

"There, there. I'm here."

Taking a deep breath and wiping her eyes on the napkin, she said, "I needed that hug, Nana. It's so good to be home."

"I heard about Lorraine. Belle told me. And you're not wearing your ring."

"And there's more. This has been the worst week of my life."

Anna listened with shock as Sarah related the happenings with college and art. "Something is not right here. We need to get to the bottom of it. This will ruin your career."

"It already has. Mr. Darwin threatened to fire me if there were any more complaints."

"I've never seen you so defeated. We will work things out. I'll start with Belle and Lady Cardish."

"We'll see." Sarah smiled at the change in Anna. She had a glimpse of the old feisty Anna that Grandpa Bill loved so much.

"Where's Dad? I almost forgot. I'm not used to him being here."

"He's sleeping and…"

"Sleeping! And what else?"

"Your dad is having difficulty adjusting. I had Dr. Gregory take a look at him. His symptoms are the same as shellshock. He needs rest and time. Come on, let's go wake him up. He'll be happy to see you."

As Sarah walked into Anna's living room, she was a child again. Sandy lay sprawled on the sofa, he looked red or she saw red; red cheeks, red nose and eyes rimmed in red.

Anna called out, "Sandy, look who's here."

Sandy sat up, rubbed his eyes and said, "Sarah, come here. Give your old dad a hug." Sarah hugged him, grimacing at the smell of stale alcohol.

"Dad, you've been drinking. I thought you'd given that up."

"Just one to get me through the day. It's nice to see you. Are you staying for the weekend? Where's that young man of yours?"

"Um…he's working this weekend." She glanced at Anna who nodded approval, obviously Sandy didn't know. "I'm going to unpack and freshen up for dinner. Dad, you need to get cleaned up and changed."

Anna walked her to the door whispering, "I'm sorry darling. I tried to look after him, but his demons only quieten when he drinks. He hasn't changed. His ordeal just made it worse."

"I'm sorry. You shouldn't have to put up with a drunk. I had no idea."

"It's okay. See you later." Sarah heard the bath water running as she closed the door. At least he'd listened to her.

**

Despite discovering her father was drinking again, she felt safe at the hotel and he had behaved at dinner the previous night. This morning she planned to meet with Mr. Grimsby. His concerns about Mr. Wexford were already confirmed. Now to find out what lazy Mrs. Brigg was up to.

Mr. Grimsby greeted her with a smile, *He's quite attractive when he smiles,* she thought, taking a seat.

"I will be quite blunt," Mr. Grimsby blurted out. "The problem is alcohol."

"It's disappointing, but I know my father is drinking. Is it affecting the hotel or guests?"

"Not directly, but it's affecting Mrs. Blaine and Mrs. Brigg."

Puzzled, she asked, "How?"

"Guests have complained of shouting from Mrs. Blaine's suite. I'm afraid he might harm her."

"I didn't see any evidence of that, but I'll look into it. And Mrs. Brigg?"

"Alcohol is her problem, too. Suzie, the head maid came to me in tears with bruises on her arm and told me that Mrs. Brigg becomes violent when she's been into the gin. I investigated and found empty gin bottles in the dustbin. Had it been summer time, I wouldn't have paid attention, but we haven't had more than six guests in the bar or restaurant in the last three weeks." He paused.

"What is it? I need to know."

"I'm reluctant to say, but your father has been a frequent visitor to her sitting room."

"Oh boy, if there is one thing a drunk loves, it is the company of another drunk. I appreciate your candour. I will deal with it. Dare I ask how the rest of the hotel is doing?"

He smiled again. "It is doing well. Chef has been trying out some new dishes. With few customers, Mrs. Blaine, Miss Jenkins and I have enjoyed some great food. January has been quiet, as expected. Miss Jenkins has several corporate bookings for February and March and an Easter program for the end of March. Would you like to see the appointment book?"

"No, that won't be necessary. I trust you, Mr. Grimsby. However, I would like you go over the accounts with me."

Mr. Grimsby took the ledger from his desk and Sarah was pleased with the current and projected income. "You have reduced the operating costs considerably, Mr. Grimsby. Well done. I think that is all, unless you have anything else."

"What are we going to do about Mrs. Brigg?"

"What do you suggest?"

"I suggest we tell her to stop drinking and get help. If she has made no attempt to stop in two weeks, she's fired with two weeks pay. And if she harms anyone, she's fired immediately."

"I agree. Go ahead and do it now. I'll be in Mrs. Blaine's office if you need me."

She stepped into the next office, pleased with Mr. Grimsby. He had surprised her with a soft streak in giving Mrs. Brigg a chance to redeem herself. She waited anxiously to hear how Mrs. Brigg had responded to the reprimand and ultimatum. "What's good for the goose, is good for the gander. I need to talk to Dad," she said aloud.

"Talking to yourself?" Anna said.

"I'm waiting for Mr. Grimsby. He's speaking with Mrs. Brigg. Nana, has Dad ever hurt you?"

"No. He gets very upset sometimes and shouts at me. It takes a while to calm him down. He sees things that terrify him."

"Did you know he has made friends with Mrs. Brigg? She has a problem with drinking. Dad has to stop, and it is so inappropriate for him to be fraternizing with the staff. Did you know about this?"

Anna nodded. "I couldn't cope, Sarah. I didn't know what to do. I'm not coping. I used to do so much."

"Nana, its okay. Mr. Grimsby is doing a great job. If I'm not here, you can go to him. Ah, here he is. Come in, Mr. Grimsby, and take a seat. How did it go?"

"At first she denied it, but when I gave her the ultimatum, she agreed to visit Dr. Gregory and assured me she wants to stay." He paused, glancing from Sarah to Anna. "It probably isn't my place but someone needs to speak with Mr. Wexford about…"

"It's all right, I'll speak to him. Thank you, Mr. Grimsby." Sarah waited until he had left. "We need to talk to Dad now."

Sandy Wexford dropped his head in shame. He was breaking Sarah's heart. She remembered how he couldn't cope when her mother died and she had always felt guilty because she couldn't take care of him. Was she doing the same things again? He wasn't a strong man to begin with, and MI6 had broken him. Drink helped him forget and Mrs. Brigg was the only friend he had.

She decided they had talked about it enough and nothing more could be done. Sarah wanted to enjoy Sunday morning and lunch with Anna. Solving the hotel problems was tame compared with college. She felt the pit of her stomach gnawing with anxiety just thinking about Monday morning.

**

The long white envelope addressed to Mr. Robin Darwin, Principal, Royal College of Art, was burning a hole in her handbag. She kept telling herself she needed to make a decision. She had made that decision the moment she fell into Nana's arms on Friday. She needed to be home.

Her heels clicked on the marble as she marched along the corridor and into Mr. Darwin's office, handing the letter to his secretary. She swung around bumping into Miss Berkley. "Good morning, Miss Wexford. You are early. Care to join me for tea in the staff room?"

"Good morning, I was heading in that direction."

"I'm glad to speak to you alone. I wanted to say that I'm sorry for what happened and I, for one, do not believe the rumours."

"That's kind of you. I did nothing wrong. I delivered the painting to Mr. Justin and he has accepted it, at least he hasn't returned it, and Lady Cardish is quite happy with her painting after I made some changes. It is of no matter, Miss Berkley, because I have made my decision. Thank you for your concern."

"Sarah, don't do anything rash. This will blow over."

"Excuse me, I'm taking my tea into the classroom as I have some work to prepare." Sarah smiled. She felt empowered; convinced she had done the right thing.

They both saw Mr. Darwin heading towards them flapping the letter. Miss Berkley looked at Sarah and said, "No, you didn't...did you?" Sarah nodded yes and waited for Mr. Darwin.

He turned on his heels saying, "My office please, you too, Miss Berkley." And he galloped back along the corridor, Sarah and Miss Berkley rushing behind him as fast as their stiletto heels would allow.

"Take a seat. Miss Wexford, I apologize if I was harsh regarding Mr. Justin's painting. I had received some misinformation. This will all blow over. Artists by nature are temperamental. You are my best teacher, and the most famous. There is no reason to resign."

Sarah wondered what misinformation he had received. "I'm curious. Firstly, why you would make such accusations, and secondly, what changed your mind?"

"I'm not at liberty to say."

"Not at liberty to say! I believe I deserve more than that."

"I will tell you that Mr. Justin is thrilled with the painting and Lady Cardish spoke highly of you. Let's consider the matter closed."

Miss Berkley said, "Yes, lets put this behind us."

"You have just ruined my art career and you want to put this behind us? I want an explanation."

Mr. Darwin hesitated. "All right, but this goes no further than this office. Cecilia Jones was behind the rumours."

"What! Madame of Le Papillon Gallery of Art?" Sarah frowned. "She never liked me, but why and how?"

"I warned you that she was jealous and devious. When the gallery was shut down, she lost everything and she thinks you had something to do with it. Her loyal servant, Mr. Sebastian planted and spread rumours that you had fallen in disgrace on the art world. Mr. Justin, already impatient about his painting, bought right into it. Lord Cardish was a mere coincidence, but it had the desired effect when Lord Cardish threatened to withdraw his funds from the college."

"Our reputations are fragile, it only takes a wrong word, a misconception or believable lie," Sarah said, almost in a whisper.

"Now that you know the truth, will you reconsider?" Miss Berkley looked at her hopefully.

"I'm afraid my decision is made. The events of the last couple of weeks certainly influenced my decision, but it wasn't the only reason. I am returning to Bexhill to take over The New Sackville Hotel. Since my grandfather died, my grandmother is not coping well and my father is not recovering from his ordeal and needs looking after." Sarah stopped talking, wondering where all these excuses were coming form. "The family has always expected me to take over and now's the time. I owe it to my grandmother. I love her and would do anything for her. My art career is over, but should I decide to paint again, I have a nice studio set up in my penthouse at the hotel."

"There is no way I can change your mind?" Mr. Darwin paused waiting for a reply. Sarah said nothing. "I see you have made your mind up, may I add, for commendable reasons. But with a talent like yours, never give up your art. Your career is not over, it is just beginning. I'm sorry, I bear the responsibility of jumping to conclusions and pressuring you at a difficult time in your life."

"Yes, you did, and I hope I never go through anything like that again. But thank you for being honest with me. Perhaps our paths will cross again. I will see my students through until Easter, giving you time to find a replacement."

"You will always be welcome here, either as a guest or professor. I am deeply sorry to see you leave."

Miss Berkley touched Sarah's arm as they walked out of the office together. "Did something else happen. You're not wearing your ring?"

"Like I said, the worst two weeks of my life. Complications have arisen." Sarah walked swiftly to her classroom.

Forty-Three

Anna's Reflective Dream

⟨decorative flourish⟩

*B*alaji poured her a second cup of coffee. She knew it would keep her awake, but reluctant to leave the safety and company of the Emily Carr Dining Room, Anna drank it anyway. She took pleasure from her favourite Emily Car paintings and her granddaughter's fine art of Bexhill.

Balaji frowned. "Is everything all right, Mrs. Blaine?"

"Yes, I sometimes find it lonely in my suite since..." *That's only half of the truth,* she thought. *Fear keeps me away from my suite.*

Sandy's behaviour had become violent of late. He couldn't stop drinking and his nightmares kept her awake most nights. She rubbed the sleeve concealing the bruise on her arm. He hadn't meant to hurt her. The demons—prison guards she thought—were attacking him. He'd lashed out, punching her in the arm. She'd talked him down, but she worried about the next time and the time after that. Sarah should be told. Maybe she could help him. He wouldn't listen to Dr. Gregory. Sarah didn't need any more trouble. Dealing with those horrible rumours and trying to keep her job were enough. If she waited long enough before returning to the suite, Sandy would be passed out from the booze and she could put him to bed and watch a little television.

Anna stared as the test screen appeared. There were no more

programs tonight, but the coffee was keeping her awake. Sandy was sleeping like a baby. Murphy's law, she thought, picking up a book and reading until she eventually slept.

Her eyes opened at five every morning regardless of how long she slept. She crept about, not wanting to wake Sandy, and slipped down to her office. Her favourite time of day and the time she missed Bill the most. Every morning when Chef tapped on the door and brought her toast and coffee, for the briefest of a moment she expected to see Bill.

She tried to be cheerful for the staff and especially for Sarah, but since Bill's death the passion had gone. She no longer wanted to run the hotel. Her knees hurt all the time and tiredness slowed her down. Most people retire long before they are seventy and enjoy the fruits of their labour. Without Bill, she couldn't enjoy anything and she still wasn't sure that Sarah would take over. How many times had Bill told her the hotel was their dream and Isabelle's, not Sarah's? But with Isabelle dead, there was only Sarah to take over.

She picked up a letter from her desk and read it for the tenth time. Skimming the introduction, she read:

Holiday Hotels is an American chain of family owned hotels. We pride ourselves on offering guests an affordable, clean and comfortable place to stay. We have selected a number of British seaside hotels that we think would convert well into Holiday hotels. I am pleased to say The New Sackville Hotel is one of those selected.
At your convenience, we would like to meet with you to discuss the potential sale...

Anna stood at her window and watched the night sky lighten to a deep blue, with a hint of sunrise along the horizon. The sea was almost glassy in the still morning. A slow, gentle breeze began to ripple the surface and small rolling waves undulated towards the shore. She wished the sea could answer her question. Should she meet with Holiday Hotels? She wanted to ask Bill but she knew his answer. He had been upset when she kept the first letter from him. He wanted to sell. Anna clung on, hoping Sarah would take over.

At one time, she almost gave up as Sarah's art career blossomed. But right now there was an opportunity to persuade Sarah to come home to safety. She didn't have to put up with the temperamental art community or the injustice of a biased art college, she could take over the hotel and paint in the penthouse if she needed her art. The truth, Anna knew, nestled in the very depths of her conscience. Her dream was almost complete and selling was not part of that dream. She threw the letter on her desk.

The hotel was springing to life. She heard Mrs. Robertson talking to Mr. Grimsby and Dorothy's cheery voice saying good morning. How could she tell her staff she was selling out? At least they would have jobs, but where would I go? *They'd have jobs with Sarah at the helm too, and I would end my days here.*

Belle was the only person in whom she had confided her thoughts on the hotel and retirement. Belle was sympathetic but not convinced it was Sarah's destiny. Did Belle think Hillcrest Hall was her destiny? Perhaps not. It had not escaped her that Sarah was no longer wearing her engagement ring.

Belle had offered Anna a home at Hillcrest Hall if she decided to sell. And, surprisingly, that had appealed to Anna. She liked the idea of helping Belle with the summer tours and gift shop. Sitting alone somewhere in a tiny flat did not hold any appeal. A broad grin spread across her face. "I wonder what old Lady Thornton would think of that? I think she would approve; she often said she would like a daughter like me." Anna laughed aloud. "But that was because she didn't approve of Belle. Well, m'lady, I think you would approve of Belle now."

Anna sat at her desk to start her morning correspondence and the letter from Holiday Hotels glared at her; she shoved it under a manila file folder as the phone rang.

"Sarah, hello."

"Nana, I wanted you to know first. I have resigned from the college. I'm coming home for good at the end of term."

"That is wonderful news, but are you sure this is what you want?"

"I've made my mind up. Mr. Darwin did apologize and the rumours were only rumours from bitter, hurtful people. I'm not happy here, so I'm coming home."

"Are you leaving your flat and moving your things?"

"Yes, Lizzy is helping me pack and driving me to Bexhill. I have to go Nana. Bye."

Anna beamed. Her dream had come true.

Forty-Four

Hard Goodbyes

⚘

I f Sarah had known how hard it would be to say goodbye to her students and peers, she might have thought twice about her decision to leave. And leaving the flat was even harder. She stood in the living room with Lizzy. Lizzy held Nicholas on her shoulder and had her other arm around Sarah. They gave one last look at what had been their start in life as young women. Sarah gave all the furniture to Mrs. D so she could rent the flat furnished and get a bit more money. Her studio and clothes were packed up in the back of Lizzy's car. One last thing to do, and she was dreading it: saying goodbye to Johnny.

When they reached the bottom of the stairs, Mrs. D distracted herself cooing at Nicholas. Johnny threw his arms around Sarah and sobbed, squeezing the breath out of her. Sarah gently pushed some space between them and said, "Johnny, look at me. You are going to be fine. We'll miss each other, but you and your mum can come and visit me and stay in a big hotel. I'll take you to the beach and we'll swim in the sea."

His wet eyes lit up. He scrubbed his face and said, "Promise."

"I promise."

Sarah reached for a large box she'd left at the bottom of the stairs and handed it to Johnny. "This is for you." Johnny looked in the box and beamed. Pulling out paints, brushes charcoal and sketch pads. Without saying a word he grabbed Sarah and give her the best big wet kiss she had ever had.

Sarah put her arms out for Mrs. D and she burst into tears, clinging to Sarah. "Oh, for mercies sake, I'm crying." Sarah smiled and gave her another hug. "Thank you for all you've done for me, Mrs. D. I'll miss you, but promise you'll bring Johnny to visit." Mrs. D nodded, wiping her face on her apron. "Now I must get on, I've got cleaning to do. The new tenant is coming next week.

Lizzy drove the car away and Sarah waved, watching Mrs. D's little row house disappear. A phase of her life was over. She wondered if she had done the right thing. She hugged the sleeping Nicholas sitting on her knee. His carry-cot, usually on the back seat, was taken over by Sarah's possessions. Lizzy glanced over. "Are you okay?"

"I'm fine. I am so thankful you offered to drive me. I know Felix wanted to but I'm just not ready to face him." Sarah sighed, "Running the hotel was always my destiny; college and Felix only complicated it. Being lady of Hillcrest Hall would not mix well with being a hotel owner." She laughed, a forced unemotional laugh. "I can still paint, if I ever decide to paint again. I'm happy in my studio at Bexhill."

"When are you going to be ready to face him? It's been more than six weeks. You haven't even asked about Lorraine—you've assumed he's guilty," Lizzy said, keeping her eyes on the busy road.

"I don't want to talk about it."

"Peter is handling the legal stuff and there have been developments. Don't you want to know?"

"I don't care. I've made my decision."

"Felix loves you. You're breaking his heart. At least tell him."

I'm not ready, she thought. *Why am I not ready?* Afraid of her own thoughts, Sarah blurted out, "It doesn't seem to count that he broke my heart." Nicholas started to cry. "Oh, sorry baby." Sarah rocked him back to sleep.

"Peter has always thought this whole baby thing was a hoax, and it looks as though he may be right. He can't find the baby's birth certificate."

"That only means she didn't register the birth or it's tied up in administration. You know, the one thing that bothered me more than anything the day Felix told me, was that he never once denied the baby was his. That says more to me than a birth certificate."

"Sarah, you are being stubborn and silly."

Sarah leaned back and closed her eyes; they drove in silence until Lizzy stopped the car under The New Sackville Hotel entrance.

"Home for good," Sarah said with a tone of satisfaction. "There's a lot to unload, Henry, and it all goes to the penthouse."

"We'll manage, Miss Sarah. Mrs. Langford, do you mind leaving the car for a few minutes?"

"I need the baby's things and that brown suitcase stays, the rest is all yours. I'm not in a hurry, but I do need a cup of tea."

Anna greeted them and immediately took charge of Nicholas. "You two go and get something to eat, I'll look after Nicholas."

"He needs changing and feeding," Lizzy said, "There's a bottle and clean nappies in the bag."

"Off you go. We'll be fine, won't we my precious little boy? Come and see what Auntie Anna has for you for Easter." Nicholas gave Anna a whopping smile.

"No chocolate," Lizzy shouted over her shoulder.

**

Boxes and bags lined the penthouse living room. Sarah shook her head, wondering where everything had come from, and more to the point, where everything was going to go. She shoved the art stuff in the studio and turned her back on it. The suitcase she dragged into the bedroom and put her clothes away. Pulling on her pyjamas, she curled up in bed with an Agatha Christie mystery. Having difficulty getting into the story, she lay back thinking of her new career at the hotel. Delighted to see Anna smiling, she was aware that her decision had had a major impact on her grandmother. Seeing Anna so happy, her dreams fulfilled, was reward enough.

Dad's another story. His behaviour is bizarre and it isn't all from drink, although the constant drunkenness must have pickled his brain. Eventually her eyes closed and the five o'clock alarm woke her. She flipped the button wondering if she would ever get used such inhospitable hours. But Nana would be in her office, and as the new manager, owner, or whatever her title was, she intended to start the way Nana expected.

"Good morning," Anna said as Sarah came into the office. "I ordered toast and coffee. You look a bit sleepy."

"I sometimes have trouble sleeping. Too much on my mind."

"Do you regret leaving the college?"

"No, Nana, I don't. I miss the students but not the college. It's...um...nothing, really."

"Anything I can help with? You're worried about Felix. Don't make any rash decisions. I can't tell you what to do, but please think things through. You have your mother's stubbornness and it got her into a lot of trouble at times."

"I'm so angry with Felix. Nana, I'm afraid if I speak to him I'll explode." Her eyes burned. "Every time I think about it I want to cry. Lizzy says there are developments and I should contact him. I can't face him."

Anna patted her hand. "It's okay, take your time. Felix has to sort this mess out. It's his mess, not yours. Wait until there are some resolutions."

"Nana, you are the first person that has said that. I keep thinking I have to sort it out. Depending on how Felix deals with this will impact our future. If we have a future." She thought but didn't say, *Am I changing my mind about Felix?*

"Sarah, I need to talk to you about your father. His behaviour is odd: he screams in fear in the middle of night and hardly leaves his room. I want him to see Dr. Gregory, but he refuses."

"I had noticed and I agree that he needs help. I'll talk to Dr. Gregory. Dad's my responsibility. I appreciate you looking after him, but it's time I dealt with it. Now, what's on the agenda for today?"

"I hate to give you a difficult job on your first day, but Mr. Grimsby has had enough of Mrs. Brigg."

"Leave it with me." Sarah glanced at the clock. "She should be in her sitting room now. No time like the present. See you later, Nana."

The housekeeper's sitting room was empty and so were a couple of bottles of gin. "She has to go," Sarah whispered under her breath as she wandered into the kitchen. Chef's kitchen buzzed with activity as the cooks created Easter cakes, tarts and chocolate bunnies. "Morning, Chef. This takes me down memory lane. My mum and Grandpa Bill worked so hard for the Easter parade."

"It's pretty much the same every year. I just follow Chef Bill's instructions." He held up a well-worn note book. "But it does seem odd not having him watching over us."

Sarah's next stop was Mr. Grimsby's office, and without further discussion they agreed that Mrs. Brigg was to be let go. He offered to tell her—when they could find her.

Back in Anna's office, Mrs. Robertson handed her the morning post. "I think these are personal, Miss Sarah. I deal with the hotel's post.

"Thank you." The air letter was from Charlotte. She stared at it, slitting the sides of the aerogramme. Would there be news of Lorraine and would it deny or confirm... She stopped—deny or confirm what? Was she afraid Felix had fathered Lorraine's child or that he had slept with her? Why did it bother her? She had known he was a playboy long before they had courted, and was she any better? She had slept with Marcus. The letter was a letdown. Charlotte chattered about her new role as vice principal, school and her new boyfriend. It was encouraging to know that Uncle Charlie intended to uncover the truth in Toronto, but the only news she already knew—no birth certificate.

Hearing a great deal of shouting coming from Mr. Grimsby's office, Sarah assumed Mrs. Brigg had been found and objected to being fired. She beckoned to Henry to wait outside the office and help Mr. Grimsby escort Mrs. Brigg off the premises. Sarah went downstairs to meet with the maids. Susie's face positively beamed when Sarah gave her the news that Mrs. Brigg was gone and that as head maid she was in charge, under Sarah's supervision, until a replacement was found.

What happened next, Sarah could not have predicted. That evening, Anna and Sarah had dinner with Sandy in Anna's suite. Because of Sandy's tendency to agoraphobia, he had stopped going to the dining room. Sarah had also limited his access to liquor, although there were days she suspected he found extra from somewhere. But this evening seemed pleasant enough, although Sandy seemed agitated.

"How did Mrs. Brigg react?" Anna asked.

"There was a great deal of shouting coming from Mr. Grimsby's office, but she did leave the premises. Susie will …"

Sandy interrupted, "Where is she? I tried to call her today."

"Dad, why would you call Mrs. Brigg?"

"She's my friend and she brings me…she visits sometimes."

"You invite Mrs. Brigg to Nana's suite? She brings you what?" She didn't need an answer. *So,* she thought, *that's how he gets extra booze and why he is agitated today.*

"I'm allowed friends. I need another drink."

"You've had your quota for the day. Dad, we had to fire Mrs. Brigg today. She's left the hotel."

Sandy jumped up and screamed, "You had no right to do that. Where's the whiskey? I know you've hidden it." He started pulling cupboard doors open and throwing whatever was in his hand on the floor; plates were smashing and food was spilling. Sarah tried to calm him and he began beating her with his fists. Anna intervened and he punched her. She fell to floor. Sarah grabbed Sandy's hands and yelled to Anna, "Call the desk and ask Dan and Lionel to come up. We need help here." She twisted his arms behind his back. Sandy sat on the sofa, staring into to space. Sarah spoke to him, but there was no response and his eyes were glazed and frightened. Whatever demons he was seeing, he was terrified.

"Dan, sit here make sure he doesn't move. I'm calling Dr. Gregory." She put the phone down. "He's on his way."

Anna was limping as she bent down to pick up the broken plates. Sarah frowned. "Nana, are you hurt?"

"No, I fell on my knee. I'm all right."

Sandy didn't move until there was a knock on the door, and then he jumped up before Dan could grab him. With an expression of pure fright, he ran around the room like a scared animal. Anna opened the door. No words were necessary. Dr. Gregory took a syringe from his bag and asked Dan to hold Sandy and within minutes they guided him to the sofa where he collapsed.

"How long has he been like this?" Dr. Gregory asked.

"An hour, maybe less." Sarah replied, shaking as the shock set in. "He went wild, throwing things punching, screaming. He was terrified."

"He needs to be in hospital. I'll call an ambulance." He glanced at Sarah. "Sarah, I have no choice. He is a danger to himself and to you and Mrs. Blaine. He needs medical care. He's a very sick man." Sarah nodded, her throat squeezed tight, resisting the tears.

"He pushed Nana over. Can you check that she's alright?"

"Of course, and how about you?"

"I'm okay, just upset." He patted her shoulder.

The attendants lifted Sandy onto the stretcher and carried him to the waiting ambulance. Dr. Gregory told them to stay put and try not to worry. He intended to admit Sandy to the Cottage Hospital and call a consultant for a professional opinion. Sarah correctly surmised he meant a psychiatric opinion. Her father's condition had a long name she couldn't pronounce, but resulted in episodes of severe paranoia and there were times he lived in a complete fantasy world, all resulting from the torture and confinement he had experienced. A few days later, needing special care, Sandy was transferred to the hospital in Eastbourne.

Sarah visited every day. She held his hand and sometimes he squeezed it with a weak smile, but most of the time he was so heavily sedated he didn't know she was there. She hoped he could be stabilized so she could bring him home. But after discovering that he'd had other episodes that Anna had not told her about, deep inside she knew the doctors were right and he would never get better. She had failed, she had failed her father. Never before had she been so desperate to feel Felix's arms around her. His soothing voice and gentle kiss, just his presence, made her feel safe. Had she failed Felix too?

Forty-Five

The Truth

⚜

*D*r. Gregory and the staff at the Eastbourne hospital had done all they could for Sandy Wexford. Three weeks of intensive treatment and he still needed heavy sedation. The psychiatrist recommended he be moved to a nursing home, a nice way of saying mental institution, or worse, loony bin. She heard the chants of innocent kids, including herself, not understanding how desperately ill these people were.

Feeling depressed after returning from a visit to the nursing home, Sarah sat on the bench watching the waves roll over the shingle beach. It was peaceful and soothing, a far cry from what she had just seen at the nursing home. Sarah paid for a private room for her father; the screaming and yelling on the ward scared him too much. He never ventured out of his room. He had seemed a little better today. He sat up in bed and she had propped him up on pillows so he could drink a cup of tea and eat a slice of cake. He smiled, enjoying each bite. He recognized her and called her Sarah, squeezing her hand. But five minutes later he called her Isabelle. She didn't mind, just pleased he was awake and peaceful. The medication kept him calm most of the time and the staff was kind. In Dr. Gregory's words, he was well taken care of, and for that she was grateful. He would never be able to function in the outside world again; this she had accepted. What she couldn't accept was failure. She had failed him by not taking care of him, and she had failed her mother too. She had no intention of failing her grandmother. Her decision to return to Bexhill was the right one, but she was lonely. She hadn't told a soul that she missed college, the staff, students and painting. And with each passing day she missed Felix more. Even if she forgave him and Lorraine went away, she would be forced into making a choice between Nana and Felix and she didn't want to do that, so in a way Felix had made it easy for her. Could they be friends like the old days?

She closed her eyes, listening to the sea and squawking seagulls. She felt someone sit beside her and immediately felt at peace. Not wanting to talk to a stranger, she kept her eyes closed, waiting for them to leave. After about twenty minutes, she opened her eyes, thinking she hadn't noticed the person move away. She turned her head to see Felix smiling and staring. She had a sudden urge to jump into his arms, but held back, remembering her earlier thoughts.

"Anna told me I'd find you here. She told me about your dad and the nursing home. I'm so sorry, Sarah, I know how much you wanted him home."

She was afraid to look at him and focused on the horizon. "It's a terrible place. The nurses and doctors are caring, but the patients, they are sad and lost." She shook her head. "Dad's okay, he has a private room. He recognized me today, called me Sarah and then thought I was Isabelle."

"From what I remember of your mother, you do look alike."

"Actually, that was the first thing he said to me the day you brought him home. 'You look just like your mother.'"

"I miss you, Sarah. Can we talk?" He moved his hand towards hers. She pretended not to notice.

"I miss you. I wish we could be friends like we used to be." Sarah kept her eyes down.

"I'd be happy to start there." Felix responded, "I've missed how we shared our problems and happy times, although there haven't been

348

many happy times lately."

"I'd like that, "she said, finally looking up at him. Her heart missed a beat seeing his eyes moist, a little sad and full of love. She felt panic. No, this couldn't happen. She had resolved to look after Anna.

"I only want to talk. I'm not staying long. I drove mother down to visit Anna. I have to go back to London before dinner. A new trial and a mountain of work. Mum's going to stay for a few days."

Sarah relaxed; a talk would be good. "What do you want to talk about?"

"Peter and your Uncle Charlie have closed the paternity suit. Can I tell you about it?" Now it was Felix's turn to stare at the horizon. He'd moved his arm across the top of the bench. He wasn't touching her, but she could feel his heat.

"Yes," she said.

"Lorraine was angry, very angry, when my father asked her to leave Hillcrest. When she returned to teaching in Toronto, she carefully concocted a story that she wasn't well and took a leave of absence. Not sick leave, because no doctor would sign a sick note. At this point, we are not clear what she was planning until your cousin told her we were engaged. At that news, she flipped and took the story further, announcing that her absence from school was because she had given birth to a baby boy and she refused to give it up for adoption because the baby was heir to Hillcrest, making me the father. Thinking I would do the gentlemanly thing and marry her, in her insane head she thought it would bring shame to my father, ruin you and she would have her man, and more importantly, her title."

Sarah looked surprised. "It doesn't make any sense. And where is the little boy?"

"There was no baby. She was never pregnant and did not give birth."

"Lizzy kept telling me Peter thought it was hoax. She would have been found out eventually. But if she kept the charade up long enough, you two could have been married. Kind of a stretch though. How did Peter find out there was no child?"

"She would not give any details of the child's name or date of birth and trying to find a birth certificate based on either Howser or Thornton revealed nothing. She eventually said the baby was born at Women's College Hospital. I don't think it occurred to her we could check and that is where Charlie helped us. The hospital had no records of Lorraine Howser having been admitted for any reason, and she would have had to use her real name for health coverage, nor did any other hospital. Charlie even checked with midwives and private clinics."

"How did Peter get her to admit the fraud?"

"Charlie did; he threatened to report her to the police for concealing a live birth. Once he quoted the penalties, including prison time, she decided to tell the truth. Your uncle is a very smart man. He had her sign a confession and apology. Perhaps not necessary, but he was afraid she might try it again. It's over." Felix paused. "Where does that leave us?"

"I don't know. Felix, there is one thing that has upset me from day one. You never denied it or considered the baby was another man's child, and because of that I was convinced it was true and you were willing to return to Lorraine."

Felix's eyes widened in shock. "I couldn't deny it. That would be lying. I admitted I slept with her. I thought it highly unlikely but not impossible that I was the father. Lorraine meant nothing to me, but an innocent child should not have to suffer because of a mistake I made." Felix's voice cracked and he cleared his throat. "I didn't know what to do. I could not abandon the child, but I was so afraid I would lose you and that part seems to be coming true. Sarah, I am sorry, I was a fool and I am asking your forgiveness."

"You don't need my forgiveness. I was blind to the truth. Lorraine manipulated you and ultimately tried to trick you. You thought you loved her and planned to marry her. I'm no better, as you pointed out to me. I loved Marcus and I allowed him to walk all over me. I knew he was no good, but I kept going back for more. He didn't even suggest marriage," she paused "and I let him make love to me anyway. Only once, but that was enough. So I am no saint."

Felix stared at the sea. Sarah had no idea what he was thinking, and given her earlier thoughts, it shouldn't matter. But it did. She watched the waves rolling erratically as the tide was turning and so was she, but she feared she had turned Felix away. Filled with love and pride, she glanced at a man who would love and care for an innocent child and risk his own happiness. Could she be failing Felix and their future family?

Felix took a deep breath and moved his arm across Sarah's shoulders. "Are we going to allow Lorraine to have the last word and split us up, or are we going to work things out?"

"It sounds simple when you put it that way."

"And it is. If you can't get past Lorraine then…"

Sarah interrupted, "Stop, this has nothing to do with Lorraine."

Perplexed Felix frowned. "What! Please, tell me?"

"Nana and the hotel." She gave a small laugh. "Remember my inheritance? I can't let her down. Whether I want to or not, I have to take over. How would we live, you in London and me here? And once we take over Hillcrest, what happens to the hotel?"

"Did you give up art to come back here?"

"Partly. But I haven't painted since the Justin Gallery episode and the college treated me badly. I can't face art at the moment."

"Sarah, I have known you a long time, and giving up is not your style. Are you sure you didn't use it as an excuse to legitimize coming back to Bexhill?"

"No, of course not. Nana needs me here." She felt threatened, Felix was challenging her rationale and she didn't like it.

"You're being stubborn. We can work something out. There are options for the hotel, and Anna can live with us at Hillcrest. Can you imagine my mother and Anna together organizing Hillcrest? Now that's a formidable thought. Have you ever talked to Anna about this?"

"I don't need to." Sarah hesitated, "Do you honestly think we can work something out?"

"Yes, I do." Felix took her hand and gently touched her empty ring finger. "Will you think about it?" Sarah nodded. Felix kissed her on the cheek and she didn't move away. He glanced at his watch. "I have to leave. I'll be back on Sunday to drive mother home.

Sarah walked back to the hotel and waved Felix off. Anna joined her.

"Nana, can we talk? I came home to run the hotel, take up my inheritance so to speak. I have always assumed this is what you wanted for the hotel, but I have never asked."

Anna led the way to her office. "Originally, the hotel dream was mine, fuelled by Bill when we bought it from Mr. Kendrick. We didn't think much about the long term as we were preoccupied keeping the place afloat in the early days. Hard work paid off, and the hotel became a success. It wasn't until your mother joined us that I thought of the long term. Your mother had a rocky start but she enjoyed marketing the hotel and learned to run it far better than I could, so it became a foregone conclusion that she would inherit the hotel and we would retire. When tragedy struck, things changed. I wanted to cling on to your mother through you. I see now I should never have done that. Your mother and I were passionate about the hotel. You are not your mother and your passion is not mine or your mother's. But not to be deterred, I selfishly stuck to the assumption you would take over. Bill knew better, but I wouldn't listen. I have known since you were a tiny tot that art was your passion. I was so excited when you said you wanted to take over the hotel, but I've watched the life slowly leech out of you and I feel guilty that you gave up your career to come back to Bexhill."

"No need, Nana. I actually enjoy the hotel. If I wasn't here, what would you do?"

"Sell. I had an offer from Holiday Hotels not long before Bill died. He wanted to sell but I said not on your life. I received another offer just before Easter. Maybe it's not such a bad idea. If you want to leave and go back to London, we can sell."

"No, I don't want to go back to London. Not yet anyway. I have some thinking to do. Nana, whatever happens, I will never leave you."

"I know that, sweetheart. By the way, Belle told me that Lorraine's hoax had been exposed. How are you and Felix?"

"We've had a good talk. Do you mind if I don't join you for dinner tonight? I'm going upstairs; I've had a long day."

Sarah was glad of the quiet in the penthouse. She wandered over to her studio corner tidied her paints and brushes and placed a blank canvas on the easel. She gazed at the Promenade. Too early in the season to be busy. The setting sun hovered above the horizon, glowing on the sea. Clouds reflected the glow, pushing the darker clouds away as though the storm had passed, leaving a sun full of hope. She started painting. She painted until the sun disappeared into the sea and the moon came up. Her passion had returned.

She stretched; tired, satisfied and happy to feel creative art pulsing through her veins once more. She went into her bedroom and opened her jewellery box. Picking up the blue pendant, she felt the cool blue lapis. *Great Uncle Bertie, it seems there's truth in following dreams.* Her eyes settled on the little blue velvet box. She hesitated, remembering how dull and lifeless it had been when she put it away. She picked it up and pushed the top open and the sapphire glowed in the moonlight and the diamonds twinkled like stars. Feeling Felix's touch on her ring finger, she slid the ring into its rightful place.

What Happened Next?

Sarah and Felix were married at Hillcrest Hall on the morning of Christmas Eve, 1964. It was a small wedding by society standards. The sighs of admiration for the bride's simple but exquisite dress by Jacob's were intermingled with mutterings of disapproval. Anna held her head high and her Cheshire cat grin matched Sarah's as they walked to the rhythm of the organ music, breaking protocol as she walked her granddaughter down the aisle. Sandy had slipped deeper into insanity, unaware of his daughter's marriage, making it impossible for him to give her away.

As planned, Sarah and Felix lived at the London townhouse. Felix continued to practice law. Sarah chose not to return to the Royal College of Art and opened her own gallery in Kensington, The Sackville Studio and Art Gallery—a fitting name as the sale of The New Sackville Hotel had financed the gallery. Remembering her unpleasant encounters with art galleries, Sarah vowed to help young emerging artists. With Miss Berkley's assistance, she devoted her time to talented artists, giving them a safe platform at The Sackville Gallery.

Holiday Hotels honoured Anna's condition of retaining the staff, but Anna's coddled society guests did not take well to the minimal services of Holiday Hotels, and within a year the property was sold a second time to a developer who converted the hotel into flats for the over 50s. The Sackville Apartments survive to this day.

Anna accepted Belle and Darcy's invitation to live at Hillcrest for as long as she wished and she became a valuable asset, working with Belle on the Hillcrest Hall summer program. Belle and Anna remained inseparable friends.

Sarah Thornton became a world-famous artist, just as Miss Berkley had predicted, and The Sackville Gallery was an overnight success.

In 1971 Sara became pregnant with twins and Miss Berkley managed the gallery during her confinement. Felix insisted she move to Hillcrest where she could be properly looked after. Alexander Darcy and Isabelle Anna were born in May 1972. Sarah continued her art career with the help of Nana Belle and Great Nana.

Shortly after the birth of the twins, Darcy died suddenly. A farm accident had given him a cut on his leg that he chose to ignore. A massive infection set in, leading to his death by blood poisoning.

Felix never did get his silk. The senior partners voted in favour of his friend Peter, and he approved of the choice. Disappointed that he had not reached his goal of Queen's Counsel but delighted in his friend Peter's success, he moved on and willingly gave up his law practice to return to Hillcrest to look after the family and take up his duties as Lord Thornton, with Lady Sarah Thornton at his side.

About Susan

Susan A. Jennings was born in Derby, England of a Canadian mother and English father. Drawn by her Canadian heritage, she settled in Ottawa, Canada where she lives and writes overlooking the Ottawa River. As an essential element of her writing, Susan interweaves British and Canadian cultures into her stories—a theme which is notably dominant in *The Sackville Hotel Trilogy*. Susan came to writing later in life; after raising five children as a single parent. While writing her memoir *Save Some For Me*, stories of a single mother, Susan was bitten by the writing bug and began writing novels and short stories. Susan is currently writing in a new genre; a contemporary romance series, but has a new historical fiction series planned for 2018. Susan facilitates workshops and retreats for novice writers and is the founder of The Ottawa Story Spinners—authors of an eclectic story collection entitled *Black Lake Chronicles* Volumes 1-6.

> ***More about Susan*** *– Follow her on social media.*
> ***Website & Blog*** *- http://susanajennings.com*
> ***Facebook*** *– facebook.com/authorsusanajennings*
> ***The Sackville Hotel News & Updates*** *- http://eepurl.com/bgY6kb*

Free Prequel - https://dl.bookfunnel.com/hj6embawkt Ruins in Silk

Acknowledgements

In some ways birthing a third novel is one of the hardest parts of writing a trilogy. Besides telling a good story, the finale must make sure that all the ends are tied up and the dramas resolved. I also found it quite lonesome at times, as I needed less help than in the other two novels. However the help I received was paramount to the success of not just Sarah's Choice but The Sackville Hotel Trilogy. Thank you to the many friends who have stuck by me, plugging away at spreading the word. Kudos a-plenty, for my loyal fans who spurred me on while waiting patiently for the next book. Speaking of patience, thank you to my trusted writing group, TOSS (The Ottawa Story Spinners), for encouragement and accolades that I sometimes needed to dispel the doubts.

I bow in gratitude to Audrey Starkes and Margaret Southall, both accomplished authors, who read the first dozen chapters of the first draft, not an easy task. Their feedback was invaluable at such an early stage. And Mark McGahey, my trusted editor who makes sense of my inconsistencies and at times indecipherable scribblings of events, as well as normal spelling and grammar mistakes. Proof readers Mary Rothschild and Myriam McCormick: a missing or superfluous comma will not escape these ladies. Thank you.

I owe a great deal to my author friends on Facebook, especially those in The Creative Penn group and SPF Group. These groups showed me how to format and select a cover designer. I would like to say many thanks to Jane Dixon-Smith of JD Smith Design for a beautiful book cover.

Cover design by JD Smith Design
www.jdsmith-design.com

More Books by Susan

The Sackville Hotel Trilogy
The Blue Pendant - Book I
Anna's Legacy - Book II
Sarah's Choice - Book III
Ruins in Silk – Prequel
*

Mystery
Blue Heron Mysteries Complete Works
*

Memoir
Save Some for Me – Memoir of a single mother
*

Contributing writer
Black Lake Chronicles Vol. 1 -6
Ottawa Independent Writers – Anthologies
*

Non-fiction
I Decided to Self-publish
*

Workshops & Online Courses
First Sentence to First Sale
*

To purchase copies of The Sackville Hotel Trilogy
The Blue Pendant - Book I

https://books2read.com/u/mlK7YP
*

Anna's Legacy - Book II
https://books2read.com/u/m2XAxO
*

Sarah's Choice - Book III Dec 2017
*

Ruins in Silk - Prequel -
99c or Free at most retailers
https://books2read.com/u/bw8DjY
*Or download your **Free copy***
https://dl.bookfunnel.com/hj6embawkt

Ruins in Silk

Ruins in Silk - Prequel to The Sackville Hotel Trilogy
'Her mother's death sets Sophie on a path of unimaginable tragedy.'
Free Download
https://dl.bookfunnel.com/hj6embawkt

Research Resources

The Royal College of Art – *One hundred & Fifty Years of Art & Design By Christopher Frayling with research by John Ohysick, Hilary Watson and Bernard Myers– Publisher Barrie & Jenkins London 1987*
ISBN 0-7126-1799-X
*

A 1960s Childhood From Thunderbirds to Beatlemania *by Paul Feeney Publisher History Press 2010*
ISBN 978-0-7524-5012-4
*

The 50s & 60s – The Best of Times *– Growing Up and Being Young in Britain by Alison Pressley 1999*
*ISBN 978-1-84317-065-***The House of Spies** *– St Ermin's Hotel, The London Base of British Espionage by Peter Mathews Publisher The History Press 2016*
ISBN 978-07509-6401-2
*

Hundreds And Thousands *– The Journals of Emily Carr by Emily Carr; introduction by Gerta Moray – Publisher Douglas McIntyre (2013) Ltd 2006. First published in 1966 by Clarke, Irwin & Company Limited*
ISBN 13 978-1-55365-172-7
*

The Emily Carr Collection *– Four Complete and Unabridged*

Canadian Classics. *Klee Wyck, The Book of Small, The House of All Sorts and Growing Pains. Publisher Prospero Books Canada ISBN 1-55267-234-4*
*

Emily Carr *– An Introduction to her Life and Art by Anne Newlands Publisher Firefly Books 1996*
ISBN 1-55209-045-0 (pbk)
*

Emily Carr On the Edge of Nowhere *by Mary Jo Hughes –Kerry Mason The Art gallery of Greater Victoria B.C. Canada 2010*
ISBN 978-0-88885-360-8
*

BBC Documentary 2015
Secrets of Her Majesty's Secret Service - Pioneer Productions

Numerous Google sites.

Printed in Great Britain
by Amazon

26166350R00212